MW00816630

THE KINDLING SPARK

Early Tales of Mystery, Horror, and Adventure

John Dickson Carr

Edited and Introduced by Dan Napolitano

THE KINDLING SPARK

Early Tales of Mystery, Horror, and Adventure

John Dickson Carr

Edited and Introduced by Dan Napolitano

CRIPPEN & LANDRU PUBLISHERS
Cincinnati, Ohio
2021

This collection is comprised of works of fiction. All names, characters, places and incidents are the product of the author's imagination. Any resemblance to real events or persons, living or dead, is entirely coincidental.

John Dickson Carr stories copyright © 2022 by the estate of John Dickson Carr.

Introduction and all Notes for the Curious are copyright © 2022 by Dan Napolitano.

All rights reserved. Printed in the United States of America. No part of this book may be used or reproduced in any manner whatsoever without written permission except in the case of brief quotations embodied in critical articles or reviews.

This book is a work of fiction. Names, characters, businesses, organizations, places, events and incidents either are the product of the author's imagination or are used fictitiously. Any resemblance to actual persons, living or dead, events, or locales is entirely coincidental.

For information contact:

Crippen & Landru, Publishers
P. O. Box 532057
Cincinnati, OH 45253 USA

Web: www.crippenlandru.com
E-mail: Info@crippenlandru.com
ISBN (softcover): 978-1-936363-70-4
ISBN (clothbound): 978-1-936363-69-8
First Edition: September 2022

10   9   8   7   6   5   4   3   2   1

TABLE OF CONTENTS

Notes on the Text

John Dickson Carr did not like to be edited. With no special concerns that Mr. Carr will return from the beyond to berate me for any of the editing here, I nonetheless must pointedly accept responsibility for the editing of this volume, which I wholeheartedly hope you will enjoy. Any errors in its presentation belong to me, not to the Master.

These are works from Carr's earliest writing days. While you will soon see the rapidity with which he progressed from a promising teenage writer to one of the best mystery writers of his generation, Carr's amateur fiction was not always well edited. Layout and continuity issues, misspellings, punctuation issues, and the like often threatened to sully the author's prose, and occasionally, to mystify his meaning.

I have performed minimally necessary line editing, correcting the text to clarify Carr's meaning only when errors were clearly present. Of course, with respect to copy editing, I have modernized certain spellings and punctuation; and because these tales appeared separately across multiple amateur publications and years, I have homogenized their different presentation conventions to make each part of this single collection.

The reader will also find footnotes to the ready where warranted. While looking up an unknown reference or as little as a word's definition is easier than ever in the present day, the editor wished to spare the reader the disruption of breaking away from the book to chase down any such supplemental information.

Wherever passages and their page numbers are quoted from Carr's novels, these are uniformly drawn from the U.S. first editions, first printings (Harper or Morrow). Similarly, all quotations from Douglas Greene's biography of Carr, *John Dickson Carr: The Man Who Explained Miracles*, are from its first printing (Otto Penzler Books, 1995). Quotes attributed to Greene, unless otherwise specified, are from the biography. Quotations from other sources, including letters written by Carr, cite those sources in context.

Finally, it is the editor's disposition, even when a given observation occurred independently to him, cautiously to credit others who made similar observations in earlier publications. Whether any given point in discussion is fully the editor's own original insight, coincidentally similar to another writer's, or first considered, then properly borrowed and attributed to its originator, each of the points made about Carr in this book has value, if it does, because it is presented in useful context for the reader as part of the discussion. The editor is gratefully obliged to others who have thoughtfully enriched his reading of Carr and would prefer wherever possible to refer the attention of interested readers to those other worthwhile commentaries.

Reintroducing John Dickson Carr
Read this introduction first—it is safe!

I confess, I am a reader who routinely avoids book introductions, or at best, revisits them only after reading what follows them. One can only experience naïvely the thrills and surprises of any fictional narrative once—the first time—which is an experience I cherish, even aggressively guard. Because I never wish unwittingly to compromise that initial reading by first encountering unwelcome disclosures, i.e., spoilers, I avoid and distrust introductions.

In this spirit, I have written the kind of introduction I personally prefer to read: this book's introduction deliberately avoids disclosing anything the reader might be disappointed to learn before enjoying the stories. There are not even any plot summaries of Carr's works.

A commentary follows each story, presented in a tributary nod to Carr as another installment of "Notes for the Curious." *Unlike this introduction, each commentary is written with the understanding that the reader has already read its preceding selection. These commentaries openly discuss plot points and solutions, even in rare cases (where unavoidable) details of some of Carr's later (professional) works. In instances where solutions to Carr's later mysteries are discussed, the reader is warned. Explicitly.*

In short, many revelations await! Read confidently: none in this introduction will spoil your enjoyment of the stories that follow, or of any of Carr's professional works.

Rather than trading in plot summaries, then, what this introduction will do is to acquaint the reader with: young John Carr's early literary style and techniques; his exploration of genres; recurring elements in his early works; and these early writings' relationship to one another, to their literary influences, and to Carr's beloved professional detective fiction. N.B.: Most line-by-line commentary, most of the study of his increasing writerly sophistication from tale to tale, and most of the closely drawn connections between Carr's amateur and professional fiction, will be left to the commentaries following the stories.

Understanding the title of this edition is helpful to perceiving one of the important recurring themes of the stories collected in it. The title derives from a 1923 Carr tale, "The Kindling Spark," not included here. "The Kindling Spark" is a literary coming-of-age story set nearly a decade before its publication, one without the decency to include even one mysterious corpse—but which does depict, with good amateur prose and great passion, the disillusioned passage into adulthood of Jimmy O'Brien, a recent college graduate working as an editorial newspaper writer courtesy of a family connection. In the story, O'Brien is baptized into adulthood with alcohol, through romantic disappointment, and by facing his generation's going overseas to fight in the Great War. The story climaxes with Jimmy's abrupt awakening into adulthood: "In that instant the Jimmy O'Brien who had been made by environment dropped away. Something flared up inside him: it burned to a crisp the meek soul of him and surged out in a white-hot wave. Jimmy's Irish blood, ignited by alcohol, was on fire."

Of course, Jimmy metaphorically represents the creative writer, and what's more, O'Brien is specifically a surrogate for the sixteen-year-old who authored him. "The Kindling Spark" is written by a young author for and about his generation facing its incipient adulthood in the early twentieth century. As Douglas Greene documents in his biography of Carr (pp. 12-13), the fourteen-year-old John had, during summers and evenings—his position secured, Carr claimed, through a family connection—written unsigned coverage in the *Uniontown Daily News Standard* of murder trials and sporting events. For his merits, Carr was promoted into writing an editorial column (attributed) for the paper, "As We See It." It is obvious how Carr is drawing on his personal history to create Jimmy's—and on himself personally to create Jimmy. Jimmy's metamorphic recognition of an ugly world, unresponsive to the childish hopes to which he has subconsciously clung, displaces the naïveté Carr assigned to him at the story's start:

> Jimmy had few illusions. One of them was that editorial writers could mold public opinion; that was a secret sense of power in which he exulted. He…clung to the frayed old [adage] which said that the editorials were the backbone of journalism… Jimmy's editorials were good, as editorials go, but Jimmy himself was a failure.

The kindling spark Carr grants Jimmy is the same one, no doubt, Carr experienced himself, and through some of the same vehicles: an emerging awareness of an indifferent, even dangerous world over which the author's pen wields no material power; having exited the cocoon of a privileged education, the feeling of being slight and unimportant in the wider world; the early (ab)use of alcohol; and the pains of early romance: coupled fear and desire for women. The literary fruits of Carr's kindling spark, for the most part happier than Jimmy's, are the tales included in this collection, as well as others not included here.[1]

---

1 This collection, ten tales (including the chapbook story accompanying the limited hardcover edition), represents only a third of Carr's amateur fiction

The stories of this volume in which the protagonists are Carr's stand-ins usually have happier tones and outcomes than "The Kindling Spark." Consider "The Cloak of D'Artagnan" (1924, included as the bonus story with the limited edition): its protagonist, Terence O'Riordan, is, like Jimmy and Carr himself, a youth of Irish descent. (Carr's great-grandfather Nicholas, born in Ireland in 1819 to a Scottish-Irish family, emigrated to the U.S. and settled in Allegheny County in the 1840s.) O'Riordan is as good an avatar for Carr as the reader will encounter in the young author's first three years of fiction. Like him, O'Riordan is of somewhat slight stature, obsessed with the desire to play cavalier, and even took fencing lessons at school. (Greene makes similar observations in the biography, pp. 38-39.)

Of stylistic interest, "The Cloak of D'Artagnan" includes an amateur dip by Carr into character dialect (Terence's father speaks in brogue); Carr would rely on it in the tale (and sometimes in his professional novels, the earliest instance of which is *The Blind Barber*, 1934) to generate humor. Over time, Carr would do much more with dialect than merely elicit laughs: Carr obsessively studied and reproduced dialects throughout his career, using them to bring color and dimension to characters. Carr especially well exploited differing dialects as easily recognized markers of economic and class strata, which brought with them into the narratives their corresponding underlying conflicts and tensions, without having to belabor these disparities more openly. For instance, in *The Devil in Velvet* (1951), we infer Kitty's true personality because, despite her initially outwardly meek demeanor, Kitty speaks thieves' cant and disrespectfully addresses her master in front of the other servants using the familiar "thee" and "thou." "It is noteworthy how many different speech patterns Carr reproduced," observes Greene (p. 346). Of course, Carr was not the first or last author to do so, nor was the technique's use so pervasive or pivotal in Carr's works as to make him an author for whom culture or class disparities were a theme. Rather, this attention to detail shows Carr to be the strong technician he was, adeptly incorporating methods used effectively by writers he admired, often since youth—in this instance, perhaps most prominently, Dickens, not otherwise an author of whom we usually think as a literary ancestor of Carr. Dickens was, though, and in more than one way. Knowing this can broaden some of the ways in which we read and appreciate Carr.

Carr's convincing reproduction of idiomatic speech crossed

---

titles. Douglas Greene published nine of Carr's others in two twentieth-century collections, *The Door to Doom and Other Detections* and *Fell and Foul Play*. Tony Medawar published *Grand Guignol* in 2020 as part of his third volume of *Bodies from the Library*. The remainder are professionally unpublished.

both class and time: consider how frequently, from his earliest novels through the later ones, recreating the speech and vocabulary of a time period was critical to establishing the mood and credibility of Carr's narrative. There are, of course, the opening words of *It Walks By Night* (1930): the mid-fifteenth-century description of lycanthropes by an Archbishop, come down through the darkness of time to prepare Jeff Marle for the emergence of a shuddersome horror in modern-day Paris. Dr. Fell's first adventure, *Hag's Nook* (1933), relies similarly on the nineteenth-century diary of old Anthony Starberth, the first of the family to die according to its mysterious curse of broken necks. Likewise, Sir Henry Merrivale (H.M.)'s first adventure, *The Plague Court Murders* (1934), features as a prominent clue an eighteenth-century letter composed with convincing fidelity. Most saliently, two decades later, Carr's textbook recreation of period English would be central to the success of his historical romances. S.T. Joshi's appreciative recognition of Carr's linguistic accomplishment in these is worth noting:

> Carr's reproduction of seventeenth-, eighteenth-, and nineteenth-century idioms in speech and writing is not only academically flawless but entirely lacking in self-consciousness or pomposity: Carr did much study in the idiomatic and colloquial speech of these periods, to the point that he must occasionally supply footnotes elucidating archaic slang terms.[2]

"The Cloak of D'Artagnan" is a tentative flirtation by Carr with dialect; before relying upon its use as a professional, he improved his skill in the poetry and stories of his school days, including some historical romances not gathered here: "The Harp of Tairlaine," "The Red Heels," "The Dim Queen," "The Blue Garden," and "That Ye Be Not Judged." The verisimilitudinous voice of a character and the character's period was essential to Carr whenever he set scenes and moods to immerse readers convincingly in the past. Carr's accomplished professional work, especially the historical mysteries, had their stylistic roots in these amateur tales. In the present collection, in addition to "The Cloak of D'Artagnan," the reader will encounter Carr's ear for varying patois in "The Marked Bullet," "The Devil-Gun," "The New Canterbury Tales," and Grand Guignol.

The crime driving the plot of "The Cloak of D'Artagnan" (without revealing too much) is a comical one inadvertently facilitated through a charade concocted by young O'Riordan. At the story level, it serves as an entertaining element in a lighthearted romance—but

---

2 *John Dickson Carr: A Critical Study*, Popular Press, 1990, p. 128. All subsequent excerpts are drawn from the same edition.

more meaningfully, it arbitrates a decisive moment in his maturation: O'Riordan's confrontation with the unexpected crime (and criminal) in a climactic brawl. The fight transforms his planned pretense of heroism into actual heroism. The reader is given to understand this will, in contrast to O'Brien's despondent coming of age in "The Kindling Spark," more happily initiate the central character into adulthood.

"The Cloak of D'Artagnan" is not the first of Carr's tales drawing on fencing—"The Will-o'-the-Wisp," 1922, is—but the reader can easily anticipate that these stories were literary ancestors to Carr's early novel, *Devil Kinsmere* (1934, written as Roger Fairbairn), which is rife with swordplay, period vernacular, and humor. All these are ancestors of the later historical romances *The Bride of Newgate* (1950), *The Devil in Velvet*, and *Captain Cut-Throat* (1955), in which the heroes matched not just wits, but blades, with their adversaries.

As with "The Cloak of D'Artagnan," one important recurring character element we will find throughout Carr's early stories is that *they are acts of wish fulfillment*: in tale after tale, we will meet protagonists serving not merely as conventional perspective characters for Carr's reader (who, in this well-known literary approach vicariously experiences these imaginative adventures), but for Carr himself. These stories unfold the kinds of adventures both Carr and his anticipated readership (others his age) wished to experience. This thread of wish fulfillment culminates in *Grand Guignol* (1929), which (like its creator) began as a sort of precocious youth, then matured precipitously into adulthood as *It Walks By Night*. The narrator of the novella, Jack (Carr's college nickname), as we will see in the discussion following *Grand Guignol*, serves not only as the conventional perspective character (the "Watson") through whose eyes the reader watches the plot's progress, but also as the culminating personal surrogate for the amateur author, gleefully imagining himself as part of a colorful and adventurous murder investigation.

While John Dickson Carr did not, in his professional years, abandon novelistic self-echoes, he manifested them less longingly and less idealistically than those he created during his teenage years. Any given "Watson" may be the reader's sympathetic stand-in, but is not, as he is so frequently in these amateur tales, a thinly disguised, aspirational Carr. Consider *The Eight of Swords* (1934), which features not one, but two characters the author based upon himself. (The first Carr reader to publish these following observations was Douglas Greene, in pp. 142-144 of the biography; he echoed and expanded on them in his 2021 introduction to the Penzler Publishers edition.) One, the central character, is Hugh Donovan, a young man who has done everything abroad *except* studied there as intended, and who swilled his own Prohibition-era moonshine in the U.S. Carr did both of these. By the time he wrote *The Eight of Swords*, Carr was a more experienced resident of England. Having shed his youthful anticipations, Carr gently uses Donovan in the novel to mock his own Anglophilia as it existed just a few years earlier. The second character, Henry Morgan, is a successful mystery writer whose views on fiction and writing style are clearly Carr's own. While both characters are *reflections* of Carr, neither serves much in the way of personal wish fulfillment.

With or without wish fulfillment, Carr's protagonists in these early stories are also following a related calling familiar to readers of his detective novels, the aspiration to (again, in the words of Douglas Greene, p. ix) "Adventure in the Grand Manner." The reader will more than once note this yearning expressed overtly in the tales included here, occasionally expressed every bit as strongly as it is famously by Dr. Michael Tairlaine early in *The Bowstring Murders* (1933):

> "What pleasures have I ever got?" the tall, frail man demanded. "Why can't I dance and sing bawdy songs and play the rowdy like any sane human being? Did I ever have any childhood?—and now I'm old. It took me this sabbatical year to realize how old. And what adventures did I ever have?" (p. 4)

"The Kindling Spark," in being a literary (not a genre) tale, absent of any high adventure or even the ambition to it, having instead a central psychological theme, is an experiment and an exception among the writings of (even the young) Carr. As Greene explains, and as regular readers of Carr know:

> Carr himself did not think that psychological analysis is the proper role of either fiction or biography... Carr felt strongly that clinical or formal psychology had no legitimate place in literature, even in nonfiction. (p. xiii)

With its metaphorical awakening of the creative writer, echoing the author's own, in fact echoing that of his entire generation, their young world disfigured by the recent war, while "The Kindling Spark" is an exception to Carr's general distaste for psychological tales, it is also an aberration because—and this is important—it does not reflect Carr's strong disposition toward Romanticism. Most of Carr's early stories, in fact, are acts of adventurous rebellion against "realist" or "lifelike" storytelling, which Carr noted, "I won't buy at any price" (letter to Nelson Bond, March 8, 1967). Carr's youthful works take place in the same world his professional novels do, where the lo-cal laws of Romanticism dictate that adventure—not the humdrum daily concerns of personal finance, doubt, and introspective anxiety concerning the future—is the likeliest outcome of this day and the next. Resultingly, the fledgling author's characters go where teenagers perennially dream of going and experience the romantic adventures we all dream, from adolescence onward, of living.

The reader need not be overly devoted to reading texts biographi-cally or psychologically to understand how natural this impulse is in any teenage author—it is a common enough motif in youthful fiction—or to recognize its ongoing presence in Carr's professional works, what-ever the age of the author. In assessing and amplifying a theme of Douglas Greene's in his "Sleight-of-Hand: John Dickson Carr Was the Man Who Explained Miracles" (a December 1994 interview for the periodical *The World and I* concerning Greene's then-soon-to-come bi-ography), John C. Tibbetts commented concerning the older Carr:

> He also felt that the world had lost whatever sense of adventure and romance it had had in his youth. Ever gallant and fastidious, he affected old-world manners and fiercely clung to politically conservative views. His detectives Fell and Bencolin likewise seemed holdovers from an earlier, more chivalrous and mannered age. And his books, particularly *Hag's Nook*, *The Four False Weapons* and *The Bowstring Murders*, are populated with surrogates for Carr—desk-bound young men who hunger to escape the mundane life for action, color, and thrills.

While, of course, Carr was never, as his frustrated protagonists were, a conformist in his own life plans, this observation is one central to reading Carr in any period of his career. As Carr aged, often, his surrogates would, too, even to the point of wish fulfillment occur-ring literally within the narrative (instead of indirectly, through circum-stances). The elder academic Nicholas Fenton, in *The Devil in Velvet* is transposed not merely backward in time via a wish (a bargain with the devil), but also again into youth, by possessing the body of his seven-teenth-century noble namesake at the height of that baronet's lusty intemperance. Twentieth-century Fenton is reinvigorated, struggling at times to control moods, appetites, and passions—hormones—he has not experienced for decades. In *Fear Is the Same* (1956), near the novel's conclusion, we learn that Philip Clavering is not simply a world-class pugilist (a career Carr admired distantly, examined first in his 1925 high-school story, "The God of the Gloves," another literary tale not included in this collection), but also has "degrees to teach history and English" (p. 284). Suddenly, Clavering is yet another Carr surrogate who has lived through a fantastic adventure, one precipitated by a verbally expressed wish to travel back through time.

Carr's grandson Wooda McNiven assessed the mystery stories selected for this volume as being "from the mind of a teen who was inspired by the genre and its famous practitioners up to that point" (letter to Douglas Greene, July 9, 2021). McNiven is on point, although the present collection, happily, includes *several* genres that inspired the young Carr: mystery, naturally, but horror, too, as well as contemporary and historical adventure. The collection reflects Michael Dirda's general assessment of Carr: "His tastes were clear from an early age: he reveled in mystery, adventure, and romance, and liked best of all to combine them."[3]

In writing these early tales, Carr was in part emulating specific authors who influenced him, and their works he loved—which means, at a level beyond their fictional import, *the tales in this collection can also be read as the wish fulfillment activities of a young author:* Carr reads Poe and tries his hand at writing supernatural tales of horror; he reads Conan Doyle and Chesterton and begins dabbling with mystery and detection; he reads the Hanshews, McCutcheon, and Hope, and responds by penning a breakneck Ruritanian adventure, Carr's longest and most ambitious composition up until that point in his young career. Specific influences on specific works will be discussed in more detail following each story, of course, but the key point here is to recognize that *in reading the variety of stories written by a young Carr, we watch him trying on, like so many literary vestments, the different genres and techniques of the writers whose works* he "gobbled up so eagerly as a boy in my early teens" (letter to Nelson Bond, March 3, 1968). In these stories, young John Dickson Carr is exploring what kind of writer he himself might become, and writing in which genres. The John Carr you will meet in this collection is *one who neither yet knows nor has decided that he will become a writer of detective fiction and historical romances*—which latter, of course, the older Carr candidly confessed were "really detective stories in disguise" (letter to Oscar Baron, April 3, 1972). Carr was rather, by his own formulation (from the same letter) "reading with pleasure when I was a boy in Pennsylvania, toying with the notion of adopting the profession I did adopt."

This reveals an important consideration for reading the young Carr: today, we view him primarily through the lens of the Golden Age of Detection, both consciously and passively measuring Carr's

3 *Mystery & Suspense Writers: The Literature of Crime, Detection, and Espionage*, Scribner's (1998), p. 114.

works and techniques according to the conventions of interwar-period mysteries. After all, Carr was a master of detective fiction, and nearly one hundred years later, still the greatest-ever practitioner of its sub-genre, the miracle crime. *But that John Dickson Carr we take for granted and read according to this conventional framework did not exist between 1922 and 1927, and only began to emerge in 1928. The John Dickson Carr whom you will meet in this book's selections can be better understood by his participation in the tradition of Romanticism.* Carr's works exhibited Romantic characteristics throughout his entire career—but contemporary readers do not generally view Carr through that wider literary-critical lens. We view him more narrowly as that Golden Age of Detection fiction writer.

Neglecting to read Carr as a Romanticist, inspired by the Romantic writers he read formatively, prevents us from connecting Carr to a broader and more "mainstream" (less defined and confined by genre) literary tradition, prevents us from recognizing and exploring those interesting influences upon him—not to mention from venturing new, worthwhile, comparisons between Carr and others in the tradition. There are, for instance, and as previously intimated, tantalizing comparisons (too far out of scope here) to be made between Dickens (a Victorian writer, of course, but in dialogue with Romanticism) and Carr. The two writers have commonalities, yet Dickens is one of the English tradition's ultimate "literary" writers while Carr, read narrowly as a writer of puzzle books, usually receives only back-handed consideration in the academy, if any.

A compelling demonstration of this is the anecdote that opens Roger Herzel's essay on Carr for Charles Alva Hoyt's unfortunately titled *Minor American Novelists* (1970). It relates Herzel's admission interview at The Hill School, where Herzel was surprised and disappointed to encounter a staff member's very parochial view of that school's famous alumnus:

> "Ah yes, John Carr '25," said the elderly master who was my guide. "I remember him well. A bright boy, but a bit of a discipline problem." He paused to laugh reminiscently. "He was a talented writer, and had literary ambitions, as I recall. But nothing ever came of it." (p. 67)

In the mind of the old Hill School master, detective fiction had no relation to literature: it was, by being genre fiction, entirely separate from literature—and wholly beneath it.

Despite the affection this book's editor and reader share for Carr, it would be disingenuous to cast him as an underappreciated figure deserving a place in the first rank of our tradition alongside Chaucer,

Shakespeare, Dickens, the Brontës, Hawthorne, Wharton, Faulkner, and all the other "literary greats" who usually fill out canonical curricula. This admitted, if we understand Carr as a participant in the Romantic Movement, we can shed the misguided wisdom of lowered expectations and the devaluation (if not disregard) of Carr as a "mere" genre writer. Doing so opens wider, and worthwhile ways of reading and considering Carr's fiction. The result may not be that we find Carr to be a greater or more important writer than we did, but we will likely find him an even more interesting one: Carr becomes more closely connected to than we realized, and comes into dialogue with, socially and artistically important movements, comes into fertile comparison with their representative authors and well-regarded works.

While it is true that reading Carr as a Romanticist does not change his works' characteristic lack of engagement with the inner emotional lives of their characters or with the existential questions and interpretive ambiguity that confer upon literary classics their durability, this lack of engagement does not distance Carr's fiction, either, from prevailing Romantic works or their antecedents and inspirations, some of which sit firmly within the sphere of conventional literary interest, recognized among the first and second tiers of the tradition. Examples include Homer's *Odyssey*, Malory's *Le Morte d'Arthur*, Mary Shelley's *Frankenstein*, the historical romances of Sir Walter Scott, the novels of Dumas père, and for that matter, the historical romances of Conan Doyle, which Doyle considered his best work, and upon which he hoped to enjoy a lasting literary reputation.

Carr himself, in considering Doyle's publication of "Habakkuk Jephson's Statement" (1883), cannily observed that it was:

> the first short story by Dr. A. Conan Doyle to appear in a magazine which wore editorial ermine and published only work of literary merit. If it were written today, when we have grown perhaps too sophisticated for our own good, the story would be called science fiction.[4]

We can see that Carr sardonically understood that the boundaries between literary fiction and genre fiction, like the banks of a great river, could shift their positions over time, although the characteristics and merits of works themselves remained fixed. Carr deplored the dismissive consignment of certain styles of writing to "genre" fiction, which left its readers less prepared to discern and appreciate creative elements that might just be as worthy of readers' attention as those in "literary" fiction.

---

4 Introduction to Conan Doyle's *The Poison Belt*, Macmillan, 1964, p. 9.

The perception of Carr as a genre writer worth little (or no) literary consideration, rather than recognizing his place among later Romanticists, can be assessed as a disparity of interrogatives: works elevated in the orthodox literary tradition are more concerned with *why* than with *how*, or even sometimes than with *what*: some revered works have minimal plots, staking their value instead upon closely explored human feelings and behavior. Carr, who scorned psychology as a central element of fiction, generated originality in his narratives by exploring *what* and *how*, and narrative tension (as with all murder mysteries) through *who*:

> Next to Why, the important question is the problem of How?—the discovery of something new which will be the basic trap of your story....Last comes the question of Who? Who is the murderer? The reader likes to pin the murder on some unlikely person; the writer must fool him, if possible, and fix it to a prominent character whom the reader overlooks.[5]

While he acknowledged the precedence of *why*, as Douglas Greene documents (p. xiii), Carr felt that detective stories "should tell '*who* or *how*' rather than the not-very-appealing *why*'." In Carr's novels, "why" is subject to an implied agreement between author and reader. Just as we have an everyday understanding of what motivates the actions of others in quotidian life—not every action is the result of complex emotions or thought, and indeed, most are not; and in any event, we do not usually construe others' actions through an intimate acquaintance with their private thoughts and inner lives—we can have a perfectly serviceable understanding of the motivations of Carr's characters. In the broadest sense, after all, there are a limited number of motivations upon which creative writing focuses: love (and jealousy), desire (including greed and revenge), death, religion, beauty (including nature), and identity conflict (culture, xenophobia, war). Carr was uninterested in exploring the quieter variations of these impulses; an arm's-length understanding of *why* sufficed for him. Consider Carr's defense of detective-fiction characterization in "The Grandest Game in the World":[6]

---

5 *The Mystery Writer's Handbook*, ed. Herbert Brean, Harper, 1956, pp. 169-170.

6 Carr's longest and best-known literary critical essay, which described and espoused the fair-play mystery. It was written, all 16,000 words of it, as the introduction to an abortive 1947 anthology Carr was to select and introduce for the publisher Crown: *The Ten Best Detective Novels*. Ellery Queen published an abridged version of the essay in a limited edition sixteen years later upon the occasion of the eponymous magazine's twenty-second anniversary; publication

No speech in the book is included just because it sounds mysterious, or because it makes a given character look guilty, or because the author doesn't know what the devil his character does mean and simply throws in the words to fill up space. Not at all. In turning over the pages afterwards, the reader can see for himself—how rare it is!—just what each character was *thinking* at any moment....That is why the story pulses with vitality all the way through, and springs into living vividness at the end. The veil is twitched away; the masks are removed. Human beings walk here, and no sawdust dolls, because the author has described voice-inflections, shades of feeling...He has not forgotten to study his characters merely because he is writing about them in reverse. That turn of the eyes—of course! That momentary hesitation when Betty puts her hand on the window-ledge as though to steady herself—naturally! (p. 10)

Carr found more interest and variety in exploring the exciting and outré circumstances resulting from reliably primary motives than in scrutinizing the motives themselves. Certainly, one consequence of this is that Carr's works contain less of the thought-provoking ambiguity and sympathetic (or antipathetic) engagement between readers and characters than literary standards do—but this is a deliberate authorial choice to write a particular kind of fiction, not a deficiency or lack of skill—and again, an approach in common with some highly regarded Romantic writers. Carr doubtless had them admiringly in mind; we will review their explicit influences in the commentaries following the selections. In short, though, in assessing Carr, we well understand that when Sir John Landervorne, in "The New Canterbury Tales," asseverates, "I sometimes wish to God that storytellers would get a bit more old fashioned. They'd be more entertaining..." Sir John is mouthing his creator's strongly held sentiments.

Interestingly, S.T. Joshi (pp. 100 ff.) also considers this hierarchical conflict of interrogatives Carr set out in *The Mystery Writer's Handbook*, but Joshi's inability to understand Carr on his own terms leads him to conclude Carr's work is uneven or limited. Joshi frequently mistakes Carr's choices for shortcomings. He does admit of Carr, "no one can deny that what he chose to do he did supremely well" (p. 112), but unfortunately, Joshi never recognizes that Carr is con-

of the complete essay would wait until the revised edition (1991) of Douglas Greene's *The Door to Doom*. Quotations here are from Queen's limited edition.

sciously following the literary values and styles of the authors he most enjoyed, most of those being commonly understood as Romanticists.

The theme of the highest interest to Carr, which he shared with many of his role models, was the persistence of, and struggle against, human evil. This is well known. Late in his career (*The House at Satan's Elbow*, 1972), Dr. Fell, who has seen much of it, asks (p. 168), "Don't you believe in human evil?" In Carr's fiction, human evil often seems to be manifested by the supernatural, which vies with human agency in the narratives to explain this problem of evil. Evil is, of course, a central problem of Romanticism, particularly of the Gothic romance.

Let us specify what terming Carr a Romanticist means. Although the two words are intertwined etymologically and in their subject matter, Romanticism is not the exploration of what is sentimentally "romantic." In the Anglo-American tradition of Romanticism, its earliest practitioners were the school of English poets familiar to any readers who have taken secondary and college literature courses: Wordsworth, Coleridge, Byron, Keats, and Shelley. While many labels describing literary and artistic movements are not self-created or self-applied— for instance, Monet, Cézanne, Renoir, Seurat et al. did not invent the term Impressionism or declare themselves Impressionists—as it happens, Samuel Taylor Coleridge inspired the term Romanticism in his *Biographia Literaria* (1817). In Chapter XIV, Coleridge summarized his contributions to the seminal work he and Wordsworth coauthored, *Lyrical Ballads* (1798), as "directed to persons and characters supernatural, or at least romantic."[7] The label Romantic grew out of this explanation, and stuck. Still, this chapter of *Biographia Literaria* contributed much more to our literary understanding than merely a term used in potted histories and college texts. It also identified the essential quality and accomplishment of creative writing, on which Coleridge and Wordsworth agreed: "the power of exciting the sympathy of the reader by faithful adherence to the truth of nature, and the power of giving the interest of novelty by the modifying colours of imagination" (p. 174). That is the generative soul of Romanticism, and in service to its ends, Coleridge in this chapter also famously conceived the all-important condition, still in effect today, that the writer's work must include, "a semblance of truth sufficient to procure for these shadows of imagination that willing suspension of disbelief" (p. 174)—because Romantic works "give the charm of novelty to things of every day, and…excite a feeling analogous to the supernatural, by awakening the mind's attention from the lethargy of custom, and directing it to the loveliness and the wonders of the world before us" (pp. 174-175).

---

7 *Biographia Literaria*, Leavitt, Lord & Co., 1834, p. 174. All subsequent excerpts are drawn from the same edition.

Subsequent practitioners of Romanticism—especially fiction writers such as Mary Shelley, Sir Walter Scott, Charlotte Brontë, Melville, Hawthorne, and Poe—expanded what we have come to recognize as the defining characteristics of Romanticism, which include: the importance and power of the imagination; the sublime (grand, lofty, transcendental, inconceivably terrible, or other subject matter so outside everyday experience that it startles us and inspires unfamiliar awe); a primitivistic appreciation of the natural world; the supernatural; the picturesque; sentimentalism; the exploration of extreme mental states, including love, fear, obsession, irrationality, and manias; an admiring interest in revolutionary thoughts and periods, whether intellectual or political; and cultural heritage, particularly gallantry and other ideals that define a culture according to its highest self-estimation.

Romantic fiction, including Carr's, was frequently intertwined with the Gothic. Of course, Poe is an exemplar, and in this context he was both the best-known practitioner and the most significant influence upon Carr. (There were other Gothic writers who perceptibly influenced Carr, including M.R. James, Ambrose Bierce, F. Marion Crawford, and E.F. Benson.) Of Carr's connection with the Gothic, Greene notes (p. 109), "More than any other writer after Poe, Carr showed in his works the connection between the gothic novel and the detective story."

Gothic fiction has its own set of defining characteristics, which are so compatible with Romantic principles that the phrase, "gothic romance" is perhaps generally better understood than the unaccompanied literary term "Gothic." The important characteristics of Gothic writing include: a nightmarish atmosphere of horror, suspense, or dread, especially with the (apparent) presence of the supernatural; a preoccupation with the past, which intrudes upon and threatens the present; the ascendancy of imagination and emotion, often placing terror into conflict with romance, or even commingling them; and physical settings that manifest these moods, which as literary devices typically symbolize and reflect characters' inner fear and agitation in the surrounding environment, e.g., centuries-old castles, ruins, barren landscapes, or any chilling site wrapped in tenebrous light, decay, or loneliness.

Nineteenth-century American authors whose writings consistently exploited both these traditions—including Poe, Hawthorne, and Melville—have sometimes been called the school of Dark Romanticism, which was defined, in part, as a reaction against the optimism of the Transcendentalists and their belief in the perfectibility of humanity and its harmonious relationship with nature. Dark Romanticists are concerned with the intrinsic weakness of people, their susceptibility to evil, and with humanity's conflicted relationship with nature. Given this, Dark Romantic works are set uneasily in indifferent, sometimes hostile environments peopled with flawed, disturbed, and even self-destructive characters. Significant works in the tradition— much of Poe of course, but also academic standards such as *The Scarlet Letter* and *Moby-Dick*, can be readily and richly interpreted along these lines.

So can Carr's works. Carr is an inheritor of all three of these literary traditions; they seeped into much of his fiction—especially during the 1930s and 1940s—during which he wrote two-thirds of his total output, despite continuing to write novels until 1972. Carr's participation in the Gothic, for instance, is not merely atmospheric; it is significant, as Joanna Kokot cogently argues:

> Contrary to most contemporary detective tales, Carr's novels do not present a crime as a mere (no matter how complicated) puzzle, an intellectual problem to be solved both by the fictitious detective and by the reader. The references to the conventions of Gothic fiction are at the same time references to a model of reality where the mimetic order has been violated by an alien element which is terrifying because it undermines the very essence of the universal harmony.[8]

The lurid passages from Carr's novels and stories that one can recall and cite, comfortably fixing him into this context, are numerous. From time to time, Carr—ever lighthearted and opportunistically hurling some outrageously, even gruesomely funny detail into the midst of the grave and the frightening—flirtatiously acknowledged his place in the Gothic tradition openly. Consider the explanation in *The Curse of the Bronze Lamp* (1945) of the novel's Severn Hall, in which Carr silently traces the roots of his literary ancestry:

> This passion for the "Gothic" was started, about the middle of the eighteenth century, by a certain Mr. Horace Walpole. Walpole bought a modest villa at Twickenham, and gradually set about enlarging it in what his romantic soul imagined to be a medieval manner. Darkling towers, stained glass—"lean windows fattened by rich saints"—a profusion of antique armour and weapons, gladdened his heart at Strawberry Hill.

---

8 "John Dickson Carr's Early Detective Novels and the Gothic Convention," *Lublin Studies in Modern Languages and Literature*, 2019 (43/2), pp. 61-74.

> Mr. Walpole presently wrote a novel called *The Castle of Otranto.* And he began a literary fashion which, with the assistance of Mrs. Radcliffe and "Monk" Lewis, lasted well into the nineteenth century.
> Our great-great grandmothers thrilled to these romances. "Is it horrid?" asks one of them eagerly, in Miss Austen's gentle satire. "Have you read it? Are you sure it is horrid?" (p. 28)

The Romanticism underlying Carr's embrace of the Gothic is distinguished from the literary schools that preceded and followed it in its consistent emphasis on the transformative power of the imagination. Probably the best critical explication of Romanticism's core principle—and one faithfully tied to Coleridge's original formulation—is the eponymous metaphor of M.H. Abrams' 1953 seminal study of Romanticism: *The Mirror and the Lamp.* (A 1953 study may not represent the cutting edge of twenty-first-century academic discussion, but it more than suits our purpose when placing Carr, a twentieth-century writer, into the context of his literary predecessors.) Abrams' thesis is easily summarized: before the Romantics, literature was perceived as a mirror being held up to the world, reflecting it accurately. Romanticism, instead, embraces the primacy of the author's imagination, which the writer casts over the landscape, illuminating it with the light and shadow of imagination, thereby transforming the landscape, not mirroring it, and transforming our perception of it. Romanticism depicts the world not "as it is," but as the artist's imagination insists it should be.

All experienced readers of Carr recognize this insistence (the world not as it is, but as the imagination makes it) is centrally characteristic of him. Greene, for instance, as quoted by John C. Tibbetts in their 1994 interview, said:

> Carr saw the world as it should be, as he wanted it to be... From his earliest high school writing, he yearned for that kind of world. He hated realistic writing. He didn't think the purpose of literature was to describe things the way they are—he said in college he didn't want the thump of the janitor's mop of [sic] the "hard-boiled stuff."

It is important, especially in Carr's case (because of the fantastic circumstances in his fiction), not to mistake Romanticism with a simple lack of realism, or to conflate Carr's work with unconnected fantasy. Carr despised the banality of *realism,* but he cherished *believ-*

ability. Greene offers insight into why Carr, while not being a realist, always remained believable:

> Carr was less interested in whether a story is probable than in whether it is entertaining and believable…. Carr…made his stories believable by a punctilious attention to detail. When he described a room, he included enough vivid points so that, for the reader, the room is real. When he talked about such things as tarot cards, a watch in the shape of a skull, strange poisons, a transatlantic voyage or swordplay, he wrote with the authority of an expert. His early stories are as completely researched as his later historical novels, so that even though the crimes *seem* humanly impossible, the settings and the other trappings of the mystery are real.[9]

As Carr himself put it, "The reader…is quite willing to believe in Santa Claus, but you must give him a glimpse of the old gentleman's boots coming down the chimney."[10]

While Carr did not, of course, declare or limit himself to being a practitioner within a literary school—which would, in fact, run quite contrary to his iconoclasm—nonetheless, from the first, Carr clearly championed the primacy of imagination both within his fiction and outside it (in his critical writings and correspondence). Stefano Serafini puts his finger on one key expression of this from Carr's amateur period, the collegiate story "The Murder in Number Four." In it, Bencolin mouths views we recognize as one of Carr's own principles for detective fiction:

> Bencolin affirms that, "the great detective is the one who can visualize the board as it *has been* when he finds the pieces jumbled. He must have the imagination to see the opportunities that the criminal saw, and act as the criminal would act"…Reason, Bencolin maintains, "reduces the thing to the silly restricted rules of mathematics," whereas crime is a [sic] "ugly, terrific play of opposite imaginations."[11]

Kirkus Reviews, in their review of Greene's biography, seemed puz-

9 *The Door to Doom and Other Detections*, Harper and Row, 1980, p. 10.

10 "The Detective in Fiction," *The Writer*, June 1932 (44/6).

11 "Murder, Mayhem, and Madness: John Dickson Carr's Gothic Detective Stories," *Clues: A Journal of Detection*, Fall 2020, pp. 29-30.

zled by Carr's works being "simultaneously florid and analytically precise," in reflection of "Carr's personality, by turns punctilious and devil-may-care."[12] To any regular reader of Carr, this is a puzzling critique. Yes, Carr's writing is (as with most or all authors) an evident extension of his personality, and of his literary perspective. We readily understand how and why—according to tradition and disposition— Carr paints for his readers a world terrorized by inexplicable murders committed within a gothic twilight colored in reds, purples, and blacks. These murders are solved, and the reliable bulwarks of sanity and social order buttressed, by the cold daylight rationality emanating from the detective's mind. As we shall see, the style supporting these works harnesses not just (Dark) Romantic and Gothic conventions, but more generally, literary antithesis and incongruity. These tools are, especially as Carr uses them, both playful and propulsive of suspense. Understanding Carr's literary roots, his personality, his style, and his views, one wonders at *Kirkus Reviews*' question, not the answer. The answer is evident.

The youthful Carr's experimentation with multiple genres and techniques led him naturally into the Romantic and Gothic traditions, simply because he was emulating the writers whom he most admired and writing in the fictive areas most stimulating to him. Carr was never an acolyte, either: he quickly grew past any such tendencies (which we can detect in his earliest stories). Carr's course toward his professional career was one of a young author rapidly discovering his interests and strengths. Happily, because the seeds of the accomplished writer he would become did germinate rapidly, most of Carr's amateur stories are not overly indebted to, or constrained by, notions of literary tradition; neither are they compromised by excessive borrowing of plots; nor are his amateur tales generally enervated by too much or too clumsy, obvious borrowing from the authors he emulated. There are discernible exceptions, of course. Carr was not a fully original or masterful writer from the first moment his pen touched paper. Still, there is gratifying originality and skill in Carr's first tales, perhaps more than we might have the right to expect. As Douglas Greene (p. 39) ironically observes:

> In looking at his *Hill Record* stories as a whole, it is
> surprising that John Dickson Carr's least effective
> stories are the types that he excelled in writing as an
> adult—detective and supernatural stories. In none of
> these was he able successfully to combine plot struc-

---

12 *"John Dickson Carr: The Man Who Explained Miracles,"* *Kirkus Reviews*, Feb 1, 1995, pp. 129-130.

ture and atmosphere. But [in]...the best of his efforts... some of his descriptive passages are so good, some of his story ideas so compelling, some of his characterizations so sharp, it is easy to overlook the fact that John was between fifteen and eighteen years old when he wrote these stories. It is also easy to fall into the trap of expecting too much maturity in them and to feel let down when we find that his attitudes were still those of a teenager. He was, nevertheless, a very talented teenager.

So the reader should be prepared, perhaps, to be as, or more, entertained by the young Carr's non-mystery fiction as by his earliest efforts at detective tales. Certainly, one of the pleasures in this collection is seeing these other, less expected sides of Carr, the detective novelist we feel we understand so well as the master of the miracle crime.

While, as we noted, the teenage author's technique and prose included some predictably amateurish aspects he would need to outgrow (and did), some of Carr's identifying characteristics of style emerged swiftly in his high school and college efforts, presaging tendencies and techniques of his mature writings. For instance, from the beginning, Carr loved subtly reusing details; in some cases, these were borrowed from favorite authors. Carr helped himself to narrative elements as broad as premises and as specific as character names.

Consider M.R. James as one case study. His *Ghost Stories of an Antiquary* (1904) seems particularly to have influenced Carr. Even as a fledgling writer, Carr was too interested in developing his own *plots* merely to copy others', but he did enjoy borrowing *premises* from the tales he relished as a reader and then, as a writer, re-fashioning those premises into his own stories. Carr borrowed several premises from the tales in M.R. James's first collection of ghost stories. James's "Canon Alberic's Scrap-Book" was probably one inspiration for Carr's "The Devil-Gun" (included in this volume, with detailed discussion following it); as Greene suggests convincingly in the biography (p. 86), James's story "Number 13," concerning a hotel room that mysteriously appears, disappears, and reappears, became the "lost gallows in a lost room on a lost street" in *The Lost Gallows* (1931); and G.W. Thomas proposes (in *Dark Worlds Quarterly*, July 14, 2020) that "The Treasure of Abbot Thomas" is the "obvious" inspirational source of Carr's *Hag's Nook*, "with its evil clergyman (changed to a prison warden), crytpograms [sic], and a treasure in a well."

Carr almost certainly further appropriated the character name "Anstruther" from James's story, "The Rose Garden" (*More Ghost Sto-*

ries, 1911), in which the ghost of Charles II's Lord Chief Justice, George Jeffreys (famously, "the Hanging Judge") troubles Mr. and Mrs. George Anstruther. An Anstruther of no disclosed given name appears in Carr's 1926 "The Devil-Gun"; another Sir George—not likely James's character, but perhaps related—goes in the company of Carr's featured detectives during two early Carter (Carr) Dickson novels, *The Bowstring Murders* and *The Red Widow Murders* (1935).

In fact, Carr relished reusing characters and names—often clearly the same characters, sometimes not—early and often throughout his career. Carr's first significant recurring character is of course Henri Bencolin, not yet promoted to *juge d'instruction*, who appears in this collection in "The New Canterbury Tales" (1927) and the novella *Grand Guignol* (1929). In Carr's college literary journal, *The Haverfordian*, Bencolin had already appeared twice before the former in short stories published in 1926 and 1927; he would appear again in two more before the latter. (None of those four is included here; all were published in Douglas Greene's *The Door to Doom and Other Detections*.) Bencolin would of course go on to feature in five of Carr's professional detective novels. His friend Sir John Landervorne accompanied Bencolin in three of the *Haverfordian* detective stories, in "The New Canterbury Tales," and, most memorably and consequentially, in *The Lost Gallows*, Carr's second professional novel.

Other, less certain character echoes abound starting with these tales told in school. Perhaps Patrick O'Riordan, the bibulous, one-armed secret service agent who first appeared with Bencolin in "The Fourth Suspect" and reappears in "The New Canterbury Tales," is related to Terence O'Riordan, Carr's avatar in "The Cloak of D'Artagnan." Remembrance of Cyril Merton, a suspect with whom Bencolin crosses paths in "Shadow of the Goat," is later summoned by the detective in both "The New Canterbury Tales" and *Grand Guignol*. This strategic re-use brings subtle fullness and consistency to the young Carr's fictive milieu; he continued employing the technique in the professional novels. Consider how Michael Tairlaine recognizes H.M.'s name upon first hearing it in *The Red Widow Murders*: "His friend John Gaunt had mentioned it—almost (for Gaunt) with admiration" (p. 24). Gaunt is, of course, the featured detective, a Sherlockian former Scotland Yarder, of *The Bowstring Murders*, according to Sir George Anstruther, "probably the greatest criminological genius England ever had" (p. 72). The Sherlockian Gaunt's complicated and understated admiration of H.M., nicknamed "Mycroft," is also a subtly clever echo of the relationship between Arthur Conan Doyle's originals. Similarly, Douglas Greene points out that in *Death-Watch* (1935):

Dr. Fell calls on an old French friend who "used to be associated with Bencolin at the Prefecture in Paris." This statement connects the Bencolin and Fell books—despite their differences, they exist in the same world of Carr's imagination" (p. 148).

There are more echoes: the alert reader reasonably wonders whether Bencolin's friend, the old writer Ludwig von Arnheim ("New Canterbury Tales," and the detective figure of "As Drink the Dead," 1926, included in *The Door to Doom and Other Detections*), is any relation to the detective's old rival, Baron Sigmund von Arnheim, who contends with Bencolin just four years later in *Castle Skull* (1931)—or for that matter, whether Baron von Arnheim's name is borrowed from Sir Walter Scott's Baron Arnheim, featured in the 1829 supernatural tale, "Donnerhugel's Narrative." (Of interest, S.T. Joshi, p. 14, connects Carr's two Arnheims, but improbably decides they are the same character, despite their markedly different ages, physical appearances, careers, and social stations.) Is Ken Blake, who appears in *The Plague Court Murders*, *The Unicorn Murders* (1935), *The Punch and Judy Murders* (1937), *The Judas Window* (1938), and *And So To Murder* (1940) actually an older incarnation of the romantic protagonist of Carr's "The Gordon Djinn"—the young newspaperman-turned-detective-story-writer protagonist of a 1925 *Hill Record* tale (not included here), which is humorously resolved either by magic (a djinn) or by drunkenness (gin), depending on what the reader believes? Across decades of writing, Carr less ambiguously traces the family line of Lafayette ("The Will-o'-the-Wisp," 1922) by featuring that Revolutionary legend's nephew in "The Gentleman from Paris" (1950).

One of the most entertaining examples of continuity in Carr's corpus, decades removed from his school days, demonstrates Carr's love for historical games. In *Captain Cut-Throat*, Carr places a delicate, rose-agate snuffbox in the shape of a pocket watch, a gift from the Emperor Napoleon himself, into the hand of the spymaster Fouché. This is the same snuffbox Carr's loyal readers, having read 1942's *The Emperor's Snuff-Box* more than a decade earlier, realize will be destroyed nearly 140 years after the events of *Captain Cut-Throat* during the commission of a domestic murder in a fictional Paris neighborhood. Nor let us forget that Fouché himself first turns up in Carr's novels residing in a portrait on the wall of H.M.'s office (*The Plague Court Murders*).

This is not the entire catalogue of playful Carrian echoes, not even of those related specifically to the amateur stories. Other instances are documented in the commentaries. Having noted this, we should not overlook perhaps Carr's most significant character-name appropriation: Patrick Butler, whom Carr first encountered as a schoolboy reader of Chesterton's "The Man in the Passage" (1913, collected the following year in *The Wisdom of Father Brown*).[13] Not only did Carr borrow Butler's name, but the Irishman's profession (King's Counsel), too, featuring the barrister in *Below Suspicion* (1949) and *Patrick Butler for the Defence* (1956). Surely, Carr enjoyed the implicit jest of having the barrister whom Chesterton created collaborate with Dr. Fell, the detective whom Carr created in the likeness of Chesterton. Along with Napoleon's snuffbox, this is one of the best examples of Carr's lifelong sportiveness with recurring elements. Some, similarly to these two, firmly connect different narratives across decades; the significance of other echoes is more open to speculation. In any event, Carr perpetrated such small whimsies for nearly a half century, from practically his first fiction to his last.

Another amusing pattern: one must note that Carr, always proud of his heritage, never neglected even an improbable opportunity to insert an Irish character into the midst of a narrative, which we will see several times in this collection. One of the funniest and most unexpected such insertions during Carr's professional years occurs in *The Four False Weapons* (1937), when a young, deskbound, adventure-seeking Richard Curtis, having traveled to Paris, enters a private gambling establishment run by the venerable Marquise de la Toursèche:

> "You are Mr. Curtis?" she said, pouncing. She pronounced the name in the English way; then she presented the man with dim eyes by some title Curtis did not catch. "We are always glad to welcome any friend of Philippe de Maupasson. I have seen you at Le Touquet?"
>
> "No, madame."
>
> "Or at the home of the Marquise de Bourdillac?"
>
> "I fear not, madame," said Curtis, a little disturbed at all these great names, and also at the way she was firing out her machine-gun questions.
>
> "You are English?"
>
> "Yes."
>
> "From London?"
>
> "Yes."
>
> "I am Irish," said Madame unexpectedly, in English; and she laughed. Her laughter was a part of the same

---

13 Predictably, Greene notes the same in *The Chestertonian Review*, Vol. X, No. 3, "A Mastery of Miracles: G.K. Chesterton and John Dickson Carr," p. 314.

gusto. Yet her speech had a rusty and disused note, more foreign than French, and seemed to jar her like the works of a clock. "You see my name on the card—Deidre, though poor Philippe takes liberties there. The O'Dowd was my father, more years ago than you would guess. I am one of the lost seven hundred and seventy-seven tribes." (p. 226)

What is the significance of all Carr's puckish borrowing and minor repetitions? Apart from milieu-building, a Carrian practice most readers overlook, the repetitions reinforce what we already knew: Carr enjoyed games. As Martin Edwards observes, "For Carr, playing games was a lifelong passion."[14] These little connections and echoes are also small demonstrations of Carr's credo that the friendly competition between author and reader in detective fiction is "The Grandest Game in the World." Such repetitions are not red herrings, but they are deliberate attention grabbers, not coincidences Carr forgetfully committed. As the reader will see in some of the commentaries, Carr could be quite calculating in their use. He reminded readers in "The Grandest Game in the World" that (his emphasis), *"Once the evidence has been fairly presented, there are very few things which are not permissible"* (p. 20). Any distracting game Carr could play with the reader's attention was, in this sense, a manipulative, fair-play gimmick. Carr wished to keep the reader guessing which obscure bits might turn out to be consequential. For instance, is the Emperor's snuffbox an important physical clue, a misdirection drawing the reader's attention away from another physical clue, or both? By tantalizing loyal and attentive readers with the snuffbox's unmentioned history and peculiar physical characteristics, Carr induces confusion, helping him slide proximate clues past the reader that much more subtly.

Carr's mischievous propensity also demonstrates his delight in gratifying any loyal, eagle-eyed readers who uncover his subtle seeming continuities. What's more, Carr's acquisition of character names from authors he admired is a tribute to them and his quiet placement of himself into their tradition.

The general revelation, though, behind these small ploys is of the author's waggish spirit. Recall that most of Carr's early novels were part of the Harper's Sealed Mystery series, each installment of which interposed a printed tissue barrier between the disclosure of the final needful clue and the book's conclusion, in which the solution was unveiled and explained. That printed seal gleefully challenged the reader to break it in order to learn the murderer's identity, or to leave the seal in place and return the book for a refund. What an apt pairing of pub-

---

14 *The Golden Age of Murder*, Collins Crime Club, 2015, p. 369. All subsequent excerpts are drawn from the same edition.

lisher and author!

Carr played authorial games with authorial names, too, not just with his characters'. In his college literary journal, *The Haverfordian*, Carr frequently wrote both anonymously and pseudonymously. At times and with their consent, to hide the overabundance of his output, Carr borrowed the names of other journal staff (Frederic Prokosch, Ira Rutherford, Francis Jameson, George Rogers), and perhaps even once that of a professor, William Reitzel. As Prokosch confessed years later, "Carr was the instigator of all this nonsense" (what Prokosch called "prankish pseudonyms") "and the rest of us merely consenting co-conspirators."[15] The name games didn't end there, either; other *Haverfordian* contributions of his appeared under nearly arbitrary sets of initials and several pseudonyms, the most entertaining of which is Eric Hirth—a character from Carr's second high-school publication, "The House of Terror" (included in this collection). Carr would go on professionally to use, propose, or consider the use of nearly a dozen pseudonyms: Nicholas Wood (considered, and later reclaimed as a Detective Inspector in *The Gilded Man*, and a tribute to his father); Christopher Street (proposed to Morrow); Carr Dickson (used once by Morrow); Piers Henderson (suggested by Hamilton); Roger Fairbairn (used once by Hamilton and Harper); Cartwright Dixon (proposed to Morrow); Carter Dickson (used by Morrow); Neill Cream (a real-life serial killer, considered by Carr); and Robert Southwell (used for a single radio script). What's in a name? Mystification, apparently.

Carr's borrowing and reworking of premises, without being overly derivative of those premises' specific plots, also remained characteristic of him throughout his career, serving Carr especially usefully during that decade and a half or so during which he wrote radio scripts. For more than fifteen years, Carr both adapted other writers' tales as source material and reworked earlier scripts of his own into new ones as he moved from one radio series to the next. Some radio scripts he even later expanded into novels.

Where adaptations were concerned, these reliably reflected the writers whom Carr most admired (which we learn from Carr's writings in other contexts). Carr adapted Robert Louis Stevenson's "The Body-Snatcher" (1884) and "The Sire de Maletroit's Door" (drawn from Stevenson's collection *New Arabian Nights*, 1882) for the radio horror series *Appointment with Fear*. (In fact, he first adapted "The Body-Snatcher" for *Suspense* the year before.) Carr penned his most adaptations for *Appointment with Fear*, but they were relatively few, ten of the fifty-one scripts he wrote for the program. He based those,

---

15 As cited by Greene in the biography, p. 46.

in addition to the works by Stevenson, upon tales by Poe, Chesterton, Conan Doyle, Ambrose Bierce, and Melville Davisson Post. *How* Carr adapted his sources is a reminder of his determination to be fresh and original. Even when he borrowed, Carr departed markedly from the originals, taking what Greene has fairly observed a great deal of liberty such that they "are so altered that they are essentially his own stories. Carr took a single part of each of the plots…and wrote a new plot around it" (p. 289). These adaptations nonetheless point clearly to the writers whom Carr most admired. His talent for recycling also helps explain, in part, how he could be so prolific: Carr would occasionally reuse a gimmick, but was able to disguise it so cleverly that even his experienced readers were unlikely to recognized it before Carr revealed the solution. So his gift of taking whatever material he had at hand, rotating it to an unfamiliar angle, and refashioning it into something seemingly new served equally well whether he borrowed from others or from himself. Like a card magician, Carr used one dexterous set of skills to create multiple illusions, each illusion seemingly different from the rest.

This leads us to another mechanicism of interest to observe in the young Carr, and how it changed, grew, and improved during his professional years: Carr's fiendish inventiveness, his construction of the miracle crimes and their solutions for which he is most highly and often praised. Many readers of the Master will be familiar with Carr's boast to his Brooklyn housemate Tommy Tomlinson, "I've had exactly one hundred and twenty plots outlined, for emergencies, since I was eleven years old."[16] It is unfortunately tempting to believe, in one or two of Carr's earliest amateur mysteries, that their mechanics were indeed conceived by an eleven-year-old: as noted earlier, Carr's youthful mysteries, perhaps because in part we measure them with his later brilliance in mind, are the least impressive among Carr's early efforts. Without any disclosures here as to the specifics, in the commentaries following this volume's pertinent selections, we will treat more in detail the kinds of solutions Carr employed, as well as their relative originality (because, as noted, Carr was not above reusing one he particularly liked), sophistication, and success. As a generalization, though, the reader of this collection will recognize the early stirrings of Carr's gift for weaving his ingenuity throughout a work, with just enough clues provided at different points of the narrative to maintain a lively pace and provide a satisfying denouement, which in the detective-fiction novels, always included a detailed explanation of how the central crime was perpetrated. S.T. Joshi summarizes this well:

16 Robert Lewis Taylor, "Two Authors in an Attic" (Part II), *The New Yorker*, September 15, 1951, p. 44.

The real secret to Carr's narrative structure—and accordingly, to his intense readability—is his ability to explain parts of the puzzle throughout the course of the work, so that as the end approaches only the problem of who (or, more frequently and pertinently, how) remains to be answered. If Carr had saved the solution of the entire puzzle to the end, it is quite possible that nearly half the book would be devoted to the elucidation... (p. 131)

As Joshi also does in his book, any reader interested in Carr's technical excellence should revisit Robert Lewis Taylor's summary of Carr's narrative construction methods:

First...he draws upon what he calls a "clue outline," marking points in the narrative at which he plans to plant the signposts to the guilt of whichever fiend he is building. Then, with elaborate pains, he makes working sketches of the characters, sometimes promoting minor players to star roles, and the reverse, as he goes...He jots down snatches of dialogue as he visualizes the characters and hears their speech in his mind. Plotting is easy for Carr—he habitually sees the entire network of human relations as a slough of intrigue—and the blocking out of the separate scenes is perhaps his favorite chore.[17]

The reader of the present collection will discover indications Carr began developing this approach during his amateur years, certainly no later than *Grand Guignol*, but arguably as early as 1922. Carr's early mysteries, although short, show suggestive glimmers of this kind of planning.

It may not be overstating his virtues to claim that as a technician, Carr's writing skills rivaled most canonical poets', and were leveraged to similarly disciplined formal standards as demanding as the ones those poets honored. As a constructor of narrative, Carr successfully challenged himself to compose some of the best-written narratives in his specialty form, the detective novel. As with great writers of short stories or sonnets, Carr's technical execution was astonishing for its rigor and discipline, delivered in the guise of an engrossing narrative that did not draw attention to its mechanics, and which was richly soaked in pleasing components: the gothic; the

---

17 Ibid, p. 40.

comic; the historic; the romantic; striking images; clever dialogue. The studied carelessness of construction in Carr's detective novels is non-pareil.

We do not admire Shakespeare for inventing the sonnet or inno-vating with it, which he did not; we admire him for the superiority with which he exploited the existing form. We can likewise admire Carr for the same kind of high accomplishment in detective fiction. If Greene had only acknowledged Carr's uniting the Gothic and detective fiction more than any writer after Poe, he would have underpraised Carr, but he also notes, "Carr combined genres in a way that not even Poe had done before him, and that few authors would do after him" (p. 85). In the long form (where Poe never ventured in detective fiction), Carr met and overcame technical challenges that detective short-story writers do not face in trying to create and sustain mood, characterization, and atmospheric setting—most pointedly, in constructing a sophisticated, long-form detective story worthy of its novel length. Carr became one of the last great practitioners of the Gothic romance, perhaps *the* last one—which in his commingling it with the detective-fiction format, Carr revivified for modern audiences. Carr understood he was doing this; he wrote:

> I am inclined to think that these detective-exploits are one of the few branches of romance left to us. If you read some of these strange and eerie crimes, you will feel that sense of awe and terror of which I have spo-ken as the chief requisite of fiction. Crime is sordid, yes—like birth and money and fundamental things. But in the magical ingenuity by which the brain of man resolves it, we penetrate a world of romance not far from the Arabian Nights.[18]

To Carr, the mystery came first, but his participation in the tradi-tion of Gothic romance was a literary inheritance he wished to pre-serve and invigorate. Mainstream fiction had long since moved along from the Gothic romance until Carr remade it with the detective novel. "I can fancy him pacing those halls at night, reflecting the plan he had evolved, chuckling at an irony which was in line with the tales of the medieval writers he loved."[19]

Carr was not alone in blending these genres in the early twentieth century, but Carr was, consistently, the best. His accomplishment still stands, in the next century, at the heights of general mystery fiction,

---

18 "The Detective in Fiction," *The Writer*, June 1932 (44/6).

19 *It Walks By Night*, p. 280.

too: Carr was not a niche writer who created obscure works in an area in which nobody else was writing, or one without much of an audience. Carr's technical ability to do all he did, painstakingly in mainstream fiction, is admirable. Other authors wrote *individual* novels that probed the boundaries between the supernatural, the horrifying, and the criminal; Carr was a relentless *practitioner* in this domain, one with unmatched formalistic capability.

We should not overlook, either, that Carr was something of a detective-fiction experimentalist, too. Whether we summon to mind Carr's debut, *It Walks By Night*, for its innovative combination of fair-play detection, suspense, and horrifying atmosphere; or *The Blind Barber*, not only for its hiding clues beneath hilarity, but for Dr. Fell's enigmatic armchair taxonomy of those clues, which he uses to explain the solution; or *The Burning Court* (1937) for its unique but satisfying subversion of Carr's own genre; or *The Murder of Sir Edmund Godfrey* (1936) for its re-presentation of history as detective fiction; or *The Arabian Nights Murder* (1936) for its seamless combination of the fair-play detective novel with a multiple-perspective narrative; or *The Three Coffins* for its astonishingly breaking the fourth wall with Dr. Fell's locked-room lecture; or *The Judas Window* for its fusion of locked-room and courtroom novels; or, of course, Carr's arguable invention of the historical detective novel beginning with *Devil Kinsmere*, extended in the 1950s by Carr's peculiar (but again, wholly satisfying and original) time-traveling twist, we come to recognize that Carr's technical virtuosity was versatile, too. Indeed, just as the young John Dickson Carr experimented with broadly different genres—poetry, literary fiction, nonfiction, horror, fantasy, adventure, humor, and mystery—so the older Carr continued, experimenting with refinements in narrative approach and genre-bending that kept his efforts consistently interesting (to both himself and to his readers).

Why, then, if Carr was a participant in broader and historically interesting literary traditions, as well as being among the best writers in his widely popular genre, do we find ourselves a century after he first began writing, and fifty years after he published his final novel, still making an argument for Carr's place in the conversation? It certainly is not a want of skills; Carr's are worthy of comparison with more accepted, better remembered writers (candidly, his are sometimes superior), inside and outside the mystery genre. For those of us familiar with him, we also recognize that the issue is not Carr's readability, either, which remains high. Reading a John Dickson Carr novel is engrossing and entertaining, which is as much as we ask of a number of writers more broadly known. The simplest answer is that Carr never broke through the general cultural barrier, which is usually the qualifying characteristic for any author perceived primarily as a genre writer (no matter whether or how many non-genre books that author may have written). While he sold well enough, Carr was not a bestseller, nor did he produce that one iconic book or character that resonated beyond his audience of mystery readers and authorial peers. Agatha Christie remains well known today because her books sold (and still sell) on a magnitude beyond not just most authors in her genre, but of most authors altogether. As well, the many adaptations of her works into film and television have helped perpetuate Christie's popularity. Seeming destined to be remembered forever, would Conan Doyle be generally known if he had not invented Sherlock Holmes? Would Dumas be remembered without *The Three Musketeers*, or Stevenson without *Treasure Island*? C.S. Forester wrote dozens of serious works, including histories and literary novels, all mostly forgotten and few still culturally relevant today. Nonetheless, Forester's creation of Horatio Hornblower and the Age of Sail adventure genre have made him a popular-culture giant. John Huston's adaptation of *The African Queen* into an enduring film classic has also burnished Forester's legacy. Unlike these and other more generally recognized authors, the difference in Carr's recognition likely comes down to the fact that he never achieved that broader cultural breakthrough. None of Carr's detective novels crossed the genre divide into general readership the way some of Christie's did. It may not help that in his other work, Carr looked, perhaps a little backwardly, to radio, instead of looking forward to television and film: there have been fewer opportunities to carry his name forward in the new media that came to dominate the latter half of the twentieth century. So as good as Carr's work is, there is not one, simple, powerful creation of his that achieved recognition outside the genre. While Carr's *reputation* has not languished—those who read Carr understand his excellence—his *renown* has. And when a special-interest audience reads a writer in a specialized (genre) context, the writer tends to stay stuck there. There are worse things than being remembered in the same breath with G.K. Chesterton instead of Agatha Christie, but let us not conflate Carr's quality with his fame.

In the end, despite a lack of broader recognition for Carr, when we consider who some of the more interesting and gifted storytellers of the twentieth century were, we may non-hyperbolically class Carr among them—and unlike many others of interest, through the early tales collected here, we have the opportunity to witness how his gifts began to grow.

Carr's amateur tales confirm, for instance, how quickly the brisk, page-turning pace of his narratives began emerging. From the first, Carr tried to conclude almost every section or chapter with a dramatic crisis or revelation that left the reader wishing to learn immediately what follows.[20] In his first extant story, a 1921 high-school mystery titled, "The Ruby of Rameses" (featuring a blind French detective who may have been something of a first draft for a recurring character, discarded), Carr concludes the opening section with the discovery of a corpse:

> Obediently he drew back a few feet, flexed his muscles for a spring, and hurtled forward like the human juggernaut he was. With a splintering crash the door yielded to his onslaught, precipitating him into the room on its top. One glance into the spacious, vaulted apartment sufficed to tell that my worst fears had been realized. Slumped forward on the floor beside his chair was the still figure of Brandon Pollard, his muscles curiously lax, his eyes wide open in a fixed, unseeing stare. Shaking off the momentary dizziness which assailed me, I sprang across the room, thrust an arm beneath the recumbent figure, and seized one already clammy wrist. Well I knew, however, what I should find. Beneath the dim stain on the shoulder of that timeworn dressing-gown there was a new, fresh one. The heart that lay beneath it was at peace.

The reader of the present collection should note that whether a story is mystery, adventure, or horror tale, how consistently Carr ends each section (chapter), as he would throughout his career, with a crashing dramatic disclosure.

Another lifelong Carrian touch detectable in these amateur works is a technique Carr borrowed from and attributed to Conan Doyle's invention (in his *Life of Sir Arthur Conan Doyle*, pp. 234-235):

> …the enigmatic clue…it is a thundering good clue at that. It is the trick by which the detective—while giving you perfectly fair opportunity to guess—nevertheless makes you wonder what in sanity's name he is talking about. The creator of Sherlock Holmes invented it; and nobody except the great G.K. Chesterton, whose Father Brown stories were so deeply influenced by the device, has ever done it half so well.[21]

---

20 This is commonly understood and commented, but also pointedly detailed by Joshi on pp. 130-131.

21 Joshi makes the same observation, pp. 109-110.

The universally familiar example of this is the curious incident of the dog in the night-time, from Conan Doyle's "The Adventure of Silver Blaze." Carr, though he acknowledged and credited his predecessors, would go on to rival, if not surpass, their accomplishments in exploiting the enigmatic clue. All Carr's detectives emulated Holmes, uttering their own frequent, wool-gathering mystifications. The reader will encounter Carr's earliest exploitation of this happily maddening gimmick in *Grand Guignol*.

Among all Carr's well-recognized methods and their inspirations, the genesis of one particularly characteristic device may come as a surprise: the author whom the young Carr highly admired whose presentation of the final-twist solution most closely anticipated Carr's own novelistic style was neither Arthur Conan Doyle nor G.K. Chesterton—in fact, the author is not generally considered a mystery writer at all! (More on this when we discuss that author.)

Which writers, then, influenced Carr in his early years, how, and which most strongly? The list of influences upon the voracious young reader and budding author is long and, happily, well documented (in Carr's correspondence and critical tracts). Aside from his native gifts, probably one of the reasons Carr found his own unique voice and style so quickly is because as a developing amateur, he drew in one way or another on as many as thirty role models.[22] This is surely one reason that Carr's young fiction is more varied in kind and tone than his professional works are. He was, as we noted earlier, exploring widely, and so his early writing was not beholden to only one or two influences, nor was it yet narrowed to a single, greatest passion.

Discussion of some of the less important (less lasting) influences upon Carr will occur in context following the selections in this volume where those writers' influences can be plainly discerned. Their influence, for the most part, diminished as Carr matured as a writer. In his

22 As a note for the curious, here is an extended list of authors Carr identified as his young favorites: Brian Oswald Donn Byrne, John Buchan, James Branch Cabell, G.K. Chesterton, James Curwood, Floyd James Dell, Charles Dickens, Arthur Conan Doyle, Alexandre Dumas (père), R. Austin Freeman, Jacques Futrelle, Anna Katherine Green, Zane Grey, Thomas and Mary Hanshew, O. Henry, A.S.M. Hutchinson, Washington Irving, Rudyard Kipling, Gaston Leroux, Natalie Sumner Lincoln, L.T. Meade, E. Phillips Oppenheim, Isabel Ostrander, Eden Philpotts, Edgar Allan Poe, Melville Davisson Post, Arthur B. Reeve, Sax Rohmer, Robert Louis Stevenson, and H.G. Wells. We can also confidently add Ambrose Bierce, F. Marion Crawford, Anthony Hope, and George Barr McCutcheon to this list—although if Carr, in writing, singled out any of these authors for praise, the editor has not been able to locate such references.

March 3, 1968 letter to Nelson Bond, Carr wrote of them, some by name, affectionately yet dismissively:

> The disillusionment of rereading in later years needn't be commented on. Always excepting Sherlock Holmes and Father Brown (these were my salvation), what appalling guff it now seems! How naive, how clumsily plotted and written, with never a clue in sight!
>
> The joke is that some of these people had really ingenious ideas. You may remember the all-but-forgotten name of Jacques Futrelle, an American despite his French name, whose Thinking Machine stories (some good ideas in fair journalese) ended when he went down with the <u>Titanic</u>. You may remember Thomas W. and Mary E. Hanshew, whose stories of Cleek, the Man of the Forty Faces, gave us several clever murder-methods hidden in prose of a hilarious nature. You may remember Arthur B. Reeve's Craig Kennedy. You may remember Anna Katharine Green, Isabel Ostrander, and other lost ladies now well lost.

Carr did nonetheless, occasionally during his professional career, offer subtle nods to some of his childhood favorites whose influence had since fallen away. For instance, the ship in "Cabin B-13" (Carr's radio program) is the *Maurevania*, named (if spelled slightly differently) for the fictional country where Thomas Hanshew set Hamilton Cleek's Ruritanian exploits. In *The Punch and Judy Murders*, Evelyn jokes that Ken, on the run repeatedly from the police, is "The Man of the Forty Races" (p. 140).

As to the authors whom Carr accounted as being the most significant and enduring influences upon him, the reader may be surprised to learn their names, which include some who are essentially forgotten today. Even by Carr's prime years, they already were. Among the remaining familiar writers, in this late day, we tend to read only a few famous pieces by them—so we may not have ready insight into how their less-remembered works influenced Carr.

Our conventional, comfortable perspective is to consider Carr the literary descendent of Poe, Arthur Conan Doyle, and G.K. Chesterton—all of whom *are* literary ancestors of his, this is no error, of course—but it is also an oversimplification, one that reinforces a narrow perception of Carr as merely among a second generation of mystery writers who were the imitators of the genre's great inventors.

Chesterton alone among these three was embraced by Carr as one of his greatest influences. In a letter to Nelson Bond, on March 8, 1967, Carr divulged the authors who had been most influential upon him:

> Well, we both admire the late James Branch Cabell, underlining the truism that nothing fluctuates like the literary stock-market. Those nowadays quoted highest—Proust, Joyce, D.H. Lawrence, Henry James—I won't buy at any price. Those who most influenced me—Stevenson, Chesterton, Cabell, Donn Byrne, O. Henry—seem to be nowhere at all. Not long ago I read a biography of the last-named by a University of Texas professor with so low an opinion of his subject that the reader wonders why he bothered to write it. O. Henry's stock is at an all-time low because there are two things the pundits can't forgive him (a) he was popular; (b) he used surprise endings. That, in egghead eyes, means complete damnation.

Carr's iconoclasm is on full display in this letter, both in his selection of literary ancestors and his dislike of establishmentarian literary standards. Let us examine each of these writers Carr named and understand how genuinely significant each one's influence was, lastingly, upon him. This will help us not merely to read the young Carr we encounter in this volume, but to read the familiar professional with unfamiliar eyes.

James Branch Cabell (1879-1958) is as forgotten as any author Carr ever loved—but he was an especial favorite of Carr's. By the time Carr corresponded first about Cabell with Nelson Bond, almost a decade after Cabell's death, Cabell had firmly fallen into obscurity. A year after Carr's initial mention, on March 22, 1968, he wrote again to Nelson Bond concerning Cabell:

> I believe we are fellow members of the new Cabell Society. The founder, Dr. Rothman, has written to ask for an article on Cabell and how he 'affected my early years.' And I don't know what to say, since my favorite works might be considered curious choices. Much though I enjoyed the saga of Manuel and his descendants, my fondest memories are of <u>Beyond Life</u> and the three books of short stories.

Carr, with his writer's viewpoint, appreciated Cabell differently than most, even than some of Cabell's more devoted readers; he derived his own individualized legacy from Cabell. Nor did Carr ever resolve the dissonance concerning his appreciation for Cabell: Bond made some minor early contributions to Rothman's *The Cabellian* (published twice a year between 1968-1972), but Carr never did.

Even without those further confessions Rothman solicited, we can confidently grasp much of Cabell's appeal to Carr. Modern readers should be warned, though: on the surface, *Carr's writings were nothing like Cabell's, neither those of the young nor those of the mature Carr.* It wasn't only that the works and strengths Carr appreciated in Cabell were less common: Carr did not imitate Cabell, either in narrative style or in genre. Carr internalized Cabell, instead, valuing Cabell's unique voice, perspective, and literary-critical epistemology. This latter is very important. Cabell was a self-proclaimed twentieth-century Romantic, a holdover writing fantasies and medieval narratives in faux-archaic diction. We can trace these same broad tendencies in Carr, but practiced quite differently—and candidly, much more effectively. Nonetheless, when we look for where the young Carr acquired his preoccupation with medievalism, with gentility, with archaic diction, and with the forms of Romanticism generally, we cannot discover them, for instance, in Poe or Chesterton, nor can we account for their emotional importance to Carr through Doyle's works. Cabell was Carr's most significant literary parent in these considerations.

Cabell wrote not just fiction, but criticism; his preeminent analytical publication, which we have seen Carr explicitly admired, was *Beyond Life* (1919). This treatise helped shape Carr's sensibilities about the role of literature in modern life. Carr learned as a teen what his character Jimmy O'Brien did: that any attempt directly to change the world with the editorial pen, not the sword, was futile. Through Cabell, Carr discovered the kinds of narratives and characters the young Carr felt were worth writing, and reasons they were worth writing. Cabell helped Carr channel his passion to write.

Cabell was a writer's writer, more consistently admired by other authors than by the public or critics—whose pillories Cabell would drolly incorporate into the review notices of his subsequent titles. It is a great and confusing treat to read the derogatory notices for previous works—even disparaging advance notices of the present one—prefacing the pages of Cabell's latest issue. Among the writers who favored Cabell, a number remain well-known to twenty-first century readers: H.L. Mencken, Sinclair Lewis, Robert Heinlein, and even Mark Twain, whom Eugene Saxton (in a 1920 letter) informed Cabell praised the stories in Cabell's volume *Chivalry* as "masterpieces... wonderfully well written." Cabell also wrote his *Domnei: A Comedy of Woman-Worship* in fulfillment of a request from Twain.

While this is meant as no judgment of Cabell's merits, it is unsurprising that he fell into obscurity. Cabell's highly artificial diction and narrative style are quite difficult for modern readers to follow, let alone enjoy. Yet he remained in Carr's favor throughout Carr's life. On April 3, 1972, Carr wrote to Oscar Baron, a Yonkers-based bookseller to whom Carr was referred by another bookseller as "one skilled in the detection and capture of second-hand volumes sought by your clients." Carr hoped to reacquire, among other boyhood favorites, copies of Cabell's *Beyond Life*, *Chivalry*, *Gallantry*, and *The Line of Love*—the very books mentioned fondly to Bond.

So what was the lifelong resonance Cabell had for Carr, which we can trace from his amateur fiction all the way through Carr's historical romances? Let us focus on *Beyond Life*, which was somewhat unique in being a literary colloquy—one of more than 350 pages! The book's literary discussion takes place between a successful novelist and a young editor, and it concerns literary and philosophical aesthetics. The setting for the book is the author's library, which paradoxically includes unwritten masterpieces and "intended versions" of well-known books, these versions being as great as their authors wished them to be, rather than (as Charteris, the fictional author explains) being "the ordinary standards for inducing sleep!"[23]

Most of *Beyond Life* is a thinly veiled monologue spoken by Charteris to espouse Cabell's own sensibilities. At its best, *Beyond Life* is epigrammatic and still resounds in the sensibilities of contemporary readers; in many (most) passages, unfortunately, the book seems dated and stilted. *Beyond Life* is ambitious, both in its length and its philosophical breadth; it essentially tries to establish a full-blown epistemology of art, one that verges on arguing for itself as a secular religion.

In fact, Cabell treats with creativity in a very literal sense, according art (chiefly and explicitly, Romanticism) a demiurgic role in the formation of human culture and ethics. Although Cabell doesn't express his ideas using this specific term, to him, Romanticism is the *genius* of culture, in the strictly received Romantic sense: the Romantic movement considered *genius* the mechanism by which art was created from nothingness. ("Genius" and "genesis" are, after all, etymologically kin: genius is ultimately derived from the Latin *gignere*, "to beget.") The artist positions Romantic *genius* as an echo of the Biblical divine creation: God created the world, which the artist recreates and glorifies through art. Cabell argues that art, in effect, *invents* the human (not the physical) world and our mores, shapes our conduct. Consider this representative passage:

23 *Beyond Life*, Robert M. McBride and Company, 1924, p. 14. All subsequent excerpts are drawn from the same edition.

Now art, like all the other noteworthy factors in this remarkable world, serves in the end utilitarian purposes. When a trait is held up as desirable, for a convincingly long while, the average person, out of self-respect, pretends to possess it: with time, he acts letter-perfect as one endowed therewith, and comes unshakably to believe that it has guided him from infancy. (p. 44)

What has any of this to do with John Dickson Carr? It was not just Cabell's high-level Romantic sensibility to which the young writer subscribed, although he did. Carr doubtless believed Cabell's associated principle that, "The most of us, indeed, at various removes, quite candidly derive our standards…from romantic art" (p. 147). This is an important inheritance, because it becomes part of *why* an author writes. The artist argues for the world as it should be, and eventually, people internalize the artist's vision and bend toward it. Every more-than-casual reader of Carr recognizes his subscription to this principle.

G.K. Chesterton, in his own coincidental assessment, makes the same argument as Cabell concerning the writer's ability to shape thought on a cultural scale—and the more interestingly, Chesterton offers his thesis directly in the context of detective fiction, writing in his 1905 essay, "Detectives and Detective Fictions":

…everybody's mind in dealing with a fact, like the Merstham fact,[24] for instance, is probably really influenced, mad as it may seem, by contemporary detective fiction. That this is so, because in every age men are *always* more influenced by romance than by reality."[25]

Carr, of course, was doubtless familiar with this essay and only the more reinforced by it in these views.

There is little doubt that many of Cabell's/Charteris's artistic pronouncements were ones Carr might have proffered himself—and in some cases, using altered words, later did. For instance, compare Cabell's assessment of literary realism to Carr's. In *Beyond Life*, Charteris attributes to Wilson Follett (the writer whose guide to mod-

---

24 Chesterton refers to the murder, only two months earlier, of Mary Sophia Money, found mutilated in a Merstham railroad tunnel. The case electrified the British public, but remained unsolved.

25 *Illustrated London News*, November 4, 1905.

ern American usage was completed and published posthumously by Jacques Barzun), and embraces, this view:

> ...since the novel of things-as-they-are calls for no constructive imagination whatever in author or reader, the present supply of "realism" is nothing but the publisher's answer to a cheap and fickle demand; and since the imaginative element in art is all but everything, the only artist who has a chance of longevity is he who shuns the "vital", the "gripping", and the contemporary. (p. 15)

What sentiment could be more characteristic of Carr? Perhaps the fifteen-year-old had exactly that passage in mind when, in his May 4, 1922 column of "As We See It" (*Uniontown Daily News Standard*), he wrote:

> ...we have no use for the so-called "realistic" novels which rob life of all that is beautiful and shows it in distorted sordidness....Why is the market flooded with such stuff as *Main Street*, *Potterism*, and *The Beautiful and the Damned*? And prodigious wonder, why do these books rank as best-sellers? ...So it is our contention that any imitation author can write a realistic story; but it takes a true master—one who knows his reader—to write a problem novel.

For the young author, too, Cabell's argument that art creates our identities and manners had a certain subtle influence. Instinctively following Cabell's sensibilities, which so accorded with his own, the teenager began to write about who he wished to be and what he wished the world to be: he began utilizing fiction as a vehicle of wish fulfillment. By spinning tales of romance, adventure, and mystery, which spoke to the essential world as it should be in Carr's eyes, and then becoming the hero at the center of them by proxy, Carr entertainingly envisioned in himself the magnanimity—literally the greatness of mind, heart, and even of creativity—toward which the teen writer aspired. While he had come to realize the writer could not change the world, at least through the narrow act of editorial writing, Carr recognized the existential and the emotional importance of fiction through Cabell—both through Cabell's critical formulations and through the anachronistic short stories that Carr remembered with partiality throughout his life. An artist could shape generations of intellectual progeny and the direction of culture itself, rather than merely "reporting" on it through cheap fictional realism.

Like Cabell, in an inheritance of Romanticism, Carr wrote most of his characters as types, albeit types updated for the twentieth century. As LeRoy Panek itemizes them:

> As for the other characters in the books, they are the usual collection: eccentric noblemen or millionaires, lawyers old and young, a retired colonel or two, a wealthy spinster or two, a brace of physicians, some clergymen, a variety of wives, some newspaper men, an odd engineer or scientist, film stars, several scholars, a few art dealers, and a writer or two. It is the same crowd that one meets in most of the detective books of the period. [26]

Although it would be putting too much on Cabell to accuse him of being the sole influence upon Carr in this next respect, Cabell seems strongly to have affected Carr's handling of women as types. Of course, in Romantic fiction, there are more Sir Walter Scotts and Conan Doyles than there are Brontës; in other words, *most* Romantic fiction, from a character development standpoint, is of the second literary order (or lower), handling its female romantic interests as types, women effectively interchangeable between one story and the next for lack of rounded individuality or any existence beyond the male gaze. It was hardly only Cabell. While young John Carr learned from multiple authors having fundamentally the same disposition how to incorporate and write about women characters, Cabell held strongly considered and starkly expressed opinions that likely encouraged Carr, susceptible to Cabell's artistic viewpoint, to draw most of his female characters as either spinsters or hellions (Carr's sardonic formulation in *The Plague Court Murders*, p. 24). In considering Carr's problematic handling of women, Greene comments on Carr's relationship with his mother (p. 9), which was one simultaneously of fear and suasion:

> When he was an adult, his mother could drive him out of a room by addressing him as Johnny, and sometimes did so. Probably the most fundamental part of their relationship was that she did not understand a boy who often lived in his own world...She wanted John to behave like a perfect child, while John himself admired the heroes of romance who did not

---

26 *Watteau's Shepherds*, Bowling Green University Popular Press, 1979, p. 168. All subsequent excerpts are drawn from the same edition.

have to be concerned about what the world thought.

The consequence of this, Greene argues (p. 44), is that, "Attracted to women, he also feared them. Female characters never become real in these early stories; good or bad or both, they remain dim figures of romance."

Carr may have acquired his schismatic disposition toward women domestically, but he also acquired it pointedly in his formative readings. Cabell, in addition to offering the expected, formulaic romantic types in his stories, also presented critical-theoretical formulations about the relationships between men and women, both in life and in art. In *Beyond Life*, Cabell characterizes the male-female relationship as, "*domnei*, or woman-worship...a man's mistress [is] an ever-present reminder, and sometimes rival, of God" (p. 49). Cabell offers an extended argument in support of this, which amounts to defining the image and purpose of a woman's existence through male eyes in a men's world:

> ...it was the very essence of *domnei*, that the woman one loves is providentially set between her lover's apprehension and God, as the mobile and vital image and corporeal reminder of Heaven, as a quick symbol of beauty and holiness, of purity and perfection. In her the lover views all qualities of God which can be comprehended by merely human faculties...And instances were not lacking...where the worship of the symbol developed into a religion sufficing in itself, and became competitor with worship of what the symbol primarily represented... (pp. 77-78)

Cabell did not settle simply for putting women on pedestals, either. In a rather Old-Testament manner, he accounts for the presence of evil in the world as a distinctly feminine one:

> Yes, in life the "wicked" people are rather pitiable, and quite hopelessly tedious as associates. I suspect that the root of most evil is, not so much the love of money, as the lack of imagination...the romantic have always fabled that by whole-hearted allegiance to evil this life in the flesh—by "jumping", as the Thane of Cawdor put it, any possible life to come, —might be rendered vastly more entertaining, and might even afford to the sinner control of superhuman powers. Men have always dreamed thus of evading the low levels of everyday existence, and of augmenting their inadequate

natural forces, by entering into some formal compact with evil. Hence have arisen the innumerable legends of sorcerers and witches....Witchcraft, if it were not indeed the first manifestation of "feminism", was practiced almost exclusively by women. (pp. 56-57)

For Cabell, and epigonically to Carr, women have potent binary capacity for divine elevation or for evil, whether as Lady Macbeth, Eve's predecessor Lilith, or as Eve herself. Woman is the object of a man's adoration and his necessary object of pursuit in the quests for love and eternity: "that...the groans of a lover be perpetuated in the wails of an infant" (p. 76). But is a woman the steppingstone to gallantry, divinity, and eternity, or is she the irresistible agent of man's corruption and destruction by evil, which she innately manifests? To Cabell, and perhaps to the impressionable Carr, every woman—particularly if she is a character in Romantic fiction—is both. In Cabell's conception, every woman is some sort of witch, whether

> "...white witches" who could help, but not hurt; "black witches," who could hurt, but not help; and "gray witches", who could do either at will....in dreams man has shown no aversion to the witch-woman... but, to the contrary, man has always clung, with curious tenacity, to the notion of some day attaining the good graces of that fair-haired and delicate-voiced witch who is a bane to men, and yet sometimes takes mortal lovers. (pp. 61-69)

We can understand how this might have resonated with the domestic upbringing of the young Carr, inculcating representation in Carr's stories of his simultaneous desire for women and his fear of them. This reductive distortion of women plays out frequently in Carr's fiction, for which he has often (and for the most part, fairly) been criticized. Cabell's witches are incarnated in Carr's books, in which even the women characters embrace this same troublesome standard. Consider, for instance, a lover's dialogue from *The Bride of Newgate*, which even preserves the archetypal and supernatural Cabellian dichotomy that explains women:

> "Damn you," Darwent presently said in a choked voice. "I understand you now. I should have understood you long ago."
> "Un—understand me?"
> "Cold and arrogant? Your trouble is that you're

too stimulating. You're a wine that has three stages
of headiness. You're Madam Circe and Mother Eve.
You're never placid; you're fierce-kiss-and-run-away;
you're angel and incubus, enough to—"
"If this is your method of damning me," whispered
Caroline, "go on and on and on and on!" (p. 194)

For Cabell, in fact, a modern woman, a thinking, independent
woman, is a threat, a menace on the order of a Biblical plague:

And had you vocally denied my doctrines on the
ground of their ugliness, I would have flung full in
your face earthquakes and cloudbursts and hyenas and
rhinoceroses and diseases and germs and intellectual
women...and I would have given you untrammeled
leave to deduce from the ugliness of these things that
they are all untrue... (p. 329)

Again, we cannot place all the blame for Carr's insufficient handling of women on Cabell—Carr imbibed similar, if generally less malignant, interpretations of women in most of the other authors and
works he read formatively. Of course, too, there remains Carr's personal responsibility: he was a product of his generation who did not
rise above the accepted views of, and places made for, women in his
day. He was no George Bernard Shaw; Carr's personal genius was not,
like Shaw's or Dickens', in helping illuminate the path progressively
toward social reform. Greene pithily summarizes the case against Carr:

With only a few exceptions—especially Eve Neill in
The Emperor's Snuff-Box—his women are described
from the viewpoint of men, and much more obviously
than the male protagonists they are types rather than
individuals. Carr's stories written at Haverford show
him attracted to but afraid of women. Over and over
he had used the image of the seductive woman who
lures men to their destruction...He objected to anyone...who seemed to take the romance and mystery
out of sex. (p. 278)

While the purpose here is not to excuse, but rather more closely
to examine, Carr's handling of women characters, his works feature
occasional, interesting exceptions to his general failing—albeit never
for the sake of improving the place of women or consideration of
them. As Greene observes, Carr's best-constructed female character,
who assumes (especially for Carr) some genuine sympathetic depth as

the perspective character in the novel, is Eve Neill of *The Emperor's Snuff-Box*. Greene sees this book as "the only instance in which Carr came close to successfully adopting a woman's viewpoint" (p. 266). At the level of an entire novel, Greene seems correct.

On the other hand, Carr's novels are infrequently strewn with other women who sympathetically defy male-oriented gender conventions. One example is the nineteenth century's Caroline Ross, the titular bride of Newgate (created by Carr about a decade after Eve Neill). Caroline is to an incomplete degree a progressive, twentieth-century sort wholly out of, and ahead of, her time. In the opening chapter, needing to satisfy her grandfather's will, Caroline schemes to marry a convicted murderer, Dick Darwent, who is scheduled to be hanged the next morning. (The will requires Caroline to be married by her twenty-fifth birthday or to be disinherited.) Though assisting her, her lawyer, Eliss Crockit, finds Caroline's plan unworthy and degrading. Caroline has what we see as a decidedly more modern view on the transaction:

> In marriage, it's understood, the husband has a certain 'right.' I will not grant *that* right to any man.... That aspect... I have always considered rather ridiculous and faintly revolting. But under your precious law, the husband has still another right. Everything I own becomes his property, even to the house we stand in at this moment.... It's not fair. It's *odious*... which is the more degrading: their style of marriage, or mine? (pp. 11-12)

Even more shockingly for her time, Caroline later declares she would "free women from being bond slaves: yes, and give them rights equal to men" (p. 193). Caroline is not, all the same, an earthquake, a cloudburst, or a germ: in the end, she is sympathetic.

In the context of her time, Eve Neill is a more believable character than Caroline, but both women rebel against longstanding constructs surrounding marriage and sexual relations, which were still persistently dominant by the time Carr penned these novels.

Eve's strength as a central character is not only her feminine progressiveness, though: Eve is, for the most part, as roundly realized by Carr as any of her male counterparts who lead other novels. She may not be drawn to the literary standards of a Henry James or a D.H. Lawrence (those authors Carr assured Nelson Bond he wouldn't "buy at any price"), but Eve is sufficiently dimensional and sympathetic to be a legitimately engaging protagonist.

In an inversion of Carr's typical formulation of an affianced couple, in *The Emperor's Snuff-Box*, it is Toby, not Eve, who is the clichéd gender type, available for our disapprobation. For his unthinking (and selfish) acceptance of the double standard concerning male versus female fidelity, Eve castigates Toby as a Uriah Heep (p. 191). Dr. Dermot Kinross, a criminal psychologist, later unsparingly sketches Toby's profile:

> "Mentally and emotionally, he's still fifteen years old… His ideas of sexual morality might have come straight from the fourth form of his old school.
> "There are plenty of Tobys in this world…They're looked on as rocks of staunchness, models of solidity…He's a good fellow to play golf or have a drink with. But I doubt whether he'd make the best possible husband for…well, leave it at that." (p. 292)

It is worth diverting momentarily to acknowledge Douglas Greene's observation of how *The Emperor's Snuff-Box* is a noteworthy departure by Carr from his earlier, consistent derision of Dr. Kinross's profession:

> This is why Dermot Kinross comes into the story. Carr had become more open to the tenets of psychology since his earlier sarcastic references to Viennese doctors, but he saw its role in explaining the *how* rather than the *why* of human behavior. Thus *The Problem of the Green Capsule* was subtitled "Being the Psychologist's Murder Case" not because it had to do with inhibitions or obsessions or Oedipal complexes, but because the clues involved how witnesses saw things. (p. 267)

In other words, Carr recognized that by embracing psychology a little more, he could better exploit some of its interrogatives—write even more baffling mysteries.

In *The Emperor's Snuff-Box*, Carr may be perpetrating some character name-play that underlies the distinctions between the key characters: Eve Neill is of course the Biblical Eve, the archetypical figure of rebellion against the established sexual order—Cabell's source of sin and evil—while her fiancé Toby's surname is Lawes, reminding us of his (very English) defense of the traditional order. (Eve's Irish surname is another subtle endorsement by Carr of her good character.) In his own understated but inimical way, Toby is just as caddish as the reprehensible Ned Atwood, Eve's ex-husband, who tries to reclaim Eve from Toby by sneaking into her bedchamber late at night and coercing intercourse. As openly acknowledged in the novel, those are (not to Carr, but to some) the "acceptable" ethics of a former husband or an admired rake; Atwood's unwelcome presence in his ex-wife's bedchamber and his attempt to rape her, in Toby's eyes, compromises not Ned, but Eve. Eve's former and intended husbands are two sides of a very ugly coin.

We can add Lady Helen Loring, from *The Curse of the Bronze Lamp*, to the rolls of Carr's better female characters. Like Caroline and Eve, she too is consciously a barrier breaker, pursuing a professional life, rather than a husband and a marriage, with her "hands like a navvy…from working at the [archaeological] digging" (p. 188). Helen is the evident professional superior of her fawning colleague, "Sandy" Robertson, who makes an initial impression of being a hapless traditionalist in addition to being an ineffective archaeologist. His nickname, another Carr name game, is suggestive of Robertson's bland lack of stolidity. In accordance with his tone-deaf male perspective, Sandy stumbles over himself in the opening pages awkwardly (and not for the first time) proposing marriage to Helen. She has other priorities—and a better man, one we learn respects Helen in her fullness of character—in mind.

Carr gives Helen her due early and often: "She could work with a spade at the diggings, as hard as any hired *Rieses*.[27] She could discuss rubrics and canopic vases as learnedly as Professor Gilray himself" (p. 2). Helen is, in fact, a central driver of the plot's progress; her incision, observations, and activity rise to the level of challenging H.M. himself. Although Carr begins, seemingly predictably, by describing Helen as a blonde with luminous brown eyes and undeniable sex appeal, his description is a disarming one, even a bit of misdirection: unsuspecting readers will not take Helen seriously, as some of the novel's male characters fail to do, mistaking her for one of Carr's usual female accessories. This will only lead to readers' being surprised by her. They, as Carr does, will come to admire Lady Helen for more than her sex appeal.

One must also count among Carr's uncommon women Jennifer Baird, of *Fear Is the Same*, mysteriously transported back through time with Philip Clavering. Not only does she co-occupy the role of perspective character with Philip, but Jennifer has a few very un-Carrian moments during which the reader listens to her thoughts and is moved by them. The best of these is Jennifer's prayer for Philip's

---

27 A laborer, but not, as might be expected, an Arabic word. Carr's use here is likely an allusion to the infamous Nazi construction project in Poland between 1943-1945, which was performed with forced labor.

safety during a climatic encounter:

> Her lips moved soundlessly.
> "O, Thou," it was a trembling through her, "bid us go from this cage in which we are held. Lead us back to our own space and time. Set us free from this dirt, and cruelty, and snobbishness…
> "Is my lover, my husband, forever to be beaten to his knees? He stands up again; he defeats them, and I am glad. But there is much blood on his head; he is changing every hour before my eyes, and I am afraid. Let him go! And, if I be considered at all worthy, let me go, too." (pp. 233-234)

This may not only be the most poignant portrait Carr draws of a *woman* in all his fiction, it may be the most touching, the most human moment he gives to *any* of his characters, in any work. The passage is an extraordinary exception by an author who rarely peers very far into the emotional minds of his characters. As such, it is all the more wistful to us in witnessing the depth of which Carr was capable as a writer, but to which he almost never plumbed.

These several women are not the exhaustive catalogue of those in Carr's works who challenge our (mostly correct) assessment of Carr as an author who did not write women very well. There are others, not only in his professional novels, but in his amateur stories, too. The reader will encounter one or two in this collection who, while hardly feminist role models or fully the heroes of their own narratives, will nonetheless somewhat subvert their received places as male accessories, and without being hellions, either. They are the smallest seedlings that bore a few strong offshoots we have seen growing later in Carr's career. As such, they are worth our attention, because with few exceptions, the adult Carr did not write female characters with any more sophistication than the teenage Carr did.

Admittedly, Carr was still a relatively sheltered thirty-five (by twenty-first century standards) when he wrote *The Emperor's Snuff-Box*. It is tempting to imagine Carr taking small, enlightened steps forward during the following decade, just as he would in his personal life come to recognize his wife, Clarice, as the strength of their marriage. In *Fear Is the Same* (nearly fifteen years after *The Emperor's Snuff-Box*), perhaps insufficiently and certainly not definitively, Carr finally moves meaningfully away from depicting women as mere Romantic types, or as Cabell's witches—and he brings along his male protagonist with him. Carr puts a short, extraordinary confession into the mouth of Philip Clavering, whose understanding of women, not just of one woman,

changes during the novel—something unprecedented for Carr. Clavering admits to Jennifer, "I discovered what a less stupid man would
have discovered long ago, that love and tenderness and passion may
all exist in the same woman" (p. 195). Without endeavoring to excuse
Carr's general shortcomings in the handling of women, let us conclude the discussion of it on that final, lovely note.

The influence of G.K. Chesterton upon Carr is much better
generally understood and documented than that of Cabell. Given
this, there is no need to dwell at length upon their literary kinship,
or to anticipate breaking much new ground concerning Chesterton's
outsized influence upon Carr. Even most casual readers of Carr are
aware, for instance, how closely Dr. Fell was modeled on Carr's literary idol, which speaks more to Carr's veneration of Chesterton than
even the most closely reasoned literary argument could. In response
to a character background inquiry by a correspondent whose identity,
other than his first name "Allan," no longer survives, Carr confirmed
in an August 7, 1967 letter:

> Dr. Fell was modeled on my literary hero, the late
> G.K. Chesterton. G.K.C. died in 1936, it's true; but
> several Dr. Fell novels had appeared by that time. He
> knew he was the original of the character, and did not
> mind. However, I still work under one self-imposed
> restraint; Dr. Fell has never been allowed to do or say
> anything which would have embarrassed the living
> Chesterton or his friends.

He further encouraged Allan, "If you're not familiar with the
Collected Father Brown stories, read them at once... You seem to
enjoy my efforts at the 'miracle' problem; try Chesterton and see how
the thing is done by a master."

Despite readers' broad and well-documented understanding of
how singularly Carr admired Chesterton, a few points are worth our
attention here: some comparative assessments of the two; considering Chesterton in his own words, as Carr did—which passages Carr
enthusiasts will recognize spoke uncannily both to the young author
Carr and about the professional one; and observing some of Carr's
more interesting invocations of Chesterton and tributes to him.

The first critical intuition of Chesterton's influence upon Carr
was Dorothy L. Sayers' 1933 review of Carr's *The Mad Hatter Mystery*:

> Chestertonian...are the touches of extravagance in
> character and plot, and the sensitiveness to symbol-
> ism, to historical association, to the shapes and co-

lours of material things, to the crazy terror of the incongruous.[28]

As is so frequently the case, much of the most helpful and concise
analysis concerning Carr's debt to Chesterton comes from Douglas
Greene. In a 1984 article for *The Chestertonian Review*, Greene draws a
complementary affinity to Sayers' between the two writers:

> Carr never used his stories to advocate a theology, or
> to debate one, but all his writings present a consistent
> attitude, one which can be called Chestertonian: a re-
> spect for the past, a love of incongruity, an emphasis
> on fairplay, chivalry and generosity.[29]

Greene also pithily summarizes an essential similarity between the
works of both authors:

> Carr...borrowed Chesterton's basic structure of the
> puzzle. Father Brown does not bother with the physi-
> cal clues that his predecessors...reveled in. To Father
> Brown guilt and innocence are not determined by ciga-
> rette ashes or ballistics but by...the pattern which the
> events form. Chesterton fools the reader by making
> him see the wrong pattern....Carr's tales are similar in
> that they depend on seeing events from the wrong an-
> gle.... Both Chesterton and Carr...had a vivid feeling
> for physical images, and they often introduce objects in
> their stories which seem to be clues but which, in fact,
> merely make the true pattern of crime more difficult
> for the reader to discern.[30]

Carr not only enjoyed having his detectives, in the manner of Father Brown, disdain physical clues; he also delighted in finding ways
to deprive them of too-easy physical evidence. In *Fire, Burn!* (1957),
Carr exploits Detective Inspector Cheviot of Scotland Yard's passage
back 110 years in time to vitiate the detective's modern investigatory
methods:

> Even as he did so, the full helplessness of his position
> swept over him.

---

28 "Mystery Out of the Ordinary," *Sunday Times*, Sep. 24, 1933, p. 7.

29 *The Chestertonian Review*, Vol. X, No. 3, "A Mastery of Miracles: G.K.
Chesterton and John Dickson Carr," p. 309.

30 Ibid, pp. 310-311.

He could not take photographs. He had no chalk, no magnifying lens, no tape-measure…
Not a modern ballistics expert on earth could identify a bullet fired from a smooth-bore barrel…he could never prove from what pistol the shot was fired.
Fingerprints…were worse than useless here…every person in the house was wearing gloves.
His fine advantages had crumbled to ruin. He was left alone to his own wits. (p. 68)

In learning how to write detective fiction, it was not merely by emulating the Father Brown stories that Carr relied upon Chesterton, but also by imbibing the great essayist's literary ideas about the genre. Chesterton wrote on the order of four thousand essays covering many subjects; naturally, these included a few seminal tracts concerning detective fiction. Consider the following excerpts from Chesterton's essays and how naturally Carr must have accepted his tenets; as with some of Cabell's pronouncements, it is easy to imagine Carr having written these passages himself, so fully did he internalize Chesterton's arguments.

The true object of an intelligent detective story is not to baffle the reader, but to enlighten the reader; but to enlighten him in such a manner that each successive portion of the truth comes as a surprise. In this, as in much nobler types of mystery, the object of the true mystic is not merely to mystify, but to illuminate. The object is not darkness, but light; but light in the form of lightning.[31]

…in the classification of the arts, mysterious murders belong to the grand and joyful company of the things called jokes. The story is a fancy; an avowedly fictitious fiction.[32]

It is useless for a thing to be unexpected if it was not worth expecting… The climax must not be only the bursting of a bubble but rather the breaking of a dawn.[33]

The detective story differs from every other story in this: that the reader is only happy if he feels a fool.… The essence of a mystery tale is that we are suddenly

31 "Errors about Detective Stories," *Illustrated London News,* August 28, 1920.
32 "How to Write a Detective Story," *C.K.'s Weekly,* October 17, 1925.
33 Ibid

confronted with a truth which we have never suspected and yet can see to be true.[34]

Of course, Carr paid homage to Chesterton in his fiction, some
examples of which we earlier observed (adapting Chesterton for radio
and borrowing the character Patrick Butler), but additional instances
merit acknowledgment.

Carr's *The Peacock Feather Murders* (1937), more directly titled for its
inspiration in the UK edition as *The Ten Teacups*, draws its premise from
the opening pages of Chesterton's *The Club of Queer Trades* (1905), in
which, in the style of Conan Doyle, Chesterton tantalizes the reader by
hinting at an unrecorded adventure: "Of the Ten Teacups, of course
I dare not say a word." Carr did dare, appropriating the undeveloped
premise and making it his own.[35] (Carr would of course do the same
with some of Conan Doyle's teasers, both through his collaboration
with Doyle's son Adrian on *The Exploits of Sherlock Holmes*, 1954, and in
The Curse of the Bronze Lamp, inspired by the mention in "The Problem
of Thor Bridge" of "Mr. James Phillimore, who, stepping back into
his own house to get his umbrella, was never more seen in this world.")

With *The Unicorn Murders*, Carr pays extended homage to Chester-
ton on multiple levels. The novel is worth considering in a little detail.
At the most general level, *The Unicorn Murders* playfully recalls the first
Father Brown story, "The Blue Cross." Carr borrows that story's premise, a grand battle of wits between the French super-detective Valentin
and the super-criminal Flambeau. In his novel, Carr pits Gasquet, the
French police's finest, against the mysterious super-criminal Flamande.
Greene makes the same connection (p. 132) and suggests that Gasquet
is modeled on Bencolin. If so, this offers readers the latitude to interpret *The Unicorn Murders* as a passing of the torch between Bencolin
and H.M. who, of course, outshines the *Sûreté*'s Chief Inspector.

Employing an echo of himself, Carr also perpetrates an inside joke
on Father Brown: a young mystery writer, Owen Middleton, while
speculating about Flamande's identity, turns Chesterton's basic premise on its head. Middleton suggests, "It's easy enough to make a clergyman the murderer" (p. 85).

More centrally, *The Unicorn Murders* honors Chesterton for that
most vital of techniques Carr learned from him: the trick of deceiving
readers into seeing the mystery from the wrong angle. Carr puts into
H.M.'s mouth an overt metaphorical representation of this signature
method of bamboozling readers:

---

34 "The Ideal Detective Story," *Illustrated London News*, October 25, 1930.

35 Also observed by Greene in the biography, p. 158.

For instance, you know what this house reminds me of? I had a friend once, who had lots of money and an awful primitive sense of humor. He had one room fixed up in his house for a side-splittin' joke. There was a carpet on the ceiling; chairs and tables were bolted to it upside down. The floor was papered over, and out of it stuck the spike and globes of a chandelier. The windows were nearly to the ceiling, and the door was a good way up—in short, it was an upside-down room. Well, he'd take a friend of his on a guzzlin' party. When the feller had slid under the table, he was carried to this room while he was asleep. The idea was to watch him next morning, when he woke up on the floor and had a good look around before the booze had evaporated. This humorous friend of mine said the drunk's first gesture would always be the same. He'd give an awful yell and make a grab for the chandelier. Y'see, he was afraid he would fall up to the ceiling.... (pp. 146-147)[36]

Greene (p. 30) records that Carr sometimes claimed that in his Hill School days, he and his friend Macon Fry built such a room and then perpetrated this prank on their inebriated schoolmates. Carr eventually admitted that this school-days claim was only a tall tale inspired by an old joke book, but what Carr could not do with Fry in the real world he learned from G.K. Chesterton to do in his fictive ones—and in *The Unicorn Murders*, Carr teases the reader with the conspicuously Chestertonian metaphor.

In a late chapter of *The Unicorn Murders*, one of the French police responds to Ken Blake's inquiry about whether the police have gathered any fingerprint evidence:

Auguste laughed outright. "The chief, monsieur, pays little attention to such trifles. He says they are outmoded, and psychologically unimportant. If any fingerprints are ever found anywhere, we can be sure they were never left by the right person. In any case, there were no fingerprints at all. Would you expect Flamande to leave any? What a joke! He would have painted his fingers with liquid rubber." (p. 239)

Once again, the reader aware of Chesterton's tutelage recognizes

---

36 LeRoy Panek, in *Watteau's Shepherds* (Bowling Green University Popular Press, 1979, p. 174), makes a similar observation, but not in the context of Carr having learned it from Chesterton.

this technique Carr learned first in the Father Brown stories: the trick of making physical clues irrelevant, even when they are to be found.

Colonel March, Carr's recurring short-story detective, who also reflects Carr's admiration of Chesterton and Father Brown, makes his debut in a story reminding us of this: "The New Invisible Man" (published April, 1938). The tale, explaining how a pair of unworn gloves can animate themselves and murderously fire a gun, is a winking homage to an early Father Brown story, "The Invisible Man" (1911). In the original adventure, there is a seemingly invisible murderer—and, for good measure, a vanishing corpse, too. Because Carr loves to borrow premises, not plots, in his version, he invents not only fresh characters and a new plot, but a different miracle solution, as well. Carr wrote eight other Colonel March stories. The first seven were collected in Carr's *The Department of Queer Complaints* (1940); the final two appeared in his collection *The Men Who Explained Miracles* (1963).

In the present collection, the reader will most strongly detect Chesterton's mentoring spirit in *Grand Guignol*. Chesterton's lack of apparent influence upon Carr's earlier mystery tales, which do not fully rise to the level of detective fiction, is an interesting absence: each of the earlier mysteries has perceptible analogues in other authors whom young Carr admired (and which will be discussed following each selection). As Greene noted, though, it is mildly surprising that among all Carr's amateur fiction—particularly those tales Carr wrote before college—his mysteries are perhaps his least successful efforts. The present editor suggests a possible correlation between Carr's election of Chesterton as his detective fiction role model and Carr's rapidly improving mastery of the genre, beginning in 1926. As Carr imitated Poe, Melville Davisson Post, and others *less*—and Chesterton *more*—he began finding his successful long-term approach to writing detective fiction. This is almost certainly the key reason Carr counted Chesterton among the handful of authors most influential upon him—especially because Chesterton's influence on Carr never waned. In his March 3, 1967 letter to Nelson Bond, after commenting on and gently dismissing the likes of the Hanshews, Arthur B. Reeve, and the "ladies now well lost," Carr reaffirmed:

> But none of this really matters. Conan Doyle and G.K. Chesterton, who could write, make up for the ineptitude of the ninety-and-nine who couldn't write; they preserve faith unshaken to this day.

Chesterton's essay "A Defence of Detective Stories," clearly indicates not only what Carr admired about him, but also, what Carr admired about Robert Louis Stevenson. Carr credited Stevenson in the same manner Chesterton did, perhaps *because* Chesterton did: even if Carr did not have Chesterton's "Defence" explicitly in mind during his decades-later correspondence with Nelson Bond, Carr had nonetheless so thoroughly internalized Chesterton's viewpoint that he expressed it in the same essential terms (literary authors versus popular ones). We have already seen what Carr wrote; more than a half century earlier, Chesterton wrote:

> We may dream, perhaps, that it might be possible to have another and higher romance of London, that men's souls have stranger adventures than their bodies, and that it would be harder and more exciting to hunt their virtues than to hunt their crimes. But since our great authors (with the admirable exception of Stevenson) decline to write of that thrilling mood and moment when the eyes of the great city, like the eyes of a cat, begin to flame in the dark, we must give fair credit to the popular literature which, amid a babble of pedantry and preciosity, declines to regard the present as prosaic or the common as commonplace....A rude, popular literature of the romantic possibilities of the modern city was bound to arise. It has arisen in the popular detective stories, as rough and refreshing as the ballads of Robin Hood.[37]

In what ways, then, did Stevenson come to be one of the most influential writers upon John Dickson Carr? Of course, all Carr's tales of youths pursuing adventure in the grand manner are in the tradition of Stevenson's *Treasure Island*, in which the newly fatherless teen Jim Hawkins sets out on an adventurous sea voyage to find a dead pirate's buried treasure.

It is not the subtlety of this influence that must be acknowledged—there is none—but rather the *persistence* of this book's influence upon Carr, even into his professional career. Every young Carrian hero yearning for adventure is Jim Hawkins *redivivus*. As with Carr's occasional, sly acknowledgements of Gothic romance, he occasionally openly confesses his connection to Stevenson, too. When in *The Arabian Nights Murder* Detective-Inspector Carruthers disappointedly learns an after-hours party at a museum was convened not to open an ancient tomb, but rather "just to look at some manuscript sheets," Jerry Wade (the museum founder's scion) consoles him:

Shake hands, Inspector...I feel exactly the same way.

---

37 *The Defendant*, R. Brimley Johnson, 1901, p. 121.

Under your blue coat beats the soul (so to speak) of a
kid reading *Treasure Island*. I sympathize with you, sink
me if I don't, at being roused from your dream of coffins… (pp. 81-82)

Stevenson's influence didn't translate into Carr's simplistically borrowing explicit storylines or plot elements, or even in the imitation of
Stevenson's prose style (as the teenage Carr imitated Poe in shades of
purple). Instead, Stevenson influenced both the young and the mature
Carr as Doyle and Chesterton did: he was a role model who conjured
a fictive world in which the outré and the singular were the everyday
fare of adventure. As improbable as any plot's circumstances might
be, they were eminently believable within the bounds of his narrative—and they were thrilling. Stevenson's Romanticism was loam for
detective fiction, and his adventurous tales clearly antecedents to Carr's
own evocative narratives.

Although he wasn't writing detective fiction, Stevenson's stories
were often wrapped in mystery. Consider, for instance, his collection
of stories, *New Arabian Nights* (1882). One tale introduces us to a "Suicide Club," a collection of emotionally broken men, all of whom wish
to die without dishonor. The chance deal of a deck of cards selects
which will die—and which other member, murder him. Greene (p.
158) alertly reminds us that *The Peacock Feather Murders* refers openly to
New Arabian Nights and the Suicide Club.

In another *New Arabian Nights* adventure, the "Story of the House
with the Green Blinds," an anonymous benefactor will bestow £500
a year upon a young London clerk, Francis Scrymgeour, provided the
clerk honors two conditions: he attend a particular performance of the
Comédie Française using a ticket left for him, and that the unnamed
benefactor have absolute approval over the selection of Scrymgeour's
wife.

These and other conundrums in *New Arabian Nights* are premises
worthy of Conan Doyle himself. While technically not detective fiction, Stevenson's *New Arabian Nights* stories are certainly mysteries,
mysteries investigated and resolved by a central character, Prince Florizel of Bohemia. He is the amateur consulting detective who comes to
the aid of troubled protagonists throughout seven of the collection's
stories. Prince Florizel's adventures well suit the definition of a mystery story that the *other* Chesterton, Cecil (1879-1918), offered in 1906,
as part of his own defense of detective fiction:

The detective or mystery story need not, of course,
be primarily concerned with detectives. Some of the
best stories of this type…have not the shadow of a

detective… The real distinguishing feature is that the reader should be confronted with a number of mysterious facts of which the explanation is reserved till the end. Now this reservation of the final solution, in order to pique the reader's curiosity, excite his ingenuity, and lead him on to an unexpected climax, is a quite legitimate artistic effect.[38]

Then, of course, Stevenson's volume has that key gothic characteristic of reincarnating the past in the present, which Carr loved. Greene elaborates on the allusive quality of the *New Arabian Nights*:

Stevenson's theme was taken from the Arabian Nights tales about Caliph Haroun al-Raschid, who at night went disguised through Baghdad seeking adventures. In *New Arabian Nights*, Prince Florizel of Bohemia wanders through London finding exotic and romantic adventures in "Baghdad-on-the-Thames." (p. 129)

Greene also reminds us (p. 131) how al-Raschid is explicitly summoned to mind by Dr. Michael Tairlaine in the opening pages of *The Red Widow Murders*. Tairlaine asks jocularly whether the host mysteriously inviting him into adventure is the ancient Caliph. His laughing host, in a rejoinder, identifies himself as Prince Florizel of Bohemia. (In *The Arabian Nights Murder*, Carr also steps back to the Arabian Nights and directly borrows the legend of Haroun al-Raschid, which he employs as a colorful legendary background for the novel's twentieth-century crimes.)

Carr's novels would continue to refer explicitly to Stevenson (also noted by Greene, p. 441), particularly to *New Arabian Nights*, as late in his career as Carr's penultimate novel, *Deadly Hall* (1971). And as Greene observed (with reference to Carr's adaptations for radio of Stevenson's stories), "Stevenson would have been astonished at the changes in his story, but they reveal that within thirty-eight-year-old John Dickson Carr the young romanticist still lived" (p. 289).

Stevenson's influence on the young (and older) Carr went beyond its subject matter, which is why his impact on Carr was more than superficial. The young Carr also recognized in Stevenson's writings that sense of nobility, of gentility, which Carr personally carried all his life, and which drew him to authors whose works championed it. Greene reports of Carr, "he was unfailingly generous about helping his friends" (p. 306). Prince Florizel, an object lesson for the young Carr, never turns away anybody in need, either—indeed, he seeks out

---

38 "Art and the Detective," *Temple Bar* (London), Vol. 2, Issue 10, pp. 322-323.

the vulnerable to assist them. Florizel values and demonstrates loyalty, not rank: he is as much a gentleman during his life as a commoner as when he is a royal prince. Like his Shakespearean namesake, Stevenson's prince does not mindlessly conflate nobility with lineage.

Similarly, the lessons of *Treasure Island* for Carr are more than Jim Hawkins' skin-deep aspiration to adventure. Consider as one example Ben Gunn, who is barely recognizable as man instead of beast. Despite this, Gunn never loses his English civility, telling young Hawkins when they meet:

> Marooned three years agone…and lived on goats since then, and berries, and oysters. Wherever a man is, says I, a man can do for himself. But, mate, my heart is sore for Christian diet. You mightn't happen to have a piece of cheese about you, now? No? Well, many's the long night I've dreamed of cheese—toasted, mostly—and woke up again, and here I were.[39]

If Ben Gunn is *Treasure Island*'s Caliban, his confession echoing his misshapen analogue's admission, "that when I waked/I cried to dream again" (*The Tempest*, 3.2.142-143), Gunn is also, in opposition to the Shakespearean character he superficially resembles, the novel's presentation of innate human nobility. Stevenson offers Dr. Livesey, in complement to Gunn, as the book's embodiment of reason, gentility, and civilization. Upon learning of Gunn's request, the doctor neatly finishes Stevenson's lesson:

> "Well, Jim," says he, "just see the good that comes of being dainty in your food. You've seen my snuff-box, haven't you? And you never saw me take snuff, the reason being that in my snuff-box I carry a piece of Parmesan cheese—a cheese made in Italy, very nutritious. Well, that's for Ben Gunn!" (p. 145)

Even Long John Silver, leader of the pirates, is clearly separated from his fellows by his seeming to be of distinctly better character than they. Throughout the novel, the reader wonders whether Long John, though unlawful, is a personally honorable man, or whether, like Dickens' Uriah Heep, he merely mouths the niceties of decency only to catch his victims the more unaware. It is the former: Long John always clings to certain tenets of honor. Stevenson imbues him with a surprising nobility that drives dramatic tension. Silver is more anti-

---

39 *Treasure Island,* Duke Classics, 2012, p. 114. All subsequent excerpts are drawn from the same edition.

hero than villain. Israel Hands, by comparison, is simply treacherous. Hands lives by the same motto as Billy Bones: "dead men don't bite"; neither of the two hesitates to break his word, whether Bones's default on his rent at the Hawkinses' Admiral Benbow Inn, or Hands' attempt, through a false pact, to lull Jim Hawkins into a fatal complacency.

Silver is redeemable because he does not and will not go back on his word. This, not merely Long John's cunning, is the reason that the mutineers instinctively accept him as their leader. During his negotiation for a flag of truce with Captain Smollet—who disdains to bargain with a mutineer but disavows treachery under any circumstances—Silver finds the captain's declaration an acceptable substitute for a formal agreement of truce: "'That's enough, cap'n,' shouted Long John cheerily. 'A word from you's enough. I know a gentleman, and you may lay to that'" (p. 148). Later, in his own negotiations with the mutineers, who fear for their safety to approach him, Long John echoes, as his own principle, Captain Smollett's uprightness:

> The door opened, and the five men, standing huddled together just inside, pushed one of their number forward. In any other circumstances it would have been comical to see his slow advance, hesitating as he set down each foot, but holding his closed right hand in front of him.
> "Step up, lad," cried Silver. "I won't eat you. Hand it over, lubber. I know the rules, I do; I won't hurt a depytation." (p. 220)

Then, of course, there is the model provided for youthful readers by Jim Hawkins himself. When Dr. Livesey, who has been granted a private interview with Hawkins while the latter is held hostage by the pirates, encourages him, "Whip over, and we'll run for it," Jim objects: "I passed my word" to Silver not to attempt an escape. He reminds Dr. Livesey, "I should have been dead by now if Silver hadn't stood for me," and chides the doctor, "you know right well you wouldn't do the thing yourself—neither you nor squire nor captain and no more will I. Silver trusted me; I passed my word, and back I go" (p. 233).

Thus, Jim reminds the doctor, and the reader, that there are differences between *civility* and *honor*, and between *honor* and *lawfulness*. Jim recognizes the common ethic that has bound them all, and by which a person's soul and sanity survive, whether marooned alone for three years, or through forming a common bond with one's shipmates, or even forming it with one's enemies. The truly noble man, Stevenson reinforces for the reader—and for young John Carr—is not a product of his station or his civility, but of his inviolable honor, his innate gentility.

The same lesson is evident in Stevenson's *The Strange Case of Dr. Jekyll and Mr. Hyde*: when one loses one's innate nobility, one ceases to be fully human. Of course, in that novel, the inner deformity is visibly represented by the physical disfigurement of Jekyll into Hyde. Surprising to those who have not read the novel (relying instead upon our general cultural awareness of it), this transformation is a *diminution*: Dr. Henry Jekyll is handsome, "a large, well-made, smooth-faced man of fifty, with something of a slyish cast perhaps, but every mark of capacity and kindness—you could see by his looks...warm affection."[40] That slyish cast is of course Jekyll's inner moral weakness, which tempts him to transform into Hyde—who, by contrast, is the physical embodiment of turpitude:

> There is something wrong with his appearance; something displeasing, something down-right detestable. I never saw a man I so disliked, and yet I scarce know why. He must be deformed somewhere; he gives a strong feeling of deformity, although I couldn't specify the point. He's an extraordinary looking man, and yet I really can name nothing out of the way. (pp. 11-12)

After the transformation, Hyde is "dressed in clothes far too large for him, clothes of the doctor's bigness" (p. 82). Neither literally nor metaphorically can Hyde fill the doctor's shoes. In every sense, his evil diminishes and deforms him. Although Stevenson does not work the metaphor nearly so explicitly in *Treasure Island*, this is probably the same reason that Long John Silver lacks a limb: he is a man incompletely moral, hobbled by his evil, but struggling against it to live according to his own noble principles.

It is this same innate nobility, the essential compass within each individual, which ethically guides Carr's detectives to set their own rules, letting sympathetic criminals go free, or goading murderers into suicide rather than sending them into the hands of the state for lawful trials, etc. Examples abound, including Bencolin's famous declaration (p. 206) in *The Four False Weapons*:

> "My dear young lady," said Bencolin very gently, "I can tamper with the law when, where, and how I like. I have tampered with the law when, where, and how I liked, and I will do it again."

---

40 *The Strange Case of Dr. Jekyll and Mr. Hyde*, Charles Scribner's Sons, 1886, pp. 30-31. All subsequent excerpts are drawn from the same edition.

Each of Carr's other major detectives also tinkers with the law according to his own sense of justice, much like Sherlock Holmes: "I am not retained by the police to supply their deficiencies," Holmes declares in "The Adventure of the Blue Carbuncle." More than one close reader of Carr (most notably, and probably earliest, Douglas Greene in *The Door to Doom and Other Detections*) has argued, convincingly, that Carr's detectives do not solve crimes for the sake of upholding the law or the conventional definition of justice. If Bencolin, alone among them actually an officer of the law declines to do so, why should we expect anything more from Carr's amateur, consulting detectives? Rather, the crimes Carr's detectives solve and punish, in whatever form, threaten rationality and social stability. As Bencolin despairs in *It Walks By Night*, "if there is no meaning in any of these incidents, there is no meaning in all the world…" (p. 65). These are what Carr's detectives defend. Greene argues that "the crimes with their hints of black magic challenge our belief in rational cause and effect," making Carr's detectives almost "exorcists; they dispel the devils and demonstrate that the seemingly supernatural events were created by humans for human motives."[41] Greene further argues that Carr "did not believe in a static world in which middle-class values of law and order are protected, but rather one in which high adventure is possible."[42] This is, of course, the world of Robert Louis Stevenson, which the reader Carr loved, and which the writer Carr perpetuated.

While we have no confirmation that Carr read Stevenson's *Memories and Portraits* (1887), it seems likely; as with Cabell and Chesterton, a number of Stevenson's literary viewpoints (and his preferred authors) provide insight not only into his own fiction, but Carr's. Consider, for instance, Stevenson's embrace of Dumas's d'Artagnan:

> …in the character of d'Artagnan…that spirit of morality, which is one of the chief merits of the book, makes one of the main joys of its perusal, and sets it high above more popular rivals…d'Artagnan has mellowed into a man so witty, rough, kind and upright, that he takes the heart by storm. There is nothing of the copy-book about his virtues, nothing of the drawing-room in his fine, natural civility…I do not say there is no character as well drawn in Shakespeare; I do say there is none that I love so wholly. There are many spiritual eyes that seem to spy upon

---

41 *The Door to Doom and Other Detections*, Harper and Row, 1980, p. 22.
42 Ibid, p. 23.

our actions—eyes of the dead and the absent, whom
we imagine to behold us in our most private hours,
and whom we fear and scruple to offend: our witnesses and judges. And among these, even if you should
think me childish, I must count my d'Artagnan—not
d'Artagnan of the memoirs whom Thackeray pretend-
ed to prefer—a preference, I take the freedom of saying, in which he stands alone; not the d'Artagnan of
flesh and blood, but him of the ink and paper; not
Nature's, but Dumas's. And this is the particular crown
and triumph of the artist—not to be true merely, but
to be lovable; not simply to convince, but to enchant.[43]

Of course, we know Carr also loved Dumas, and d'Artagnan;
whether he came to him through Stevenson, we do not know.

As to the act and purpose of reading itself, Stevenson enjoined:

In anything fit to be called by the name of reading,
the process itself should be absorbing and voluptuous;
we should gloat over a book, be rapt clean out of ourselves, and rise from the perusal, our mind filled with
the busiest, kaleidoscopic dance of images, incapable
of sleep or of continuous thought. (p. 247)

What could be less like reading Henry James (an author with whom
Stevenson, like Carr, occasionally took specific issue)?

Assessing his own boyhood favorites, Stevenson united them as
Carr later would his own: "Different as they are, all these early favou-
rites have a common note—they have all a touch of the romantic"
(p. 250). Stevenson's further, extended exploration of this idea only
sounds more like Carr's own expression of the virtues of fiction:

The desire for knowledge…is not more deeply seated
than this demand for fit and striking incident. The dull-
est of clowns tells, or tries to tell, himself a story, as the
feeblest of children uses invention in his play; and even
as the imaginative grown person, joining in the game,
at once enriches it with many delightful circumstances,
the great creative writer shows us the realization and
the apotheosis of the day-dreams of common men.
His stories may be nourished with the realities of life,
but their true mark is to satisfy the nameless longings

---

43 *Memories and Portraits*, Charles Scribner's Sons (New York), 1895, pp. 242-
244. All subsequent excerpts are drawn from the same edition.

of the reader, and to obey the ideal laws of the day-dream. The right kind of thing should fall out in the right kind of place; the right kind of thing should follow; and not only the characters talk aptly and think naturally, but all the circumstances in a tale answer one to another like notes in music. The threads of a story come from time to time together and make a picture in the web...these epoch-making scenes, which put the last mark of truth upon a story and fill up, at one blow, our capacity for sympathetic pleasure, we so adopt into the very bosom of our mind that neither time nor tide can efface or weaken the impression. This, then, is the plastic part of literature: to embody character, thought, or emotion in some act or attitude that shall be remarkably striking to the mind's eye. This is the highest and hardest thing to do in words; the thing which, once accomplished, equally delights the schoolboy and the sage...Compared with this, all other purposes in literature, except the purely lyrical or the purely philosophic, are bastard in nature, facile of execution, and feeble in result.... In the highest achievements of the art of words, the dramatic and the pictorial, the moral and romantic interest, rise and fall together by a common and organic law. Situation is animated with passion, passion clothed upon with situation. Neither exists for itself, but each inheres indissolubly with the other. This is high art; and not only the highest art possible in words, but the highest art of all, since it combines the greatest mass and diversity of the elements of truth and pleasure. (pp. 255-261)

In this peroration, Stevenson, one of the great Romantic novelists and an admirer, like Carr, of their Romantic predecessors, delivers not only his own literary *Summa Theologica*, but that of Carr, too—and in good part of Chesterton, and even recognizably of Cabell. This is a common thread running through the skein of all Carr's most admired writers.

Brian Oswald Donn Byrne (1889-1928), an Irish novelist and short story writer, was another of Carr's literary idols who is all but forgotten today. Unlike Cabell, Chesterton, and Stevenson, Donn Byrne delivered no treatises on his literary aesthetics; but when we examine his fiction, we understand readily why Donn Byrne's influence was strong upon Carr.

To begin, it is easy to recognize that the Irish novelist's focus on traditional Irish storytellers and characters, blended ably with his Romantic use of historical themes, appealed to and inspired young Carr, also proud of his Irish heritage and seeking to express it in his own fiction. Donn Byrne took a contemporary approach to the medieval narrative. Like Cabell, he was not period-faithful, but his works are much more accessible to readers in their earthy expression, their bawdiness, and their delivery with a wry sense of humor.

Among the five authors Carr named most impactful upon him, Carr's own humor is most like Donn Byrne's. Donn Byrne may have inspired Carr to combine, however improbably, humor with genres to which it was otherwise less commonly matched.

One novel the young Carr likely loved, Donn Byrne's reinvented origin of a familiar historical legend, is *Messer Marco Polo* (1921). It describes the journey of a young Marco Polo to China in pursuit of love, and is filled with evocative, even lyrical descriptions of an idealized past—into which, nonetheless, the sort of sly, modern humor Carr fancies creeps into the narrative without violating the sense of time and place. Carr frequently strives to achieve the same effect. In Donn Byrne's novel, Marco Polo's familiar legend is recounted through a framing narrative: in modern New York, a resident Irishman, formerly of County Antrim (which, incidentally, provides the surname of a married couple in *The Punch and Judy Murders*), listens to an old countryman and clansman, Malachi Campbell of the Long Glen. Campbell delivers his own version of Polo's tale, because, says the old bard:

> The scholars can tell how many are the feathers in a
> bird's wing, but it takes me to inform the doctors why
> the call comes to them, and they fly over oceans with-
> out compass or sextant or sight of land.[44]

"The New Canterbury Tales" is of a kindred spirit in narrative structure, tone, and humor, perhaps in part inspired by this novel, although we can and will trace stronger, more direct influences upon that story cycle in the discussion following it.

Messer Marco Polo's main action commences when Polo's father and uncle decide to grant Marco's request to return with them to China, which they initially refused. Marco has asked because, after hearing tell of her from a Chinese sea-captain, Marco seeks idealized Christian love incarnated in the person of the Khan's daughter. The Chinese princess, Tao-Tuen, is known popularly as "Golden Bells" for her soft, sweet voice. (Donn Byrne's book, while certainly trading on the same

---

44 *Messer Marco Polo*, The Century Co., 1921, p. 13. All subsequent excerpts are drawn from the same edition.

Romantic stereotype of women as most other medieval and Romantic narratives, unlike Cabell, does so absent of cynicism.) Marco's father Nicholas and uncle Matthew have been charged by Kubla Khan to return with theological emissaries from the Pope to debate religion with the great ruler, but they cannot, because of the Papal interregnum. So, in Venice, they discuss alternatives, the first of which, suggested by Nicholas, is Matthew himself.

> "Oh, sure, they'd never listen to me," Matthew laughs—"me that's drank with them, and deludhered[45] their women, and gambled until I left them nothing but the sweat of their brows. I'd be a great one to preach religion to them. Why, man, they'd laugh at me. But I tell you what, Nicholas. There's a bishop in Negropont, and I know where he lives, and I know his house and everything. What do you say, Nicholas? We'll just throw a bag over his head and tie him on a horse. Oh, sure, he'd give grand discourses to the Great Khan!"
>
> "Have sense, Matthew; have sense. You're always too rough; always ready to end an argument with a knife, or just lift what you want. Have sense, man; you can't kidnap a bishop like you'd kidnap a woman."
>
> "Well, I don't see why not," says Matthew. "It would be easier, too, because a woman will scratch like a wildcat. But if you're set against it, I won't do it," he says. "Well, then, how about young Marco?"
>
> "My sound man Matthew! my bully fellow! Sure you were never at a loss yet! Young Marco it is; sure, 't is the elegant idea. There's not a man born of woman better for the job." (pp. 59-60)

As the princess Tao-Tuen is the idealized Romantic woman, so, of course, will Marco prove to be her worthy Romantic lover. The reader can, doubtless, perceive the connections stretching back to the epic historical legends inspiring Donn Byrne (including, as backstory, the Crusades), through Donn Byrne's contemporary retelling, and connect these to Carr's own preoccupation with tales of chivalry, both past and modern, told for modern audiences. (We will encounter multiple instances of this in the present collection of young Carr's fiction.) While Donn Byrne wrote no literary criticism, as many authors do, he placed in this novel some of his own artistic views (views Carr clearly shared) into the mouth of one of his characters,

---

45 Not a typo; this archaic word means, "deluded."

the minstrel:

> But a story is how destiny is interwoven, the fine and
> gallant and the tragic points of life. And you mustn't
> look at them with the eyes of the body, but you must
> feel with the antennae of your being. (p. 131)

Donn Byrne's modern stories also seem to have left their imprint
upon Carr. In his 1915 collection *Stories Without Women (and a Few with
Women)*, the author included two modern boxing tales, "An African
Epic" and "A Man's Game." The premise of these may have inspired
Carr's 1925 story, "The God of the Gloves," published in *The Hill
Record*, and reprinted in *The Haverfordian* two years later under a fellow
student's name. Like "The Kindling Spark," "The God of the Gloves"
is one of young Carr's infrequent literary tales set in the twentieth century, as much focused on character as on action. There is a superficial
resemblance between "The God of the Gloves" and "A Man's Game":
both plots pivot on cheating in a championship match. Despite this,
they and "An African Epic" have much more at stake: all three focus
on a turning point in the protagonist's life, cast in larger, interpersonal
and social consequences, which of course somehow all hinge on the
outcome of the boxing match. Certainly, Carr, who took such delight
in dramatizing every thrust, feint, and parry, carefully, technically observed, in his fiction featuring fencing matches, must have enjoyed following Donn Byrne's lead in meting out a plot and character revelations, blow by blow, in "The God of the Gloves." We should note, too,
that Carr's *Fear is the Same*, three decades later, features pugilism at its
climax.

There will be additional discussion of Donn Byrne in the story
commentaries, but we have, at a high level, finished sketching why
Carr acknowledged him so strongly as a literary ancestor. Their cultural affinity, their shared literary heritage of medievalism and Romanticism, their compatible senses of humor, and Carr's likely admiration
for Donn Byrne's clear narrative technique, occasionally capable of
ascending to lyricism without false notes, all define this bond. True,
Donn Byrne was the least innovative and consequential of Carr's most
cherished authors—a number of Donn Byrne's novels were mere
potboilers—but Donn Byrne's romantic Irish spirit clearly sang to
Carr's—and of course, we well understand that conventional literary
merit was never on Carr's list of important criteria for favored authors
and works.

This brings us to the last of Carr's greatest influences, O. Henry.
At the most superficial level—but still valid—we remember that Carr
always valued a twist ending; even today, we still recognize O. Henry as

one of the ablest practitioners of dramatic irony. There is no doubt that in this context, Henry was nearly as great a practical influence upon Carr as Chesterton was.

O. Henry's stories being sardonic and often comical, while the young Carr's were aspirational and atmospheric, we generally find *contrasts* between his works and Henry's, whose tales often rely upon entertainingly dashing grand expectations, not fulfilling them. Characters in Henry's tales having similar aspirations to Carr's usually differ with Carr's by having entirely worse luck. Consider James Clancy, in *Cabbages and Kings* (1904), who aspires to adventure in the grand manner. After meeting a charismatic Guatemalan, he sets off to become a revolutionary liberator in that country. Were Clancy a Carr character, he would experience a life-defining, heroic adventure—and almost certainly meet a nubile heroine and, in the denouement, marry her. Instead, for all his high-minded politics and ambition to adventure, Clancy finds himself deceived into becoming an enforced laborer, building a railroad on behalf of the corrupt politician who seduced Clancy by exploiting his naïve assumptions and worldview.

Where Clancy's adventure aligns with Carr, despite this, if not very specifically, is where we find O. Henry's general influence on Carr: that characteristic concluding twist. It is no exaggeration to say that Henry, as much as any writer (again, even Conan Doyle and Chesterton), taught Carr the value of an unexpected ending. As we will see in this volume's selections, young Carr's use of this literary tool in his earliest mystery stories is more clearly an emulation of Henry than of the detective-fiction writers with whom we commonly affiliate Carr. While not all Carr's earliest mystery stories are devoid of fair-play clues, for the most part, they are in fact *mystery* fiction, not *detective* fiction. They do not (as Carr later would, in a style then closer to Doyle and Chesterton) provide all the clues to the reader necessary to solve the crime, clues revealed at the same time to the reader as to the story's detective.

While we do not usually think of O. Henry as a writer of mysteries or crime fiction, he did, in fact, write more than a few stories straying into the genre—albeit, in Henry's inimitable way, so not providing much of a role model for the mature Carr. The young John doubtless read with special interest, for instance, Henry's three Sherlockian pastiches: "The Adventures of Shamrock Jolnes," "The Sleuths," and "The Detective Detector." All were originally published before Carr was born, but the first two were collected in Henry's *Sixes and Sevens* (1911), and the final one in *Waifs and Strays* (1917). These stories, like many of the contemporaneous Holmes pastiches, are pure silliness.

Given that O. Henry was the favorite writer of Carr's father, Wooda, whose large library in Uniontown likely included all O. Henry's books, it would be surprising if, by the time the teen began writing, he hadn't read all of Henry's fiction. Among the volumes in his father's library, Carr would certainly have fixed on Henry's *The Gentle Grafter* (1904). Despite its being one of the nineteen added titles in 1967 that rounded out the original 106 Haycraft-Queen cornerstones (1948) into 125 Queen's Quorum titles—indeed, joining some of Carr's own titles on that list—*The Gentle Grafter* probably only provided the young Carr enjoyment and a reaffirmed appreciation of O. Henry. Like the Holmes pastiches, the book has no clearly discernible stylistic influence upon Carr, no special resemblance in plot or technique even to what the amateur Carr wrote, let alone the professional. Rather, *Gentle Grafter* is a collection of garrulous tall tales of con artistry, as told in the first person to an anonymous narrator, which chronicles the career of their teller, Jeff Peters. Although enormously likable, Peters is an unredeemed antihero; he is not the Hanshews' Cleek, reformed for the love of a woman, or Flambeau, apprehended and made penitent by Father Brown. Peters' self-interested adventurism is hardly comparable to the gallant demeanor and yearning toward grand adventure common to all Carr's most representative characters.

Nor do the narrative tone or character voices in this collection resound in Carr's fiction. Consider as a representative sample of *The Gentle Grafter* the following drunken splutter by Tucker, Peters' frequent partner. In the story "A Midsummer Masquerade," while perpetrating a fraud, the inebriated Tucker cannot recall whether he should be impersonating the Arctic explorer Lieutenant Peary or the Duke of Marlborough. So hilariously, he slurs together both:

> "It was in the spring of last year that I sailed the Castle of Blenheim up to latitude 87 degrees Fahrenheit and beat the record. Ladies," says Andy, "it was a sad sight to see a Duke allied by a civil and liturgical chattel mortgage to one of your first families lost in a region of semiannual days." And then he goes on, "At four bells we sighted Westminster Abbey, but there was not a drop to eat. At noon we threw out five sandbags, and the ship rose fifteen knots higher. At midnight," continues Andy, "the restaurants closed. Sitting on a cake of ice we ate seven hot dogs. All around us was snow and ice. Six times a night the boatswain rose up and tore a leaf off the calendar so we could keep time with the barometer. At 12," says Andy, with a lot of anguish

in his face, "Three huge polar bears sprang down the hatchway, into the cabin. And then—"[46]

It is easier to imagine Henry channeling Twain than Carr channeling Henry. Other than acknowledging Carr's emulation of Henry's brisk narrative pace and his trademark surprise endings, in fact, a reader can hardly see any resemblance between Henry's "crime" writings and Carr's own. Such comparisons amount to barely more than generalities, leaving the reader with a small mystery: why did Carr number Henry among the select authors who most influenced him?

In fact, there is one O. Henry work of seemingly peculiar influence upon Carr: *Cabbages and Kings*, Henry's first book-length publication and his only novel. Unfamiliar readers may be interested to note that *Cabbages and Kings* coined the phrase "banana republic." The setting for this book is the fictional South American country of Anchuria, which has an economy wholly dependent upon selling its fruit to industrialized nations, chiefly the United States.

The novel's inception is helpful to understand. O. Henry's real name was William Sydney Porter. *Cabbages and Kings* was inspired by his time living as a fugitive in Honduras for six months beginning in 1896; the novel was written in a Trujillo hotel during this exile. Porter was accused of embezzling funds from the First National Bank of Austin. Whether or not he did, Porter skipped bail and fled the United States. When he returned and stood trial, Porter was convicted and sentenced to five years in prison. It was during the three years he served (being released early for good behavior) that Porter invented the pseudonym O. Henry. Aided by a friend in New Orleans, who forwarded Porter's manuscript submissions to publishers (so they did not seem to come from a convict), Porter successfully published fourteen short stories, laying the groundwork for his successful post-prison career as a writer. His first book, published in 1904 as O. Henry, was *Cabbages and Kings*. In the novel, not only the less-advanced nation's economy, but its politics, inevitably come unduly under the control of the large trading company, the Vesuvius Fruit Company, which buys and resells Anchuria's natural resources.

On the surface, *Cabbages and Kings* is a loosely interwoven series of individual character sketches set against the background of Anchuria's personal, political, and business machinations, with the predictably resulting corruption and conflicts. Of course, being a work by O. Henry, the novel's tone is comic and ironic. Most of the action, which has outsized consequences for Anchuria, takes place almost improbably not in the country's capital, but rather, in a sleepy little coastal town, Coralio, where the American Consul is located (but

---

46 *The Gentle Grafter*, Doubleday, Page & Company, 1920, p. 97.

where there is not even a good harbor to facilitate trade).

Beyond understanding the novel according to conventional reading terms, we can read *Cabbages and Kings* as a mystery novel, one that has some relation to and influence upon Carr's developing technique. Of course, Carr was intimately conversant with Henry's first published book, holding it as a favorite; as late as December 29, 1939, in a letter to John Cheatle, he evoked *Cabbages and Kings*, borrowing its malapropic misstatement of the Homeric Lotus-eater metaphor in Chapter X. In that chapter, an old railroad hand, Halloran, serves up the metaphor to James Clancy as an explanation of why he declines to join Clancy's escape attempt from their enforced labor. Halloran confesses that he has become a "lettuce-eater":

> 'Tis the tropics that's done it. 'Tis like the poet says:
> "Forgotten are our friends that we have left behind; in
> the hollow lettuce-land we will live and lay reclined."[47]

This comic formulation remained with Carr for nearly a quarter century after he first read *Cabbages and Kings*. Excited by his early success in radio drama, Carr wrote to Cheatle, "I have been bitten by the bug. In O. Henry's words, I have ate the lettuce. I am going to write more radio plays."

Cabbages and Kings, as it moves from humorously portraying one Coralian denizen to the next, develops a subplot around a Carr-worthy crime: $100,000 stolen from the country's treasury by its absconding president, Miraflores. The full explanation of the theft and how it completes the stories of some of the novel's central characters is reserved until the closing chapters. While the final explanation is not fair-play, it is clever enough—and of course, it is a surprise. A reader of Carr and *Cabbages* easily sees how young John Carr would have taken specific inspiration from this singular book. Henry's climactic revelation is layered on top of *multiple earlier clues* concerning what happened to the missing money. As in a mature Carr novel, the revelation of the final, true explanation in *Cabbages and Kings* serves to reframe every earlier, seemingly damning fact. The solution cleverly makes the reader recognize having misapprehended the clues and accused the wrong suspect, finally seeing the full solution from a different, definitive, angle.

In each of his more than three hundred short stories, Henry, as is practical for the format, usually incorporated a single twist ending. We find the same approach in some of the young Carr's short mystery fiction: each has its surprise ending, and as with Henry, not always earned. Of course, as Carr matured, he gained admiring notoriety for his ability not merely to surprise, but to mislead the reader by the in-

---

47 *Cabbages and Kings*, Doubleday, Page & Company, 1915, p. 176.

corporation of multiple potential solutions, each suggested by clues appearing progressively and fairly throughout the narrative, and each tentative solution seeming to fit the facts of the crime—all of them finally superseded and debunked by the last, most surprising, and most complete explanation. In this, Carr was applying the technique he likely encountered for the first time, with enduring gratification, in *Cabbages and Kings*. Of course, Carr developed the technique to a consistently masterful level not achieved by Henry or by most of Carr's detective-fiction predecessors or peers. "The majority of detective writers usually rest on the one big surprise," he says, "but I prefer the double. It's more ingenious."[48]

Worth noting, Greene credits E.C. Bentley's *Trent's Last Case* (1913) and Anthony Berkeley's *The Poisoned Chocolates Case* (1929) for initially popularizing and then perfecting the false-solution mechanism in detective fiction, and in doing so, being influences upon Carr. There is no reason to argue against these being available examples for Carr—although, of course, in the case of the latter, the young author was already layering his own false solutions into *Grand Guignol* that same year. What we do know is that Carr had a special passion for O. Henry, one demonstrably not exhibited by a resemblance in prose or a borrowing of premises, even where such borrowings might have been available to Carr given Henry's compatible subject matter, for instance, *The Gentle Grafter*. Perhaps O. Henry's so-strong influence upon Carr rests solely upon the surprise ending—but it seems impossible that Carr would have overlooked the clever construction of one of his favorite books, a book to which Carr was still casually alluding a quarter century after he first read it. Rather, it seems Carr's ardent appreciation for Henry would have magnified this technique of the novel in his attention, making Carr the more likely to adopt and experiment with it.

As with Donn Byrne, O. Henry's influences upon Carr may not have been varied and numerous, but clearly, they were in any event strong and lasting. We have witnessed in his correspondence how the older Carr, long since a successful writer, retrospectively correlated to Bond and others their impact upon his emergence as a writer.

We should also invoke, in tallying up explanations of Carr's amateur writings, his introduction to the MWA's (Mystery Writers of America) 1952 anthology, *Maiden Murders*. This anthology collected, based upon an idea first suggested by Ellery Queen, the first short stories by the organization's members. Whether Carr declined to provide "The Ruby of Rameses," or whether it was not selected by the

---

48 Robert Lewis Taylor, "Two Authors in an Attic" (Part I), *The New Yorker*, September 8, 1951, p. 39.

committee (who narrowed *Maiden Murders* to twenty selections for the sake of length) we do not know. Carr did, in any event, write the book's introduction. Although the introduction speaks, as intended, aptly to the tribulations of all neophyte mystery writers, we can detect in it Carr offering a bit of autobiography when he explains the mindset of young, first-time writers who "meant business":

> A new window had opened. A fiery new idea hummed in our heads. On the beach, say, lay a fine fresh corpse, strangled, with only its own footprints leading out across the damp waste of sand. We might not yet be able skillfully to maneuver with that corpse: no, not yet. But one fine day we would. One fine day, by thunder, we would succeed!
> And then one fine day, we did.[49]

Enjoy these stories now, written by an improbably young, improbably talented John Dickson Carr.

---

49 *Maiden Murders*, Harper & Brothers, 1952, p. xii.

The House of Terror (1922)

I

Melford paused. Above him loomed Heatherby House—gaunt, grim, and forbidding. One slim tower thrust itself boldly across the face of the moon, but the house itself lay wrapped in shadow. Even the park had a wild, unkempt appearance; the statues seemed to brood and the fountains to have long since hushed their clamor. No leaf stirred in the trees; not even the eerie wail of a night bird disturbed the stillness.

Melford's frown deepened as he perplexedly surveyed the silent house. For a moment he stood lost in thought. Then, shifting his travelling-bag to his other hand, he strode onward up the path, aiming angry kicks at the pebbles beneath his feet. Swallowed up in the shadows which clung close about the house, he mounted the short flight of steps communicating with the terrace and jerked savagely at the bell-pull. Again and again he awoke the echoes within, but still his strained ears could catch no sound of an answering step.

Melford swore volubly under his breath. After having come down from London to take over his lately acquired estate, and having tramped a good three miles over roads which were none of the best into the bargain, he found Heatherby House deserted. The fact demanded explanation. He had been enjoined by his late grandfather's solicitor to present himself at the manor-house on the twenty-first. True, Spencerton's consent to meet him there had been tacit, but the lawyer had led him to assume as much by hinting at matters hitherto undisclosed to be revealed to him when he took possession of the estate. But even if Spencerton himself were not in attendance, surely some of the servants must be about! The attorney had given him to understand that his grandfather's entire staff of retainers had consented to remain at Heatherby House in the service of its new master. Yet even they appeared to have deserted the place, as rats desert a sinking ship. For some reason the simile impressed him.

Melford ruminated. He must of necessity gain entrance to the house, but how? An unlocked window, perhaps. That was his sole remaining hope. Descending the terrace steps, he frowningly scanned the unprepossessing facade of the house. Tier upon tier of vacant, unshuttered windows stared blankly down at him. Must he risk his neck testing them all in search of one possibly left unlocked? He groaned. Then, of a sudden, he brought himself sharply erect, involuntarily crushing in his hand the cigarette which he had half-lifted toward his lips. In the window of one of the lower rooms had suddenly appeared what might have seemed nothing more than a white blur, devoid as it was of all semblance of human shape, had it not been for the Thing's eyes. Evil, malignant eyes they were, glowing like red-hot coals and seeming to Melford to sear his very flesh. For a moment they remained fixed upon him—burning, blood-red, awful in their unwavering intensity; then figure and eyes slowly resolved themselves into darkness.

For a long moment Melford stood stock-still, his breath coming in short, labored gasps, his every muscle paralyzed. Then, arousing himself to action, he leaped up the steps, darted along the terrace, and, pausing before the window in which had appeared the apparition, peered into the Stygian gloom within. Almost instantly he heard the spiteful crack of a pistol and a long, silvery tinkle of falling glass as a bullet tore its way through the window-pane and sliced a strip of felt from his hat-brim.

Dazedly Melford groped his way to the balustrade of the terrace and leaned weakly upon it for support. The unexpected attempt at his assassination had been the last shock to his shattered nerves. It seemed ages before the sense of nausea which overcame him passed. Then, rising, he was off toward the stairs when—it came, he felt sure, from somewhere close at hand: a hideous, choking cry, swelling up in shrill crescendo on the night air to terminate abruptly in a short, gurgling sob!

His weakness forgotten, Melford spun round and was off in the direction whence had come that horrible cry. Some would-be assassin's bullet had all but found his brain; perhaps someone else had not been so fortunate. His vest-pocket flashlight was out in an instant, its narrow beam playing hither and thither about the terrace. Perhaps twenty paces further he discerned before him the pillars of a loggia, and, hurrying forward, he directed the disk of light from his torch within. Half prepared as he was for what had happened, he shrank back with a low cry.

Before him, face upward on the flagstones, was the body of a man. His vest and shirt-bosom were dyed a dull crimson, and a thin stream of red trailed off across his coat. Close beside him Melford caught the evil glitter of a long, slender dagger, its haft wrought in the semblance of a serpent twining about the trunk of a tree, and its polished blade stained with blood. In the man's outflung right hand he convulsively clutched a crumpled envelope; his left was empty, but beside it lay a broken cuff link. Yet it was not these indications of a violent death which held Melford spellbound, but the face of the murdered man; for the face he saw in the misty rays of his flashlight was that of Basil Spencerton!

II

Weak and almost fainting, Melford clutched at the pillar behind him and there clung until he had to some degree recovered his composure. Even then the recollection of the horrors he had undergone almost overwhelmed him. He had switched off his light; the ensuing darkness seemed a thing of evil that had gripped him by the throat and was slowly strangling him. Almost frenziedly he pressed the controlling button of his torch; he could not bear to be alone in the dark with that still figure whose outstretched hand almost touched his foot. The thought of flight assailed him, but he rejected it as cowardly. He must discover the cause of each and every one of these mysterious events before he quitted Heatherby House, he told himself grimly. Falling on his knees beside the silent form, he lightly touched one wrist. Then, with a startled exclamation, he laid a hand on Spencerton's forehead. No, he had not been mistaken: both wrist and forehead were stone cold. The man had been dead at least an hour.

The fact could only mean that the scream he had heard had not come from the murdered lawyer. Who, then, had uttered it? With a puzzled shake of his head Melford gave up the problem and turned his attention to the envelope upon which Spencerton's fingers were closed in a vise-like grip. With no little difficulty he contrived to remove it; to his surprise it was addressed to himself.

Written in his grandfather's small, neat hand, the superscription read:

"To my grandson, Calvin Melford, to be delivered to him on his taking possession of Heatherby House."

Without further ado he tore open the envelope and drew therefrom a closely written sheet of notepaper. The missive was dated a week before old Sir Geoffery Melford's death, and ran:

My dear Calvin:

This communication will seem to you like one from the grave. I write it because I feel the shadows closing about me—the dread shadows of death. But before I am summoned to my long home I wish to make you my confidant in a matter which I have never even so much as spoken of to anyone else.

"I am neither a nervous nor an imaginative man, and I never believed in ghosts—until I saw that

THING. But it hates me in death as Philip Darworth hated me in life[1], and wherever I go its eyes burn into my soul as his did that night when, as I stood over him with my hunting crop, he swore that if I killed him he would not rest quiet in his grave until he had hounded me to suicide. Well, I won; he has not driven me to kill myself, but I'll not last a week. But if you wish to learn of the act—I will not call it a crime— that caused this THING to dog me, go to the safe in the library—you know the combination—and on the upper right-hand shelf you will find a document which will explain all.

GEOFFERY MELFORD.

Here the letter terminated. Melford felt bewildered. What did it all mean? The mention of the "Thing" suggested the apparition he had seen in the window through which his unknown assailant had fired—but the contrast between a nocturnal visitor from the Land Beyond and so material a matter as a pistol shot was almost ludicrous.

The glint of metal on the floor caught his eye, and, leaning over he picked up the cuff link lying broken and blood-stained within reach of Spencerton's fingertips. Slowly he turned it over. It was of polished silver, and set off in the center with a single jet-black opal which flashed and scintillated in the light from his electric torch. For a moment Melford stared like one stunned at the costly trinket in his hand. Well he knew to whom it belonged! Sir Eric Hirth[2]—here! The thing was impossible! Yet the evidence of the cuff link was incontrovertible; and, if Hirth were really at Heatherby House, there could be no question of why he had come. Sir Eric's threat of the previous day, when, accused of cheating in a game of whist at one of Lon-

1 Greene notes in the biography: "This is a paraphrase of the opening lines of one of Carr's favorite ghost stories, F. Marion Crawford's 'The Screaming Skull'...'No, I am not nervous or imaginative, and never believed in ghosts, unless that thing is one. But it hates me as it hated Luke Pratt'" (p. 25).

2 "Eric Hirth" would become a community pseudonym at *The Haverfordian*, writing poetry and prose not clearly Carr's. Hirth's initials were also listed among those of the authors of "The New Canterbury Tales." In the March 1928 *Apologia* column, the prankster editorial team even provided Hirth a fictional background as a resident of Long Island. In the same column, they contrived a mock controversy over January's authorship of "The Dark Banner" (not by but attributed to Carr), and "The God of the Gloves" (by him but attributed to George P. Rogers).

don's ultra fashionable card clubs, Spencerton had given the nobleman a terrible beating, came back now with full force.

"I'll get you," the enraged and humiliated Hirth had sworn; "I'll get you, and get you before I'm many hours older! Don't forget that!" But if it had been Sir Eric who had struck the fatal blow—and there was no positive evidence that he had—why had he taken the trouble to come—

Abruptly his musings came to an end. At the farther end of the loggia a rectangle of light suddenly outlined itself on the darkness as a door was flung violently open; and a wild, disheveled figure darted out into the night, vaulted the balustrade of the terrace, and sped off across the moonlit lawn. Perhaps sixty yards from the house Melford saw the unknown stumble, fling wide his arms in a gesture of despair, and pitch headlong to the ground, his obvious horror finding vent in one final fear-stricken cry: "Those eyes! My God! Those eyes!"

III

Kneeling beside the prostrate figure, Melford directed the beam of his flashlight[3] on the man's face. No, he had not been mistaken: it was Sir Eric Hirth. He had swooned from sheer fright, as Melford ascertained after a hasty examination. Bewildered, the new master of this house of terror passed a hand across his eyes. What, he asked himself again, did it all mean?

Rising, he gazed thoughtfully down at the recumbent figure. It would be merciful to let time rouse him; and, too, it was possible that if wakened he might be inclined to be ugly. Melford felt it imperative that he inform the authorities at once of the crime at Heatherby House. If a telephone were available, so much the better; he could reach the village lying three miles south of the estate, and, later, Scotland Yard.

Returning to the house, he entered the spacious, book-lined room from which Hirth had made so hasty an exit. A solitary candle on the mantel shelf cast weird, dancing shadows about the apartment, and Melford felt an unaccountable impulse to glance over his shoulder at each scurry of the rats behind the wainscoting or creak of the boards beneath his feet. To his relief a telephone of archaic pattern hung against the wall nearest the door, and after what seemed to him an interminable length of time a crisp voice over the wire informed him

---

3 Readers of Carr's novels, especially *The Plague Court Murders*, might have thought Carr's inconsistent use of the terms "electric torch" and "flashlight" began after he moved to England. This story shows that, curiously, Carr always used them interchangeably. He also sometimes preferred British spellings before ever visiting the UK.

that he was speaking with the local "constable." Melford briefly explained the situation, and with a promise to come at once to Heatherby House the officer rang off.

Melford glanced about him. An antiquated iron safe stood against one wall. Taking the candle from the mantel shelf, he crossed the room, knelt before the box-like affair, and deftly twirled the knob. A few quick turns and the heavy door swung open. On the upper right-hand shelf lay a folded paper, addressed in bold letters to himself. With a half apprehensive glance about him, Melford put the candle on the massive center table and threw himself into a chair facing the loggia door. Opening the manuscript, he began to read:

Why Philip Darworth hated me I cannot say. I am sure I did nothing to offend him; perhaps it was one of those unaccountable dislikes that all of us have felt. But few ever carried a mere personal dislike as far as did Darworth. He owned the neighboring estate, and never lost a chance to harass me—turning my tenants against me, casting slurs on my name, angering me in a thousand petty ways, until at last I could stand it no longer. I visited Darworth and bluntly demanded what he had against me. He replied with an insult, whereupon I knocked him down. His rage against me knew no bounds, and he swore that the next time we met he would kill me. I left his presence without a word.

About a week later I had sat up reading until well after two in the morning, the servants having retired, and was about to seek my bedchamber when there came a knock at the front door. It was Darworth, just drunk enough to be ugly. I let him in, and he swaggered into the library, a sneer on his handsome face and murder in his eye.

"Melford," he snarled, "my creditors are getting after me and tomorrow I leave the country. Understand? Tomorrow!"

"Well?" I queried, truculently. I knew he meant trouble.

"And before I go," he went on, his hand stealing toward his pocket, "I intended to settle up an old score. You remember what I said when we met last?"

"Perfectly," I returned.

"So," he continued, "as I've taken my wife's jewelry—the finest collection in the country—to pay my passage to America, I may as well be hanged for a wolf as a lamb. Therefore"—he whipped out a pistol —"therefore, I'm going to kill you!"

Without hesitation I lunged at him. We grappled. The pistol was, luckily, uncocked, and I twisted it from his hand. It fell to the floor, and Darworth followed it after a momentary exchange of blows. There he lay, furious and panting, while I took my hunting crop from the table and bent over him.

"Darworth," I said, coldly passionate. "Darworth, you miserable skunk, I ought to kill you without mercy. But I'll give you one chance for your life. I see your hand stealing toward that pistol; what's more, I'll give you the opportunity of using it. The moment you get a grip on that gun I'll strike. If you can bring it up in time to shoot me before this crop lands, well and good. But remember— the minute I see your fingers tightening about it, I swing! It's somewhat of a duel. Now!"

"Melford," he grated hoarsely, "if you get me, I'll make you endure a living death! Mark my words I'll never rest quiet in my grave until I've driven you to suicide!"

"Go on," I ordered shortly. "You'll have to face the issue; there'll be no dodging now!"

His hand was on the weapon; I saw his fingers close about it until the knuckles showed white beneath the skin. In that instant I struck. A faster man than he might have beaten me to it, but he had not even time to pull the trigger.

The next minute I looked down upon all that was mortal of Philip Darworth. My blow had crushed his skull.

Instead of frenzy, a sort of awful calmness seized me when I knew that I was a murderer—that my hands were stained with the blood of a fellowman. I dragged his body out of the house, and down to the high-road, and threw it into a clump of bushes about a hundred yards from my gates. He had thousands of pounds worth of jewelry on him, and this I took, to make the police think the murder the work of a highwayman and to divert suspicion from myself. The hunting crop I carefully cleansed; the stains of blood on the floor I washed out; the jewelry I hid.

Suspicion never once turned in my direction, but Darworth made good his threat. He is constantly at my elbow, his eyes burning into mine, his lips set in a malevolent smile. But he won't win; he shall not! And never, until I have passed into the Great Unknown, shall my crime become known.

For a moment after completing this astounding document Melford sat as though turned to stone. His grandfather—a murderer! The thing was incredible! Yet—it must be true. He shuddered. In this very room, had that strange duel been enacted. It— Of a sudden he leaped to his feet and spun quickly round. Yes, he had heard it plainly. A footfall outside—not the loggia door, but that behind his back, communicating with he knew not where; then a rattle as of a hand laid on the knob, and a creak as the door swung slowly open!

IV

On a sudden impulse Melford blew out the candle and crouched down beside the chair in which he had been sitting. The intruder had evidently not noticed the light: Melford saw a dim figure hastily cross the room and, drawing out an electric torch, direct its beam on the safe from which he himself had taken his grandfather's manuscript. He saw the newcomer start violently as his eyes fell on the open safe; saw him thrust a trembling hand within; and heard him breathe a fervent prayer of relief as his exploring fingers found that for which they sought. Almost lovingly he brought forth a small, dingy wooden box. Flinging back its lid, he let its contents cascade out into his palm. With bulging eyes Melford stared at the tangled heap of jewels which flashed and glowed like bits of living fire—diamonds, rubies, amethysts, opals, turquoises—stones of every size and description—lay in a blazing pile before him. And through Melford's mind rang one short sentence in his grandfather's statement: "The jewels I hid." This, then, was the collection of stones that Sir Geoffery Melford had taken from the dead body of Philip Darworth. Someone else knew his grandfather's secret!

Melford thought quickly. He must restore the jewels to their rightful owner—Darworth's widow, even at the price of Sir Geoffery's honor. It would entail a fight, but his recompense would be in discovering the identity of the mysterious intruder. His mind made up, he crept slowly toward the unknown man, who, oblivious to his surroundings, was still contemplating the stones. Then…

Melford could not stifle the horrified cry that rose involuntarily to his lips as his eyes fell upon that which lay within a foot of where the unknown knelt before the open safe. In outline resembling the figure of a man, the Thing crouched in a huddled heap on the floor, one hand lifted as though to ward off a blow. Its eyes blazed fiendishly, its pallid face was set in an expression of implacable hatred, and its body, though blurred and indistinct in contour, shone with an infernal light of its own. There was blood upon its forehead, and, as the Thing slowly raised itself on one elbow, Melford shrank back in terror at the ghastliness of the apparition. But if the effect on him was great, upon the intruder it was absolutely demoralizing. With the shriek of a lost soul he sprang to his feet, his hand spasmodically closing over the jewels, and leaped for the door. In that instant Melford acted. As the vague figure flitted past him he thrust out a foot and sent his man crashing to the floor. The other's flashlight had been broken by the fall, and the darkness was intense. Guided by the unknown's heavy breathing he closed with him as the former sprang to his feet. For a moment they reeled about the room—Melford striving to get in a blow that would render his adversary unconscious, the other battling frenziedly to free himself from his assailant's grip. The man's strength was almost maniacal; with a last convulsive jerk he wrenched one arm loose and drove straight for Melford's jaw. The blow landed with a sickening thud: Melford felt his senses reel, but despite his grogginess he clung grimly to his opponent. Again the man's arm flashed forward. This time Melford sensed its approach, and when his antagonist, almost carried off his feet by the impetus of his swing, momentarily relaxed his hold, he dodged under the other's arms and planted a jolt beneath his ear that sent him spinning half across the room to crash into a low chair and pitch backwards to the floor. In the same moment he heard a tramp of footsteps in the loggia and a blinding shaft of light cut through the gloom and came to rest upon him.

"Mr. Melford?" One of the trio standing in the doorway advanced into the cone of light and gazed inquiringly at the bewildered Medford. "Why—man, what's the matter? You look ill!"

"I—I think I am," responded Melford, sinking wearily into a convenient chair. "You're the constable, Mr.—?"

"Brant," supplemented the other: "I am. This is the coroner, Doctor Ennisthory. Your friend, here"—indicating the third figure in the doorway—"we found on the lawn. He was in need of medical attention; scared half to death," Ennisthory said. "He's better now, but—"

"There's another," interposed Melford, "who, I think, needs your attention also. That's it, Doctor; light up"—as the medical man applied a match to the candle on the table.

As the wick flared up Ennisthory bent over the still figure lying in a crumpled heap near the door. With an amazed exclamation he raised his head.

"Hawley," he announced succinctly. "Old Sir Geoffery's butler! And where did he get those jewels?"

"Stole them," was Melford's brief reply. Rising, he crossed to the lifeless form and gazed frowningly down upon it. Then, laying a hand on the doctor's arm, he indicated the fingers that still retained the jewels. "Look —how clean his hands are! Almost shining! And"—bending over—"do you see that red smudge on the edge of his sleeve? Suppose Spencerton found him with the jewels—denounced him as a thief. Then this Hawley, to prevent exposure, stabbed him with the first weapon that came handy. Logical, isn't it?"

"And dragged his body into the loggia?" suggested Ennisthory. "Perhaps—perhaps. I've often seen that dagger you described to Brant—Sir Geoffery used it as a letter opener."

"I suppose, in the light of this new theory, you'll let me go?" Sir Eric Hirth, still somewhat shaken but defiant and disdainful as of old, stepped forward from the doorway.

"I—I—" Brant gulped and stood at a loss. "I don't know what to do," he confessed at length. "The evidence looks black against you, sir, but when we find a man with a handful of stolen jewels whose hands are newly washed and whose sleeve bears a bloodstain—well, as I say, I don't know what to do."

"I think," began Ennisthory, "it would be better to arrest Hawley—"

"Why not the real murderer?" At the words, spoken in a ringing, electrifying tone from the doorway into the interior of the house, a sudden start ran around the group. Turning with one accord, they beheld a tall, gaunt figure, bearing over its arm a white, flimsy something which gleamed dully in the wan candlelight, and holding in its hand a light mask of paper mache. With a knowing leer the man advanced into the room.

"I'm tired of playing ghost," he resumed, "and, because I wasn't handed a square deal, I'm going to snitch. I know who killed Spencerton. I saw them out there in the loggia. But before I tell, I want you to listen to my own story.

"I'm an American; hired by two people working in cahoots to play ghost and scare old Melford away from the house so they could find a collection of jewels hidden somewhere about the place. One of those was the butler—the other the murderer of Basil Spencerton. They found the jewels, but I wasn't successful, and when a new master came to the house they decided it was time to act. Well, one of those men double-crossed the other and came here tonight to get the sparklers for himself. That one was the murderer. The other, true to the bargain effected between them, discharged the servants for the night and waited for his confederate to come so that they could split the treasure and beat it to America. The murderer came here about an hour before you"—indicating Melford—"and Spencerton, arriving on the scene, caught him picking the lock of the loggia door. The man had just got the door open, and as he slipped inside his hand fell on a sharp letter opener lying on a table beside the entrance. As Spencerton ran forward he sprang at him and drove the knife home. Then, half crazed by his crime, he fled.

"Perhaps half an hour later that fellow Hirth arrived. He had followed Spencerton with the intention of killing him, and after wandering about the house in search of his victim he stumbled over the body in the loggia and gave vent to an awful cry. Ghost as I was, it nearly froze the blood in my veins. I had just finished appearing to Melford—and shooting at him through the window to add zest to the thing. Then Hirth ran into the house, and I proceeded to scare him out of his wits with my flashlight eyes. A little later the butler, who had hidden himself in another part of the house, concluded that his partner had got cold feet at the last minute and came down to get the jewels. I 'appeared' to him to tell him what had happened, but his nerves had been so upset by what he had heard that he up and ran. I don't know about his washing his hands, but whatever that stain on his sleeve is, it's not blood."

"But the murderer?" prompted Ennisthory hoarsely. "Who is he?"

A grim smile overspread the man's face. The tension was so great that it threatened any moment to snap. Melford leaned breathlessly forward; Hirth gazed thoughtfully at the man; Hawley, who had in the meantime struggled upright, glared defiantly about; Ennisthory nervously drummed the table-top; Brant suggestively fingered his handcuffs.

"As I say," went on the pseudo-ghost, "I know who killed him." Suddenly he leaped forward, and, seizing one of the group by the shoulders, swung him about before the others. "Gentlemen, the murderer of Basil Spencerton!"

Before them stood revealed the man who had colluded with Hawley to get possession of the jewels, who had double-crossed his confederate, and who had struck down the lawyer—Constable Brant himself!

Notes for the Curious: "The House of Terror"

"The House of Terror" is of plain interest because it presages the writer Carr would become. It is a mystery (albeit not a fair-play detective story) draped in macabre trappings. The story is an early step along the path that Carr would travel through the several Bencolin novels, to *Hag's Nook*, *The Plague Court Murders*, *The Three Coffins*, and to other frights beyond.

Poe is of course a key inspiration behind "The House of Terror"; its imagistic language is openly imitative of his. Notably, Carr remembers the "vacant eye-like windows" upon the House of Usher's bleak face with Heatherby House's own "vacant, unshuttered windows" that "stared blankly down." Carr would rely upon this windows-as-eyes metaphor more than once in the amateur fiction, not remaking the image of the haunted manse fully into his own until *Castle Skull*, in which architecture, not imagination, anthropomorphizes the structure:

> Then Castle Skull grew in size, though it seemed even farther above our heads. Massive walls, battlemented and fully a hundred feet high, were built into the hillside… In the centre of the walls, built so that the middle of the battlements constituted the teeth of the death's head, reared the vast skull of stone. The light was too dim to make out details, but I saw the eyes. I saw the two towers on either side, horribly like ears...
> (p. 24)

The frightening descriptive prose in "The House of Terror," which would later become a professional strength is, by comparison with Carr's professional prose, underdeveloped. This early story is replete with stock imitative phrasing that might have appeared in numerous stories by numerous amateur authors. There is the obligatory gloom of the atmosphere; nearly half a dozen cries, one of which, a "low cry" echoes the "low, moaning cry" at the climax of "The Fall of the House of Usher," and more than one passage filled with unoriginal phrasing, e.g.:

> Evil, malignant eyes they were, glowing like red-hot coals and seeming to Melford to sear his very flesh. For a moment they remained fixed upon him—burning, blood-red, awful in their unwavering intensity; then figure and eyes slowly resolved themselves into darkness.
> For a long moment Melford stood stock-still, his

> breath coming in short, labored gasps, his every
> muscle paralyzed. Then, arousing himself to action,
> he leaped up the steps, darted along the terrace, and,
> pausing before the window in which had appeared
> the apparition, peered into the Stygian gloom within.

Again, in both his vocabulary and the descriptive density of
the prose, Carr is openly imitating Poe; in observing this, we need
not too strongly criticize the young author. Perhaps the opposite is
true: how swiftly Carr passed out of this phase is a testament to his
early potential. What Carr had yet to realize in writing this story is
that conveying what characters *fear* and *imagine* is often more terrifying than explicitly describing what they *see*. So Melford, arriving at
Heatherby House for the first time, encounters grim and frightening
sights without his (or the reader's) being much frightened by them.

In contrast to the leaden unoriginality of the prose in "The
House of Terror," the professional Carr could create frightening imagery more economically, and in fresh language. Consider *The Plague
Court Murders*, which conjures atmospheric chills to better effect. The
house at Plague Court, for instance, having an ancient, dark history,
is frightening in the suggestive impression it conveys, not because of
any clichéd physical spookiness:

> The house—or what I could see of it—was made of
> heavy, whitish blocks of stone, now blackened with
> the weather. It had almost a senile appearance, as of
> a brain gone, but its heavy cornices were carven with
> horrible gayety in Cupids and roses and grapes: a
> wreath on the head of an idiot. Some of its windows
> were shuttered, some patched with boards. (p. 20)

The paradox of Plague Court's architecture, its "horrible gayety,"
only reinforces the intangible dread the mansion provokes. Carr has
since learned that he can well afford to let Plague Court's windows
simply be windows: their being shuttered or boarded, as with the edifice's weather-blackened white stonework, is more disquieting than
if the house's face resembled a human one. Carr tries less and ac-
complishes more.

Carr introduces us to the Darworth family in this story; we will
encounter them again for more than a decade. There is a familial lack
of ethics: the Darworths are a bad lot who, each generation, seem to
come to deservedly bad endings—sometimes twice. As we have seen
here, Philip, whose inexplicable malice persists—perhaps supernaturally—after his death, meets his ugly end while trying to murder his

neighbor. Roger Darworth, of unknown relation (based upon mention of an inheritance, perhaps Philip's grandson), first appears in the *Haverfordian* Bencolin case, "The Ends of Justice." The opening lines there reveal that Darworth, in addition to being a spiritualist of questionable reputation (Sir John Landervorne calls him a "stagy fake"), is that story's miracle-crime murder victim. "The Ends of Justice" also offers us a second hereditary echo: the unwelcoming object of Darworth's attentions is one Cynthia Melford. What her relation is, exactly, to Geoffery and Calvin is unclear, but it is not coincidence. One can hardly blame Cynthia for her inherited aversion to the Darworths, either: Roger's perverse form of wooing includes sending Cynthia "a dried arm from a dissecting room in a flower box."

Roger Darworth makes the leap from Carr's amateur fiction into his professional works by being resurrected for H.M.'s first outing, *The Plague Court Murders*. There, too, he is a grifting spiritualist, but once again, Roger does not survive very long: his locked-room death is the crime that changes the case from a Detective Inspector Masters investigation—Masters is a noted debunker of bogus mediums—to a murder puzzle only H.M. can piece together.

As the young Carr searches for his ideal style, "The House of Terror" and each early mystery story experiments individually with how its solution is discovered and explained. In this story, there are no advance clues, whether to explain the Thing haunting Heatherby House or to uncover the identities of the criminals. Grasping after the same surprise-ending effect he enjoyed in O. Henry's fiction, and after a climactic close like the thrilling ones in Poe's tales, Carr elects to resolve this mystery with a sort of thunderclap, a closing exclamation: it is a "reveal," not a detective-story solution. The unnamed American knew of the criminal conspiracy and witnessed the murder, all of which he simply discloses. Nobody else detects these, especially the reader. Similarly, whether or not Philip Darworth's spirit actually came back to haunt Geoffery Melford, or whether only Melford's conscience did, is left ambiguous, unexplained.

As a professional, Carr would never leave such an important plot element unexplained—and of course, part of his gift is depicting a situation that seems susceptible *only* to a supernatural explanation and putting it back into the realm of ordinary human evil. Still, Carr was only fifteen years old when he wrote "The House of Terror," and it was only his second story ever. So the reader can afford to be forgiving!

In consideration of the mature Carr's professional practices, the explanation in "The House of Terror" is noteworthy, because it violates Carr's self-imposed rules of engagement between author and reader. In "The Grandest Game in the World," Carr's first rule (p. 21) is: "The criminal shall never turn out to be the detective, or any servant, or any character whose thoughts we have been allowed to share." How good or original, after all, can any murder mystery be if "the butler did it"? Carr also arguably violates his third rule: "The crime shall be the work of one person"—but Carr admits of that rule, "the murderer in some instances may be allowed to have a confederate." Whether or not the reader believes Carr violated both rules, all of us, including young John Dickson Carr, easily sense how underwhelming the ending to "The House of Terror" is. Carr clearly recognized this quickly: he would never return to the use of a simple, unprepared reveal.

The Will-o'-the-Wisp (1922)

It was an ugly night—raw and blustery, with a fine, drizzling rain that beat an eerie tattoo on the windowpanes. At my desk in the outer office I sat immersed in the fatiguing business of evidence-sorting. The battered clock above my head cheerily ticked off the minutes as its hands crept slowly round the dial to one. Only when it proclaimed the hour with a faltering, throaty stroke that seemed to drag itself out interminably before it died away did I thrust aside the mass of papers before me and push back my chair. Wearily stretching my cramped legs, I yawned luxuriously. Then, rising, I crossed the room to the window and peered out into the night. A mist had settled down on the thoroughfare outside, blurring the uncertain light of the streetlamps and making mere specters of the neighboring houses. Through the fog I could dimly discern the bold outlines of the adjacent courthouse, and, standing grim and stark in the narrow yard surrounding the edifice, the wooden statue of a famous French dignitary who had visited the town in the first quarter of the last century—the Marquis de Lafayette.[1]

Wearily I dropped into a chair beside the window. Elbows resting on the sill, I supported my chin in my cupped hands and stared out into the welcome darkness. The low rustle of the wind in the chimney fell on my ears like a lullaby. Outside the blended roar of the elements resembled the deep-throated rumble of a pipe organ. Lulled into a sort of dreamy repose by the indescribable music of the storm, I fell to musing. Again the statue of Lafayette caught my eyes. The immobile figure in the courthouse yard took on a new significance. That statue had been fashioned after a pulsing, virile man; that inanimate form was the counterpart of a person whose hand had helped shape the destiny of America.

Could it but speak the speech of the man it represented, what secrets might it tell? What might it say of Lafayette, the Man? What—

---

1 The statue here of the French aristocrat who fought for the colonies in the Revolutionary War, even commanding American troops, is modeled directly on the statue in Uniontown, which Douglas Greene documents in the biography: "Uniontown was also proud of its past. In the narrow yard outside the courthouse was a gilt-covered statue of the Marquis de Lafayette, erected to honor that statesman's visit to Uniontown in 1825. As a boy, John Carr looked at the statue and thought of romance—of swordsmen, and honor, and dedication to a cause." (p. 2)

with an effort I roused myself. I suddenly realized that I was falling off to sleep. Putting down the alluring temptation to yield to the drowsiness that possessed me, I struggled resolutely to my feet.

The sensation I experienced as I turned away from the window I shall simply pass over. I believe it beyond mortal ability to describe my feelings at that moment. Sufficient to say that for an instant I would have felt no sense of pain had I been prodded with a red-hot poker. When the mist had ceased to swim before my eyes, I became aware that my temples were pounding like trip hammers in my head, that my heart seemed to jump at every beat, and that I was trembling violently from head to foot.

For gone was my dingy, commonplace law office. In its place I saw a long, low-roofed room whose oak-paneled walls glistened dully in the blaze of a hundred candles. The magnificent chandelier, its clinking glass prisms flashing like so many diamonds suspended in the candlelight, was dazzling to the eye. Full-length mirrors shone in the yellow glory of the tapers. Heavy portieres of crimson velvet shrouded the windows. The polished floor, newly waxed for dancing, almost reflected the glittering assembly that thronged the spacious room. A colorful gathering, this; although one that seemed like some shadow of the dim, forgotten past that ere long would dissolve in the darkness from which it had emerged. The gayly attired men and women appeared like figments of a bizarre dream—fantastic shadow people that would be whisked away with the morning. Yet that I dreamed or that I was the victim of a hallucination I refused to believe.

Almost frenziedly I glanced about me. What was I to do? Instinctively I felt that I was out of place in that richly clad throng. Yet, although no one appeared to have noticed me, I thought myself the cynosure of all eyes—especially after a swift glance at my clothes convinced me that if some awful power had in reality swept me backward into the dusty past it had not altered the ordinary business suit I wore. To make my way from the room in an attire so markedly different from that of anyone present would be the worst possible move under the circumstances. And, even if I did succeed in escaping observation, where would I go? If I were not the victim of a hallucination, then this was my native town perhaps a hundred years before I was born. That being the case, I had no home. A panic was gaining possession of me; I felt an almost irresistible impulse to rush from the room, shouting at the top of my voice as a vent for the conflicting emotions that surged within me. As I stood irresolute in an agony of doubt a hand was laid on my shoulder. Swiftly I swung about.

Confronting me stood a slim, petite slip of a girl with a wealth of bronze-colored hair and long, brilliant eyes of a beryl hue. Somehow, those haunting eyes destroyed the ingenuous appearance she would have possessed without them. They added an almost sinister aspect to her Lorelei[2]-like face. I put her down at once as a girl dangerous in the nth degree. She was the sort of beauty who is not content with being merely coquettish, but must stir up trouble among her suitors, ostensibly to test their love for her, but really in a spirit of malicious delight at being quarreled over. Just now her lips were parted in a dazzling smile which but for those uncanny eyes might have made her face seem one of the most ingenuous imaginable and her tone was the essence of naivete as she said:

"What's the matter tonight, Rupert? Rather pensive, aren't you?"

I wet my lips with the tip of my tongue. What was I to say? Evidently I had been mistaken for someone named "Rupert" and, for the present, it might be best to keep up the deception. I took the plunge.

"You think so?" I parried warily. "What is there for me to be pensive about?"

I had made a bad blunder, I saw in an instant. She arched her eyebrows in surprise.

"Evidently," was her reply, "you don't consider the visit of the Marquis de Lafayette of any moment. From your conduct this evening I would have inferred otherwise."

The Marquis de Lafayette! Well, I had learned something. I found my panic fast diminishing as I set my brains to work on a question I might ask her which, while eliciting some useful information, would not betray me. At length:

"Did you expect me here tonight?" I queried, studying her intently from beneath the lowered eyelids.

"Of course." She looked up in surprise. "Your father, I know, is too weak to stir out of the house, but then only the last time I was over to Brixley Rouse he said, 'Marcia. I'm fully aware you jilted[3] my son when Juan Alvez began paying court to you and I know it's still a sore spot with him. But I'll make him come over to your place the night Lafayette's in town if I have to order Sam to drive him over with a horsewhip! I have no doubt he doesn't want to go, but then I'm hanged if I shall let people say a Brixley didn't meet the Marquis when he visited here!' That's just the way he said it, Rupert; it was too funny for anything! I told him you wouldn't refuse to come over just because

2 In German mythology, a siren of great beauty living upon a Rhine rock; as in The Odyssey, she seduces mariners to their destruction when they navigate toward her irresistible song and their ships are wrecked.

3 A subtle word choice by Carr, since the verb derives from the pejorative noun having the original meaning of a harlot or unchaste woman, or any woman who offers false sexual encouragement (and then dashes that hope).

our little—affair—er—" Brazen as she was to have gone even this far, she found it impossible to go on and dropping her eyes, plucked nervously at the plume of her fan.

"Of course I wouldn't, Marcia," I hastened to assure her, inwardly elated at the information I had secured. It was clear to me now that the real Rupert Brixley had not, after all, come to the reception, which, I gathered, was being given in honor of the Marquis by the girl's father. I began to thoroughly enjoy the situation into which I had been thrust. My earlier terror was completely gone. I felt that I could play my part to the finish. The wine of the only adventure I had ever experienced in the course of my drab, prosaic life mounted swiftly to my brain; I felt gay, confident, reckless.

"Where is the Marquis?" I queried, glancing about the room. "Has he come yet?"

"What?" There was genuine surprise in her tone. "Do you mean to say you haven't met him?" And before I could reply she had seized my arm and was piloting me across the crowded floor toward a sequestered group near the door, volubly reproving me for forgetting to meet Lafayette when he had been presented to the company "not ten minutes ago." Something like my old panic returned when my thoughts suddenly reverted to the clothes I wore, but I rightly surmised that in the prevalent excitement at the presence of so distinguished a guest my attire would go unnoticed. Fortunately, I traversed the floor unembarrassed by any comment. Into the center of the group near the door Marcia pushed her way.

"Father," she said rapidly to a sleek, rotund, little man with a bustling air of authority suddenly thrust upon him, who was in a high state of flustration at his own importance and whose rubicund face looked not unlike a cherry-cheeked apple set on top of a towering front of collar. "You haven't introduced Rupert Brixley to the Marquis! I'm surprised at you! Do so this instant!"

"Oh—er—yes." The little man nodded sagely. "Yes, certainly." He assumed his most dignified air, and, taking me paternally by the shoulder, hauled me up before the central figure of the group as a bailiff drags a recalcitrant prisoner into the courtroom.

As the great Lafayette touched my hand and murmured something stereotyped, I unobtrusively took in every detail of his appearance. An impressive figure he was, tall, lean, clean-limbed; with a sort of little hardness in his carriage that gave one the impression of tremendous physical strength held in check. His square-cut, smooth-shaven countenance; jutting, aquiline nose high set between cold gray eyes; firm thin-lipped mouth about which were cut deep furrows; and high forehead surmounted by a wave of silken brown hair, slightly grayed at the temples; all told of a man cynical, firm, authoritative, ruthless in the bent of purpose. He seemed to forget me the instant our perfunctory introduction had been concluded, turning to chat with a gaunt, sharp-featured woman in funeral black who stood solicitously at his elbow. I swung back to where Marcia had stood, to find her prattling vivaciously to a short, burly young man with the face of a bulldog and the biceps of a prize fighter, who appeared completely under the sway of her magnetic smile. She seemed to be exerting her potent wiles to the utmost on him—a fact I found difficult to account for. I stood watching her for a moment in silence, my earlier impression of her character confirmed. I was engaged in a debate with myself regarding the best course of action under the circumstances, when a hand descended on my shoulder and fingers of steel tightened about it in a grip that made me wince. Whirling about, I found myself looking into the swarthy yet fine, delicately molded face of a young man scarcely out of his teens, whose glossy, almost unctuous, black hair and eyes of a like color betrayed his Spanish descent. His voice was not quite steady— "Come over here, Brixley," he requested in an almost inaudible voice.

As I followed him without demur to a plush sofa in a secluded corner of the room I could not help noticing the marked strain under which he was laboring. His dark eyes glowed balefully through narrowed lids; the muscles about his jaw stood out like whipcords; yet he strove to appear nonchalant and unconcerned. It was only when I dropped down beside him that the full torrent of his passion burst forth like a pent-up flood when the dam is broken.

"Brixley," he ground out in a voice which, while low-pitched, was so pregnant with a deep-seated, vital hatred that I involuntarily shrank from him, "this is bad business—d—d bad business!"

"What?" I demanded, on my guard instantly.

"Marcia's attentions to this fellow Lafayette and his idiot secretary," he jerked, his eyes singling out Marcia as she chatted with the stocky young man I had noticed before. "I can't stand it; and, by God, I won't stand it!"

"Why," I ventured cautiously speaking conservatively lest I betray myself, "I didn't know she was paying any particular attention to either. There's no harm in her talking with the little fellow; and as for the Marquis, I haven't seen her even speak to him."

"Then you're blind!" he flung savagely. "How long have you been here?"

"Not long," I answered warily. "Why?"

"Well," was his vibrant rejoinder, "she's got that man Lafayette so infatuated—" He paused, his wrath choking him, and glared vindictively at the object of his anger, who was placidly talking with the woman in black.

I studied the infuriated young man intently. If I were not mistaken, this was the Juan Alvez, for whom Marcia had thrown the real Rupert Brixley over. The Spanish blood in him boiled in his veins like molten lava at the thought that in the space of a few short minutes the volatile Marcia had cut him dead in favor of the Frenchman. Yet it was incredulous that a cold, hard-headed man of the world such as the latter should take the coquetries of the girl seriously. It was a tribute to her wiles if Alvez were not so blinded by his own passion that in every glance he saw a hidden meaning, in every word a veiled endearment. I more than suspected that the latter possibility was the true one. However, even the love-mad Alvez could scarcely have been worked up to such a pitch of fury without a better reason than an idle flirtation on Marcia's part. There must be another and a deeper reason.

"But surely you must know Marcia well enough to suspect she'd be more or less inclined to flirt with every man she met," I reproved hoping to draw him out. "There's no use getting yourself worked up like this. It'll do you no good, and if you keep on you're likely to create a scene. Quiet down. You're exaggerating matters to yourself."

"You think so?" A baleful smile curled his lips. "You didn't—you didn't see him kiss her right here before everyone, did you?"

I leaped up. In a flash I saw through it all. A French mannerism on the part of the Marquis had been misconstrued by the lovesick Alvez.

No doubt the girl had rendered some service to her country during the American Revolution, and the Frenchman, on his visit to her home, had taken the liberty of appropriately thanking her for it.

"Alvez," I said earnestly, "you've come near making an egregious ass of yourself. It's a French custom to salute one deserving of an honor with a kiss. Don't you understand, man? He didn't mean anything of a personal nature by it. Do you supposed a man like Lafayette would be affected by the attentions of a provincial belle?"

It was not the most polite speech under the circumstances, but certainly it was the most logical. I settled back, confident that even Alvez would understand.

"You're a great little peacemaker, Brixley," he said in an ominously quiet voice which, in contrast to his earlier tone, sounded like the hush that broods in the air after the thunder has heralded the storm, "but you can't smooth matters over so easily. Not by a long shot!" He sprang up. "I'll call the hypocrite out!"

He was trembling like an aspen leaf, and his jet-black eyes burned feverishly in his sheet-white face. Unsteadily he lurched toward the group near the door. I leaped after him and seized him by the arm in a grip that made him wince.

"Alvez, for heaven's sake, don't!" I entreated, striving vainly to force him back into the seat. "You're making a mountain out of a molehill! Do you want to break up the reception by calling out a man who's done nothing to offend you? Think, man!"

For a long moment he stood immobile.

"As you will," he complied in a low voice. "I'll wait until after the ball. Just now, however—" his teeth came together with a snap and his words shot out like the hiss of escaping steam, "I'm going to get drunk!"

Swinging round on his heel, he vanished in the crowd. Slowly I retraced my steps to the spot where Lafayette, the officious little man, and the woman of unprepossessing appearance were engaged in what seemed a politely heated debate. Unostentatiously I took up a position by the former's side.

"I tell you, sir," the rotund gentleman was saying, "Things have come to a pretty pass hereabouts when a lone bandit can snap his fingers at the whole community!" He paused for breath, his facing growing redder with each word, gulped, and resumed: "Why, sir, the audacious fellow does things Turpin[4] would never even dream of attempting! He's clever—I'll give him credit for that—and elusive as a streak of light. That's why they call him the Will-o'-the-Wisp. Why, confound him, no stage line in the state will be responsible for valuables carried by its passengers, he's that feared! I'm told he's operating in this district now. God help the town if he ever hits it! Why, this very night I hired a couple of stalwarts to watch the house and shoot at sight anyone who tries to enter nefariously. I thought because of your visit, and the reception, and all that he might think it a propitious time for a raid. Well, sir, if he does come,"—the little man grew so vehement that his tight-fitting collar gave out an ominous ripping sound— "he'll meet with a warm reception!"

Lafayette smiled a pitying smile.

"My dear Mr. Gallivan," he said in his flawless English, "your country is indeed in a deplorable state if such a daring criminal cannot be apprehended. Now, in my native land your Will-o'-the-Wisp would

---

4 Dick Turpin, the legendary English highwayman of the eighteenth century, whose life and adventures were heavily romanticized, in ballads, theater, and fiction after his execution and into the nineteenth century. Carr discussed Turpin in his essay "Stand and Deliver," which was the first in a series Carr intended for a book of histories about motley lawbreakers. Douglas Greene printed Carr's essay in *The Door to Doom and Other Detections.*

be under lock and key within a week. Really, I cannot conceive of such a slackness of the law anywhere else than in these United States."[5]

The gaunt woman frowned darkly and Gallivan's rosy face turned scarlet.

"Perhaps, sir," flashed the latter, "your country has never been plagued with a criminal genius like the Wisp."

"Now if he should by any chance come here tonight,"—the Marquis's air was patronizing— "I might do you the favor of showing you how a Frenchman deals with men of his ilk."

"And what would you do, sir?" was Gallivan's laconic query. Lafayette pursed up his lips.

"Well, my dear sir," he began, "I should in all probability—"

"Go on, Monsieur the Marquis," rang out a voice from the doorway behind him; "what would you do?"

I glanced up. As one still some distance from Niagara Falls hears the faraway thunder of the cataract, so I heard the concerted gasp that went up from the assembly. For in the doorway legs wide apart and slim body in a slouching, listless attitude, stood a man whom I recognized without the aid of Gallivan's hoarse cry:

"My God! The Will-o'-the-Wisp!"

The intruder wore a broad-brimmed hat pulled well down over his eyes, and a mask concealed the lower part of his face. A dark cloak was draped about his shoulders; he wore heavy riding boots against whose sable background I caught the evil glitter of a sword scabbard; and a neatly gloved hand holding a pistol protruded from the folds of the cloak.

"Please proceed, my dear sir," softly enjoined the masked stranger. "I believe you were telling your excellent host and hostess, the good Mr. and Mrs. Gallivan, how you would capture the Will-o'-the-Wisp?"

I glanced toward Lafayette. His whole body has stiffened suddenly, and the crouching attitude into which he had dropped reminded me of the pose of a panther about to spring.

"Is that a challenge?" he questioned quietly.

"You may regard it as such. I am here. In what way do you propose to capture me?"

"I know of none now," returned the Marquis equally. "You have me covered. I can do nothing. From the way Gallivan talked I would have imagined the Will-o'-the-Wisp an above-board fighter. Now I

---

5 At the time of this visit to Uniontown (1825), Lafayette, at the invitation of President Monroe, was on a grand tour of the United States honoring the nation's 50th anniversary. Lafayette was 67. Carr has taken some liberties with both Lafayette's vigor and his attitude toward the United States, which he still loved well in 1825.

find that he is one who must take an adversary from behind."

"Yes?" the unknown's voice was cold and hard as steel. "What would you consider a fair position, then?"

"You are wearing a sword. Give me one, and I'll guarantee that within two minutes I'll spit you like a rat!"

"That is an unfair proposal. If I win, I would yet have to make my getaway. If, on the other hand, you win, I am lost."

"I pledge my word as a gentleman," threw back the Frenchman with a quiet earnestness that could not be mistaken, "that if you are victorious and I am not seriously hurt, I shall aid you to escape. Do you agree?"

The Will-o'-the-Wisp bowed.

"It shall be as you wish," he responded quietly.

The buzz of comment in the room rose to a confused babel of voices as Lafayette swiftly removed his coat and dispatched Levasseur, his secretary, with a few hurried words of instruction; while the stranger flung off his cloak, tossed aside his pistol, drew from its scabbard a long, slender, flexible dueling sword, and stood calmly awaiting his challenger's pleasure. In a trice the stocky young man had returned with a naked rapier of a pattern similar to that of the Wisp. Then, as the two antagonists advanced to the center of the room, a profound hush fell over the gathering. As the combatants tested their weapons with the rapid movements of practiced duelists, one could hear the tingling swish of the swords through the air. A short nod from each indicated the readiness of the other, and at a tense "On guard!" from the Frenchman the blades crossed with a slithering hiss that sent an electrified start through the audience. I became conscious that Juan Alvez had elbowed his way to my side, and felt his whiskey-laden breath fan my cheek, but my entire attention was riveted on the fighters. Their slim blades wove in and out like shuttles of light as they maneuvered for an opening. No sound disturbed the deathlike stillness save the metallic clash of sword on sword. On the face of the challenger was a supercilious look that seemed to say, "You can't beat me; I am undefeatable," yet to my unpracticed eye it seemed that the Wisp was far outplaying him.

At length the inevitable break came and with stunning suddenness. Lafayette had been forced to retreat by his adversary's lightning-like attack, until he was now within a foot of the outer ring of spectators. Now his blade described a movement that no eye, least of all mine, could follow. Through the other's hitherto impregnable defense it wormed its way; a prolonged slithering sound cut in on the silence, and the unknown's rapier described a flashing arc in the air, to spin across the room and clatter along the floor. Disarmed, the

Wisp stood like a tiger at bay. Slowly, remorselessly the Frenchman advanced, his merciless blade poised for a thrust that would terminate his opponent's career.

Suddenly, and with the sensation of one unexpectedly doused with cold water, I became aware that Alvez, at my elbow, was coolly levelling a pistol at the oncoming Lafayette. Without an instant's hesitation I leaped forward and turned the gun from its course with a sweep of my arm—just as it vomited forth its winged messenger of death. The report still rang in my ears and the acrid smoke still stung my eyes when a mighty shout went up from the spectators. For on the floor, motionless, was stretched a silent figure—but it was not that of the Marquis. The diverted bullet had struck down the Will-o'-the-Wisp!

Alvez was still staring into space, the smoking pistol clutched in his icy fingers when I reached the side of the recumbent form. Lafayette and Gallivan were there before me, and the latter, kneeling beside all that was mortal of the bandit, gently drew down the mask. The next instant I saw his face blanch white as new fallen snow; his eyes seemed starting from his head; and he reeled backward into my arms with a cry that would have pierced a heart of stone.

"Great God in heaven!" he shrieked. "It's Marcia!"

For a long moment the silence was so profound I could distinctly hear the cheery ticking of my watch. Then Juan Alvez tore his way through the fringe of awed onlookers and flung himself upon me.

"Brixley!" he cried, "Brixley, you've killed her! Why didn't you let me shoot him? Not twenty minutes ago Marcia disguised as the Will-o'-the-Wisp told me she intended to teach this conceited fellow a lesson. Somehow she won me over and made me promise to aid her. But when I agreed to stand guard with a pistol in case anything unexpected happened, I didn't think of—this!" Wild-eyed, he whirled on Lafayette, and before the astonished Marquis could make a move to stop him he had seized the Frenchman's rapier and with a mad gesture of farewell had plunged its needle-like point into his own breast. Then with a mocking laugh he pitched headlong to the floor. From somewhere within the spellbound group a woman's shrill scream cut in hideously on the silence as the young man's body twisting over beside the still, cold form of the girl, rolled sightless eyes upwards. Louder—louder grew the scream, beating painfully on my eardrums as I gazed uncomprehendingly down on the two silent figures. A mist swam before my eyes. I reeled backward, that haunting cry still ringing in my ears. The brilliantly illuminated ballroom seemed fading—fading—

Bewilderedly I raised my head. The rain ceased. Dawn crept in at the windows, putting to shame the sickly glow of the electric lights. Shaking off the clinging fumes of sleep, I glanced about me. Again I saw my dingy, commonplace law office. Turning back to the window, my eyes fell on the statue in the courthouse yard. And, as I gazed on it through the mists of early morning, I suddenly became aware that a heavy coal-truck was lumbering off down the thoroughfare below my window, its siren giving vent to another such shriek as had re-called me from my wanderings in the shadowland of the past.

Notes for the Curious: "The Will-o'-the-Wisp"

The reader is warned: While this commentary contains no actual spoilers, it mentions some important details from Carr's 1950s novels, *The Devil in Velvet, Fear Is the Same,* and *Fire, Burn!.* If you have not read one or more of these titles, you may wish to read them before reading the following remarks.

"The Will-o'-the-Wisp" is Carr's third short story, written directly following "The House of Terror." Carr's evident progress is striking; in a number of ways, it is a much better story than its predecessor.

In simple matters of mechanics, note that the young author's language, including his use of tropes, is stronger. Consider, for instance, Carr's exchanging the various stock images regarding faces and eyes in "The House of Terror" for Marcia Gallivan's Lorelei-like features in this story. Carr's description of Marcia is neither casual nor gratuitous. It is symbolic foreshadowing: like a mythical siren, Marcia will lure a man willingly to his death. This more thoughtful use of personal imagery is a great improvement over Carr's borrowing Poe's "blood-red" eyes, purely for effect, in the earlier tale.

Carr uses an equally apropos simile when Mr. Gallivan introduces the unnamed narrator, in the guise of Rupert Brixley, to Lafayette: "taking me paternally by the shoulder, [he] hauled me up before the central figure of the group as a bailiff drags a recalcitrant prisoner into the courtroom." The narrator, an attorney, calls to mind a comparison natural to his profession. Compare this with the less organic cliché Carr puts into the mind of Melford, the perspective character in "The House of Terror":

> The attorney had given him to understand that his grandfather's entire staff of retainers had consented to remain at Heatherby House in the service of its new master. Yet even they appeared to have deserted the place, as rats desert a sinking ship. For some reason the simile impressed him.

Of course, Carr has not in "The Will-o'-the-Wisp" entirely shed his reliance on formula—in one instance, the narrator expostulates with Alvez, "You're making a mountain out of a molehill"—but the strength of the writing in this effort is perceptibly greater, demonstrating to us, not for the last time, the remarkable rapidity with which the teenage author was improving.

Nor are the measures of improvement here confined to Carr's

prose. Although "The Will-o'-the-Wisp" is not a mystery story, the "reveal" in it benefits from something "The House of Terror" did not: fair clueing. The ending of this story feels earned. Despite being almost one hundred words shorter than the earlier story, "The Will-o'-the-Wisp" offers two hints to prepare the reader for its climax. The first is when the narrator notices Marcia interacting with one of the party guests:

> I swung back to where Marcia had stood, to find her prattling vivaciously to a short, burly young man with the face of a bulldog and the biceps of a prize fighter, who appeared completely under the sway of her magnetic smile. She seemed to be exerting her potent wiles to the utmost on him—a fact I found difficult to account for.

With the Lorelei metaphor, the narrator formed his suspicion of Marcia's manipulative nature; here, that suspicion is confirmed. This glimpse prepares us to believe that Alvez, Marcia's suitor, will assist in her seemingly mad stunt of impersonating the Wisp and dueling with Lafayette. Alvez will even point a gun at the great man and attempt to murder him.

As to Marcia's impersonation of the Wisp, Carr offers us a first-rate clue to her deception before the mask ever comes off: "In a trice the stocky young man had returned with a naked rapier of a pattern similar to that of the Wisp." *The pattern on Lafayette's borrowed rapier is the same as that on the Wisp's because both have been supplied from the Gallivan family's armory.*

Marcia is, of course, a *belle dame sans merci*, one of Carr's typically problematic women; she is one of Cabell's black witches. We understand Marcia's *goal*, to humble Lafayette, but not very well her *motivation*. We might imagine Marcia's thoughts run similarly to Caroline Ross's...

> I was so hoity-toity, so sure my feelings were above other women's. Men were odious, and I could not endure the touch of one. My will power was supreme! My will power would conquer all! (p. 192)

...but even Caroline's strongest stances and actions have perceptible, believable motivations. In keeping with the siren-like identity Carr assigns her, Marcia is malignant and conniving simply for the sake of devilry: " She...must stir up trouble in a spirit of malicious delight at being quarreled over." Albeit in a formulaic way, love redeems Caroline, but Marcia is elemental. She never changes.

"The Will-o'-the-Wisp" is Carr's first story featuring swordplay as a pivotal element. Of course, for all his career, Carr's love affair persisted with "swashbuckling stuff, not altogether free of gadzook-ses or the like, but at least historically accurate." This description doubled as both Carr's summary of the historical romance he wrote in Paris in 1927 (then destroyed)[1] and the confession (pp. 4-5) Carr assigns to Jeff Caldwell, his historical-novelist surrogate in *Deadly Hall* (written almost fifty years after "The Will-o'-the-Wisp"), con-cerning the kinds of novels Jeff aspires to author. Where writing that "swashbuckling stuff" is concerned, Carr pulls off his first attempt here marvelously.

What is most significant about "The Will-o'-the-Wisp," as we briefly noted in the introduction, is that, essentially, *Carr's invention of the time-traveling historical romance begins with this short story, in 1922,* nearly thirty years before Carr published his first such novel, *The Devil in Velvet.* All the essential elements are present in this story, however abbreviated.

To begin, the protagonists of all these time-traveling tales retain memories of their original selves and of the twentieth century, despite assuming the identities of others. This creates similar, fundamental bases of dramatic tension: each perspective character sees the time and situation the way the reader would, both being twentieth-century (or later!) visitors to the past; each lead character is concerned about making anachronistic mistakes and being discovered; each time trav-eler is involved in events that might change history.

Given this, it is instrumental that these characters meet historical-ly significant people and interact with them. Famous historical figures become indispensable participants. When Carr began writing histori-cal mysteries in the 1950s, he practiced a great conservatism about such characters' use. In his afterword to the first, *The Bride of Newgate,* the author made a point of drawing the reader's attention to the fact that, "no famous historical character appears in the story at all" (p. 303). But in the time-traveling historical romances, Carr brings them directly into the plots: even Charles II himself appears briefly—and consequentially—in *The Devil in Velvet.* Although they are less famous than royalty, Robert Peele, Colonel Rowen, and Richard Mayne (the founders of Scotland Yard) appear and participate throughout *Fire, Burn!.* In *Fear Is the Same,* the Prince Regent himself is a significant character. It is part of the stakes of every Carrian time-traveling ad-venture that history itself might change: will Lafayette be slain in a duel? Shot? Will the protagonist prevent it?

---

1 As reported by Greene in the biography, p. 63.

One reason Carr relies on the stakes of history may be that the time-traveling historical adventures have comparatively little mystery. While essentially still fair-play, the presence of mystery serves in each narrative more to add color to a ripping adventure than the obverse: using history superficially to dress up just another detective novel. In any event, we can observe confidently that both the young Carr and the mature Carr leveraged the same core elements in these time-traveling narratives. "The Will-o'-the-Wisp" is not as well written as the novels of Carr's maturity—including, most pointedly, lacking the professional novelist's expertise in recreating the dialects of earlier centuries—but the short story's ancestry of them, and the joint testimony of them all to the yearning for adventure in the grand manner as a persistent theme across Carr's career, surprise and delight readers with their freshness.

Each time-traveling account also employs a simple, similar mechanism for traveling into the past. In *The Devil in Velvet*, as in "The Will-o'-the-Wisp," the gateway between the twentieth century and the past is merely sleep, a drowsy slip backward in time. In the novel's opening, Nicholas Fenton awakens in the seventeenth century:

> In his half-doze he could not remember drawing the curtains of the bed, which was three hundred years old. And it floated through his mind that he had swallowed rather a large dose of chloral hydrate, as a sleeping draught. (p. 1)

In *Fire, Burn!*, Cheviot's passage to 1829 is occasioned by bumping his head stepping out of a taxi sometime in the mid-1950s. In *Fear Is the Same*, as in *The Devil in Velvet*, the passage back through time is precipitated by an express wish. (Fenton sleeps his way back into the seventeenth century, but this is facilitated by a bargain with the devil.)

Although *Fear Is the Same* is more problematic than the other three—two characters, not one, are transported back in time, returning to the present with shared memories of their experiences, and leaving the reader no obvious way to dismiss the reality of their adventures—generally, in the time-traveling novels, Carr follows the template set here in "The Will-o'-the-Wisp" by leaving sufficient ambiguity for the reader to decide whether the adventure in the past actually occurred. Did Nicholas Fenton strike a fantastic deal with the devil? Does the devil even exist? Or did Fenton simply have too strong a sleeping draught? Did Cheviot travel back to 1829, or did he concuss himself and hallucinate? Did Philip Clavering and Jennifer Baird actually visit the eighteenth century, and by doing so, gain supernatural insight into their strikingly similar twentieth-century dilemma? In a sense, this is like asking whether Dorothy truly traveled to Oz—it is beside the point. Carr is narratively uninterested in whether time travel is possible, or in inventing any elaborate explanation for it to "convince" the reader. He stakes nothing on its reality. Rather, in each tale, it is the journey out of time, the adventure itself, that matters.

The theme of wish fulfillment is one reason, of course. The unnamed narrator of "The Will-o'-the-Wisp" wishes the statue of Lafayette could disclose to him the great man's thoughts—which, had the narrator lived in the nineteenth century and seen Lafayette on the grand tour, might well have happened. During the tour, Lafayette reminisced publicly, for many eager Americans, about his adventures liberating a new American nation. The unspoken (and under-developed) need of this young attorney is to be better reconciled with his own time and place. Nicholas Fenton exclaims of his journey back through time (p. 3): "'Wished' is a mild word. God! How I longed for it! How I writhed on a bed of nettles, as men scarify themselves for money or women for social position!" Cheviot confesses to himself that his travel back to the nineteenth century is because he has longed to meet the famous beauty Lady Flora Drayton, whom he has loved helplessly across time. His nineteenth-century love affair with her prepares him to return to his twentieth-century life, a life of unspecified emotional troubles he will resultingly resolve. And Jennifer Baird's wish, an agonized prayer, immediately precedes the conveyance of her and Philip (p. 38) back into the Georgian era: "Oh, if only we could be out of this! If only we could go back a hundred and fifty years in time, and forget it!"

Of course, it is the characters themselves who change, not history with a capital "H." This Carrian genre is more than the mere repetition of formula: given where each time-traveling character's story concludes, we come to understand that the wish fulfilled in each story was actually for the resolution of internal personal conflict, which the time-traveling protagonists did not immediately recognize. The disembodied voice that responds to Jennifer Baird, for instance, hints as much (p. 38): *Would it be any different if you did go back?* Carr offers us a highly unusual and entertaining vehicle for explaining how these characters develop, better understanding themselves and their lives through changed perspectives, not changed history. The remarkable circumstances are merely the mechanisms. As with period-faithful dialogue, "The Will-o'-the-Wisp" under-develops this element compared to the mature novels—its main character's alteration is perceptible, if inexplicit—but this 1922 reverie is unambiguously their starting point.

Let us examine more closely the proposition that the historical romances are more character-driven than the regular detective novels, using *The Devil in Velvet* as our reference. Nicholas Fenton of Cambridge, the eponymous lead of the novel, is another literary echo of Carr himself: a middle-aged historian and fencing enthusiast who yearns so powerfully for a past he admires (in this case, the Stuart period) that, making a bargain with the devil, Fenton travels back to that time and attempts to change history. But this novel is no youthful fantasy, and Fenton is no adolescent instrument of wish fulfillment. Instead, Fenton's romantic vision of the past is chastened and subdued by the age's gritty reality. Without rejecting it—this novel is a fully Romantic one—Carr nonetheless gently mocks the genre by subverting clichéd expectations, whether Fenton's or the reader's:

> "I dare suppose," he said, "as in so many romances, the King immediately fell captive to your charms? And did your bidding?"
> "Nay, 'twas no such thing," replied Meg, with a faint touch of injury or even anger. (p. 314)

Distinctly unlike his youthful works, or even early novels like *Hag's Nook* in which adventure in the grand manner remains exalted while Carr's surrogates come down to earth, in *The Devil in Velvet*, the scales fall away entirely from the principal character's (and the reader's) eyes. Fenton's "adventure" is at times a compromised, middle-aged confusion. Of course, in the tradition of Faustian literature, no deal with the devil ever unfolds happily and without impediments as the bargainer hoped—but whether *The Devil in Velvet* narrates an actual time-traveling romance or merely a sedative-fueled hallucination, the result is the same: what would have been a boldly colorful, swashbuckling success for one of Carr's younger protagonists instead unwinds in muted grays and deflated expectations: several of Fenton's victories are adulterated with astringent consequences.

Further, unlike the younger heroes of Carr's youthful stories and early novels, Fenton struggles against the realization that dark menaces do not simply threaten us from without, seemingly supernaturally, but rather significantly, from within ourselves. Whether or not the devil exists, he is not Fenton's real adversary. As Greene (p. 352) insightfully argues:

Professor Fenton's struggle to keep Sir Nicholas at bay can be read as an attempt to control the beast within all of us. When Fenton almost loses his temper, Carr says, "Professor Fenton, as though fighting to shut down a coffin lid with some rolling horror inside, felt the struggle cease and the lid click shut." In many of his novels, Carr had controlled his fear that the universe may indeed be chaotic by providing human, material, and rational explanations for seemingly impossible events. In some books, however...human rationality was not enough, and chaos threated to burst through. In *The Devil in Velvet* we see that the chaos, the irrationality, may not only be part of the universe but also be within us as humans.

This puts *The Devil in Velvet* into conversation—after three decades of Carr's life, as the theme of wish fulfillment speaks, in weary, middle-aged experience—back across the decades with its youthful, time-traveling ancestor, "The Will-o'-the-Wisp."

Greene and others see setting his 1950s novels in an earlier age as a way for Carr to keep his own perspective relevant at the mid-century: "The hero of each of them is transported from the twentieth century to an earlier, more romantic era when adventure was possible and gentlemanly values were respected" (p. 344). This is surely a factor; after all these decades, Carr was still consonant with Chesterton in identifying what was wrong with the twentieth century. Chesterton's explanation was pithy: "What is wrong is that we do not ask what is right."[2] A war-weary age had learned calamitously that the world no longer operated according to inviolable codes of personal conduct.

Extending Greene's observation, "The Will-o'-the-Wisp" demonstrates for us, as the true starting point of this genre, that Carr's 1950s historical romances were not, as has sometimes been over-simplistically characterized, Freudian retreats from the homely modern day, nor expressions of Carr's disaffection after World War II with the UK's march toward socialism. "The Will-o'-the-Wisp" is a fresh-faced, adventurous romance from the mind of a fifteen-year-old teenager. The older Carr did indeed despise social changes in the UK after WWII, but he wasn't reacting to these changes, as an author, by facilely abandoning the present as an unworthy setting for murder.

---

2 *What's Wrong with the World*, Dodd, Mead and Company, 1910, p. 7.

Of course, while other interpreters may not, Greene knows this; in a December 13, 1967 letter to him, Carr explained the 1950s shift in subject matter this way:

> It's true that during the middle and later nineteen fifties, following a severe illness, I seemed to be losing the joy and zest and drive that had carried me hitherto. Writing, once a breeze, became hard work except for certain moments in books I particularly enjoyed: <u>Fire</u>, <u>Burn</u>! as an example. Then for no discernible reason, all the original joy returned with a whoop just over two years ago. It is probably only a coincidence that this occurred when I left England for good and settled here in South Carolina.

So the joy for Carr was in returning not to a place, or running away from one, but in returning to a genre that had interested him since his youngest days, one he relished for its own intrinsically Romantic qualities. Consider again the aspirations of Jeff Caldwell, who is almost an autobiographical character, so closely modeled is his background upon Carr's own:

> "I want to write historical romances, as I always have... There's one other kind of novel I'd rather like to try, though I don't think I ever can.... Detective stories, about who killed whom and why. There's always a market for blood and thunder, and I love it!" (pp. 4-5)

It is true, all the same, that Carr recognized a post-WWII readership less beguiled by the traditionally cozy settings of the interwar period; he explained this in a letter nearly a decade later (February 2, 1963) to Jan Broberg, in sentiments very like those he would place into Jeff Caldwell's mouth:

> It's hard to care who stabbed Sir Oswald in a locked library or to imagine the reader will care either. But a writer must enjoy what he is doing, or he can't expect to communicate enthusiasm. If his secondary interest has always been history...he may generate enthusiasm by combining the two techniques.

If any kind of retreat, Carr's 1950s historical novels were a retreat not from socialism, but from *horror*, too much of which readers had experienced through the recent war's brutality. Carr no longer felt, as he did when he wrote the Bencolin novels, that an interesting narrative could be based upon combatting unimaginable horrors with more human ones like the Mephistophelean *juge d'instruction*. A novel's threats needed to be less frightening than they had been in Carr's 1930s and 1940s works. Greene makes this same connection:

> One of Carr's purposes in writing mystery and historical dramas for the BBC was to relieve the horrors of the war by presenting cozier and, with the solutions at the end of each play, more manageable horrors. Carr said about his *Appointment with Fear* series, "These plays are, frankly, forms of escapism. The present war is seldom or never mentioned; the action takes place against a peacetime security."[3]

In fact, the entire landscape of mystery fiction was shifting after WWII, not just Carr's works. Genres were beginning to proliferate and fragment. Suspense and espionage fiction were both on the rise: in the increasingly popular works of Eric Ambler, for instance, the amateur detective was replaced by the amateur spy.[4] As to mystery and suspense novels, they incorporated as key elements psychology and the economic and class struggles of its protagonists. These were mysteries decades removed in time and worldview from Sir Oswald's locked library.

WWII itself even furnished the background setting for any number of mystery novels. Consider Ira Levin's Edgar award-winning *A Kiss Before Dying* (1953), which draws on all the "new" elements Carr did not. In it, Bud Corliss, returning from service in WWII, is determined, in any way necessary, to leave behind his working-class background. He seduces the daughter of a rich businessman. Trouble, crime, and suspense result. Corliss is no hero, either: he's an antihero. In much post-WWII fiction, the darkness represented is no longer situational or atmospheric, nor is it occulted behind the eyes of a murderer trying to blend into an otherwise sane world in which truth and normalcy are underlying postulates, defended and restored by the detectives who apprehend murderers. Characters like Corliss are not the kind Carr would ever have conceived, nor novels like Levin's the sort he would ever have written.

We can recall somewhat emblematically, as well, that while Carr's

---

3 "Adolf Hitler and John Dickson Carr's Least-Known Locked Room," *The Armchair Detective*, 1981 (14/4).

4 As an amusing aside, consider Greene's Appendix 4 (pp. 463-464) in the biography: "John Dickson Carr—Spy?"

generation of successful mystery writers often crossed media to write radio dramas, after WWII, writers like Charlotte Armstrong, Ambler, Daphne du Maurier, and others joined Raymond Chandler in writing screenplays for television and films (some of these authors even adapting their own works). This is not an insignificant distinction. The fiction of these authors readily lent itself to adaptation for the screen. They wrote visual scenes, not wool-gathering discussions.

Nelson Bond, who had also written for television, received permission from Carr to adapt one of Carr's novels to the stage. Bond explained in his April 12, 1967 letter to Carr that the latter's fiction presented some practical impediments to being transposed to the stage:

> You may be wondering how I am coming on with my project of adapting one of your books to the stage. Well, dammit, I'm not coming along at <u>all</u> well! And this has nothing to do with the quality of the books or the subject matter; it is simply that the action moves about so fluidly that any of the stories would adapt easily to the screen or to television, but less easily to the stage. In a play, we cannot just go merrily galloping off from place to place, but must confine the action to a limited number of sets. So, without performing major surgery (which I am not about to do) I find myself baffled so far.

There is truth to Bond's observations about the fluidity of Carr's narratives, and as Carr enthusiasts know, some few works of his were adapted to the screen. In the main, though, Bond was mistaken that Carr's detective novels might readily translate to the screen—certainly not faithfully. Most, as we see in hindsight, were not adapted, either. This is for a reason Bond overlooked: a Carr novel, unlike a Chandler or Ambler novel, is not a series of set pieces that straightforwardly translate into screen scenes of action and suspense. Instead, a Carr detective novel is one that often transitions from the investigation of a crime scene into a long, sedate dialogue about what the clues mean. Carr novels feature action much less frequently than they do ratiocination.

This was even true of Carr's historical romances. Carr related to James O'Brien in an April 22, 1955 letter, "When the hero goes into action, he uses his brains and not his fists completely to shatter and destroy the villain, who, in turn, is usually the tough-guy type who has now become almost an American hero." Yes, Carr's historical romances include more set pieces and physical action than his classic puzzlers featuring Bencolin, Fell, or Merrivale do, but as Carr confessed to Oscar Baron, these novels are still, in some real sense, mysteries. Carr's heroes are not action heroes. Even his most agile swashbucklers unknot their Gordian mysteries with reason, not a sword. Again, deferring to Douglas Greene (p. 345), we recognize, "The strengths of his historical fiction resemble those of his puzzle novels—strong plotting, vivid though not detailed characterizations, and a colorful sense of setting."

The time-traveling historical romances—as unlike Carr's earlier works as they are on the surface—are, in fact, the logical post-WWII descendants of those Golden-Age puzzlers: they seem, in retrospect, if not quite inevitably, to be the mystery novels a Romanticist would write following WWII. Romanticism routinely glances away from the present age, commenting upon it only obliquely by revisiting the noblest times past.

This is an important point to discern clearly: Carr's interest in in the past is a fundamental, lifelong part of his identity as a Romantic writer, not a post-war retreat from the present. *After all, was even the early novelist ever really writing about his contemporary society?* Are the Bencolin, Fell, or H.M. novels taking place in any less fictive a setting, despite taking place superficially in "the present," than the time-traveling historical novels are? If anything, Carr, an enthusiast of history, is more careful in his historical fiction not to transform the past than he otherwise is not to transform the present. In his contemporary works, after all, London and Paris, and even rural America, exist in a twilight of gothic horror that is adjacent to their dull realities. As Greene has notably characterized it, in Carr's milieu, present-day London becomes Baghdad-on-the-Thames.

Understanding all this, we also understand that "The Will-o'-the-Wisp" is probably Carr's second-most important amateur work, after only *Grand Guignol*. It is the surprising disclosure to today's readers, a century after it was written, of the origins of Carr's 1950s renaissance. It is the very first instance of a peculiarly Carrian genre, one that helps us better comprehend those distinguishing works of his maturity.

The Marked Bullet (1923)

Handreth was restless. He lay half submerged in the feathery sea of bedclothing, tossing into grotesque positions and entwining himself in the coverlet like a mummy. Still sleep would not come. At length he opened his eyes and stared up at the canopy overhead, hot and irritated and uncomfortable. The moonlight peeped pallidly in at the window near the head of the bed, stirring uneasily on the ghostly outlines of the heavy, stolid, impassive furniture. A breath of wind trembled through the curtains, making the pool of moonlight writhe, but it conveyed no coolness to Handreth. Thoughts jostled through his mind in a way that wearied him without bringing sleep. Finally he slid down from the high bed and crossed to where the pale oblong of the window cut open the blackness. The night air whipped through his pajamas and ran a prickly finger up his spine. It fanned his face soothingly, and, kneeling on the low window seat, he leaned out.

On either side ivy patched the walls of the house, like scars on its stolid gray face. The blank eyes of its windows looked furtively toward the low line of the marshes, shivering in the mist. The whole place huddled together, the ivy whispering, and shrank from the moon, as though it had done something it was afraid of. There was a curious air of deadness about the grounds: Brandon Hall was like the silent specter of a dead house in a magic forest. Below the dingy trees shivered and cowered and moaned, the moonlight scampering through their aisles in terror. Handreth stirred impatiently. Rotten place for a house-party, this—like a desert island…he leaned farther out. A pale yellow was trembling on the terrace under the window of the room below. Somebody was moving around in the library.

There was an element of companionship in the thought that another person in the house was wakeful. Handreth rose and groped his way to the bed. He touched the electric switch at its head, bathing the apartment with a warm rose glow that seemed out of place in that grim room of dark furniture and darker portraits, whose faces peered distortedly down from the blackened paneling, like ghosts out of a fen. Handreth pulled on his bathrobe, dropped a flashlight into his pocket, and thrust his feet into his slippers. Then he turned off the lights once more and ventured cautiously toward the door.

A breath of wind shuddered in the hall, brushing his ankles clammily as it crept past. The corridor was a vast, draughty place of blended grays and blacks, fretted with streaks of pale light from a Gothic window at its far end and alive with crawling shadows.

A pallid finger thrust itself through the gloom and pointed out the face of a woebegone portrait immediately opposite Handreth's door. It looked alive in the wan illumination, leering and grimacing down at him. Handreth closed the door softly behind him and shuffled down the hall. His hand was on the button of the flashlight when he stopped short suddenly and listened. Somewhere before him a footfall rustled on the carpet—a mere ghost of a sound that drifted back to him as though from miles away. Somebody was creeping down the stairs...

He drew back quickly and re-entered his own room. That footstep might have been made by a guest on an innocent enough errand, but he knew instinctively that it had not. He groped after his valise, and when he straightened up from bending over it held an automatic pistol, its barrel curiously long and thick. Noiselessly he returned to the hall. There would be no use arousing the house unless...

At the gaping mouth of the stairwell he paused in his stealthy progress and peered over, straining his ears for a repetition of the sound. At the bottom of the dark sweep a ragged edge of moonlight clung to the lowest step, and the great Gothic windows of the lower hall shot gray paths across the floor, but nothing moved there. One wan beam lay across the library door, bringing it out sharply in the gloom. A thread of yellow lay under the sill. Handreth began a cautious descent. From somewhere in the black void a clock ticked hoarsely, as though it had a cold. A sigh wheezed up from its throat; then, very deliberately, it began to strike. One, two...

Handreth started violently and almost dropped the flashlight. A sharp crack rocked the silence like a physical force, the echoes snatching it up and rolling it through the house until every window seemed to chatter and every room to have its separate reverberation. In the night stillness the hall quivered to it; as it trembled away there was a stirring in one of the bedrooms, and a light slid out under the door. Somebody began to call shrilly. Another light winked up.

Handreth bounded down the stairs. His eyes were on the library door. A pistol shot, if he had ever heard one...and it had come from there! Something darker than the surrounding gloom flickered before him as he reached the bottom of the steps.

"Who's there?" These words cracked out in a sharp staccato. Simultaneously the yellow knife of his electric torch ripped open the gloom and came to rest in a quivering disk on the face of the person before him. The latter clung to the newel post and threw up a slim hand.

"It's Julia Mansfield," she flung back, her voice sobbing and breathless. She lowered her hand slowly, and he saw that her face was chalky. "In the library…Mr. Brandon…I think…"

A yellow glimmer sprang up and moved across the Stygian gulf of the hall. The arm of light reached around and picked out the white of a startled face, like that of a materialized spirit at a seance.

"What's the trouble?" Landridge's shrill accents shook uncontrollably. He held the candle high, throwing a golden halo about his head.

"Something's wrong in here." Handreth crossed to the library door and swept the light over it. Then he rattled the knob and pounded.

"Open the door!" he shouted. "You in there! Open the door!"

The candle flame fluttered over the impassive wood as Landridge appeared at his elbow. Handreth gave a last wrench at the knob and turned to the butler. He spoke breathlessly.

"We've got to force the door. God knows what's happened…" He thrust the electric torch into his pocket and seized the knob once more. His shoulder thudded against the wood. It shuddered and let out a thin crackling sound. Then the ancient lock ripped open and flung him into the room. Landridge, peering around the frame, saw him staring at the huddled heap in the center of the apartment; a mass of gray and black from which a thin hand shot out, fingers digging into the carpet like claws. A candle fluttered on the table near him, and its flame gloated on the thin crimson stream that was crawling across the rug from under the silent thing…

Handreth faltered a little as he crossed to its side and peered down. The ghastly face leered distortedly up at him. It was Curtis Brandon, and he had been shot through the heart.

*****

It was a grim-faced group that had gathered in the library. Dawn was painting the marshes gray and paling the blaze of the electric lights. Wrayburn stood on the hearth rug, looking like a great vulture as he stared down at the dull blotch on the floor that marked the spot where had lain the body of the master of Brandon Hall. His hands were clasped behind him; he stood with leathery face outthrust, and gaunt frame drooping.

"You think, then, that it was suicide?" he queried deliberately.

Constable Marden had been pacing restlessly. He wheeled his bulk about and shrugged.

"I think it was suicide," he replied, "because it could not have been murder."

"But there is no weapon…"

The other gestured impatiently.

"I know it. But, on the other hand, murder would have been impossible. Let me show you." He surged across to the door and indicated the bolt with a blunt finger. "Bolted on the inside, you see. When Mr. Handreth broke the door open he tore the socket clean from the wood...so." He pointed at the splintered screw holes. "As I have been able to understand it, Mr. Handreth was on the stairs when the shot was fired. He did not lose sight of the door the whole time—and nobody came out. Even if he had not been there, it would have been impossible for anyone to have gone out and locked the door on the inside. Just a moment!" He waved Wrayburn into silence and crossed to the great Gothic window. "Now notice this. The only window in the room. Secured by two heavy catches, both of them intact. Couldn't possibly have been put on from the outside. And note the string of cobwebs from the sash to the frame. The window couldn't have been raised without breaking that. You see? If the murderer didn't go out by the door, and he didn't go out by the window, then it wasn't murder...You searched the room?"

"Immediately." Handreth nodded. "There was no one hiding here."

The coroner, small and wiry and ferret-like, spoke suddenly.

"Would it have been possible for anyone standing by the door to have gotten out unnoticed immediately after Mr. Handreth forced it open?"

"It would not," said Wrayburn positively. "There were half a dozen people in the hall. Landridge was squarely in front of the door, and Mr. Travis, here, and myself were only a few feet behind. Nobody came out after the door had been opened."

"How about a secret entrance?" the doctor pursued. "Any such thing here?"

"I have made certain of that." Marden dug his hands into his pockets and frowned heavily at the table. "I assure you there is nothing of the kind. I overlooked nothing in my examination. Walls and floor and ceiling are all intact. Not even a crack. Fireplace bricked up." He shrugged. "The room might have been made of concrete, to all practical purposes. And yet I can't find a trace of a weapon."

"Would Brandon have had time to have hidden the weapon after shooting himself?" Handreth asked abruptly.

Coroner Wayne shook his head.

"Clean through the heart," he said soberly. "Death was instantaneous. He couldn't have lifted a finger after the bullet hit him. It was a thirty-eight..."

Marden waved him into silence. He rolled a cigar into his mouth and fished in his capacious pocket for matches.

"It's the damnedest thing I ever ran against! It couldn't be suicide and it couldn't be murder. Suicide's the safest bet. That's what

I'd call it...but what verdict can a coroner's jury bring in?"

"You're absolutely certain there's no weapon?" Wayne persisted doggedly.

"Absolutely. If there had been we'd have found it."

The little doctor gestured helplessly.

"Murder then. There's always a chance that something's been overlooked in a murder case. You can't slip up on suicide."

"That," Wrayburn opined, "will just raise hell. You'll get everybody here tangled up in the thing. There'll be no end of trouble for nothing."

Marden jerked up his head.

"And what if it does," he demanded. "I propose to get at the truth. Something happened in this room. Suicide or murder...it happened. There'll be an inquest, anyhow, and your friends will have to testify. In the meantime, I'll snoop around a little. Can you furnish me with a list of the names of everyone here—servants, too?"

"Is all this necessary?" Travis queried. He had hovered in the background, moving restlessly about the room during the conversation. Now an outraged sense wrung the question from him. He glowered under the constable's scrutiny. He knew that he looked disheveled, and it annoyed him, even before a police officer. His neat mustache drooped a little; his colorless hair was scraggly without oil; and his hasty toilet made him look lopsided. He rushed on indignantly: "You mean to go running around nosing into everything and making everybody feel like a criminal. You know none of us killed Curt...and you'll bring a lot of reporters around. Confound it, why have you got to—" He realized that his peevishness was getting the better of him, and his voice trailed off lamely. A dull red crept up his cheek.

"It's very necessary that I do it, Mr. Travis." Marden looked at him steadily. Then he turned to Handreth.

"I should like those names, please...and tell everybody that I wish them here in the library immediately after breakfast. In the meantime, I'll have a further look around. Has Mr. Brandon any near relatives?"

"A niece and a nephew. Miss Julia Mansfield and Mr. Arthur Brandon...you met him coming in. He'll be downstairs in a few minutes."

"His heirs?"

"So I should imagine. There are no other relatives that I know of."

"Do you know of anyone who had cause to wish Mr. Brandon dead?"

Wrayburn's head came up. His eyes flashed a warning to Handreth.

"No one, Mr. Marden," the latter responded firmly.

For one moment their glances clashed. Then the constable lowered his eyes slowly. He had opened his mouth to speak when somebody coughed at the door. Landridge had sidled in. He stood there looking from one to the other of the occupants of the library, his bent frame so angular as to give his frayed suit the appearance of being draped on a wooden figure. His eyes were set so far back that his head looked like a skull. He bowed a little and kneaded his long fingers.

"I beg your pardon, sir. I might be able to tell you something, sir."

"About this?" Marden barked.

"Yes, sir." Landridge had been butler at Brandon Hall so long that he had almost contrived to efface his cockney accent. In his excitement a tinge of it crept back into his speech. He gripped his fingers hard and went on: "I thought as 'ow you might be interested. It's about somebody wanting to kill the master, sir. It's about Mr. Arthur and Miss Mansfield, sir."

"Well?"

Landridge shot a glance at Wrayburn. The latter had half stepped forward and seemed about to speak. Something flickered over the butler's face.

"Well, sir, the other night I was a-makin' the rounds to shut up the 'ouse," he hurried on, "and I saw there was a light in the library. The door was near closed, but I could 'ear somebody talking inside. It was the marster, sir, and 'e was in a hawful temper, sir. I could hear him a-walkin' up and down and a-ragin' frightful, as you might say, sir. I could not 'elp 'earin' what he said…"

"Who was he talking to?" Wrayburn flung the query.

"That's what I'm a-tellin' of, Mr. Wrayburn," returned Landridge with dignity. "It was either Mr. Arthur or Miss Julia, Mr. Marden, sir, but I cawn't say which. Mr. Brandon was a-sayin': 'I kept you here,' he says, 'I kept you here, and I did everything for you, and this is the way you repay me. I've 'ad my suspicions for a long time, you that was so meek and innocent and lovin' all the time, you that made such a fuss over your uncle—you young viper! You thought you 'ad me when you got that prussic acid and put it in my brandy… oh, I saw you; don't try to lie, you little fiend!' Then the other person said something in a voice so low I couldn't distinguish it, and that fair made the marster crazy. 'You been tryin' to kill me for the money I give you in the will,' he shouts, 'and now you don't get a damned shilling! I'm not bringin' disgrace on myself by showin' kin of mine to be…' Then the other person said something again, and the master moved toward the door. I left, sir."

For a moment after he had cut short his breathless discourse the room was so still that Handreth heard his watch tick. Then Wrayburn leaped forward.

"You damned liar!" he shouted. "You damned, treacherous liar!" He seized Landridge by the shoulder and spun him around. The butler shrilled and retreated against the table, his hand groping for something along the side.

"Get away!" he babbled. "I'll show you! You want proof that one of those darling relatives killed him, do you?" His voice had risen shrilly, and the hand on Wrayburn's arm quivered. "Well, then, look 'ere!" He pressed one of the oaken rosettes carved into the wood, and beside him a long, shallow drawer slid out. In it lay an automatic pistol.

An expletive shot from between Marden's lips as he snatched up the weapon. It was a thirty-eight-caliber Colt. He broke it open.

"One chamber empty," he announced tersely. "Look at this!" His finger indicated a name cut neatly into the steel on the grip. The name was Arthur Brandon.

*****

"And I found—this," Marden concluded. He threw on the table a handkerchief, streaked with dirt and crumpled into a tiny wad, and a small, neat, compact pistol of the barrel design. He was very grim.

"It amounts to this: one of these two is entirely innocent and knows nothing of the whole rotten business. The other," savagely, "is a devil. I couldn't imagine a person in this world who looks more incapable of any kind of crime than Mr. Brandon or Miss Mansfield. And yet one of them tried to poison old Mr. Brandon and finally shot him for his money. Then one deliberately set out to throw suspicion on the other. Either Arthur shot him and planted this pistol and the rag used to clean it in his cousin's room or else Miss Mansfield is guilty and left the weapon in the secret drawer." He gestured helplessly. "God! What a business! What a rotten, sordid business! To think that one of those..."

Wrayburn had been pacing restlessly, like a caged animal. He swung around.

"Must a policeman be an idiot in real life as well as in the stories?" he snapped. "Can't you see...can't you understand..."—he groped desperately for words— "isn't it plain that neither one of those could do a thing like that? In God's name, man: it's not possible! You're putting the characters of people like Arthur Brandon and Julia Mansfield against the word of that lying thief of a butler!"

"But the two pistols; the fact that only they could profit by Brandon's death. It's clear circumstantial evidence."

"I believe you wished to see me?" The voice was low and soft and pleasant. Marden glanced to the door. A young man stood there. He was pale as the collar he wore, and his face seemed to have aged in a short space of time. His eyes were very dry and very bright, like sapphires set in marble. There seemed to be some internal pain that was racking him. The hand that he raised to smooth his hair back from his finely chiseled brow was long and thin, and it trembled pitiably. Behind him stood Handreth, his eyes conveying a warning to Marden. The youth stepped into the room. He walked with a slight limp, and one hand held jealously close the curious short cloak that he wore.

"Mr. Arthur Brandon?" Marden asked awkwardly.

"I am told you wished to see me about my uncle's death." He spoke the word thickly. "I am sorry I could not get down sooner."

Marden turned to Wrayburn and Handreth. He was very grave.

"In what I am about to do," he said slowly, "I shall seem heartless. I am afraid you would not approve. Therefore I shall ask you to leave the room and allow me to query Mr. Brandon alone." His eyes flickered steel.

"I see," Wrayburn snapped. His lip curled. "You want to bully…"

"I want to get at the truth." The words cracked out like whiplashes: "And now will you go?"

Wrayburn bowed stiffly and motioned to Handreth. Together they left the room. Marden watched the door close behind them. Then he turned to Brandon.

"Mr. Brandon, do you own a revolver?" He whipped out the question.

"Yes. Why?" The other raised a startled face.

Marden drew from his pocket something bulky wrapped in a handkerchief. He opened it, disclosing the pistol engraved with the other's name.

"Look at this. Don't touch it! Tell me if it belongs to you."

Brandon stared down at the weapon. He was gripping a chair back fiercely.

"It is mine," he announced very quietly. "You don't mean to…"

"Somebody shot your uncle. He used this weapon." Marden leaned forward slightly. His eyes bored into those of the man before him. "After he had used the weapon, he rubbed his hand along the grip to smear out possible fingerprints. He made indistinguishable blurs of those on the handle. But"—the word cracked out— "he forgot the trigger: wide and smooth and glossy. He left half the print of the first finger of his right hand, Mr. Brandon…did you know that?"

"I see the implication," Brandon said dully. "I didn't kill my uncle." He jerked up his head suddenly. "I didn't kill him because under your conditions I couldn't have." He faltered a little; then, very slowly, he drew back his cloak. "I—I haven't any right hand. I lost the arm at Chateau Thierry…"[1]

*****

Marden and Wayne dawdled over their coffee in the breakfast room, the only splash of modernity in the house. The morning sunlight was painting a warm tracery on the floor through the French windows, but none of the guests save Wrayburn and Travis and Handreth had come down yet. Marden recounted his interview with Arthur Brandon. Wayne was silent.

"You see how it is," the constable finished. "The fingerprint wasn't his…and that leaves the girl."

"I'd believe almost anything before I'd believe that," declared the coroner. He leaned back in his chair and stared hard at his cup. "Marden, you're taking too much for granted. Everything hinges on that butler's testimony…"

"Except the two pistols."

"One of which Brandon did not fire," Wayne reminded him dryly. "It's just possible that there is some explanation for the weapon you found in Miss Mansfield's room. Landridge is a malicious old devil, anyhow. You may talk about appearances being deceitful, and all that…but I'd swear that girl isn't crooked."

"She may have done it in a sudden rage, or something like that—on the spur of the moment. Women are the queerest things on God's green earth. Talk about weakness and lack of nerve all you please; I tell you that an infuriated woman can raise more hell than a half dozen men…I've seen it done. When a woman stands up and points a gun at your heart and threatens to shoot, you're all right; she couldn't hit you even if she did fire…which she wouldn't. It's when she sees red and turns her head away and begins to pump lead into the air that you always get plugged."

"But even if she did do that," Wayne argued, "what about the pistol in the secret drawer? Unless it was coincidence, I'd say it was a deliberate plot to throw suspicion on Arthur Brandon. According to your theory she couldn't have done that. And that brings us right back to where we were. Marden, that girl is either entirely innocent, or she's the worst she-devil I ever ran across. I think she's innocent."

---

1 Fought on July 18, 1918, but the presence of Brandon, an Englishman, there is curious: at that battle, the Germans faced the French and the American Expeditionary Force. British forces did not fight at Chateau Thierry.

"It can easily be proved. The fingerprint…"

"The fingerprint won't tell you a confounded thing. You've just got half of it—enough to prove that it wasn't Arthur Brandon, and not enough to identify anybody by. You couldn't convict a person on half a print."

Landridge slid in like a well-trained ghost to remove the coffee cups. Marden allowed him to get almost out of the room. Then:

"Landridge!" he called suddenly.

The butler started a little and turned around. He came back to the table.

"You were wanting something, sir?"

"Yes. Put those cups down, Landridge, I want to talk to you."

The other set down the tray. His restless fingers plucked at the cloth.

"It's about what you told us early this morning," Marden resumed. "You realize what a serious thing it is to make an accusation like that, do you?"

" 'Twasn't an accusation," the butler returned a trifle defiantly.

"You accused either Mr. Brandon or Miss Mansfield of being an attempted murderer and in all likelihood a successful one later. You will be prepared to swear to all this at the inquest?"

"Yes, sir." Landridge's tone was dogged. "Hevery bit of it, sir. Hit's true, I'm a-tellin' you. I heard it just as plain…" He shrugged.

"Where were you when the shot was fired?"

"Hin my room, sir. I 'eard the shot and I thought…"

"Mr. Handreth says you came into the hall with a candle not longer than five or six seconds after the report. Your room is at the back of the house. How did you get there so quickly?" Marden leaned forward slightly and flung out the query.

Landridge's hand clenched suddenly. A startled flash showed in his eyes.

"Hi…hurried, sir. Mr. Handreth must have been mistaken!"

"Mr. Handreth was not mistaken. You're lying, Landridge."

"I'm not!" His voice rose shrilly. It held a note of desperation. "I thought I saw somebody out on the lawn…a burglar, likely. So I put hon my bathrobe and went downstairs…You hask Mr. Handreth who else was in the 'all besides me, if you want to know. Ask 'im who cried out that something was wrong in the library. It was Miss Mansfield, that's who it was, and he's a-tryin' to shield 'er!"

Something was bound to snap. A voice broke the tensity then, shattering it like a thing of plaster that clattered noisily down about their ears.

"I beg your pardon." The man in the massive figure, reminiscent of hewn granite, seemed to spread out and fill the door, but he moved with the smooth, lithe ease of a panther. Under a towering cliff of forehead he peered at the occupants of the room with eyes that reflected the light oddly like opals. His hair reminded the constable of a mane. He seemed to radiate power; it pulsed in a sort of aura about him—dominating, irresistible. One sensed something fierce and dynamic in every detail of his appearance. He dug his rugged hands into his pockets and stared across at Marden. Landridge seemed to crumple up and vanish instantly.

"I did not know you were...cross-examining," he apologized. "Perhaps I had better introduce myself. I am Sir Lionel Barnstow. I think I can tell you something bearing directly on your investigation, Constable."

Marden bowed slightly and a little awkwardly. Sir. Lionel Barnstow! Sir Lionel Barnstow, one of the most picturesque figures in England. Author, explorer, sportsman—a dozen other things. He seemed to be the personification of every man's secret desires. He had penetrated farther up the Amazon than any man in England. He had shot big game in Africa and involved himself in an uprising in India. In his earlier years he had once held a mission post with a Gatling against an Afghan regiment. A white seam followed the curve of his jaw where a knife had ripped it open during a street fight in Cairo. His age was baffling; though he seemed to have been on the front pages of newspapers for innumerable years, still his turbulent soul continued to shoot the rapids of life in the frail canoe men call nerve. During the late war they could tell you of the Mad Ace who drove into a squadron of German planes singlehanded...

But he was speaking now in his quick voice.

"I thought it best to communicate with you at once. Wrayburn told me this morning that he had called in the police...Well, sir, it's about last night. After the house had retired I went out for a smoke and a stroll in the garden. I left at half-past one; I remember seeing the clock in the hall. It was quiet and peaceful out here, and I must have walked around for about half an hour. I was returning to the house when I noticed that there was a light in the library. The window was made of some rough, heavy leaded glass, set off with a coat of arms in the center, so that I was unable to see into the room. Suddenly I saw a sharp silhouette against the yellow light, and it was that of two struggling figures. One of them tore loose as I watched; then both vanished, and I heard the report of a pistol. I dashed around and into the house, arriving in time to find Brandon shot. That is all. You see that under the circumstances it could not have been suicide…"

For a long time Marden was silent, tapping the table thoughtfully.

"We have already determined that it was not suicide, Dr. Barnstow,"[2] he said at length. "The evidence…You have no idea as to the identity of the other person you saw? Was it a man or a woman?"

"I cannot say to a certainty. The figures were distorted by the candlelight. I got the impression that it was a man, however."

"Mr. Marden!" The voice quivered across the room arrestingly. Landridge was standing at the door of the breakfast room, and this time he was kneading his fingers fiercely. His pale eyes flickered brimstone, and Marden thought he could see the malevolence overflowing his mouth and trickling down the corners in little slimy streams. There was triumph in his cracked voice. "What did I tell you?" he shrilled. "I told you it was one of them two, didn't I? Just you go up to that girl's room! She's gone! She's run away, that's what she's done."

Marden's chair went over with a crash as he sprang up. "What do you mean?"

"She's run away!" the butler babbled. "Room all turned upside down; maid found it when she took breakfast up. Everything thrown around; clothes out of the drawers where she packed up…"

His voice trailed off as Marden pushed past him into the hall. At the foot of the staircase stood a little, faded, mouse-like woman who seemed all gray and black: Mrs. Saker, the housekeeper, according to the list Handreth had given to him. Wrayburn was leaning against the newel post, talking earnestly to her. He stared at Marden as the latter hurried up the steps. At the open door of Julia Mansfield's suite a trim maid hovered; she turned to go as Marden came into view, but he detained her. She came back hesitatingly. Her finely molded face was a little pale, and despite himself the constable wondered at its delicate, patrician beauty. He was looking into eyes the color of seawater in the sunlight…

"You discovered Miss Mansfield was gone?" he demanded.

"Yes, sir. I brought the tray up, sir." Her eyelids drooped, and their black lashes stood out vividly against the alabaster of her face.

---

2 The original editing of this story is problematic, not just on small points such as the mishandling of Sir Lionel's title. In the original text, the discussion with Barnstow is placed in the next chapter, at 12:30 A.M., when neither Landridge nor anybody else is with Marden, who is quietly investigating a late-night noise. So the discussion is a non-sequitur, one followed even more inexplicably, by Landridge's dramatic disclosure concerning Julia Mansfield. As originally edited, Marden had already been contemplating the disclosure. The editor has concluded that both conversations were meant by Carr to occur here in the breakfast room and moved them appropriately.

She spoke quickly, almost incoherently.

Marden glanced into the room. Drawers had been pulled open, their contents overflowing and billowing on the floor in a delicately tinted sea. An open closet door disgorged a gush of filmy stuff. The bureau had been swept clean, as though its things had been thrown promiscuously into a valise. Marden turned back to the maid.

"You haven't any idea where Miss Mansfield has gone?" he asked quickly.

"No, sir!" The girl tugged at the edges of her apron. She was obviously frightened. "I just came up, and...she wasn't here, sir!"

"What's your name?"

"Milly—Mildred Lane, sir. Sister of the cook."

"Very well, Milly. You may go."

Marden turned thoughtfully back to the stairs. He met Wayne and Wrayburn coming up. The latter showed his excitement.

"Absurd!" he rapped. "Absurd, I tell you! She couldn't have..."

Marden answered Wayne's questioning glance with a sober nod.

"I'm afraid she's gone. If we had only known—but nobody would have thought anything like that. Now there'll be hell to pay."

"There will!" Wrayburn agreed savagely. There was something agonized in his tone. He turned about slowly and began to descend the steps. Marden followed in silence.

Handreth met them at the bottom of the stairs. He looked a mute query at Wrayburn, and the latter's head sagged. He seemed completely crushed.

"See here, Mr. Marden: what do you propose to do about—this?" Handreth got the question out with an effort.

"I shall swear out a warrant for Miss Mansfield's arrest," responded Marden very steadily. He looked straight into the other's eyes, and Handreth saw no sign of weakening there. This man was the law...

"Very well," he said almost inaudibly. He held himself in with an effort.

Wrayburn had sunk into a chair. He was staring straight before him, his tongue moistening his lips with a little dry, parched sound. Now he got up unsteadily. The man could not have been more than thirty-five, but he looked very old and very worn as he stood there, gripping the back of the chair fiercely. His lean face was rigid.

"Constable." The word came out huskily. "You want to arrest the murderer of Curtis Brandon. I can't let an innocent person suffer. That is why"— he choked a little— "I am going to confess. It was I who killed him."

*****

Under the yellow splash of the lamp Marden gazed down at the two letters under his hands. Then he picked up the slip of paper Handreth had given him and studied the names on it. At length he returned once more to a perusal of the letters that Wayne had found among the papers of Curtis Brandon.

Somebody in that house was masquerading under an assumed name. Somebody in that house was a detective—an operative from Scotland Yard. Which?

Again he read the letter from Chief Inspector Moreton, dated a few days before the tragedy. It was brief and rather cryptic, but Marden gathered enough to tell him that, at Brandon's request, one of his most efficient operatives had been installed as a guest at the house party.

"Under the circumstances, I think you are warranted in the belief that this person has designs on your life. The poison episode could have been no accident. So I am taking steps toward sending to you a man whom you will find both clever and discreet. He can be relied on to keep watch on this person, whose name I believe you said was—"

Marden flung the letter angrily from him. Torn in half at the very word he would have given so much to know! Whose name had filled up that blank? Was it Arthur Brandon, or was it Julia Mansfield herself, who had set out deliberately to remove the only obstacle between a fortune and him or herself? There could be no doubt now that Landridge had been telling the truth.

But what of Wrayburn and his inexplicable confession? Mardon's mind reeled kaleidoscopically. Two people confessing to a murder, one tacitly by flight in the face of evidence; the other voluntarily, with not a shred of proof against him! If Wrayburn were guilty, why did he maintain his stubborn silence as to by what means he had done so? Why did he fail to reveal his motive for such a deed? Marden knew that he must arrest him—that tomorrow he must remove him…but what of the girl? Why her flight? Why the pistol in the drawer of her dressing table?

Marden rose and moved restlessly about the room. Fame lay within his reach if he could find the key to this puzzle. But the key: was there one? It seemed that everyone in the house was conspiring against him. Everyone had something to tell, and nobody would tell it except under pressure. Then there was this unknown operative from Scotland Yard…one of the guests? A perpetual question mark was forever staring him in the face. If he could only find out to whom Brandon had willed his money…

There was the answer! Idiot! Marden's fist thudded down on the table. Of course Brandon would have cut off the one he suspected! It would be the last link in the chain. There might be some explanation for Miss Mansfield's disappearance beyond that of fear of the law—but the evidence of a will in her cousin's favor would be incontrovertible proof. Who would know? Travis, naturally; as Brandon's attorney, he would have drawn the will. Strange that he had said nothing about the matter before.

Marden looked at his watch. Twelve-thirty...he must have been sitting here pondering the problem for a long time. Would Travis be awake at the hour? He must be awakened if he were not.

The constable drew on his coat and crossed the guest-chamber to the door. He closed it softly behind him and stood in the corridor, brushed by a prowling wind. It was uncannily still. He peered through the light-spangled gloom at the stiff line of doors down either side of the hall. That door at the far end marked the entrance to Julia Mansfield's suite; the next one was Sir Lionel Barnstow's, next to that Wrayburn's, and next to that Handreth's adjoining his own. On the other side there was the room that Brandon had occupied, communicating with that of his nephew. Then there was a suite in which stayed some army officer or other—a Major Pemberton and his wife, both dusty, mid-Victorian, and excitable—and next to them, Travis.

Marden padded softly across the hall to the attorney's door. Travis had impressed him as insipid and self-centered, but as one who knew his business: he, if anyone, could tell...

He rapped softly and waited. Nothing stirred inside. Then he turned the knob. The door opened under his fingers and he peered into the black depths of the room. The outlines of the furniture were sketched with a flat, gray brush on the darkness. Marden crossed quickly to the bed and looked down at it. It was empty.

Perplexedly he retraced the steps to the door. Where was the man? Was he prowling around the house at this hour of the night...?

In the hall Marden stood and listened. The branch of a tree was stirring uneasily against the pane of the window down the hall—an eerie breath of sound that was like the brushing of a human body on the glass, as though someone were peering in at him. Marden bent forward suddenly. Somebody was moving around in the lower hall.

Marden held himself steady with an effort. Swiftly he went down the hall and looked over the balustrades. There was a light in the library.

He was quivering with excitement, but he descended the stairs very cautiously...Perhaps the solution of the enigma that baffled him lay in sight; perhaps…Something stirred the shadows of the lower hall. Quick footsteps echoed up to him, like noises out of a gulf. A man was silhouetted sharply against the light that built a yellow pillar out against the darkness through the half-opened door; then he entered. Marden reached the foot of the stairs and sidled cautiously across the corridor. Very slowly his head came around the angle of the door. He saw two figures in the great room.

One of them stood near a tier of bookshelves along one side of the apartment. Her sable hair, billowing about her shoulders, stood out vividly against the white wrapper she wore. She held high a dull gold candelabrum, and in the yellow glory of the shivering flames Marden thought she looked like Lady Macbeth in the sleep-walking scene. She had been intent on a book in her hand, but as the man advanced into the room she spun around quickly with a little gasp. Marden saw that it was Milly Lane, who had discovered Julia Mansfield's disappearance. The cloudy green of her eyes deepened as she stared at the man whose back was to him, and the hand that held the lights trembled. Very distinctly the newcomer's voice came back to him:

"A word with you, Miss Mansfield."

*****

Handreth sat at the window and gazed out across the moonlit lawn with its scraggy growth of trees, like the stubble of a beard on a rugged face. His thoughts were in chaos. Last night he had sat here in almost the same position, and at that same time down in the library…he shuddered a little. Tonight the house, the grounds, the sinister gray line of the marshes seemed charged with an electric something that tingled in the air forebodingly. The ivy twisted uneasily about, as though fearful of a slinking danger that would take it from behind; the trees cried softly to the moon, tossing their bodies like things held down by chains, and somewhere in the distance an owl hooted. A black shape obscured the moon for an instant as a bat wheeled crazily about the eaves, flapping and rustling as it careened against the ivy. Handreth thought of Dracula.

Then he leaned forward a little and looked hard at one of the trees. Was it his imagination, or…yes—something moved down there. A shadow lay long and black across the carpet of moonlight for an instant as the thing slunk across an open space.

Handreth leaped up. The person who was prowling around under his window might be the same as—he glanced wildly about. If he were to go down by the stairs, the prowler would have in all probability gone when he reached the spot. There was but one alternative. This side of the house lay in the shadow. He leaned out and tested the thick growth of ivy beside his window. It was his chance, but he must take it. He seized the vine and swung himself out. There was a momentary sinking sensation at the pit of his stomach as the ground below reeled about under his eyes; then he steadied himself and began the descent. The ivy sagged sickeningly and cracked beneath his hands, blistering them as he swung downward and bits of the mortar pattered about him. After a breathless descent he stood, panting and disheveled, on the stubbly grass. He steadied himself against the wall and peered out over the lawn. The figure had halted; a black splotch under one of the trees. Evidently he had not noticed Handreth.

Slowly, and with infinite caution, he dodged from shadow to shadow until he stood within a few feet of the unknown person, who was bending over something on the ground near a tree. Handreth saw him straighten up, holding something in his hands. A thin finger of light, stabbing through the trees picked out wanly the face of Travis.

"Taking the air, Travis?" he questioned very steadily.

He was moving like a ghost through the thin breath of mist that blurred the crooked black bodies of the trees. As he emerged full into the ragged splash of moonlight Handreth stepped in front of him.

The other started and recoiled back against the bole of a tree. He stared without speaking.

"Taking the air?" Handreth repeated.

The lawyer straightened up. He thrust something into his pocket and returned the other's gaze defiantly.

"Yes. The same as yourself."

"You realize, of course, the implication of prowling about the grounds at night—suspiciously engaged? Mr. Marden…"

Travis stepped forward. His hand closed on Handreth's arm and he looked straight into his companion's eyes.

"Mr. Marden must not be told," he said quietly. "It is absolutely necessary that I be allowed to do as I choose without anyone questioning my movements in any way. You understand?"

"Indeed! and why should you…"

"Because," Travis replied slowly and very distinctly, "because I happen to be Chief Inspector Moreton, of Scotland Yard."

*****

Marden pressed his ear to the door again.

"You needn't grow alarmed," the man's voice said gently. "I wanted to see you alone sometime. Why are you posing as a maid?"

Marden could visualize the girl standing there as he heard her cool, defiant tone. She must be looking straight into his eyes.

"I have reasons of my own, Mr. ..."

"No names, please," the other enjoined quickly. "Walls have ears. You were very clever about it, Miss Mansfield. It was dangerous, too. You had to keep out of the sight of all the guests. You might have gotten away with it if I hadn't heard you talking with the housekeeper. Yes, it was a nervy thing to do. If you were caught..."

"I am caught—now." There was a dry, bitter sting in the words.

"You think I would give you away?" came the quick query.

"Then you won't...?" Something full and vibrant seemed to rise higher with each word. Marden heard the girl move forward impetuously.

"Of course not...Why did you run away?"

The silence dragged out in an interminable pause. Marden began to fear that they had heard his heavy breathing, and he edged away slightly. Then Julia Mansfield began to speak quickly and a little breathlessly.

"It was for the best. I suppose it was a mad thing to do, but—but there was no other way. I did it so that I would not have to testify against someone for murder."

"Arthur Brandon?" The question crackled out.

"Yes," replied Julia listlessly. "I suppose I oughtn't to tell you—"

"Go on," the quick voice insisted.

"I heard him having words with Uncle Curtis not long ago," she rushed on. "I didn't see either, but there was a terrible row. I—heard them in the library. Uncle Curtis accused Art of trying to murder him, I think. Art struck him—and then his pistol was in the desk drawer..." She was stumbling over her words, and now her voice trailed off. Marden could almost hear her short, jerky breaths.

"I am going to tell you something—Julia!" The man's voice was very low and very steady, but there was that in it that made Marden stiffen involuntarily. "You needn't have done that. Arthur is innocent. It—it was I who killed your uncle."

*****

In that grim room of grimmer memories the Brandon household had assembled. A dusty bar of sunlight, striking across the room like the illumination of a prison cell window, rested on the desk at which sat Marden. He was leaning back and staring at the row of chairs before him. Landridge balanced himself on the edge of one, returning the constable's gaze defiantly; Wrayburn, very pale and very calm, looked steadily down at the floor; Travis, looking a little bored, chatted with Handreth; Sir Lionel Barnstow's massive head, thrust forward, was regarding Marden speculatively. A little group of servants huddled in the background, with Major Pemberton hesitating at the door, but neither Julia Mansfield or Arthur Brandon was present.

When Marden got to his feet the breath of conversation stopped suddenly. The constable began to speak—slowly at first, then with increasing rapidity until his words were crackling out like electric things.

"There is but one explanation for the crime we have here at Brandon Hall," he said. "I did not know that explanation—until last night." He leaned forward slightly. "Two people were in this room then. One of them confessed to the murder."

He paused. A tingling shock quivered about the group. Something in the air seemed to be tightening, like a net.

"Even in the light of this explanation, several things remained in doubt," Marden went on deliberately. "After these two persons had left the room, I found on the table something that one of them had been examining, and had left there when—that person left. Then I knew." The final sentence ripped across the room. Marden's arm whipped up, bringing before the eyes of the spectators a delicate volume of Shakespeare. In the back a ragged, scorched tear yawned where some terrible force had ripped asunder the delicate vellum of the binding.

"It meant," Marden continued, "that two shots had been fired. Let me tell you how it happened. Someone in this room knew Curtis Brandon had had trouble with either his niece or nephew—and he did not know which. So on the night of the murder he confronted Brandon in the library, getting him downstairs on a ruse, and threatened to expose the scandal unless Brandon paid him a certain sum of money... Don't try to escape, Landridge."

"It's a lie!" The butler's voice shrilled out desperately. He leaped to his feet, and there was the look of a trapped animal in his eyes. "It's a lie! I didn't kill him. I—"

"Arthur Brandon's pistol was in the drawer," Marden went on inexorably. "Driven into a frenzy, Brandon seized that. There was a short, sharp struggle, and Brandon fired. Terrified, Landridge ran to the window and leaped out, just missing Sir Lionel Barnstow... There, Wayne, snap the handcuffs on him!"

Strange men seemed to be pouring through the door suddenly. Wayne burst through the fringe of spectators; something clicked sharply; and there was the crash of an overturned chair as a member of the group leaped to his feet, handcuffs gleaming at his wrists. Cowering back before them stood Handreth.

"Yes, you shot him!" Marden's voice rang out. "You shot him because you were madly in love with Julia Mansfield, and you hated her uncle for the way he treated her. You thought by marrying her to get the money she would inherit... Yes, you did, Handreth. I heard your confession—how you had a pistol when you went out into the hall that night, with a Maxim silencer on the barrel.[3] You came to Brandon Hall with the intention of killing Brandon, and the silencer was handy. You thought Julia Mansfield was downstairs with him when you met her, and it drove you almost crazy. When you heard the shot you rushed over to the door, a plan already forming itself in your mind. Landridge had come around through the back door and was with you. In the meantime, Brandon had quickly reclosed and locked the window, brushing the cobwebs back across the sill to make it look as if they had not been disturbed.[4] He heard you pounding, and he was halfway across the room when you opened the door. I believe you were half crazy—anyhow, you fired just as the door flew open, the silencer pointing out between the folds of your bathrobe. Nobody saw him fall; the guests were just rounding the turn of the stairs, and Landridge was cowering back, terrified. Then you hid the silencer in a tree, where Travis found it, as he told me today. You allowed Wrayburn to confess to the crime. He was madly in love with Julia Mansfield. You didn't plant the pistol in Julia Mansfield's room; it was Landridge, vindictive to the last in a grudge against her, who did that—"

Handreth had suddenly jerked his arm free of Marden's grip. The constable saw him convey a small, gray pellet to his mouth, and the next instant he sank exhausted into a chair, his thin lips contriving to articulate:

"I did—what I did. It's too late for an antidote now!"

---

3 Later, Carr would be very precise with timetables, and the solutions to some of his novels, such as The Bowstring Murders and Poison In Jest, would depend upon clear representation of which suspects were where and when. Here, Carr gives the impression, by placing the lawn scene between Marden's trip from the top to the bottom of the staircase, that Handreth was in two places at once: out on the lawn with Travis/Moreton shortly after Marden did not find him in his room, and downstairs moments later in the library with Julia Mansfield. Unlike the earlier editorial error, there is no way to correct this. It is a problematic handling of the timetable by the young Carr.

4 This is an improbable (at best) locked-room clue that the later Carr would have found a more believable way to manage (or avoid). Also, why would Brandon do this, in any event?

Notes for the Curious: "The Marked Bullet"

The reader is warned: This commentary discusses vital clues in Carr's *The Curse of the Bronze Lamp.* If you have not yet read that novel, the editor strongly encourages you to do so before reading the following remarks. This commentary also discusses the solution to Carr's first mystery story, presently unpublished. The editor deems this an acceptable trade-off.

In considering Carr's skill in handling this, his third mystery story, it is necessary to acquaint the reader with some facts concerning his first one, "The Ruby of Rameses," which was also Carr's first short story. Both are locked-room murder mysteries. In both, the weapon of choice is a gun with a Maxim silencer, inspired by Arthur B. Reeve's "The Silent Bullet"[1]—and the ability of which to elude the notice of witnesses at close range the teenage author optimistically overestimated. Both stories share an ending, too. Here are the closing sentences of "The Ruby of Rameses":

> I saw him convey a small, grayish pellet to his mouth,
> and the next instant he sank exhausted into a chair,
> his thin lips contriving to articulate:
> "I did what I did. It's too late for an antidote now!"

Like "The Ruby of Rameses" and "The House of Terror," "The Marked Bullet" is heavily reliant upon overwritten, stock language. Brandon Hall, like Heatherby House, has blank-eyed windows and Stygian darkness. Every portrait seems haunted, its ghostly subjects peering down at the living. Carr resorts several times to the gesture of a head being jerked up, which we will see perhaps a bit too often in his amateur fiction. We need not dwell on a young writer's shortcomings, but those in this story demonstrate that for an author already working to better effect in other genres—his next story would be "The Kindling Spark," a striking, youthful character study, one much better written—Carr still struggles to construct mysteries. The originality of this mystery is low, all the more so given that Carr reuses the same locked-room mechanics and the same closing lines from his first mystery. He seems a bit stalled.

To the degree that "The Marked Bullet" differs in technique from the earlier tales, it does so in its unoriginal resemblance to stories by Carolyn Wells and the "lady waltzers" of whom Carr was later dismissive:

---

1 Greene makes this connection to Reeve on page 17 of the biography.

> Many books written during that decade begin with the murder and present characters who are easily recognizable types—Chief Suspect, Least Likely Person, Suspicious Servant, Ne'er-Do-Well Nephew, Greedy Cousin, Helpless Damsel, and so on. The detective interviews all the suspects…and examines myriad bits of physical evidence. There is little tension in the plot, and indeed in some books almost nothing happens. This type of story has been called the "chess problem," or less kindly, the "humdrum."[2]

This noted, leveraging some "chess-problem" mechanics, "The Marked Bullet" moves closer to being a fair-play mystery than its predecessor. Carr provides several clues throughout the story that the reader can use to deduce the murderer's identity. In fairness, too, it is a better narrative: "The Marked Bullet" may be unoriginal in language and technique, but it is an interesting story. Carr also begins to demonstrate his comfort in developing such stories by having a greater number of relevant scenes played out over a substantially longer story than ever before: "The Marked Bullet" is almost twice as long as any Carr tale that preceded it.

Even more so than in "The House of Terror," Carr transgresses in this story what would later become his first commandment for the fair-play mystery: "The criminal shall never turn out to be the detective, or any servant, or any character whose thoughts we have been allowed to share." The story begins by sharing Handreth's thoughts, and Landridge has his own criminal culpability, too. Landridge's guilt is less surprising, Handreth's relatively more—but it is hardly a fully earned surprise, as the murderer's identity routinely will be in Carr's novels.

A new ploy here by Carr, used reasonably well, will be reused in *Grand Guignol* (and *It Walks By Night*): like the unnamed waiter who drops his tray after discovering the dead body in Fenelli's club, ruled out as a suspect because the fingers of his right hand have been amputated, Arthur Brandon is removed from suspicion in "The Marked Bullet" because of his missing right hand—but did Arthur earlier attempt to poison his uncle? This is another loose end, like Darworth's haunting of Geoffery Melford in "The House of Terror." The later Carr would always cleverly tie off such ends.

One more pattern alert readers will have detected is the young Carr's penchant for serving justice through the murderer's suicide. Three of his first four amateur stories leverage this plot device, one

---

2 Douglas Greene, *The Door to Doom and Other Detections*, Harper and Row, 1980, p. 14.

not even a detective tale. Better handled, this mechanism's use will extend into Carr's professional novels. (The editor omits listing specific titles for the obvious reason.)

Firmly on the black side of Carr's technique ledger, his work here with Landridge's cockney accent, including the moments in which it betrays the butler's agitation, is quite good.

A few clues, a minor new plot device, a cockney accent, expanded plot development and a better read overall are not very cogent recommendations for this early detective story—so what is of great interest to readers of Carr, if anything, about "The Marked Bullet"? It is that *this story is part of what is perhaps Carr's grandest joke in the re-use of his own materials during his entire career.* We have remarked in some detail how Carr liked playfully to reuse anything from a character name to a plot device to a premise. In *The Curse of the Bronze Lamp*, he does all three, and the object of that novel's homages, more than two decades later, is this story from Carr's high-school years.

In "The Marked Bullet," the lovely young heiress, Julia Mansfield, "disappears" by disguising herself as Milly, a maid in her own home. Despite noticing her patrician beauty, Constable Marden, when he questions Milly, fails to detect Miss Mansfield. *Julia Mansfield is also a character in* The Curse of the Bronze Lamp, *a shopkeeper among the suspects in the disappearance of Lady Helen Loring. In that novel, Lady Helen vanishes by assuming the false identity of Annie, the between-maid, in Lady Helen's own home, Severn Hall.* Like Julia in "The Marked Bullet," Lady Helen remains undetected in her own household merely by dint of her assumed station and demure conduct.

Both women, too, are the objects of attentions by murderous adventurers who scheme illegally to marry them for money: in this story, Handreth, and in *The Curse of the Bronze Lamp*, Sandy Robertson. (We would be remiss if we did not wonder whether Carr remembered Handreth in 1935 and gave him a sister, Lucia, in *Death-Watch.*)

Julia and Helen's disappearances are according to that most Shakespearean of devices: nobility disguising themselves as servants. (Like Shakespeare, Carr loved to play with disguise as a plot device, which readers will encounter many more times in his works.) Helen even echoes Shakespeare ("For the apparel oft proclaims the man," Hamlet, 1.3.72) with her rhetorical question, "Don't I know...that clothes and a name make the woman?" (p. 192)—a declaration with implicit credibility given the underlying English psychology ever since Queen Elizabeth's Sumptuary Laws.[3] H.M. observes that for

---

3 The 1574 law, the "Statutes of Apparel," followed by at least eight other royal proclamations, determined the colors and kinds of fabrics citizens were

Lady Helen Loring to complete her disguise effectively, she merely needs to "put on the clothes, drop her hoity-toity accent, and sling in a few words of dialect" (p. 193). In "The Marked Bullet" and *The Curse of the Bronze Lamp* (among other works), we must appreciate the importance of Carr's eye and ear for distinctions between economic classes and his practical exploitation of them.

permitted to wear based upon their wealth and social rank. These regulations were repealed in the early seventeenth century, but even without the force of law, their influence lingered for generations.

Ashes of Clues (1923)

I

The long corridor outside the dressing rooms was deserted now. A single dusty electric bulb glowed yellowly at the far end, making ghosts of the gaunt props that lolled beside the wings. A door slammed somewhere distant, and quick footsteps echoed through the great theater. Picking his way carefully along, a man traversed the hall. He paused at the illuminated door and knocked. In the long silence he tapped on the floor nervously with his cane. In the great, high darkness the echoes of his own footfalls still seemed to come back faintly to him. There were creakings; water dripped slowly somewhere.

"Come in," a quick voice snapped beyond the door.

The man hesitated a moment; then he stretched out his hand, turned the knob and slipped in, closing the door after him. The room was narrow and ill-ventilated; tobacco smoke writhed about the green-shaded lamp above the dressing table. Chair tilted back against the wall, the only other occupant of the apartment sat gazing at him. The newcomer's eyes strayed over the floor, littered with withered costumes. A bottle of ink lay overturned on a white toga, staining the linen with a great blue blotch. A greasepaint box, stepped on and smashed, had rolled almost to the threshold. Odds and ends of property were stuffed into corners; a bust of Julius Caesar was draped with a red wig, and a pair of muddy shoes sprawled on a delicate gilt chair. The newcomer's eyes ran over the untidy room quickly; then they fastened themselves on the man who sat motionless opposite.

"Well?" the arrival said. "I'm here. What do you want?"

"A great deal." The harsh voice rasped back startlingly. "Sit down."

Slowly the newcomer backed into a chair. He regarded the other furtively. The latter stared hard at him for a moment; then he reached over and pulled open a drawer of the dressing table. His hand remained inside.

"There's always been a great likeness between us," he went on. "A touch here and there—you'll acknowledge, I think, my artistry in making up—and not even your wife could tell us apart...or your friends."

The other looked up suddenly. A startled flash showed in his eyes.

"What are you getting at?" he demanded. "I came here tonight just to oblige you, Saunders—"

"To oblige me!" Saunders snapped. He leaned forward, and his voice shook. "To oblige me! Shut up!" His voice had been rising steadily, until it resembled something between a scream and a snarl. He flung over his chair and leaped up, crouching like a panther before his companion. "You used to be called 'Maddon' when I knew you. There was a little business out in Arkansas...I got five years and you came east. No, you weren't mistaken; I could be dangerous, all right. You'll find out just how dangerous...Sit down!" His hand whipped out of the drawer, and it held an automatic pistol. "You listen to me. I'm going to kill you. You used to say I could impersonate anything on two legs. I've impersonated you a lot since you got worth it...and now I'm going to do it for good!"

"Saunders!" his guest shouted. He sprang backward and groped for the door, overturning a table with a crash that rolled and thundered through the theater. He looked like a man on the scaffold waiting for the trap to drop. "Saunders...have you gone—"

"A few changes in my appearance and nobody can tell us apart," the actor cut in breathlessly. "Then I'll step into your place; and I can fill it, too! You're just a common crook with an education. When the first performance of Brin's new production goes on tomorrow, apparently I will be missing. I'll hide your body after I've taken all the things you have on you, and if they do find it they'll take it for me. Do you understand? It will probably decay before they come across it, and that—"

The other had spun round and rushed for the door. Fire spurted from Saunders' weapon; the report thundered along the walls. A tiny, blackened hole appeared in the back of the man's head, and his body crumpled suddenly. The dressing table chattered as the inert heap thudded to the floor. Across the room the smoke hung silently.

For a moment Saunders stood motionless, staring down at the huddled thing on the floor. He swallowed hard; with a little shudder he shook himself, glanced about cautiously, and thrust the pistol into his pocket. Hesitatingly he crossed to the side of the dead man. Once he turned to glance at himself in a mirror, and he noticed that he was pale. But it was the likeness between the still face peering up at him and his own that held him.

He lit a cigarette to quiet his jangling nerves, pacing back and forth, his lips forming soundless words. Then he sat down resolutely at the dressing table. From a drawer he brought forth a curious collection of articles, which he laid systematically before him. Settling to work, his quick fingers moved like lightning. In the powder-dusted light his lean face was slowly undergoing a transformation beneath the cosmetics. Lightly, almost imperceptibly, he applied them, until, as he rose with a grunt of satisfaction, the likeness to the countenance of the dead man was startling. Saunders' theatrical genius was in impersonation, and he knew that he could fill the role he was calling on himself to play. Of a sudden his old personality dropped away. He was willing himself into another nature.

Before the mirror he posed, walked, gestured, and rattled out fragments of conversation in a voice that was anything but his own sharp, harsh tone. Satisfied, he produced an immaculate evening suit from a wardrobe and donned it. Now the clay had been shaped, and the transformation was complete. With an effort he went through the murdered man's pockets, swiftly, surely, transferring the articles therein to his own person.

Suddenly he jerked himself upright, his heart giving a sickening start. A door banged to somewhere in the building. Panic crept into his blood, but he held himself steady. He stepped to the door and locked it. Quickly he crossed the room, pulled aside the curtain of the wardrobe, and disclosed the stolid face of a high iron safe set into the wall. The dusty door creaked open. Saunders picked up the limp body and trundled it across to the safe. There was no time to lose now. He flung the articles of clothing in after the body; the pistol he thrust into his pocket. Clanging shut the door, he twirled the combination knob and stood leaning weakly against the wall, his throat throbbing. A last look he gave about the apartment; he trod out his cigarette and caught up the cane and gloves of the other man. Then he snapped off the light. Unsteadily he groped toward the door, opened it, and peered cautiously outside. It closed softly after him. Only the moon struggled through a grimy window, dripping a white pool on the other, darker stain on the floor.

II

Detective Sergeant Mattison took several strides about the room. Then he turned back to the nervous group at the door.

"It looks like murder," he said grimly. "When did you last see him?"

"Yesterday afternoon." The stage manager, flustered and disheveled, wheeled round excitedly. "One of the most important parts… and the understudy is horrible!" He gestured helplessly. "If it gets out before the performance the whole thing will be wrecked. Senator Brin's money and Mr. Maynard's reputation—"

"And a man's life," Mattison interrupted coldly. "Do you see this bloodstain? Murder, I tell you…well, Williams?"

The policeman who had lately entered shook his head.

"We've searched the whole place, sir. No sign of him here."

"Senator Brin!" It was the stage manager's agonized voice. A newcomer had shoved through the knot of awed performers at the door.

He flashed a startled glance about from beneath his level brows.

"The police? What is it?"

"Mr. Mattison says it's murder!" wailed the stage manager. "And you're likely to lose every cent you have in the production if the thing gets out... It affects audiences something terrible!"

"Murder!" the other rapped. He glanced about the room. "Saunders?"

"I'm afraid so, Senator," Mattison put in. "Mr. Delancy, here, called me in; it hasn't gotten out yet...and you needn't worry. There may be nothing in it. But we can't find the man Saunders. He wasn't at his lodging house last night; and there's blood—"

Brin sank into a chair. He raked the floor nervously with his cane.

"I see no reason why the performance shouldn't go on. It may be another of Saunders' strange ideas. What do you think, Delancy?"

"It isn't very pleasant," the tall, blond young man at Mattison's elbow said slowly, "but, as you say, I think we should go ahead." He drew himself up a little. "My wife and I will try to make up for any deficiencies in the cast."

Brin's eyes strayed to the fragile beauty of the slim girl who stood behind Delancy; then back to the man whose meteoric rise to fame had made him invaluable to the producer. He nodded. "We can go on, I guess."

"Senator!" Another figure brushed into the room. John Maynard crossed to where the other sat. "They tell me something's happened."

"Nothing that will interfere seriously with the play," Brin assured him quickly. "It may prove a grave matter to the police. Saunders has disappeared. There's blood on the floor—"

"You mean he committed sui—"

"No. Murder, Mr. Mattison of the police department thinks." Brin drew out his watch. "Seven-thirty. It's all right, John. Your play will get over; don't worry. In an hour we begin. Better hustle along."

Slowly the members of the company filed out. Delancy put his wife before him and took a long look about the dressing room before he closed the door and left Brin and Maynard with the detective.

"Lord! I was scared!" Maynard confessed. "The way the stage manager talked over the 'phone I thought the roof had fallen in or something...and it isn't so trivial, at that. But I was up in the air. Tonight means whether I'm a complete success or a grand flop as a playwright. What's that?"

Mattison had suddenly swooped down on something among the litter. He held up the coat of an ordinary dark suit. An exploring hand in one pocket disclosed a package of cigarettes and two letters addressed to Mr. George Saunders. Mattison stared hard at the former.

"He was a genius, that man," Maynard asserted soberly. "He had the most wonderful gift of impersonation I ever saw...he used to do tricks imitating prominent people before Brin here dug him up."

"He did?" Mattison's head jerked up. He frowned in thought for a moment, and then he smiled grimly.

Brin rose a trifle awkwardly.

"You'll have to excuse me," he apologized. "I've a box—wife and daughter and a couple of friends. I'd like to see them in. And no word of this matter, if you please, until after the performance." He went out quickly, leaving Mattison gazing thoughtfully after him.

"Look here!" The detective swung quickly to Maynard. "Is there a photo of this man Saunders around here anywhere?"

"There ought to be," the other answered. "You want it for the papers? I don't know...I think all of them he had are in character."

Mattison was already rummaging, in the dressing table drawer. He held aloft a bundle of faded photos triumphantly. "This the man?"

Maynard nodded, and again the smile played over Mattison's lips.

"Good Lord!" he exclaimed. For a moment he stood lost in thought. Then: "Tell me: what is this play of yours about? What was Saunders?"

"A sort of fantastic conception. Modeled more or less on this Egyptian craze.[1] There's a temple scene. Delancy as the high priest and Mildred Delancy as the high priestess evoke the spirit of the future from a sarcophagus... It's the wild sort of thing that gets over nowadays."

"Good!" Mattison's eyes were shining now. "And Saunders?"

"Was the spirit that came out of the mummy case. Why?"

Mattison was very grim, but there was a ring of triumph in his tone.

"I have an idea," he announced slowly, "that before morning I'll be arresting somebody for murder...no, don't ask me. I'm taking a long chance, and staking everything on one throw. As I say, I have an idea, and if it's the right one..."

---

1 Only the year before Carr wrote this story, the British archaeologist Howard Carter had discovered the tomb of the 18th Dynasty Pharaoh Tutankhamun—King Tut. The discovery of the boy king and the alleged Pharaoh's curse ignited global interest. Newspapers vied, and paid big fees, to secure exclusive stories regarding Carter's excavation. In popular culture, Egyptian motifs emerged in clothing, hairstyles, on jewelry and fabrics, and even in architecture. Young John Carr would have been exposed to Egyptian-themed hit songs and stage performances, too.

III

A murmur rippled over the vast, dim, blurred audience. On the great stage the weirdest effects of lighting and a scene painter's art were woven into a subtle, exquisite, haunting pattern. It had all the mystery and uncanny suggestion of buried, forgotten vaults and the weaving magic of Egypt. In the cool gloom a single sinuous figure flashed back the blue of the footlights. Shadows scampered and were gone. There was a breath of music in the air. The ghosts of the past seemed to move and glide about the stolid sarcophagus in the foreground.

Even Mattison, standing in the darkness of the wings, with Maynard beside him, straining to catch the slightest hint of approval from the packed house, was impressed. Ghostly figures flashed past him in the gloom as the property men toiled endlessly to produce the carefully studied effects on the stage. Now another figure had moved into the foreground: Delancy, tall, straight, handsome, imperious. The eerie throb of drums began to swirl and send a tremble through the spectators. Slowly, lithely, perfectly, the woman began to dance, her body moving with the sinuous ease of a snake. Suddenly she darted down and flung wide the swinging lid of the sarcophagus as it stood upright.

Simultaneously the great velvet curtains rushed together: a blinding shaft of light ripped through the gloom; and Mattison's handcuffs flashed and clicked as there rolled from the mummy case the dead body of John Maynard...

IV

"From the time I found the cigarettes I knew that Saunders had not died," Mattison explained to an interested audience in the dressing room. "Upon the surface of the bloodstains on the floor there were some fine particles of cigarette ashes. That meant that a cigarette had been smoked there after the murder. Then when I found the half-smoked end itself, I proved it to my own satisfaction. In Saunders' coat there was a pack of that same brand: very unusual; Cuban, I think. So it was fairly plain that since a murderer would not likely smoke his victim's cigarettes, and since that particular kind was so rare here as to be almost unique, that Saunders was not the victim, but in all likelihood the assassin, granting, of course, that a murder had been committed. When I learned of Saunders' phenomenal success at impersonation, and saw his photo, which is so like Mr. Maynard, I was more than suspicious. Lately used cosmetics scattered on the dressing table confirmed it. But the final stroke was when I unearthed the safe. I communicated with Brin, who alone outside of Saunders had known the combination, and there we found Maynard's body. But the likeness was really so strong between Maynard and Saunders that the latter could not swear that it was the actor whom we found in the safe—so you see there was no really tangible proof. I had recourse to the very theatrical experiment, which surprised a confession from Saunders and in reality did not injure the play itself, inasmuch as the audience assumed it as part of the action. It was bad taste, perhaps, but it was necessary. The surroundings all went to help.

"The cleverest of them slip up, you see. If I hadn't found the ashes on the bloodstain he might have gone on in Maynard's place—until somebody else found him out. Anyhow, in an investigation you can't afford to discard anything—not even ashes of clues."

Notes for the Curious: "Ashes of Clues"

The premiere (and unfortunately, only) issue in 1995 of the John Dickson Carr Appreciation Society's journal, *Notes for the Curious* (edited by Tony Medawar, who has of course been a leader in digging up out-of-print or never-professionally printed Golden Age nuggets) reprinted "Ashes of Clues." It included a prefatory note by Douglas Greene:

> John D. Carr III (as he then styled himself) was not quite 17 years old when "Ashes of Clues" was published in the October 1923 issue of *The Hill Record*. It may be accounted doubtful that in later years Carr would have wanted any of his apprentice stories made available, and modern readers must look at this story with some indulgence.
>
> Its main interest is twofold: the young Carr's attempt to manipulate a complex plot in a short space; and the many elements in the story that he would re-use in his later works. The structure of the tale is sophisticated. It's likely that Carr had read R. Austin Freeman's *The Singing Bone,* which, though published in Britain in 1912, did not appear until 1923 in the United States. This celebrated book introduced the inverted detective story in which, in the first part, the reader sees the crime committed and, in the second, follows the detective's investigations. The challenge for the reader is to anticipate the mistakes (leading to clues) that will reveal the guilty party.
>
> "Ashes of Clues" is an inverted detective story – the first and only time Carr attempted that form. Indeed the story has an additional challenge that Freeman never tried. We know who the murderer is but we don't know who he has become.
>
> The mistake that the murderer makes, revealed daringly in the title of the story, is a neatly devised clue even though other evidence gathered by the official investigator, Detective Sergeant Mattison, is concealed from us.
>
> Much of Carr's later style is already evident in "Ash-

es of Clues." The tale begins with plenty of atmosphere: the "gaunt props" outside a dressing-room
are "ghosts"; there are creaks and drips as a man
walks through the darkness, tapping (like later Carr
characters) with his cane. The young Carr cannot describe costumes tossed on the floor merely as in a
disordered pile; no, they are 'withered'. And, at the
end of the story, we hear the 'eerie throb of drums'.

The dramatic conclusion is everything that Bencolin would have appreciated, as in the first Bencolin
short story ("The Shadow of the Goat") and the first
Bencolin novel (Grand Guignol/It Walks By Night),
the story is based on masks. Carr was always convinced of the power of masks (whether literal masks
or make-up, or merely changing behavior) to hide or
even, in a sense, create a person. Some of this must
come from the early influence of Thomas W. Hanshew's extraordinary sleuth, Cleek the Man of the
Forty Faces, who – literally – could become anyone;
but more fundamentally, it is involved with Carr's
own presenting of masks to protect himself from the
outside world. In the practical, detective-story sense,
this attitude allowed him to make almost anyone the
criminal in one of his books, no matter how they appear to the reader.

"Ashes of Clues" can be read as an entertaining story in itself (certainly for an author of Carr's tender
years) but it is, I think, better read for its foreshadowing of the power as a writer that John Dickson Carr
would eventually achieve.

The editor has reprinted Greene's brief preface in its entirety
because, predictably, Greene touches pithily on nearly all the points
of interest concerning "Ashes of Clues." Greene's remarks may bear
some amplification--for instance, observing this tale's relationship to
"The House of Terror," "The Will-o'-the-Wisp," and "The Marked
Bullet" in their earlier use of masks (as did "The Ruby of Rameses"),
and perhaps the more explicit available comparison between the pivotal disguise in this story and the one in *Grand Guignol*, about which
the impersonator might have offered the same utterance as Saunders:
"not even your wife could tell us apart...or your friends"—but there
is not an excess of observations to add to Greene's.

A second point of Greene's worthy elaboration is that we witness

Carr ambitiously trying to break out of his apprenticeship in this story by hiding the murderer's new identity until the climax. Yes, Carr puts his own twist upon the inverted format this way, a format to which he would not return (at least, not precisely). So the format is not the path out of his apprenticeship. Rather, it is the already repeating disguise motif in which we perceive "the power as a writer that John Dickson Carr would eventually achieve."

This device may be the first strong hint of Chestertonian influence in Carr's detective fiction; Chesterton often featured disguise as a confounding element. By the time he wrote "Ashes of Clues," Carr had already encountered this ploy in the Father Brown stories "The Blue Cross," "The Invisible Man," and "The Duel of Dr. Hirsch." Of course, Carr's enthusiasm for Chesterton only increased: three years later, in the book review section of *The Haverfordian*, Carr contributed a review of Chesterton's recently issued *The Incredulity of Father Brown*:

> Here we have G. K. taking rabbits out of clerical hats in his most mystifying manner. These are the best detective stories of the year, and not even Conan Doyle has ever come within a pistol-shot or a knife-throw of them. We have haunted castles, winged daggers, vanishing men—and over it all the genial, lovable priest who plays detective.[1]

Years later, in "The Grandest Game in the World" (p. 20), Carr defending the element of disguise, would cite one of the stories in *The Incredulity of Father Brown*, "The Dagger with Wings," as an exemplar of exploiting disguise.

By the time he wrote that review of Chesterton, Carr was writing his Bencolin stories. As Greene observed of their quality, as compared to this ("Ashes of Clues" was Carr's penultimate high-school mystery, and better than the one that followed it, "E'en Though It Be a Cross"):

> Carr's detective tales at The Hill School had been the least accomplished of all his juvenile works, but although the solutions often strain credulity, the early cases of Henri Bencolin, prefect of police of Paris, would be worthy of many writers past the juvenile state and aspiring to become masters. This development came about because Carr had outgrown the Hanshew period of his interest in impossible crimes and had absorbed the methods of G.K. Chesterton... And

---

1 *The Haverfordian*, Haverford College, 1926 (XLVI/2), p. 81.

like Father Brown, Henri Bencolin understands the
crime by re-creating it in his mind. (p. 50)

In the present collection we will also, formalistically, witness Carr
breaking more out of his detective-story apprenticeship with "The
New Canterbury Tales," in which Carr cleverly turns the framing narrative itself into a fair-play detective story. Carr's collegiate Bencolin
tales were "of such maturity"[2] that Greene published them in 1980's
The Door to Doom and Other Detections. "The New Canterbury Tales,"
an unconventional Bencolin mystery, stretches further beyond the
boundaries of its borrowed model than "Ashes of Clues" does. It
transforms, not tweaks, the literary structure it adopts.

Mattison's tracing of the physical evidence in "Ashes of Clues"
recalls a passage from one of Carr's most influential and favorite
books, Stevenson's *New Arabian Nights.* In that book, a young clergyman's latent skills of observation and deduction unexpectedly quick-
en, entangling him with international criminals:

> The detective that there is in all of us awoke and be-
> came clamant in the bosom of Mr. Rolles; and with
> a brisk, eager step, that bore no resemblance to his
> usual gait, he proceeded to make the circuit of the
> garden...[H]is eye was at once arrested by a broken
> rosebush and marks of trampling on the mould.
> He looked up, and saw scratches on the brick, and
> a rag of trouser floating from a broken bottle. This,
> then, was the mode of entrance chosen by Mr. Rae-
> burn's particular friend...The young clergyman whis-
> tled softly to himself as he stooped to examine the
> ground. He could make out where Harry had landed
> from his perilous leap; he recognised the flat foot of
> Mr. Raeburn where it had sunk deeply in the soil as
> he pulled up the Secretary by the collar; nay, on a
> closer inspection, he seemed to distinguish the marks
> of groping fingers, as though something had been
> spilt abroad and eagerly collected.[3]

Of course, we can similarly detect Poe, Leroux, and Conan Doyle
behind Mattison's investigation of the physical clues. Stevenson is
not an inventor here, although he is an apt instructor for the young
Carr. The reader of "Ashes of Clues" witnesses Greene's point that
"Carr's grasp on the fundamentals of short-story construction be-

---

2 Douglas Greene, *Fell and Foul Play,* International Polygonics, Ltd., 1991, p. 2.
3 *New Arabian Nights,* Charles Scribner's Sons, 1910, p. 151.

came more and more sure as he wrote tales at the Hill Preparatory School and Haverford College."[4] Carr's handling in the story of a crime-scene investigation, of clue placement, and of the detective's solution are all improved in "Ashes of Clues," if not yet especially original. As Carr comes more to embrace Chesterton as a model in his subsequent detection stories, he begins finding his own, original voice, while still drawing on multiple influences so as not merely to be imitating Chesterton in the way he earlier had the Hanshews, Reeve, and others. Carr also begins daring to invent his own miracle-crime mechanics, or perhaps to draw more upon those hundred and twenty plots he claimed to have outlined when he was eleven.

While Bencolin would have appreciated Mattison's dramatic flair in unmasking the murderer, he would have disapproved heartily of the Detective Sergeant's methods: "When you add the evidence of the cigarette ashes…you add a couple of details which never interested me."[5]

4 *Fell and Foul Play*, International Polygonics, Ltd., 1991, p. 2.

5 From *Grand Guignol*…read on!

The Blindfold Quest (1923)

I
Adventure Boards the Train

"That," said Carter, pointing to a pink dot on the map, "is Bro-kovia. The pinpoint there is St. Spike, the capital. That's where we're headed for."

"But what's the idea?" demanded Cullan. "Why do you want to go running off to a little country nobody ever heard of, when we haven't even been to Rome or Naples yet? Let it go until we see everything else."

Carter rolled up the map.

"If it's like Graustark[1] or Ruritania[2]," he answered with an air of finality, "we're in for a hot time. In the stories the Americans always go to some little kingdom and start a revolution or marry a princess or something. Anyway, they always raise the devil. And when I tell you about this place, you'll agree that it's just like the ones Mc-Cutcheon and Anthony Hope wrote about. It ought to make the star experience of our trip to Europe."

"Blaah!" Baire had been hunched up in a corner of the stuffy, ill-lighted railway compartment, half dozing despite the rattle and bump of the train. Now he shook himself, opened his eyes, swung viciously at a fly that had flirted with him throughout the entire journey from Paris, and swore. "You've got a lot of idiotic notions from the movies…"

"Do you remember the Mademoiselle Ness we met at Monte Carlo?" Carter asked quietly. "You know—the Lady Katherine Ness. You got drunk and told her father you were the sacred white elephant of Siam[3]…"

---

1 The eponymous fictional country of George Barr McCutcheon's 1901 adventure novel (with five sequels, the last in 1927). Graustark is less well-known than Anthony Hope's Ruritania series, but McCutcheon's novel is more directly influential upon Carr's story than Hope's.

2 The fictional country featured in a trilogy of adventure novels by Anthony Hope between 1894-1898, the first of which is *The Prisoner of Zenda*. "Ruritanian" has come into use to denote minor/unspecified European countries, especially fictional ones (like Graustark) participating in this literary genre.

3 An ironic metaphor, since, although venerated, these rare albino elephants were malicious gifts: the kings of Siam gave white elephants to make them

"I did not!" shouted the other.

"Anyway, you remember her. She's from Brokovia. Her father is a duke or something."

Baire sat up very straight.

"Then we're going to Brokovia." He glared at Cullan. "If you say one word against that I'll break your neck... How do we get there, Bob?"

"Oh, hell!" Cullan said explosively.

"We can get a night train from Bordeaux." Carter began to study a timetable. "We'll be pulling in there in five or ten minutes. That will give us time to get the ten-thirty to St. Spike. It's just over the border."

Cullan groaned. "Idiots!" he enunciated very clearly and very forcibly. "Anyway, you won't get to see that girl!"

"Shut up!" ordered Baire. "You ain't romantic. Besides, we're not going to this burg just to see the Lady Katherine. What sort of place is it, by the way?"

Carter began to rummage around in the newspapers which strewed the floor of the compartment. Finally he smoothed out a copy of *Le Journal* and pointed to an obscure item.

"Tomorrow at high noon King Gustave IX of Brokovia will be married to the Princess Jeanne of Barnehasset, a neighboring country, in the Cathedral at St. Spike," he explained. "Everybody of consequence in the two kingdoms will be present. The marriage is a diplomatic move, I guess. The two countries have always been rather on the outs, and this union will quiet them if anything will." Another plunge into the papers produced an illustrated weekly, on one of whose pages two pictures stood out prominently. He pointed to them. "King Gustave and his bride. What do you think of him?"

"Looks like a yegg[4]," announced Cullan, scrutinizing the grim and austere figure in uniform. "But the girl is a pip.[5] It's a crime that a girl like that should get tied up to this roughneck. If we were heroes in a story, now..."

He paused abruptly. The outer door of the compartment banged open in a gush of rain, and the smoky light glistened on the mackintosh of the man who entered from the running board. He closed the door slowly and put down the valise he had been carrying. Then he pulled off his sodden cap.

"My apologies, messieurs. Messieurs will pardon the intrusion." He was breathing heavily, but his voice was low and clear. His eyes,

---

financial burdens upon the recipients and ruin them. That is why our modern phrase implies an expensive or unproductive undertaking.

4 A criminal, specifically a safecracker or robber.

5 Early twentieth-century slang for an attractive person.

oddly bright and restless, darted about the tiny room.

"Oh—hello," Baire greeted. "Sit down. You're the first man in France I've heard speak English intelligently. What'd you do? Hop the train?"

The newcomer looked out of the streaming window. The lights of Bordeaux were springing up wanly in the darkness. Suddenly he whipped round once more, and his hand, jerked out of the pocket of his coat, held a squat, ugly automatic pistol.

"When this train stops at Bordeaux," he said harshly, "certain men will enter this compartment. They will search my luggage. The contents of that valise must not be found in my possession. You will put those contents in your own effects. Then…"

"Now, look here, Jesse James," interrupted Carter, "put that thing away. It may be loaded. Let me tell you—you're a bum crook… Hey! Wait a minute!" He edged away as the weapon waved toward him. "I didn't mean anything! But if you're trying to get past the cops at Bordeaux, why didn't you jump off the train when you could?"

"You will please keep silent," came the steely voice. "If these men do not find certain things in my possession, they will conclude that they have made a mistake. You will be above suspicion as American tourists. You will not be searched."

"He ain't entirely dumb," declared Cullan, shaking his head wisely. "He knew we were Americans… But he's pretty dense. Why, even a French cop ought to know…"

"Throw up your hands, please!" The command crackled out in French from the doorway. A startled glance behind showed them the glare of the station through the rain-misted windows. The train was rumbling to a stop. And a slender, wiry little man was digging the stranger in the back with an ominous hard something.

"Search him! Here—the valise on the floor!" As the words snapped across the room two gendarmes edged through the door. "Drop that weapon. Your handcuffs, please."

One of the officers opened the stranger's satchel, glanced inside, and nodded. The little man came slowly around to face his prisoner, and the hand that held his revolver was very steady.

"The crown jewels, monsieur?" asked the gendarme in a voice that trembled.

"Yes. This man is Frederick Brotheurs, whom I had the honor of arresting once before in the Villond pearl robbery." Suddenly the little official swung around, and his eyes roved over the three faces of the travelers. A startled flash showed in his eyes, but he spoke grimly to Baire:

"And so! How do you come to figure in this?"

"Damfino,"[6] the other confessed. "Outside of the fact that this bird appears to be a terrible crook, I haven't the slightest idea..."

"Arrest him," snapped the little man. "Two birds with one stone. This is Rex Mayland. The American police will be glad to get him. He's wanted for murder in the States...and he has a hand in the theft of the Brokovian crown jewels!"

Baire leaped to his feet. He shook his finger in the officer's face. "I'm a patient guy," he shouted, "but there are limits! A joke is a joke. Look here, Sherlock—if you think you can pull any funny business with me..."

"You have always been a sportsman, Mayland. At least, you have had that reputation. And now that you're caught fairly, you squeal. Put out your hands!"

"You're crazy as hell!" yelled the accused one. Then he stopped abruptly as Carter laid a hand on his sleeve. One word passed between them, swift and comprehensive. Baire nodded, and Carter went on in English:

"I don't think this hick understands the language. Here's our chance for the Graustark stuff. And we could easily enough prove our identity. So, if we don't care, and we have the nerve..." He sprang up suddenly. *"Let's go!"*

The little man's pistol spat fire as Carter plunged across the compartment. A sweep of Baire's arm and the smoky oil lamp crashed from its bracket, blotting out the scene in darkness. Another streak of flame darted across the black void; then Carter's grip slid into place, and he sent the police official spinning across the room. There was a long rattle of falling glass as he disappeared through the door, and Carter, leaping up and around, was in time to see Baire and one of the gendarmes lurch out after him. They reeled drunkenly across the slippery platform into a babbling, rushing crowd that pressed about the train, and pitched to the floor in a writhing tangle. Brotheurs, cool and grim-faced, had rammed his pistol into the ribs of the remaining gendarme and fired. Without a sound the officer crumpled forward. Then Brotheurs caught up the satchel. He was half through the door when Cullan's quick dive brought him down. A lightning twist, and the two were up. Brotheurs, clubbing his pistol with his free hand, drove it into his opponent's face and wrenched himself free. Baire appeared through the crowd in time to crash full and square into the flying man with the valise as he made for the maze of open track beyond which a long

---

6 This is an early twentieth-century portmanteau (the combination of multiple words into one), i.e., "Damned if I know." Examples routinely in use today include the words smog, brunch, and stash.

line of arc lamps glowed whitely through the downpour. The criminal recoiled against the side of the car, whirled, and plunged across the rails. For a moment Baire stared after him. Then Carter and Cullan were at his side.

"Brotheurs!" Cullan gasped out. "He shot that cop…and he's got the valise!"

Behind them they could see at last the train guard and a swarm of gendarmes elbowing through the awed onlookers. A whistle shrilled; somebody shouted for them to stop.

"Hit for the street!" Baire cried. "There—the way he's going!"

Blindly the three stumbled across the tracks. The rails shimmered in the dancing yellow blurs from the lanterns of the pursuers; once a firearm cracked, and a track light ahead of them vanished with a jangle of falling glass. Cullan was staggering when they reached the embankment over which Brotheurs had disappeared, but he fought his way grimly to the top and stumbled to the pavement. Under an arc lamp just ahead stood a long, heavy Renault, silent and sinister. Brotheurs had gained the running board of the car as the three reached the street; then Baire was upon him. Off balance, the other flung up his arms, reeled backward, and rolled over on the sidewalk. Carter had assisted Cullan into the front seat; simultaneously, Baire jerked himself free of the fighting figure and swung to the running board. In one moment lights shot up over the embankment as the headmost pursuers scrambled into view; in the next, the heavy automobile plunged away from the curb. Down the deserted street it roared. From behind came the short, sharp spit of a pistol; there was a rush and wheeze of air, and the speeding machine lunged to one side.

"He got a tire!" Carter bellowed.

"Never mind the tires!" Baire bellowed back. "Give her all she can take!"

The din of pursuit was growing fainter. They had reeled around a corner like a drunken avalanche, and now Carter decreased the speed of the car. His companions were huddled in the front seat. In the dim light of the dashboard lamp their faces were white and strained; a thin trickle of crimson was crawling down Cullan's cheek where Brotheurs' weapon had gashed his forehead, and the hand with which he held a handkerchief to it shook despite himself. Then Carter's gaze strayed down to the floor, and an exclamation shot between his lips. There, where Brotheurs had thrown it, lay the valise they had last seen in their compartment on the Bordeaux train!

II
Death in the Night

Baire bent over and picked up the bag. There was an ugly crimson blotch on the side, and he shuddered a little. Snapping back the catch, he peered inside. His hand, diving within, brought up a tangled string of pearls that rippled and blazed through his fingers like a stream of liquid fire. He let them trickle back into the bag, which, as Cullan glanced down, seemed to flash and glow from the interior with an infernal light of its own.

"Gems!" Baire's fingers trembled slightly as he reclosed the valise. "Thousands of dollars' worth! The question is..."

"The question is," Cullan cut in suddenly and vigorously, "where are we going, and what do we intend to do about all this? Who does this car belong to, anyhow? And how soon will it be before every cop in France is wired to watch for us? Brotheurs doesn't have these stones. They'll think we stole them...and he'll probably accuse one of us of murdering that cop! Lord, what a mess!"

"Shut up!" growled Carter. "They would have accused us anyway—and then that nut got it into his head that Baire was some kind of a crook. The thing we've got to do to square ourselves is to go to Brokovia and return these jewels... Isn't that where the hick detective said they were from? Well, they'll be glad to get them, if that marriage is tomorrow. Without the crown jewels they'd sort of be in the soup. In about five minutes the word will be all over the city to watch for us. Our best bet is to get out of here right away. It isn't very far to St. Spike, and if the roads are passable somebody should be able to tell us how to get there."

"Oh, yes," agreed Cullan sarcastically. "Why don't you ask a cop?"

"It was the worst fool trick I ever did." Baire drew a deep breath. "We jumped out of the frying pan into the fire. But it might be worse. All our luggage except a couple of grips is checked to Bordeaux. We can get it. Somehow, I sort of like this thing, dangerous or not."

"You're absolutely off!" Cullan asserted from the fullness of his heart. "I swear I never saw anybody...Well, get out of it to suit yourself. We'll get the jug[7] anyhow. I'm going back and lie down. That fellow gave me an awful wallop. Believe me, if I ever see him again..."

He was steadily climbing back into the tonneau. His exploring fingers brushed something on the floor of the car, and he leaped

---

7 "Jug" is slang for jail, of course. In the eighteenth century, Newgate Prison was nicknamed "The stone jug."

back suddenly.

"There—there's somebody lying on the floor back here!" he shrilled, his voice rising hysterically. "Look—there! Quick—strike a match!"

Baire spun about. There was a sinister dark bulk on the floor, and with unsteady fingers he struck a match. As the yellow flame burst out Cullan shrank back with a low cry. Huddled on the floor was the body of a man, face twisted up grotesquely to the light. Baire had seen that lean, bearded countenance, now rigid in death, only once before, but recognition flashed home to him in an instant. Here, sprawled in the back of a stolen car and with a tiny, blackened bullet hole just above the right temple, lay His Majesty, King Gustave of Brokovia!

III

The Girl at the Palace

Down the broad Avenue of Triumph, white and dazzling in the hard glare of the sunlight, swelled a vast, inarticulate roar. St. Spike seemed filled with a rushing surge of sound that swept through its shaded streets from the Square of the Saints, where the spires of the Cathedral towered, a mighty monument to the majesty of Brokovia, to the slim, white turrets of the royal palace on the hill above the city. A great black sea of people tossed on either side of the Avenue of Triumph; the flag of Brokovia flashed above it and snapped free in the wind from the buildings which lined the thoroughfare. Somewhere a band crashed thunderously into the final inspiring bars of the national anthem. Sharp above the swell of sound cracked horses' hoofs on the asphalt; the scarlet and gold[8] of the royal guard blazed along the fringe of the crowd as the soldiers on duty there wheeled their mounts about to keep the people off the street.

Unseen and unheralded, a dusty Renault car spun around the corner of a side street and shot up the long hill toward the palace. A grim, heavy-eyed figure clung to the wheel, keeping the machine on the road despite its limp from a blown tire, and despite the strain of the terrific pace it had been keeping up. The high, delicate wall of the palace grounds sprang up through the trees; its iron-grilled gates were flung wide, and stiff soldiers like dummies stood on either side. One of the dummies suddenly came to life as the car thundered up the drive; the soldier waved his gun and shouted something unintelligible when the Renault rocketed past him, roaring up the drive like

---

8 Reminiscent of the Graustarkian royal guards' uniforms, who wear "tight red trousers, shiny boots, close-fitting black coat with gilt trimmings, and…red cap." *Graustark*, Grosset & Dunlap, 1901, p. 133. All subsequent excerpts are drawn from the same edition.

a whirlwind. Grimy and silent, Baire and Cullan stared straight ahead at the white brilliance of the palace, appearing through the trees like a fairy creation from the Arabian Nights. Soldiers in red and gold were springing up all around them, but the speeding auto did not slow down. Another and more sinister machine had swung up through the gates now: a long, low-hung black hulk bearing the insignia of the Bordeaux police department. Under a long archway tore the Renault; Carter rammed in brake and clutch, and it skidded to a stop. Staggering a little, the three leaped to the ground, hesitated a moment before the huge doorway, and then plunged inside.

A desert of polished floor seemed to stretch almost to infinity; they got the impression of a vast, dim, vaulted roof; of excited attendants rushing toward them; then Baire shrilled something and they leaped toward the spreading stairway, like a carpeted shaft down from the skies. Swords were flashing in the hall below them; shouts roared up the stairway and more dummies in red and gold were swarming up the steps, but they rushed blindly on. On the landing Carter hesitated; his eye lit on a tall, graceful vase and he swung it aloft. Pausing a moment, he whirled back on the pursuers. In the light through the landing window the vase blazed above his head; then it hurtled down like a flaming rocket. The headmost pursuers vanished in a whirl of leaping glass; there was the thud of a fall, the bump of rolling bodies, and a pistol shot. Baire had already jerked open a door on the second floor and yelled for his companions to get inside. Through the door they stumbled; it slammed shut, and the bolt clicked into place.

"How dare you!" The words rang out from behind them, quivering with anger, and in a startled instant they recognized that voice. As they whirled about, the Lady Katharine Ness stood behind them in the doorway to another room, and her eyes were blazing blue lightnings that stabbed at them like a physical force. Oddly enough in the circumstances, Baire temporarily forgot the rush of feet in the hallway outside and the imminent danger. He noticed only how the light made a shimmering halo about the gold of her head; how...

"Lady Katharine!" Carter blurted out.

"Why—it's the Americans!" stammered the girl. She looked wonderingly from one to the other for a moment; then in a flash of inspiration Baire shouted:

"They're chasing us out there! They think we're crooks, and we're not!" He caught himself up abruptly and rushed on: "They won't come in here if you tell them not to! Help us out! We'll explain...I swear we're not..."

Somebody was pounding on the door; shrill voices babbled outside. One mute look passed between Carter and the girl and the doorway. Her calm, clear voice floated out:

"Enough of that! It is I—the Lady Katharine! No one has entered here. Go, if you please!"

"A thousand pardons, your ladyship!" came the quick reply. Feet shuffled; the voice receded, and more sharp commands rattled out. The fugitives could hear doors banging all over the hall. Slowly the tumult swept away.

"We can't thank you enough," Carter said in an almost inaudible voice. He dropped into a chair and sank back. "They chased us clear from Bordeaux; got on our trail a mile or so out. And now there's the deuce to pay."

"We got mixed up with a crook named Brotheurs," Baire explained incoherently. "Things look bad, though we hadn't anything to do with it all. Now I guess we're trapped—done for!"

"I do not know what you mean," came from the girl quietly. "Nevertheless, I do not believe... Why did you come here?"

"We couldn't help it," said Cullan. "They chased us, for one reason. Everything's the matter—murder, robbery, everything."

"In an hour," Lady Katharine continued, "the king's marriage is to take place...perhaps you know of it? In the confusion you may be able to escape. I can have my car ready..."

"You don't think we're guilty?" Baire jerked his head up suddenly. "We're not, I tell you! But all that's impossible—getting away. The king will never be at the Cathedral this day! His body is down in that car we got away in. Somebody shot him last night!"

IV

Too Many Kings

"What!" the girl recoiled, and the color drained slowly from her cheek. She steadied herself on the door casing. "Why—we've heard nothing of it here! I understood the king was still...You are absolutely sure of this?"

"A newspaper photo is a bad likeness, heaven knows," answered Carter slowly. "But there is no mistake. He had papers on him—well, it was enough proof. Oh, your king is dead, all right!"

In the long silence a bugle blared somewhere downstairs. Shrill and stentorian, the cry rang through the corridors: "The king! Make way for the king!"

For a moment the four stood as though turned to stone. Then, heedless of being seen, Carter raced through the doorway toward one of the high, arched windows giving on the palace lawn beneath. The girl was beside him in an instant, and she nodded down significantly.

Below them the sunlight blazed and rippled over the bayonets of the guards assembled before the entrance door; grim, orderly, silent rows. From behind the palace a procession was turning into view, erect, stately, and flashing with barbed sabers. The hoofs of the horses crackled angrily on the driveway as the cavalry cantered easily past, plumes fluttering, sunlight glinting on gilded harness. A closed carriage was moving toward the broad marble steps leading down the terrace. It stopped, and a lackey sprang forward to open the door. From the doors of the palace a single uniformed figure stood forth, other uniformed figures hovering in the background. But not even the sight of the tall, stately woman who had stepped to the side of the man in the colors of the reigning house of Brokovia detracted the attention of the watchers in the window. For, as he turned to give an order, Cullan, Baire and Carter recognized in the erect, bearded monarch the counterpart of the man they had seen lying in the back of the Renault with a bullet through his brain!—and yet there was something about him...

For a moment he stood motionless, pulling on his gloves. Then he lent his arm to the woman at his side—regal, haughty, and yet glowing with the dark beauty of an Italian painting. Uniformed and resplendent, two of the solemn figures in the background helped the royal couple into the carriage. A hidden band crashed into "Brokovia Forever," and the officer's sharp commands snapped along the line. Slowly the procession began to move.

"Your ladyship!" said a voice reproachfully. "Your wraps!...The car is waiting downstairs. Your father..." The trim maid who had appeared in the door caught sight of the three travel-stained figures, and she let out a little squeal.

"Silence!" ordered Lady Katherine, raising her hand peremptorily. "You will call Jacques at once, Louise. These gentlemen are friends of mine. Have Jacques convey them to my brother's rooms, and let them be fitted out in the uniforms of the guard. If anyone questions your right, refer him to my father. Tell the earl that I will follow in my own car. Quickly, if you please. And no word to anyone except Jacques!"

"But your Ladyship, these may be the men for whom the officials from Bordeaux are searching..."

"Go, I tell you! I will be responsible!" The girl lowered her hand, and Louise vanished with a last protesting shrug. Their benefactress turned back to the dumbfounded Americans. "I believe you," she asserted calmly. "As for the king—there is some imposture, and we shall see. Nobody here will question your right if you accompany me in uniform. Jacques will see to that. If they have good descriptions of you…"

"They haven't!" faltered Baire. "But this plan—you don't mean to say—"

"I mean to say that we will attend the wedding. If your story is true, then—who knows?"

"It is true!" Baire's voice was almost frenzied. "Everything's seemed against us from the beginning. We were coming peacefully on the train; Brotheurs steps in with these jewels—the cr—" He caught himself up, shot a swift glance at the girl, and went on: "Well, with some stolen stones, and a hard-boiled egg from the police comes in, arrests Brotheurs, and claims I'm his accomplice. We beat it—and then found the jewels in the car along with the dead body of your king. But we didn't do anything—honestly!"

For a long time the Lady Katharine was silent. At length she nodded.

"I believe you," she affirmed, looking out of the window thoughtfully. "It coincides with something I already knew. But here is Jacques. And now if you will accompany him, you will get to my brother's apartments unseen. Once uniformed, well, I promise you we may make of this farce—something of a tragedy!"

V

Baire Plays His Ace

Up into dim blue emptiness curved the slender vault of the Cathedral. Down its majestic length, over the heads of the awed concourse which jammed it, quivered the mighty voice of the organ. It pealed out thunderously, swelling aloft in a great note of triumph that shook the walls. White-robed priests stood like ghosts in the soft glow of the altar candles, phantom figures that seemed to have stepped down from the stained-glass windows behind them. A procession was moving down the aisle through the center. At the altar it paused, spreading about the tall patriarch who stood there, dominating, awesome. The figure in white elevated a slim, blue-veined hand; misty eyes were raised; and a sudden hush stilled the tumult in the audience.

"By the grace of God and the will of the people," the trembling old voice began in a thin thread of sound, and wavered on through a chanting discourse while the two central figures before him stared straight out over the multitude; the king still commanding despite his long, graying hair and heavy beard; Princess Jeanne impassive as one of the painted figures on the stained glass. Rustlings and sighings swept over the spectators as the ceremony progressed; somebody in uniform had been elbowing through the crowd nearer and nearer the softly lighted space before the altar.

Again the marble hand of the Archbishop was lifted; his voice took on sudden fire:

"And I now confer upon thee the title of Queen of..."

"Stop!" The word ripped across the Cathedral suddenly, stilling the voice of the Archbishop and quivering through the crowd like a thunderbolt. A grim figure in uniform had pushed through the fringe of the onlookers, tense and panting. No one in the assemblage, not even the prowling officials from Paris, saw in him the worn, dusty Baire they had pursued from Bordeaux. An instant the Cathedral was silent; then two shouts cracked out like pistol shots on the heels of one another:

"Complete the ceremony!"

"I forbid it!"

The first was the king's; the last that of the metamorphosed Baire. Other uniformed men had leaped to his side; then as a shriek of alarm tore its way from the throat of the Archbishop, he had seized the king and spun him about before the audience. A quick wrench and the wig was shorn from the dark head beneath; the beard came away simultaneously, and Baire's triumphant cry rang and echoed through the edifice:

"Here's your man! King Gustave is dead, and here is the impostor!...Frederick Brotheurs, actor, jewel thief, and murderer!"[9]

VI

War

"It means—war!" rapped the Earl of Ness tensely. He leaned across the table. "We know that Brotheurs performed that amazing impersonation for his own personal welfare—but Barnehasset doesn't! Princess Jeanne fled without a word. The Ambassador from Barnehasset says it can only be a matter of hours. It was inevitable. And it means war!"

"But how was it all brought about?" queried Cullan. "We recognized Brotheurs, even through that make-up, when we got a close view of him—his eyes couldn't be mistaken. We left him lying at Bordeaux. True, we wasted enough time before we'd found the right road—and got the officers after us! But how did Brotheurs get back

---

9 Who informed Baire that Brotheurs was an actor? Perhaps he only means "actor" in the sense of "imposter," but between Saunders and Brotheurs, actors seem to be a bad lot in young John Carr's fiction.

to Brokovia—and what did he want to do that impersonating for?"

"That," replied the Earl, shaking his cotton-white head slowly, "is something we can only guess at. We've got Brotheurs, but he won't say a thing. I'll tell you what, somebody is back of all of this! There's some kind of conspiracy—I'd stake my life that Brotheurs was only a tool, and a sort of pawn that somebody in power had been playing! We know that he got away with the crown jewels by clever substitution; the Secret Service knew it, but Moverne, of the Bureau in Bordeaux, was keeping it quiet. And he killed the king— he's confessed that. But beyond such admissions he won't say a word—about how he came to be in one of the palace cars—that Renault belonged to the king, you know—and how he happened to have the body in the back. It just points to this: He's shielding some-body!—somebody higher up, to whose advantage it was Brotheurs shot the king! About the impersonation—heaven knows!"

"Anyway, we're cleared!" Carter drew a long breath. "The fellow is a sportsman. He told the truth about us. And that theatrical effect of Junie's put us in an A-number one position. Now, didn't it?"

"That little detective we knocked for a loop won't forget us, though," grinned Cullan. "Boy! I'll bet he was fightin' mad!"

The Earl smiled. He glanced cautiously about the great mirror-lined room and raised his voice. "The Crown Prince must be mad!" he said with a peculiar intensity. "This frivolity—at such a time! The king murdered! A clever criminal almost getting himself mar-ried to the Princess of Barnehasset, and Brokovia on the eve of war! I've remonstrated, but he would have this dance tonight. You would think he would at least have the respect—" He shook his head angrily, rose and crossed to one of the high, velvet-draped windows in his suite at the palace. Throwing open the casement, he pointed down to where, in the long, low east wing of the huge building, strings of electric lights spattered a trail of yellow fire on the darkness, sketching out the graceful lines of the architecture. Japanese lanterns glowed softly through the gardens there; in an ingenious system of lighting, the spray of a fountain spurted up dazzlingly like molten gold. Through the open French windows of the ballroom, occupying the whole lower floor of the wing, the men at the casement could see the polished floor shining like the mirrors that flashed on the walls. It was all like a fairy garden: a dream scene from some magnificent Arabian Nights tale, except for the one grim, suggestive touch. From the highest dim tower, like a stairway to the stars, gaunt fingers of blinding white light shot down, ever moving about the garden; shifting far out over the city, and reminding the men at the window of the sentinels posted there, keeping the searchlights trained on the area over which the threatening danger might come. From the ballroom came softly the plinks and creaks of an orchestra tuning up.

"Making merry—with the king hardly a week dead!" whispered the Earl. "And out there"—he swept an arm toward the quiet countryside, and toward where the lights of the city spangled the night—"may come disaster. The call for mobilization may come any moment. It will take our citizenry, for the army is pitifully insufficient. Barnehasset's air fleet could put St. Spike in ruins overnight...It means destruction if we go into war now! Our ministers are in the Barnehasset capital now. Crown Prince Francis has sent an apology to the king. But they've been waiting for an opportunity to strike, I'm afraid. Our border defenses are small. There are but three regiments of infantry stationed in the city now. Destruction, I tell you!"

"They must be crazy!" Carter shook his head bewilderedly. "They ought to see you couldn't help that fellow Brotheurs gumming the works. But if they want to start trouble, why, I suppose they can easily enough. Hello! Who's this?"

A short, rotund man had stepped into the room. He was in dress uniform—for the dance that night, Baire assumed as he saw him. But under the close-clipped beard the lines of his mouth were very grim and hard.

"Oh, good evening, General Patersonne," the Earl greeted him rather awkwardly. "I understood you were in London. You returned—"

"For His Royal Highness's very appropriate and brotherly ball," cut in the other savagely. "See here, Ness—is this man crazy? The king was buried yesterday. Tonight we have this festival. Do you know that Barnehasset is likely to declare war any minute?" He flung his gloves on the table, and stalked across to the window. "I'll tell you this: if that does happen, we're done for. Done for—do you understand? I brought with me from Paris Captain Longue—you've heard of him: the greatest aviation expert in France. Was an extra high 'ace' in the air service during the war. Well, he tells me that there isn't a plane in our hangars that's fit for anything more grueling than easy maneuvers! And our aircraft guns—"

"Oh, don't finish!" snapped the Earl. "I knew we were out of date. But what can we do? Francis is determined on this festival tonight. It's too late to overhaul any planes. Have you done anything yet?"

"The Fifth Alesian cavalry is on its way here. I've wired for the two regiments at Endsburg. But if they strike for St. Spike they'll smash the border defenses in ten hours. Make my excuses to Francis tonight. I'm going to Fort Gustave by auto—if you're attending the festival, you'd better go down." He pointed down to where groups, dim black figures against the light, were idling through the doors of the ballroom.

"Look!" The Earl's sudden command burst out explosively, and he clutched General Patersonne's arm. He pointed down with a hand that trembled slightly. A mud-spattered auto whizzed up the drive and jerked to a stop beside the terrace on which the ballroom opened. The music had just begun raspingly, but it was choked off abruptly as a man leaped from the automobile, vaulted the railing of the terrace, and flung himself through one of the French windows. His words tore through the still air, even up to the watchers above.

"Your Highness!—Barnehasset declared war at six o'clock this evening! They're shelling Endsburg with long-range guns, and a bombing squadron is flying on the capital!"

VII

The Navies of the Skies

The long white knives of the searchlights were stabbing the sky all over St. Spike. Pandemonium swept the streets. From a balcony of the palace, tense and silent, Baire, Cullan, Carter and Crown Prince Francis watched the turmoil. Sharp and clear below came the crackle of commands and the thud of running feet as the palace guard was gathering. Excited people swarmed through the palace; the ballroom was forgotten. Headlights glared for a moment in the driveway and were gone as a car of the general's staff whisked by. Ceaselessly from the tower the lights searched the leaden sky.

"Can't we do something!" demanded Carter desperately. "I don't care if we are Americans—we want to get in this scrap; we caused it, anyway!"

"You can do nothing now," Francis told him in his quick, sharp, slightly unsteady voice. In the light from the door behind they could see that his face was chalky. "You may—have—to—do something if Fort Gustave falls!" He turned back to the room behind, where frightened groups were gathered. The Earl of Ness, gaunt and impassive as usual, was chatting calmly with a lank, bespectacled figure whom Baire, as he followed the direction of the prince's gaze, remembered having been indicated as Longue, the aviation expert from Paris. Thrusting his hands into his pockets, Baire nodded and passed into the room. At the door he met the Lady Katharine Ness, whom he had not seen since the afternoon when his dexterous move had saved his companions and himself. She smiled.

"Rather looks like trouble, doesn't it?" was her calm query.

"Rather!" he responded dryly. "I understand they're looking for aeroplanes. If ever..."

Of a sudden the roar outside seemed to swell deafeningly. In the same instant the crash of an anti-aircraft gun from one of the towers shook the walls. Then beyond the windows a lurid glare rushed up from the outskirts of the city as though the streets had split wide and a sheet of fire spurted forth; the roar of the explosion crashed out and rumbled across the sky. Baire knew that the girl had seized his arm spasmodically, but he stared out of the window, half hypnotized. In the silence some last fragments of glass tinkled down from the shattered windows; then slivers of flame shot up all over the city and the sharp spit of the anti-aircraft guns rattled over the housetops. Once more houses were flung apart as a bomb burst in another part of the frenzied capital. Again barked the sharp staccato of the defenders' cannon, and a darting body like a flaming bird spun over in the darkness and plunged down—one of the invaders had been hit!

Baire saw Carter dash through the door to the balcony. His voice sounded in the other's ear above the thunder of the guns.

"They're not sending up a plane! Get that aviation expert!" He was flailing his arms wildly, and Baire caught some of his spirit. He swung around to where Longue stood, calmly trying to talk above the turmoil. Heedless of the fact that he had never met the man, he seized him by the shoulders.

"Where are the aeroplane hangars?" he yelled, shaking the startled aviator. "Where are the pilots? Can't anybody in this country fly a plane?"

"Why—they're not fit for use!" Longue regarded him amazedly. "They haven't the speed or the equipment or the construction for..."

"You're going to pilot one, do you understand?" shrieked Baire. "If nobody in this hick kingdom has the nerve to go up and meet 'em, we will! I never used a machine gun in my life, but..."

"Monsieur is mad! The aeroplanes could not be used!"

"They'll be used or we'll all be blown to hell!" Carter was hustling the pilot toward the door, and he thumped the other on the back wildly. "If you have the nerve they say you did in the war, we'll bust up the whole army! Come on!"

Something of his own excitement had communicated itself to Longue. The other hesitated at the door; then the smile so familiar from newspaper photos crept over his face, and he squared his shoulders.

"It is well, then. To the hangars—back of the palace. Vite![10] We may be able to do some damage—for a while, at least!"

It was a mad, stumbling race through the corridors. When they at length emerged into the air another explosion flash showed a roadster in the drive. Longue was at the wheel, and he sent the machine thundering through the grounds. The aeroplane hangars, dim, ghostly bulks through the darkness, were guarded only by a single soldier, but at Longue's quick commands lights leaped up suddenly and bewildered men appeared from nowhere to babble excited protests to the expert's orders. Now animated as a whirlwind, Longue dragged open one of the heavy doors. A three-passenger bombing plane loomed gauntly inside. Men were swarming about it now, and as in a dream Carter found headpiece and goggles thrust into his hands. Longue was shouting explanations of the ugly-looking machine gun he uncovered in the fore seat, his fingers mere flashing blurs above it. Carter vaguely knew that he was being lifted into the giant craft. Belts were encircling his waist; he got the shadowy impression that Baire had climbed into the seat behind and that Longue, still crackling out orders, was pulling on gloves preparatory to springing into his own place in the rear. His hands fumbled over the cockpit of the machine. They came in contact with the cold steel of the gun, and a little quiver shot up his spine. He tried to remember what Longue had said about its operation, but all that seemed hazy and indistinct.

It was not until the propeller began to roar and the plane to hum and vibrate that the impression of a dream was sponged from his brain. With a little jerk the machine bumped over the landing field; Carter swallowed hard and gripped the butt of the weapon. The air was ripping past his face with a low whine that blended into a hysterical screech. He peered over. The earth shot away from under the wheels; the plane lurched slightly, and righted itself into a long climb. The propeller was drumming monotonously in his ears, but Baire's muffled voice came to him through the speaking tube:

"The rest of them are coming up. They can't last, but…"

The words were lost in the steady drone of the motor and the whistle and creak of the wind. The weapon felt icy beneath his touch, but the steel trigger was reassuring. Far below the night was powdered with tiny lights, like the reflection of stars in water. A white arm reached up from a searchlight and groped about the sky. Clammy mist like a spirit hand brushed Carter's face, blurring his view through the big goggles, but just ahead he could see a long, dark body flash downward through the momentary light. His fas-

---

10   Quickly (French).

cinated gaze swerved down to the jagged line of fire crawling along the toy city underneath; then that reeled about, and he knew that the plane was plunging down. It righted itself and crept along, circling like a hawk. Carter's hand closed on the trigger of the gun. Below them a dark surface appeared; in the next instant it sprang upward. As the full broadside of the other flier was exposed, fire spurted from the Brokovian craft, its machine gun spitting and snarling like a live thing. The enemy machine hesitated, hung balanced a fraction of a second; then a knife of flame tore open its side, and it took a swift dive. Like an arrow it blazed down through the night.

Carter twisted around. One of the shafts of light whirled across the black void, and across it shot the hulk of a light Spad.[11] Carter's jubilant cry was lost in the shriek of the wind, but he knew that Baire must have seen for one fleeting moment the Brokovian arms on the flier. The crippled air fleet was rising to meet the invaders!

A stream of fire spattered out of the blackness far to the right, and spinning shapes like bats wheeled about one another as the searchlights found them. A Brokovian plane had engaged an enemy. Suddenly Carter noticed that their own craft had begun a long climb. The city lights had almost vanished now; only the white eyes of the searchlights leered up at them. The Brokovian machine was winging straight toward the south. Carter wondered how long the imperfect motor could stand that terrific pace, and he stared grimly over the side, his hands still glued to the machine gun. One could never tell when—still— He fumbled for his watch. Two-thirty. Why, they had been in the air nearly twenty-five minutes, and it seemed...They must be almost to the border, and that meant...In one blinding flash the truth crashed in on him. Longue was striking for Urbsboro, the capital of Barnehasset, and he meant to raid the city alone!

VIII

Into Barnehasset

At the far end of the vast, dim room, Princess Jeanne of Barne-hasset stood at the open window, silhouetted blackly against the pale starlight. Her dusky hair seemed to blend almost imperceptibly into the darkness behind, but her face showed wanly, as set and inflexible as that of a statue. About her was spread the seething city, its hum and throb beating up on the still night air, but its serene lights giving no hint of the activity that boiled through the streets. Already three detachments of cavalry had left by the Portan highway that led to Endsburg. The grumble of the artillery had but recently died down.

---

11 A French fighter biplane used during the First World War.

That meant…

A door crashed open, sending a broad streak of light across the floor. The woman at the window swung round, and a single word snapped out:

"Well?"

"Endsburg is holding out," came the terse reply. The man in the doorway, wearing the colors of the Barnehasset general's staff, held out a scribbled note. "We've just heard from Bayne. Their counterattack drove the line back half a mile in one part. But they can't keep it up. Fort Gustave will surrender before morning."

"The planes?"

"Terrific destruction in St. Spike," returned the other breathlessly. "We suffered—to some extent. Their air fleet came up…"

Princess Jeanne whipped round again.

"Our informant gave us to understand there would be no opposition from that quarter. He said the planes were unfit for use. If he has betrayed us…" Her lips set in a thin, firm line, and her eyelids drooped dangerously.

"I do not know," shrugged the officer. "At any rate, Your Highness, there can be but one result."

The Princess Jeanne had opened her mouth to answer when a geyser of fire lit up the room with a bursting ruddy glare from beyond the window, and like a physical force the explosion of a bomb rocked the city. The hum of Urbsboro swelled to a hysterical roar, through which shrill, agonized cries cut like knife thrusts. Debris was settling down through the rolling smoke, and whips of flame flashed up…

The Princess Jeanne recoiled as another bomb ripped wide the Hall of Justice at the far end of the city, its spires crumpling,; lit up a moment by the lurid burst, it tottered into blackness once more. The woman in the palace whirled to her half-stunned companion.

"Crippled!" she flung out the word. "He's betrayed us! Our whole fleet has gone to St. Spike. We're absolutely powerless!"

A white line of light streamed up from Urbsboro and moved about; then another, and another. Another bomb found its mark, this time close to the palace; simultaneously the anti-aircraft guns began to snarl from below. It was then that the big bombing plane bearing the Brokovian arms altered its direction, and, in the face of the shifting lights began to take a downward glide. Above the smooth, close-clipped lawns of the palace it swept down, bumping to a stop along the velvety turf. The crackle of the guns came raggedly to Carter's ears as Longue leaped down from his seat, peering about the smooth expanse of grass that merged into the terraces of the palace. Beyond the trees the reddened sky showed like the long gash of an open wound, the smoke hanging sullenly above it; and the palace itself throbbed with activity, but down here only the writhing shadows moved on the red-lit ground.

"What are you going to do?" demanded Baire's half hysterical voice. He fumbled at the belts with unsteady fingers. "To risk a landing at night and here…"

"The motor—it was beginning to miss," came Longue's low, vibrant tones. "It was our only chance, for we couldn't go back. Look there!" He flung an arm to where the lights were picking out dark bodies in the sky. "We've done damage both ways. They are shelling their own planes. Three of them followed us from St. Spike!"

IX
The Reckoning

The orderly had gone. Once more Princess Jeanne was at the window in the long, darkened room, but this time her mind was ringing. Tirelessly the searchlights prodded the heavens. She shuddered as she turned her eyes toward the stricken city. Down there…

"Your Highness!" The words floated across the room in a thin thread of sound. Through the velvet drapes that shrouded the walls a man had appeared like a ghost. His footfalls echoed on the polished floor.

"I came by the secret staircase," he explained haltingly. "I got away from the crowd at the palace and drove over the border like mad." Suddenly his voice changed, and a note of hysteria crept into it. "I shouldn't have gotten through the lines if they hadn't known me on both sides. In God's name, can't you stop the air raid on St. Spike? You promised…"

Like a striking rattler the woman spun round.

"I promised! Yes—I promised!" She gripped him by the arm as he emerged into the pale light beneath the window. "See! Look at what you've done! You have the nerve to come here after the way you betrayed…"

"Betrayed!" The word shot from between his lips. "I did nothing of the kind. But you, after what you'd said… You must stop it! I don't care about myself. But…"

"You betrayed not only your own country, but this one," cut in the woman. "Why? You were to be Prime Minister if we were successful. You furnished us the justification for declaring war with that episode in the Cathedral. Brotheurs was silent. There was nothing to fear. But you told me the aeroplanes were unfit for use. Look there!"

"I thought they were," responded the man quickly. "But those Americans—they tried them anyhow. They helped our plan in unmasking Brotheurs before we had planned to do it, so as to make justification for war full and complete. Your father declared war immediately. It was the supreme insult. If he ever knew… It was your fault! Just because you hated Brokovia you'd have war! If the king of Barnehasset knew that it was a conspiracy…"

"Stop!" Something of his own excitement was communicated to the Princess Jeanne. "You're mad! I never thought danger could make such a coward… Do you say I would be implicated—I? My father might pardon me. But if your people were to know your part in this thing, what would happen to you? And you accuse me of being responsible! Who proposed it?"

"You!" flung back the other. "You hated Brokovia, and you hated Gustave! I'm not weakening. I should have stopped at nothing if you hadn't put over that air raid!" He paused for breath, and in the tense silence the two glared through the dimness. Then a soft click drifted down to them, and the room sprang up dazzlingly. A third figure stood at the far end of the apartment. The King of Barnehasset removed his hand from the light switch slowly. He was holding himself steady with an effort.

"So it's you!" Under their craggy brows his eyes flickered like fires in caves. His grim, withered face was like that of a malignant idol. But two more words he uttered: "My daughter!" Then he closed the door behind him. He was in full uniform, and his hand strayed to his side. The barrel of a pistol glinted in the light.

The other man saw his intent, and he recoiled against the wall. The king's stony gaze shifted from the weapon in his hand to the ashen face of the figure against the paneling, his body gleaming against the dark wood like a form on a cross. Then, deliberately, he tossed the pistol upon the table. One long, bony hand went to the crossed dueling swords upon the wall beside the door. They flashed down in the yellow light; one of them the king flung spinning across the room, the other he grasped. Then he spoke suddenly:

"I could call the guard. But I prefer to kill a traitor myself…even a traitor of another country!"

Slowly the man at the window bent to pick up the weapon at his feet. An instant he held it loosely, staring at the grim, awesome figure, like Zeus on Olympus. Suddenly he tensed, rose to his full height, and stepped to the center of the apartment. There was no tremor in his hand as he saluted. Then the blades darted forward. The king's weapon was flashing like the thunderbolt in the hand of a Zeus, and his spectacular attack swept the duelists across the room. Lunging and twisting, his antagonist thudded against the wall, steadied himself, and drove desperately into a lock. The king's quick wrench sent him spinning backward, to crash into a low chair and pitch to the floor. Lithe as a cat, he was on his feet, meeting the other's bewildering attack with a marvel of swordsmanship that made the blades mere dazzling blurs between them.

In one moment the king was pressing his opponent steadily to the wall once more; in the next his own sword was clattering along the floor, and he was crouching against a table—disarmed!

The Brokovian's weapon swept about in a blinding arc; simultaneously, four pistol shots ripped across the room, and the echoes thundered back from the walls. The weapon dropped from Princess Jeanne's nerveless fingers; the man's body tensed suddenly to the shock of the thudding bullets, and he crumpled forward, sword twisted beneath him.

The King of Barnehasset found himself staring down at the crumpled figure at his feet, from beneath which a thin trickle of crimson was crawling across the carpet—and back to Princess Jeanne; to the men in aviator's caps and goggles who had appeared at the door.

The white-haired man looked very old then—and worn, and weak. One hand fluttered up; he said the same words he had uttered not ten minutes before, but now they sounded far, far different:

"My daughter!"

Slowly his eyes travelled down to the still form at whose hand he had so nearly met his end, and he knew that never again should he be in danger from that man. The Earl of Ness had been shot through the heart.

X

The End of the Trail

"And so it all ended well, after all," said Cullan thoughtfully. From his chair on the terrace he gazed out over St. Spike. "It was a mighty fine thing of the king—that apology. He didn't owe it."

"It was," agreed Carter. "But it wasn't to any great extent the Princess Jeanne's fault, I think. Ness had led her on by those idiotic letters about Gustave's threats against Barnehasset—which had not been made, or he'd have sent them to the king. It was a crazy thing, and a part of the bargain was that Gustave wasn't actually to be killed, but only abducted, while Brotheurs took his place. They were to unmask him, and so give the greatest possible offense to Barnehasset. Ness paid Brotheurs with the crown jewels… Brotheurs has confessed at last. He gave him the car; the king was abducted, but he showed fight, and he was killed. The Secret Service was wise to the fact of the theft, and they trailed him to Bordeaux; he went to another town and doubled back on his tracks, leaving the car at Bordeaux, where he stepped into our train: that was where adventure entered, and we got mixed up in the whole thing. It's been a great time, hasn't it?"

"Yes." Baire smiled reminiscently. "It was a great old war while it lasted. And I wonder if they'd have beaten us if the King of Barnehasset hadn't stepped in and explained? He's made restitution to the best of his ability and the Crown Prince showed more generosity in giving terms than I would have imagined. Ness was confoundedly clever, though, by the way he tried to get us off the track…Well, where do we go from here?"

"I am staying at St. Spike for a while," Carter announced firmly. "The Lady Katharine… We have some golf dates and things. I got you to come here, fellows—do you know why? The lure of adventure? Of course not. That wasn't strong enough. But I had become quite intimate with the Lady Katherine at Monte Carlo, and, well—I knew you'd come if I gave in to you for a while. And you?"

"To Urbsboro," replied Baire with a quizzical smile.

"And then?"

"As you say yourself," answered the other thoughtfully: "Who knows?"

Notes for the Curious: "The Blindfold Quest"

"The Blindfold Quest" is the young Carr's most ambitious, and most successful, piece of fiction so far in his amateur career. At roughly 9,600 words, it is more than twice the length of any previous story except "The Marked Bullet," which it still exceeds by almost 1,000 words. Carr struggled with the mechanics of the earlier tale, his first longer effort; in "The Blindfold Quest," he succeeds, and entertainingly.

We have already noted that the European adventure novels of McCutcheon and Hope are the two primary, among other, inspirations for this story. *Graustark* is plainly the strongest. Like "The Blindfold Quest," that novel opens on a train; its first chapter bears the title, "Mr. Grenville Lorry Seeks Adventure," which Carr echoes with his own first-chapter title. The *Graustark* narrator quickly assures us, "As it happens, Mr. Grenville Lorry did not have a dull moment after the train started" (p. 1), and the same can be said for this story's young rail-traveling Americans. Carr's narrative has other high-level similarities to *Graustark*, some of which are of course common to the genre, not simply between these two books: royals incognito and impersonated; a plot against the throne, opposed by a young American adventurer (or three); unlikely royal-commoner romances; a protagonist going in disguise as a member of the Royal Guard. In any event, Carr's borrowings in "The Blindfold Quest," like the best of them elsewhere throughout his career, are merely of premises and expected elements. None smacks of too-close imitation.

Carr was also inspired by the crowning episode of *Cleek: The Man of the Forty Faces*. In that adventure, the thief-turned-detective leaves England and returns to his ancestral country, Mauravania. There, Cleek performs Ruritanian exploits and uncovers his mysterious origins.

There is one other likely inspiration for "The Blindfold Quest," if less certain: the choice to feature a plane in battle, as well as some of the circumstance and tone of Baire and Carter's bold maiden flight, may have been inspired by Donn Byrne's "Biplane No. 2," which opens the 1915 collection, *Stories Without Women (and a Few with Women)*. In it, the protagonist, Stanton, undertakes his first combat reconnaissance. Stanton's pilot, like Longue, is "one of the best fliers of the corps."[1] Carr is not openly mimicking Donn By-

---

1 *Stories Without Women (and a Few with Women)*, Hearst's International Library Co., 1915, p. 10. All subsequent excerpts are drawn from the same edition.

rne, but the sense of wonderment during a first flight into combat is common between the two stories, with each initiate's senses dropping away to the earth and being subsumed into the droning engine and vast sky. (Remember: unlike twenty-first century readers, Carr had none of his own commercial experience of air travel upon which to draw in describing one's first flight—he was describing a reality not all that long removed from speculative fiction.) Carr assigns Carter a different role than Stanton's, gunner, but both missions are dangerous, both critical to their sides' respective victories. Stanton's enemies "knew that the aëroplane was sending wireless information to headquarters, and that it was directing the terrible fire from the batteries" (p. 23). Although Carr carves out his own narrative of flight, combat, and consequences, it is easy to believe that Donn Byrne's story was inspirationally in his mind as Carr composed the climactic air sequence for his Brokovian romance.

There are of course ongoing observations of style and theme available for "The Blindfold Quest." Carr's prose, although occasionally working too hard—"They reeled drunkenly across the slippery platform into a babbling, rushing crowd that pressed about the train, and pitched to the floor in a writhing tangle"—is generally brisk and fresher than in the earlier stories. Despite some of the early-twentieth-century slang's sounding dated to readers one hundred years later, this story is simply a pleasure to read. Carr is also more confident in drawing more of his own tropes instead of borrowing tired ones. Consider his lovely evocation of the view as the Brokovian plane climbs into the air: "Far below the night was powdered with tiny lights, like the reflection of stars in water."

"The Blindfold Quest" also seems subjectively to the editor somehow more alight with dialogue than most of its predecessors. As a percentage of word count in any given story, this is not strictly true, but the give-and-take in this story between the characters, and their distinctive voices from one to another, are as good or better in this story as in most of Carr's earlier efforts.

One other incremental improvement in style here is how effectively Carr furnishes every chapter with an attention-grabbing finish. "The Blindfold Quest" is fast-paced in a manner that belies its greater length than the previous stories. In a sense, it is the exception to how Carr would characterize his work in that April 22, 1955 letter to James O'Brien: "When the hero goes into action, he uses his brains and not his fists…to…destroy…the tough-guy type who has now become almost an American hero." In this story, it is the Americans' pugilistic impulsiveness that consistently propels the action, right from the first few minutes aboard the train when they evade the police and attempt to recapture Brotheurs.

> "It was the worst fool trick I ever did." Baire drew a deep breath. "We jumped out of the frying pan into the fire. But it might be worse... Somehow, I sort of like this thing, dangerous or not."

Baire's confession is as applicable to all of three of the Americans. Their impetuousness induces the most obvious recurring Carrian theme demonstrated in "The Blindfold Quest": the youthful aspiration to grand adventure. Carter is the first, baldly, to propose it:

> "If it's like Graustark or Ruritania," he answered with an air of finality, "we're in for a hot time. In the stories the Americans always go to some little kingdom and start a revolution or marry a princess or something. Anyway, they always raise the devil. And when I tell you about this place, you'll agree that it's just like the ones McCutcheon and Anthony Hope wrote about. It ought to make the star experience of our trip to Europe."

Of course, essentially all that Carter suggests transpires, but in the end, Carr offers us an O. Henry-like twist: Carter was intent on going to Brokovia not in the pursuit of adventure, but in pursuit of Princess Katherine, with whom he had begun forming a romantic connection. Baire had openly pursued the princess with no success; Carter, more quietly, and with some. Nor are there are any hard feelings: conveniently, Baire courts a more receptive Princess Jeanne.

If romance travels in disguise to Brokovia and Barnehasset, Carr's Romantic sense of honor travels openly, whether in the hearts of the hotheaded American protagonists or the King of Barnehasset, who puts himself in unnecessary jeopardy when confronting the Earl of Ness. The King tosses down his pistol and, instead, takes down a pair of hereditary dueling swords from the wall.

"The Blindfold Quest" was Carr's only foray into this most Romantic of modern genres, the Ruritanian adventure. One senses that his success with it was partly due to his excitement in writing the sort of story Carr had "gobbled up so eagerly as a boy in my early teens" (letter to Nelson Bond, March 3, 1968). This adventure story is, in any event, an early tipping point in Carr's amateur career. After barely two years, the young author, while still experimenting and not always succeeding, will from this point onward score more hits than misses, so to speak, whether in terms of better dramatic construction or the swiftly increasing technical skill of his writing. Much of the fiction that follows will feature well-handled historical detail, original and effective pictorial language, better psychological horror, varying dialects, more distinctive characters, and better, more effective dialogue. The spirit, too, if not the genre, of "The Blindfold Quest" will live on in not only Carr's better amateur works, but in many of his professional ones.

The Riddle of the Laughing Lord (1924)

Some said it was haunted. Some called it idle superstition. But the tower room kept its ugly reputation.

Morgan Grimm had christened his home Greytowers in imitation of the old English manor houses, which it resembled for all the world. It was one of those heavy, squatty, piles of stone, with windows peering out from behind the ivy at all sorts of impossible places, and legions of towers straggling over the roof. The place resembled a watchful old beast, the ivy patching its stolid face like scars. And it had a habit of silhouetting itself gauntly against a crimson sky, sneering above its cluster of dingy pines…or of showing black against the moon at night, soaring on its crag like a castle in a fairy tale.

Morgan Grimm built it, spending money with a lavish hand, and copying the English style of architecture. It was the showplace of the village in Maine where Grimm went during the summer, away from the roar of New York. The surf thundered on its shores; there were dull prowling winds and slate-hued skies—and Grimm loved it.

At first he had loved, too, to show visitors the tower room. He had an oriel window[1] there that had been lifted bodily from an English monastery; a fearful and horrible thing, they said. The banker's tastes had run to antiques, moreover, and he had crowded the tower room with such an amazing and diversified array that it looked like some grotesque museum created by a madman. There was a Borgian poison chalice[2], a bedstead in which three Hapsburgs[3] had been stabbed to death, a torture chair from the dungeons of Toledo[4], the

---

1 A bay window projecting outward from the surface of the edifice but not reaching the ground. It has visible architectural supports such as brackets, cantilevers, or corbels (stylized projections).

2 In another Carrian echo, Carr would, in 1926, reuse this chalice as the centerpiece of a historical detective tale, "As Drink the Dead." The reader here will meet the "detective" in that tale, Ludwig von Arnheim, in "The New Canterbury Tales."

3 A royal house (family) of Austria, whose members were monarchs in multiple European countries during a span from the 15th to the 20th centuries.

4 One site, of course, of the Spanish Inquisition, which began in 1478.

hideous picture that some crazed Genoese artist had painted of his wife after he had murdered her and while she yet lolled with his stiletto through her neck, and the statue of the Laughing Lord. The Laughing Lord constituted perhaps Morgan's prize... And thereon hangs the tale.

The evil name of the tower room began from the things in it. Then a servant left Greytowers and got out of the village itself as quickly as he could. The villagers, of course, put their own construction on it, and when the hotel proprietor told an incoherent story about strangling cords and velvet drapes and candles shining in mirrors, doubt became certainty.

The one flaw in Grimm's happiness was the hatred of his wife for Greytowers. Patricia Grimm, full-lipped, dark-eyed and glowing with vibrant youth, detested the wildness—the eerie suggestion of the place that for her husband held so much charm. Morgan Grimm resembled more a poet with a grudge against the world than the man who had whipped his way to the top of the financial ladder. Yet the brooding eyes could flame in wrath; the thin, delicate hands could be iron with set purpose. Their wills clashed frequently and tempestuously...yet Grimm always gave in to his wife except on one point. He would not abandon Greytowers in the summer. Finally matters came to a head.

"Go if you want to!" she had snapped after a stormy scene in his office at the Cyclops Trust Company. "But I'm staying here in New York! You'll not drag me up to that prison again, you morbid...thing! Tom Middleton will see that I enjoy myself, even if you don't!"

"Oh, no, he won't," Grimm had retorted smoothly. "Tom is going along with me for a week or so at Greytowers. I want to get his opinion as a sculptor on the Laughing Lord. And it's just as well. I fear you're paying too much attention to Tom, my dear."

And he had laughed when the door slammed.

*****

Tom Middleton shivered a little and drew the lap robe closer about him.

"I don't like this place one bit—with all respect to you, Morg," he said to his host in the front seat of the speeding auto. "But Blade here is probably crazy about it."

"Sure I am," Anthony Blade replied cheerfully. In the stinging wind that ripped in from the sea, thundering far below, his boyish face was aglow. He looked up at the bare, writhing trees and the leaden chaos of the sky. "Everything is all set for a ghost or a murder or something. You know, Grimm, I should have been a detective. As an amateur one I'm languishing to see your collection of gruesome relics."

"You would," retorted the sculptor. "But that reminds me, Morg—

what about this statue you wanted me to see? That's associated with a lot of tragedies or the like, isn't it?'

"You'll see." Grimm buttoned his coat still higher and increased the speed of the car, sending it skimming over the flinty road up the bleak line of the cliff. "We're almost to Greytowers now... There, through the trees. Do you see it?"

Over a fringe of cowering pines chill towers stared down through the dusk, which was creeping out of the sea like a crawling thing. The sea itself boomed louder, and the wind swaggered around corners. Blade got no more than a fleeting glimpse of the leering facade of the house before the big front door opened. Stamping and beating his hands, Grimm gave the car over to an owl-faced young man who ran to meet them, unwieldly in a huge fur coat. Then he hurried his guests inside.

In the great, wide, high darkness of the hall they could hear the wind playing on Greytowers as on a harp. At its far end a single mosaic lamp splotched the gloom like a candle in a gulf, and the shadows clutched around it. Blade could see the light glimmer wanly on the steel of a coat of mail standing like a dead figure against the wall. He got the impression of faces peering down at him from the paneling...

"In there," directed Grimm, pointing to a door through which an elfish light glowed ruddily. He flung his coat and hat to the man who had slid from the darkness like a ghost beside him. Blade, pulling off his own coat, followed Middleton through the door.

The library rose in heavy, impressive lines around them, spreading away into black nooks where the genial firelight did not penetrate. In the fireplace a wide blaze went streaming up the chimney, hanging big, beetle-backed shadows of the furniture against the walls. Prim files of books stood around them, grotesque tapestries shivered in a draught, and from the tossing night outside the wind whipped the branch of a tree against a windowpane, like a lost soul hurling itself...

"Sit down," said Grimm, pulling up a deep leather chair in front of the fire and pushing a tabouret with cigarettes and a decanter of whisky toward them. He spread out his hands to the blaze. "Ugh! Rotten night, and this place is draughty... Damn!" The burning logs exploded sharply, and Grimm gave a little involuntary jump. "Hate sudden noises like that," he explained. "Nanette will bring in coffee shortly. We'll eat about nine."

"I'm beginning to love this place." Blade lit a cigarette and leaned back luxuriously. "And now, Grimm, without wishing to seem too hasty, suppose you tell us something about this Laughing Lord. I'm curious."

Grimm's long, white fingers fumbled nervously with a cigar.

"The Laughing Lord," he began, "was a young Austrian nobleman, who lived about the time of the first Crusade.[5] He was superbly handsome, a deep scholar and thinker…and yet he was mad. Some kink in his brain made him a homicidal maniac.[6] And he had a gift of laughter; they could hear him laughing in the halls of his castle at night…when he was using the strangling-cord or the dagger or the poison cup on one of his nearest and dearest…"

"Oh, shut up!" exploded Tom Middleton. The door into the hall blew open with a bang, and the sculptor sprang up. "Damn that door! Morg, this place is—"

"You wanted to hear about it… Well, some idiot sculptor made a statue of him, laughing and staggering; fearful execution of detail. I want you to see what you think of it. Suppose we go up to the tower room now."

"All right." Middleton's voice was not quite steady, but he got up with a determined air. "I'm ready. Let's get it over with."

Middleton and Blade had a chaotic series of impressions after they left the library. There were black corridors that stretched up to the sky; reeling shadows sweeping before them like a ghost-train; long, winding marble stairs, flecked with the tiny points of light from candles, with which the house seemed to be filled. On the last flight of the stairs Tom Middleton spun about and clutched at the wall.

"I nearly stepped on something," he said wheezily. "It looked like—a spider; a big black spider. But I think it was a human hand… Oh, God, Grimm!" His teeth gleamed through his bloodless lips, and the candle-shine was bright in his eyes. "What's got into this place? This hall is—full of—live things. Live things, I tell you!"

"You're crazy!" Grimm bent down and unlocked the door. The three of them entered, Blade lending his arm to the sculptor, who was muttering under his breath.

"Gentlemen, the Laughing Lord!"

Against the vivid black of the drapes that swept the floor all around the huge room a single white figure blazed out at them. The dull candlelight rippled over the puffy, bloated face, the crawling horror of the distended mouth, the gaping eyes…body crouched and tense, hands gripping a cord.

"Look!" ordered Grimm. "See the vice grinning in those eyes! Isn't it a marvelous piece of work? And note the careful attention to

5 The end of the eleventh century, 1096-1099.

6 Carr will present the character of Laurent similarly in *Grand Guignol*: "He was a mild-appearing young man, soft-spoken and pleasant. The black spot on his brain was sadism. Usually lucid, he would have intervals in which the temptation to kill and mutilate became overpowering…"

detail."

Blade swallowed hard. Middleton let out a little choking noise.

"The mad sculptor who made that said that the Laughing Lord's character would be forever stamped upon that until he did a good deed," Grimm continued inexorably. "There he stands, among relics of wickedness"—he pointed to the monstrous, deformed shadow of the bed of ill-repute, sinister against the ceiling; to the grim and deadly trophies of villainy which lowered about him—"until some good deed liberates his soul. Oh, the irony of it!"

Involuntarily Blade shrank back. He could hear the wind hooting outside the tower, tearing at the stone. The shuddering candle flame reflected a goblin light in the windowpanes; it glittered on the reddened steel of a sabre against the wall...and it glittered even brighter in the eyes of Tom Middleton. His breath was whistling through his teeth.

"That thing," he shouted suddenly, "is alive!"

Drunkenly he swayed on his feet, flinging out an arm before him toward the figure of the Laughing Lord. Grimm sprang to his side and caught him as he crumpled, tilting a silver flask to his lips.

"If you value your life, don't touch that flask!" The words ripped across the room. A dark form whipped past Blade; the criminologist saw the flask spin and flash from Grimm's hand, and the leaping candle flame vanished, blotting out the room in darkness.

Grimm screamed just once. And as that cry trembled through the tower room, Blade heard something like a laugh... Wildly he stumbled toward the window, gripped the velvet curtains and tore them from their fastenings. A flood of moonlight gushed across the black carpet, and there, glimmering before him in the white radiance, stood the statue of the Laughing Lord. Yet gone was the hideousness from the face. It had altered, sponging away the horrid laugh, the bloated cheeks, the leering eyes. In its place the serene calm of an untroubled soul reigned, leaving no disfiguration of mania upon the handsome face. The arms were extended as though in supplication; the eyes turned out of the window...

And huddled at its feet lay Morgan Grimm, head lolling horribly. The vivid line of a cord in the leaden neck showed that he had been strangled to death.

Notes for the Curious: "The Riddle of the Laughing Lord"

The reader is warned: While this commentary contains no actual spoilers, it mentions some details slightly indicative of the murderer's identity in *The Corpse in the Waxworks*. If you have not read that novel yet, you may wish to read it before reading the following remarks.

The economy of "The Riddle of the Laughing Lord" is as laudable as the graceful handling of Carr's long narrative in "The Blindfold Quest." This story is, in practicality, a fairy tale. Carr hints this clearly enough to the reader: the central character's name is Grimm, and the setting, Greytowers, is to all purposes, "a castle in a fairy tale." These typically Carrian language games are not the extent of Carr's fairy-tale mimesis, either: his horror story is short because fairy tales are short. Like traditional fairy tales, "The Riddle of the Laughing Lord" has clearly good and evil characters in basic conflict. At its heart is magic; in its resolution, the breaking of an ancient curse. "The Riddle of the Laughing Lord" demonstrates a simple, universal lesson—a moral. It is a terrifying little twentieth-century fairy tale written for the enjoyment of grown-ups.

Of course, the story is not without minor faults, the most salient of which is the unprepared insertion of Anthony Blade into the weekend party and the ambiguity surrounding Blade's career. In the car, Blade only wishes he were a detective, but Carr calls him a criminologist in the story's closing moments—when Carr also leverages Blade a little abruptly as the perspective character. Until then, the story has been told through a conventional, third-person omniscient narrator perspective. It would not have cost Carr much exposition to introduce Blade, or much effort to clean up the narrative point of view, but none of this spoils the reader's enjoyment.

Greytowers is straight out of the Gothic tradition. We hear, in the story of its creation, echoes of the construction of Walpole's Twickenham estate (as described by Carr in *The Curse of the Bronze Lamp*) and we learn that Morgan Grimm has built it consciously to meld grotesqueries of the past with the present. The tower room's collection of grim relics and an oriel window that "had been lifted bodily from an English monastery" give present-day life to medieval abominations that otherwise would have passed away with time. Greytowers possesses genuine gothic menace: although Carr, a little predictably, continues in this story his zoetic descriptions of manor houses, he simply does so better here than in his earlier ones. No longer is Carr offering us lifeless, derivative presentations. Compare the description of Brandon Hall...

> On either side ivy patched the walls of the house,
> like scars on its stolid gray face. The blank eyes of its
> windows looked furtively toward the low line of the
> marshes, shivering in the mist. The whole place hud-
> dled together, the ivy whispering, and shrank from the
> moon, as though it had done something it was afraid
> of. There was a curious air of deadness about the
> grounds: Brandon Hall was like the silent specter of a
> dead house in a magic forest.

...with that of Greytowers:

> It was one of those heavy, squatty, piles of stone, with
> windows peering out from behind the ivy at all sorts
> of impossible places, and legions of towers straggling
> over the roof. The place resembled a watchful old
> beast, the ivy patching its stolid face like scars. And it
> had a habit of silhouetting itself gauntly against a crim-
> son sky, sneering above its cluster of dingy pines...or
> of showing black against the moon at night, soaring on
> its crag like a castle in a fairy tale.

These are surprisingly comparably worded descriptions, but that
of "The Riddle of the Laughing Lord" is more successful. While Brandon Hall—and for that matter, Heatherby House—is a stale, predict-
able specter, an echo of Poe with dead airs and no surprising qualities,
Carr imbues Greytowers with living, squirming bestiality, both in the
first moments we see it and throughout the remainder of the narrative. Its vitality is threatening, particularly when, in a literary antithesis,
Carr sets off the manor's giant, leering facade against the diminutive
"owl-faced young man who ran to meet them, unwieldly in a huge fur
coat." There is a sense of the sublime in these juxtaposed images that
increases the reader's disquieted anticipation.

Carr is playing much better in this story upon the imagination
of his readers than in earlier efforts. From the group's chaotic ascent
through shadows into the tower room hall, which seems to hide mysterious, living nightmares—did Middleton step on a human hand, a
gigantic spider, or did he hallucinate entirely?—to the story's climax in
Grimm's peculiar chamber, with its wicked relics from history, Carr's
prose generates suggestive dread.

Carr also subtly parallels the squatting, minatory presence of Greytowers, shrouded in a dusk "creeping out of the sea like a crawling
thing" with that of the Laughing Lord statue and its "puffy, bloated

face, the crawling horror of the distended mouth, the gaping eyes... body crouched and tense." As with the improvement in the use of tropes we began seeing in "The Will-o'-the-Wisp," there is a distinct utility in Carr's use of imagery here compared to previous sinister tales. In "The Riddle of the Laughing Lord," tropes reinforce meaning.

What's more, Carr cleverly links Morgan Grimm himself, too, with the statue. Grimm's exultation in Greytowers' evil reputation is, of course, indication of a "kink in the brain" like the one that turned the Austrian nobleman into the depraved Laughing Lord. Immediately after Grimm's argument with Patricia—in which she calls her husband a "morbid...thing"—as his wife slams the door, Morgan laughs. Without being too overt, Carr here conflates the laughter of the recently mentioned Laughing Lord effigy with the laughter of its obsessed owner. Given this, when the tale climaxes in Grimm's depraved emulation of the Austrian nobleman, the reader is prepared for the supernatural transference of homicidal insanity between the statue and Grimm.

"The Riddle of the Laughing Lord" is not only a clear stepping-stone from the less successful baleful tones of earlier tales to the leap forward in *Grand Guignol*, but to the professional works, too. There is an especially rich comparison to be made between this fairy tale and *The Corpse in the Waxworks*. As Joana Kokot observes, "Some locations in Carr's novels are viewed...as enclaves in the contemporary world, belonging to another time and 'haunted' by the spectres from the past."[1] Like Grimm's tower room...

> ...the Gallery of Horrors in the world of the dead with its wax figures representing people long gone. It is there M. Augustin, the owner, believes he sees a ghost of a woman once sent to the guillotine by Bencolin. As he says: "one night, months ago, when I was closing up, I could have sworn I saw Madame Louchard, in her fur neckpiece and her little brown hat, walking along the green-lit Gallery..."[2]

Concerning the murder itself, in the Gallery of Horrors...

> ...the border between what is real and what is only part of the exhibition is blurred. The dagger in Marat's chest is stained with actual blood, as it was used as murder weapon by Miss Martel's killer, while the body

1 "John Dickson Carr's Early Detective Novels and the Gothic Convention," *Lublin Studies in Modern Languages and Literature*, 2019 (43/2), pp. 61-74.
2 Ibid.

of the girl is at first mistaken for a wax figure.... Evidently, the killer lay the dead girl in the arms of the legendary creature purposely: "Is it strange then [...] that he should continue this symbolism of his? That after he had stabbed [her]...he should put her body into the arms of — *the satyr?* He was offering her there as a kind of sacrifice..."[3]

Such encroachments by past augurs upon the living world occur throughout *The Corpse in the Waxworks*, as well as in *Grand Guignol/It Walks By Night*, *The Lost Gallows*, *Hag's Nook*, *The Three Coffins*, and other Carr novels of the 1930s and 1940s. In "The Laughing Lord," we recognize for the first time the emergence of Carr's signal capability, better than anybody since Poe, to infuse expected everyday settings and the reader's mind with a gothic sense of dread.

---

3 Ibid. This article is a particular case in which, while the editor had already thought through many of its points independently, the article is so well conceived and written that it seems important to draw the reader's special attention to it.

The Devil-Gun (1926)

I

Anstruther went only once to that weird twilight by the Black Sea. But since then he can never look at a key without shuddering.

Russia is the place for minds that are not quite sane, and Anstruther has often told me that the people he saw there were not human at all. In those days before the war they were brutes who seemed all the more horrible because they had the forms of men, with their square faces and woolly caps. They would stand motionless to stare at you in the snow—that snow which is not calm and holy, as of Christmas Eve, but dreary and streaked on the black hills.

Two things only can a person say of Anstruther: he is one of the most powerful men alive, and he has a morbid dread of fire. If you give him the opportunity he will sit for hours with his big body hunched in a chair, and the grim face like stone propped on his hand while he talks about fire. It is uncanny. Fire—the agony of burning at the stake—what the martyrs suffered; you have to shut him up or he will set you shuddering. It was with this horror of fire that he went into Russia, gloomy and secretive like the country, to hunt a man who had barricaded himself there against devils.

Anstruther and his companion got a sleigh at Odessa for the drive through the most dismal country west of Siberia. You can imagine Anstruther sitting there with his big dark face unmoving under the astrakhan cap, like a god out of folklore. He says the sleigh bells jingled incessantly; just that in silence…

Where he had picked up Noel Barnstow nobody knows, though I think that it was in London. Opposite Kensington Gardens there is a little hotel called Coburg Court, and there the slim imaginative Noel told his story. It concerned Noel's father. If you remember the club gossip of fifteen years back you will recall the scandal when Major Sir Lionel Barnstow was cashiered from the Coldstream Guards. The disgrace forced Noel to leave Harrow, and probably had something to do with the subsequent death of his mother. Presently his father left England, talking hell-fury and throwing duel challenges to everybody. He disappeared into Africa, but in time there came the report that he was busy inciting the Shimla blacks to revolt, that he was a Voodoo witch doctor, that somebody was shipping rifles for an uprising that would shake the British empire. The government interfered, and Barnstow disappeared again. You might have seen him everywhere, crazy and headstrong as a comet; flaring and bursting and then slinking away… Now Noel Barnstow came to Anstruther with an account of a letter he had received from his father from Russia, written in his father's own powerful jumbled manner. It summoned him; defiantly, but with a strain of fear. At the end the paper was pricked around a blot of ink, as though the man had flung down his pen into it like a knife. Noel Barnstow wanted Anstruther to accompany him when he went to see his father, because he was afraid. He could never conceive of Anstruther fearing anything—which was right if you except fire.

They got their sleigh at Odessa, and Noel, who prided himself on being a linguist, tried hard to talk to the sullen automatons of men. The wind was terrific, so that they saw the faces through a blur of water, but up against the hard bright sky that shone in dusk there were squat black church spires like the minarets of mosques surmounted with double crosses. There was an unearthly hush, as though on the evening of the Crucifixion, but with a mighty roaring force behind it; and the big leering officers stamped and rattled their sabers, and on the steps of a church a piteous little girl, a match seller, was trying to warm herself by lighting her own matches. They saw her blue lips and white face against the gray of snow and stone… Then the sleigh swung out, the bells tinkled with some semblance of life in that stark, silent place, the faces melted into a whirl…

Noel had been talking rapidly and steadily, craning his neck to stare about. Now he leaned forward, fumbling a cigarette in numb fingers. He was a pale, handsome chap, like an ineffectual fairy-tale prince who had somehow strayed into a cold world where he did not belong. There was a strain of aristocracy in the boy; you respected it all the more because of his father, but sometimes it was a bit priggishly apparent. He said,

"I couldn't stand living in this place, Anstruther! Look at them, the brutes; watch that one blow on his fingers!…I couldn't stand living here, Anstruther; I wonder how Father does? These people—I mean—there was a Barnstow who fought at Agincourt, you know—"

It was just verging on the pathetic. Anstruther looked sideways at him; he answered gruffly, "I know."

The bells kept on jingling into night. Still the strip of sky shone white like a meteor, hurtling before them into darkness. It was all vast and empty as a cavern; lurch, swing, and the curling crack of the whip bells singing, swinging drowsily… Noel's doze was broken when the driver drew up on a level waste. He got down to light the sleigh lamps, and they saw his face by the yellow flame. It waggled[1] and cackled like

---

1 An interesting eccentricity of Carr's: nothing wiggles if it can waggle, or wobbles if it can wabble. These are real words, if less commonly used than their familiar alternatives. In this collection, the reader will encounter "waggle" twice

Punch's in a Punch-and-Judy show; it was ugly, with a misshapen big nose, and diagonally across it ran the weal of a whiplash. He twisted it toward them, peering up in the bright halo on darkness. Vaguely the horses rustled. Then in a moment they were moving on, while the bells rose shrilly.

When the moon rose it uncovered the hills like a veil. Noel kept watching the shadows with fascinated eyes.

"Look!" he muttered, "up there over the trees—it's a church. Out here in this God-forsaken place; it's a church!"

Sheer black the edifice stood, black on the moon-gray sky among its stumpy trees that were like gnomes going in to worship. It was as though one expected those gnomes of trees to move, so that in their rigidity there was something closely akin to the horrible. The wind hung quiet now. The sound of tinkling ceased, and the driver turned.

"The gentlemen must go on alone," he said. Noel stared at the sleigh lamp.

"Go on—where?"

"The man you seek," replied the driver, "lives there, for there devils may not attack him. But *I* will not go," he added, turning his scarred face.

"Buck up!" snapped Anstruther, and he put an arm around the young man's shoulders. "We'll go in; come, now…"

"But, my God! What's he mean?"

"Take your hand away from me!" cried the driver. "My masters, get out of the sleigh. I will not go farther."

"He says my father lives there," Noel babbled. "He wouldn't live there—listen, there was a Barnstow who fought at—"

"Give him his money, then! Here—hand me your valise."

They stood alone. The driver had whipped up his horses, and the lights went lurching away. They heard a sing-song chant like a prayer.

"I keep fancying that there are people all around here," muttered Noel. "Maybe there are… Anstruther, I don't want to go near the place! Listen, I visited a leper colony in Burma once, and it looked—"

"Don't be an ass!"

"I know; but there's something wrong with it…I wonder why they have those queer-shaped towers, and the double crosses. Look, Anstruther—please say something!" he added rather breathlessly; "there's one with a *triple* cross!"

He pointed, high against the dim-lit sky. Then he coughed, and began peering with eyes that were whitish under the moon.

"It's moving… I'm not crazy, I'm not nervous…I tell you that

---

and "wabble" three times. Carr continued preferring these unusual forms as a professional.

cross is *moving!*" The words kept growing louder and louder, flatly shrill.

"Now, steady—it's a man. He had his arms out under one of the crosses."

"It's looking at us…"

II

Anstruther had to knock many times on the big doors. Finally they heard steps. On a tall window above them a light ran up suddenly, so that the figure on the stained glass, a white saint, looked down at them. Then the door opened. Inside stood a Negro holding a candle, a monstrous shiny fellow who smiled and smirked and regarded them with reddish eyes. He said in an uncertain voice, like one repeating a lesson, "The master—inside—"

"He's wearing livery," mumbled Noel, not quite knowing whether to laugh. "Anstruther, he's wearing the Barnstow livery!"

The big Negro did not understand, but he continued to grin while he led them into a passage. In the torn finery he wore he was too grotesque to be absurd. They saw the light shining on ahead, through rows of pews in that forgotten church where the echoes trailed them like an army. The place had turned cold for Noel. He knew starkly that he was afraid.

The Negro stopped by a door near the nave, and a light shone out. He drew himself up pompously; then he announced, "Mist' Noel Barnstow!"

The echo boomed back. Again Noel felt the inclination to laugh, jumpily. And when they entered the room, the wild absurdity of it seemed too much. A fire burned on the hearth of a stone room, a dirty littered room with broken cups on the table and an oil lamp smoking above the mantelpiece. But before the fire stood a man. His face was almost as black as the Negro's, and looked as though it might crumble like dust—wrinkled, with staring yellowish eyes and a mane of tawny hair. But what struck Anstruther was the fact that the huge body was clad in evening clothes, with white tie and shirt front grimy. A rosary hung across the shirt front in the manner of a decoration.

"You may go, Mortimer," he announced, waving his hand to the Negro. The door closed. Noel bowed his head.

Then the man smiled with his crooked teeth, and advanced shamblingly. His eyes were grotesquely tender.

"Ain't you going to greet your old father, Noel?" he said, the eyes widening; "your old father that always loved you? We put on airs for you, Noel, we did—"

Noel took the old man in his arms. His face was white.

"Certainly, sir—certainly—"

"We want you to be at home here, Noel. My son! I c'n remember when you wasn't more'n a little thing," said the man coyly.

"Father," replied Noel with an effort, "I have a friend here, a gentleman from London. Allow me to present: Mr. Anstruther—Sir Lionel Barnstow."

The old man bowed, trying to make a flourish of it. Anstruther bowed in return.

"Delighted to make your acquaintance," Sir Lionel said. "Oh, yes, and you're from London. From London! I sh'l be happy to have you look me up there, sir—very influential there...I sh'l give you a card to the Embassy Club, if you like... Noel! Ain't you glad to see me, lad?"

There was a silence. Then another door was opened by the Negro. He cried: "Lady Corinne Barnstow!"

Again in silence a woman came through the door. She looked thin and shrunken, and her faded eyes did not smile, though the mouth took on the semblance of a grin. Her scanty, straw-colored hair had been piled high, stuck with a red plume; she wore a flowered gown of a decade past, which swept out into a train and almost tripped her. Her cheeks were heavily rouged, and she glittered with glass jewels.

" 'Ow do you do, sirs?" she greeted them, curtseying, " 'ow d'ye do... Is that Mr. Noel, now? Well, ain't 'e the grand 'andsome young 'un, though—like his father," she added with a smirk.

"Noel, here's your mother; here's your new mother!" the old man cried eagerly. "Go and kiss her, Noel; ain't she pretty, lad?"

They looked at each other, these two. Each face was beaming, and the dark wrinkled one shone with pride...And then Noel did a thing that was magnificent to the point of caddishness, for he went quietly over to kiss the painted cheek.

"—'tendin' bar, I wos, in Cape Town, and along 'e comes with 'is fine manners and captures me 'eart! Sit down, won't you... Wot wos your name, sir? Mr. Anstruther? Y' know my son, Mr. Anstruther?"— she patted Noel's arm—"Barnstow's a grand name, sir. There was a Barnstow what fought at Agincourt, y' know..."

Noel was looking very white. His father turned round and went to the table; he poured out a drink, drained the glass, and stared at them.

"Corinne," he said suddenly, "I can hear it now. It's a-walkin'..."

"My God!" Noel cried out, "My God, what are you talking about, Father?"

"It's a-walkin'; Corinne, it might stick its hand through that door... Boy," he muttered, and went toward Noel with his yellow childish eyes wide, "you've got to get us away from here. I saw it last night! Don't

you realize, Noel—it ain't alive—please, it's goin' to kill your old dad-
dy! Sit down, all of you; it won't come in while we have lights."

He stood outlined against the red fire, holding an empty glass.
Abruptly they began to think that in the old body there was terrific
insane strength.

"Get the gun, Corinne; my devil-gun... You don't know all about
it, Noel. Listen: what's the most horrible thing you can think of?
What in all the world would scare you most? Tell me, please!"

Noel did not reply, because he thought he knew. Anstruther
spoke one word:

"Fire!"

"Fire!" repeated the old man and laughed. He went on with a
rush: "I know; that's all right. You don't imagine anything more horrible, eh? But I'll tell you, you never saw this thing when it was dead.
I don't mean alive, but dead! It was a black man, a witch doctor. I
c'n remember the night I shot him—" Power was in Lionel Barnstow, a mighty force that drove his words to a cry: "Shot him! They
don't know what I did down on that river among the n—s.[2] The
n—s thought they had me cornered that night, when the jungle fever
was makin' them shrivel up and die howlin', and there was hot fog
in the trees... They'd started beatin' their drums; I could hear the
damned drums going—*boom, boom,* just like that, all around me. Flat
painted faces, n—s, with their fires burnin' by the river and shinin'
on the black water. I had an elephant gun. This Voodoo doctor came
out with his side all hunched up in paralysis, shaking his throat and
screaming to heaven—then I pulled the trigger. It tore his face wide
open, but he yelled once before he splashed back among 'em in the
reeds: one face out of that ring with their war spears... I wasn't afraid
of him while he was alive. But he didn't come back lookin' the way
he did before he died... Can't imagine a thing worse'n fire, eh? Well,
I saw this thing the other night. I came in my room, and lit the lamp,
and there it was just sittin' in my chair lookin' at me—"

It was as though a climax had come like the clang of a bell. In
an instant weirdness had changed to hysteria; everything appeared
to move in the room, for the fire had sunk. Even Anstruther stared
at the old man unwinkingly. Sir Lionel had assumed a lopsided appearance, and his yellow eyes were the chinks you see in a furnace.
He took a step forward. Then he fell—fell heavily, so that the lamp

---

2 Carr wrote the entire ethnic term here, which the editor has elided. Its use
100 years later is unacceptable. Carr puts this word into the mouth of a terrible
character—he does not otherwise use it—and at the time Carr was writing,
its use was common. There is no reason to conclude the word reflects Carr's
personal views.

shook, and lay there waving his legs in the air like a beetle.

The woman screamed, "Lionel!—Lionel!" after which she set up a wail for Mortimer. From behind a chair she had taken a squat heavy weapon. Anstruther realized that it was an elephant gun.

"Y'll have to get away, sir," she told them. "Mortimer will take you to y'r room. 'E gets like this sometimes, when hit's a-chasin' 'im—"

"You mean," said Noel, "that there is—"

"Hisaw it! Git up, 'oney; it cawn't 'urt you now; I'll shoot it agin... It was a-standin' hout in the moonlight, and it 'adn't no face..."

Sir Lionel lurched up. His lady was giving instructions to Mortimer, who had thrust his grinning countenance around the edge of the door. They saw Sir Lionel lumber toward a table; there was a splintering of wood, and he had wrenched a leg from it...

The last thing they saw as they backed toward the door was that firelit image—the figure in the dress suit, holding the table leg, erect with dignity now and crying that he was an English gentleman, and, huddled in a corner, the staring bejeweled woman with the gun across her knees.

III

Mortimer took the two guests upstairs to a room. At every turn of the steps Noel thought he heard things wild as laughter. The wind swung and shook now; it had taken on a fierce pealing note like trumpets, so that the candle flame made a fluttering sound... They saw the tall Negro's grin...

Their apartment was high up in the church. Noel almost pushed Anstruther in, and slammed the door on the Negro. He had seen much on that slow ascent. Once inside, they faced each other. It was a large room, stained damply, and with rough beds in the midst of a litter of church relics—cloths, candles, silver, and the images of saints, all dusty. At the left they saw a fireplace with a blaze; in front, dominating the wall that faced them, a monstrous window of stained glass. It represented Christ on the cross, a distorted figure, red-stained face under the crown of thorns, and all colors shining in the moon behind...

"Look at that thing!" said Noel, standing with his back against the door. "It's cold in here. Oh, it's so cold!" He shivered. "They don't expect us to sleep here, do they?"

Anstruther began to pace about. They could hear the wind... Noel remained motionless, looking at the window. The fire threw so little light that in the dark chamber the window with its colors stood out in ghastly relief by the moon... Anstruther kicked over a candlestick with a clattering noise. And Anstruther was nervous. They did not know what was to happen.

"Lock the door!" ordered the older man. He went over, turned the key, and took it out from behind Noel's unmoving body. Then he approached the fireplace.

"We'd better get to bed," he said heavily.

"I can't!—Listen, do you recall what father told us. He told us, 'I came into the room, and lit the lamp, and there it was sitting in my chair looking at me—'"

"Shut up!"

"No... You look—horrible yourself—"

Anstruther took out a cigarette. He stood leaning against the mantel with his eyes on the fire. Fire! Fire that was a menace, gnawing the wood...He bent down, attempting to get a light for the cigarette, but, as he neared the fire, his hand trembled. He was close to it now; it stared him in the face squarely. Bright, burning brightly, glaring at him.

"I thought I heard someone *climbing*," Noel was saying in a faraway voice. Anstruther saw only the fire. But he went too close; he almost cried out as his fingers were scorched by it. He leaped back, and his hand unclosed, dropping the key into the middle of the blaze...

Then he paused, turned halfway around. There was a silence so utter that it had a rush and force, as though a car were hurtling to crash against a tree. Noel stood strained, with his arms outspread on the door...

Anstruther's eyes went to the floor. On the square of the moon-brightness a shadow was rearing behind the shadow of the crucifix... Suddenly Noel darted out an arm to point. His eyes were staring and fixed.

"Get the key out—*Get it out!*" he muttered.

Anstruther turned. There was a crash from the window.

"It's breaking the glass—" went on Noel monotonously.

Another slow stroke hit the window, picking at it; the shadow hunched, and then, as the face of the Christ-figure was shattered away, another face peered in... More glass was steadily cracked away... Anstruther did not hesitate. He turned, and with a gasp he plunged his right hand full into the fire after the key.

Noel screamed. Every nerve went into his voice, every insane crying terror. He saw the whole window fall to an inrush of wind, and heard the thud as something dropped to the floor. Anstruther had pulled out his arm, half stupefied at the realization; the arm smoked and glowed... Then Anstruther seized the poker that had lain there in the blaze. Noel saw him turn with the poker uplifted, its red tip moving in the gloom—over toward the window—the red tip going forward as Anstruther lurched steadily on. Something jumped at him...

The red iron whirled and fell, staggering there in the air. The wind flung glittering snow swirling in; it shocked full over Noel, rousing him. Laughter came from under the moving poker tip. In a tangle of shadows Anstruther was wheezing; a candlestick was kicked over... And in the midst of it all there was Noel running over and pawing in the fire for the key, scattering embers about him hysterically.

The drive of wind had made an inferno of the place, whirling sparks through it. But the moonlight lay white on the floor, and only the shadow of the fight spun across it... Voices were crying below in the church; Noel thought he heard somebody singing a hymn. He had the key now, and he did not realize that it was scorching his fingers. Hands were pawing at the door from the outside... One of the beds thudded over, and the poker, spinning, shot across the room like a flaming rocket. Anstruther's gasp was a gasp of bewildered pain...

Then the door was thrown open. At the same instant Anstruther's big body came reeling out of shadows and drove to its knees among the sparks, panting. Against the window a silhouette reared up. But in the doorway, lit yellow by an upheld lantern, stood another figure—one with a red plume in its hair, and the light shining down its face. When the elephant gun crashed and blasted in fire full at that silhouette, Anstruther crawled round to peer up stupidly. The woman stood motionless by the door; she had not lowered the elephant gun, but she was croaking, "Glory be to God!—"

The thing that had come upon them by night, and whom the woman had shot in the face as Sir Lionel had shot the witch doctor, was flung back against the window ledge. They heard it slide to the floor. Now there came only the boom of the wind. Utter quiet...

With halting steps the big Negro was carrying a lantern over to the window. They saw Lady Barnstow's red plume bob after it; then there was a scream. The woman had sunk to her knees beside a shapeless thing, and she was holding it to her breast and rocking back and forth. They heard her cry, "Lionel!... Lionel!... Hi didn't mean to shoot you, honey...Lionel!—"

Notes for the Curious: "The Devil-Gun"

"The Devil-Gun" is Carr's purest horror story, although he only wrote three. "The Riddle of the Laughing Lord" was, of course, the first. His third horror tale, "Pygmalion," published in *The Haverfordian* in 1927, is a contemporary story with a horrifying twist. It is a shame Carr wrote so few horror tales, because "The Devil-Gun" is a real treat that demonstrates his potential. Of course, that potential was not entirely wasted, given Carr's gothic mysteries of the 1930s and 1940s, but it seems certain Carr's readers would have forgiven him the writing of a few more straight horror stories.

The first question about which an alert reader wonders concerning "The Devil-Gun" is whether it is a sequel to "The Marked Bullet." Is "The Devil-Gun" the story of the ignominious end of Sir Lionel Barnstow, the towering and legendary English hero who appears briefly in that mystery, "one of the most picturesque figures in England. Author, explorer, sportsman—a dozen other things…the personification of every man's secret desires"? The conclusion that it is seems sadly unavoidable, but this connection between the stories is another demonstration of Carr's milieu-building from year to year.

Part of the pleasure of "The Devil-Gun" is its inclusion of so many of the ingredients we have seen used by the young author all along, combined into another gratifying leap forward. Consider the story's participation in the Gothic, especially in its use of the grotesque: "The Devil-Gun" features textbook mingling of the familiar with the unfamiliar such that the familiar is distorted, appropriately suggestive of the repulsiveness beneath the surface. Here, of course, is a little bit of flavor shared between Carr and Robert Louis Stevenson's *The Strange Case of Dr. Jekyll and Mr. Hyde*—but really, between Carr and Poe, too, and others…essentially, between Carr and the best of the Gothic tradition.

One inspiration for this story was probably "Canon Alberic's Scrap-Book," an M.R. James chiller in which an English collector of old manuscripts encounters the titular folio, whose "unprincipled" author plundered its hundred and fifty leaves from some dozens of illuminated manuscripts. Both tales play with the concept of how imaginative horror can, improbably, physically materialize evil. The final leaf of the book in James's story includes a seventeenth-century sepia drawing depicting the confrontation by King Solomon and his guards, in horrified disgust, of a night demon—a crouching, bestial figure that has already killed one of the guards. Even viewing a *photograph* of the illustration, the narrator discloses, produces a terrifying effect upon the viewer:

I recollect once showing the photograph of the
drawing to a lecturer on morphology—a person of, I
was going to say, abnormally sane and unimaginative
habits of mind. He absolutely refused to be alone for
the rest of that evening, and he told me afterwards
that for many nights he had not dared to put out his
light before going to sleep.[1]

As to the original illustration, its malevolence is so potent that
viewing it directly manifests the demon:

He had taken the crucifix off, and laid it on the table,
when his attention was caught by an object lying on
the red cloth just by his left elbow. Two or three ideas
of what it might be flitted through his brain with
their own incalculable quickness.
"A penwiper? No, no such thing in the house. A rat?
No, too black. A large spider? I trust to goodness
not—no. Good God! A hand like the hand in that
picture!"
In another infinitesimal flash he had taken it in. Pale,
dusky skin, covering nothing but bones and tendons
of appalling strength; coarse, black hairs, longer than
ever grew on a human hand; nails rising from the
ends of the fingers and curving sharply down and
forward, gray, horny and wrinkled.
He flew out of his chair with deadly, inconceivable
terror clutching at his heart. The shape, whose left
hand rested on the table, was rising to a standing pos-
ture behind his seat, its right hand crooked above his
scalp. (pp. 23-24)

"The Devil-Gun" ends with an O. Henry-style surprise, and the
story's final revelation makes it kin to Poe's "The Tell-Tale Heart":
the tormented character has been bedeviled from within, not from
without, as he believed. Notice how much more satisfying the ending of this story is than that of "The House of Terror," which never
resolved the question of whether Darworth came back after death
to haunt Melford. "The Devil-Gun," like Carr's professional works,
resolves the supernatural ambiguity in a most satisfying manner—if,
it must be admitted, without a happy ending.

1 *Ghost-Stories of an Antiquary*, Edward Arnold, 1905, p. 18. All subsequent
excerpts are drawn from the same edition.

Carr juggles several dialects comfortably, and to intentional effect. Noel Barnstow's Queen's English carries the conscious veneer of civilization in it, and the family pride, too. Mortimer's unrefined English belies Noel's family image, the incongruity of Mortimer's station even provoking fear in the younger Barnstow. The cockney accents of the degraded Sir Lionel and Lady Corinne, in their comical absurdity, bring the family dignity fully low, deflating those hereditary airs originated in the Barnstow who fought at Agincourt—especially when Lady Corinne mentions it, reducing the pathos of Noel's reliance upon family history to mere bathos when she does so.

Clothing imagery parallels and supports Carr's use of dialect. Mortimer wearing the Barnstow family livery stupefies Noel. It is ripped and shabby, ill fitting the sizeable Mortimer; he is all the more jarring in it for his reddened eyes and grinning, unsophisticated demeanor, no proper English servant. Sir Lionel's evening clothes are notably grimy, and as with Mortimer, there is an antithesis between what the civilized English clothes represent and the figure wearing them: "His face was almost as black as the Negro's, and looked as though it might crumble like dust—wrinkled, with staring yellowish eyes and a mane of tawny hair." Carr also pairs these two by calling attention to their common grotesquerie. Of Mortimer, he writes: "In the torn finery he wore he was too grotesque to be absurd"; of Sir Lionel, "Then the man smiled with his crooked teeth, and advanced shamblingly. His eyes were grotesquely tender." As to Lady Corinne, her appearance is nothing more than a cheap pretense to a nobility she never had:

> Again in silence a woman came through the door. She looked thin and shrunken, and her faded eyes did not smile, though the mouth took on the semblance of a grin. Her scanty, straw-colored hair had been piled high, stuck with a red plume; she wore a flowered gown of a decade past, which swept out into a train and almost tripped her. Her cheeks were heavily rouged, and she glittered with glass jewels.

The prose of "The Devil-Gun" is remarkably absorbing, drawing the reader's focus into this relatively short narrative. The language in it is so concentrated that, compared with "The Riddle of the Laughing Lord," the reader's attention slows down—not the story's tempo, our attention. We feel as if we are consuming something denser and more filling. Despite how much of the storytelling is visual, few if any passages in this tale seem overwrought, as some in Carr's high-school efforts did. Nor is there any longer any easy borrowing of tread-worn language: most of Carr's tropes are original and cogent. The technical performance of "The Devil-Gun," in sum, with respect to the construction and the exploitation of figurative language, is quite strong.

Carr's use of such imagery in "The Devil-Gun" is often in the service of subtext. The central and most consistently developed figurative language is, of course, the story's religious imagery: the snow antithetically reminiscent of that on Christmas Eve; the Crucifixion references; the "sing-song chant like a prayer"; even the name of the younger Barnstow: Noel.

In contrapuntal balance, there is also plenty of devil imagery: the titular gun; the depiction of the Russian natives as devils; the elder Barnstow's talking "hell-fury" on his way out of London, which is a bit of foreshadowing. All this heaven-and-hell language prepares the reader for Sir Lionel Barnstow's moral descent and transformation, which climaxes by his crashing through the stained-glass window of the crucified Christ, his frighteningly distorted face grotesquely supplanting the Savior's.

Almost fifteen years later, Carr revisited a key element of "The Devil-Gun"—the visceral tensions between races and cultures—in *The Reader is Warned* (1939). Martin Edwards succinctly analyzes it in *The Golden Age of Murder* (p. 396): "Carr's treatment of racial issues— in a storyline touching on Bantu Fetishism—is of its time, but steers clear of bigotry. Perhaps uniquely in Golden Age fiction, the catalyst for the crimes is the first victim's casual racism."

In "The Devil-Gun," Sir Lionel, too, is destroyed by his own racism. The reader may understandably be uneasy with Carr's use of expected, even trite imagery: the drum-beating voodoo practices of the African tribesman, or Mortimer's stereotypical Negro grin. This is fair. As with his handling of women, Carr is no better here than his culturally received precepts. Still, as Edwards argues, Carr demonstrates no bigotry. We can also agree with Greene (p. 163), who assesses the potentially problematic nature of *The Reader Is Warned* by concluding, "In short, Carr seems to be saying that whatever evil beliefs and practices exist, they are not racial; they are human."

Of this story in the biography (p. 49), Greene suggests *Weird Tales* may be the general influence, but there is a more specific and telling one: Joseph Conrad's *Heart of Darkness*. Sir Lionel Barnstow's journey into Africa after he leaves London is certainly reminiscent of Kurtz's. Compare key passages concerning both:

> He disappeared into Africa, but in time there came
> the report that he was busy inciting the Shimla blacks
> to revolt, that he was a Voodoo witch doctor, that

somebody was shipping rifles for an uprising that would shake the British empire. The government interfered, and Barnstow disappeared again.

Kurtz had been educated partly in England, and—as he was good enough to say himself—his sympathies were in the right place. His mother was half-English, his father was half-French. All Europe contributed to the making of Kurtz; and by and by I learned that, most appropriately, the International Society for the Suppression of Savage Customs had intrusted him with the making of a report, for its future guidance. And he had written it, too... But this must have been before his—let us say—nerves, went wrong and caused him to preside at certain midnight dances ending with unspeakable rites which...were offered up to him...."[2]

Both men travel into the subcontinent carrying with them the European presumption of being civilizing influences. Instead, the superficiality of each's culture is stripped away and both men acclimate to tribal customs, participating in superstitious rituals, including violent ones. As to that report Kurtz writes concerning the suppression of savage customs, it encapsulates his unwinding:

There were no practical hints to interrupt the magic current of phrases, unless a kind of note at the foot of the last page, scrawled evidently much later, in an unsteady hand, may be regarded as the exposition of a method. It was very simple, and at the end of that moving appeal to every altruistic sentiment it blazed at you, luminous and terrifying, like a flash of lightning in a serene sky: 'Exterminate all the brutes!' (p. 75)

Sir Lionel Barnstow, like Kurtz, acts on the report's horrible exhortation. His descent, echoing Kurtz's, is an object lesson regarding what Conrad terms, "the heart of a conquering darkness" (p. 110). He is transformed by his own acts of unjustifiable savagery. First their commission take his sanity, then finally, his life. Kurtz's famous deathbed words may as well have been Sir Lionel's: "The horror! The horror!"

If Sir Lionel is an evident cognate to Kurtz, Anstruther is likewise one to Marlow. Anstruther, while likely related to Sir George (of *The Bowstring Murders* and *The Red Widow Murders*), is certainly not he. Sir

---

2 *Heart of Darkness*, Duke Classics, 2012, p. 74. All subsequent excerpts are drawn from the same edition.

George studies anthropologically from a careful distance what this tale's Anstruther encounters directly. Sir George is the Director of the British Museum and a Cambridge lecturer who resembles "less a scholar than a sort of cultured bartender" (*The Bowstring Murders*, p. 4). He wheezes and speaks genially. He confesses to his colleague Dr. Michael Tairlaine that he has never had an adventure, and he all but admits being unfit for one. The Anstruther of "The Devil-Gun," like Marlow, is an adventurer. Anstruther is large, terse, decisive, (nearly) fearless, and physical. Perhaps the two Anstruthers are brothers sharing a familial interest in anthropology. In any event, like Marlow, Anstruther has only one peculiar hatred, which both men associate with the same thing—death:

> Fire—the agony of burning at the stake—what the martyrs suffered; you have to shut him up or he will set you shuddering.

> You know I hate, detest, and can't bear a lie, not because I am straighter than the rest of us, but simply because it appalls me. There is a taint of death, a flavor of mortality in lies,—which is exactly what I hate and detest in the world—what I want to forget. (pp. 35-36)

Of course, each man's adventure forces him to confront that one thing he dreads and detests; the encounter is life-changing.

Noel Barnstow, too, has an analogue in *Heart of Darkness*: the young Russian trader, nicknamed by Marlow "the harlequin" for both the motley state of his clothes and his fatuousness. Carr does not offer any explicit allusion, but we can readily imagine that Conrad's description of the Russian can also serve for Noel Barnstow:

> A beardless, boyish face, very fair, no features to speak of, nose peeling, little blue eyes, smiles and frowns chasing each other over that open countenance like sunshine and shadow on a wind-swept plain. (p. 78)

Heart of Darkness, although in many senses a modern novel, is consistent with the tradition of Dark Romanticism. (Conrad was not an American writer; we refer here to the novel's essential characteristics.) As we have noted, available comparisons between Carr's works and novels like *Heart of Darkness*, novels traditionally regarded as being of the first literary order, help us understand and appreciate Carr in new and expanded ways. *Heart of Darkness* is also the kind of Romanticism Carr admired, in its stripping away of the civilized patina to reveal the more exciting (and distressing) truth underneath it—or, as Chesterton phrased it:

> ...men's souls have stranger adventures than their bodies, and...it would be harder and more exciting to hunt their virtues than to hunt their crimes...that thrilling mood and moment when the eyes of the great city, like the eyes of a cat, begin to flame in the dark...

In many Carr works, London is imaginatively transformed into Baghdad-on-the-Thames, and the characters traversing it live through gothic, Arabian Nights-style adventures. In "The Devil-Gun," by contrast, Sir Lionel (as Kurtz did) rides the River Thames, which runs into London, the heart of civilization, out of it—and then rides the Congo River into the heart of darkness, instead.

The New Canterbury Tales (1927)

Written with Frederic Prokosch

Dedication

To One Who Does Not Believe In Romance, We, Who Abhor Fact,
Dedicate These Madcap Tales, In The Hope That We Shall Find a
Few Hardy Souls Unashamed To Confess a Weakness for Ghosts
And Buried Treasure And Rollicking Foolishness.

A droning voice that does not lift or falter,
A drowsy hum from out a hot slow class—
Your spectacles, with eyes that never alter—
This is you. From you the dead facts pass.

Year in and out. Long, lank, and never-bending.
At watch-tick intervals you turn the leaves of fame;
A little rustling—that is all; it is unending—
Your lecture-notes. Always you are the same.

"After the First Crusade we must consider
The economic aspects of this act."
You talk of crowns sold to the highest bidder,
And spice your figures with the sifted sand of fact.

Year after year you gather knowledge, only
To gather more. Oh, man, have you forgot
How in the lilies Guinevere dreamed lonely
Beside the mirror lake of Camelot?

It was a stag affair, which was just as well, because your well-fed and drowsy man is apt to get reminiscent about his amorous conquests over some o'd red liquid in a tall glass, especially if he be old. And it was a hunting dinner after the fashion of a hundred years ago, in an ancient, rook-haunted, decaying manor house on the Wessex downs. They all wore red coats, with white vests and Ascot ties pulled open; there were even some dogs in the room, where a big fire blazed against the autumn wind. Unquestionably, the day had been successful enough, even from the point of view of old Sir John Landervorne, who flushed up red through his gray beard till his eyes sparkled. He had been foremost in at the death: a wild thundering figure, sharp against the greenish sky in twilight over the downs, urging his horse through mire and sticky heather. Now he sat in a corner by the fire, under the dark panel-ing and a diamond-paned window, legs thrust out, holding up a glass. The others sat near him in the tall-backed black chairs. They were tired and mud-spattered, half dozing after a meal: Dunstan, the host, who was fat and winking like a wine-barrel—Bencolin, the apologetic French detective and an execrable horseman—old Ludwig von Arnheim, the shrunken shaggy-bearded author—Patrick O'Riordan, Bencolin's Irish friend—and the American newspaperman, Stoneman Wood.

It was a curious group, because Dunstan was by way of being a celebrity hunter as well as country squire, and each man was famous in his own manner. Von Arnheim, eternally peering and snorting around himself, blinking over his old square spectacles, fumbling at his beard—even von Arnheim had pulled away from his studies among languorous-lipped ladies of the fifteenth century to come, though he hated fox hunting. He sat now with his chin in his hand, looking at the fire.

"You have a wild hard-riding country, Dunstan," said von Arnheim in his careless and perfect English. "There are legends, I suppose?"

"Legends!" cried O'Riordan, the burly, grinning Irishman, who was sitting fondling a dog under the light of a candle. "Man, the place is thick with 'em! Don't you know: we sit here like a lot of people in a story, with nothing to do except drink and talk about the days when men wore swords...why not legends? With soft-close kissing women in 'em, though, I stipulate. Wind and song and steel; that's what Wessex is. Alfred fought the Danes here. This was the place where the Great White Horse scoured. There was Alfred, and Harold, and Colan; Chesterton made a fine ballad about it, didn't he?[1] You remember Colan, who had—" He

---

1 *The Ballad of the White Horse*, Methuen & Co., 1911. O'Riordan refers to Book V, in which Colan, an impoverished Irishman and faithful Christian, carrying

threw back his head and sang:

"The little worm of laughter
That eats the Irish heart!"

"There never was a county in England," said Dunstan proudly, "that didn't have the stories." He sat back, and his fat body quivered as though with mirth, and his smile curled almost across the jovial face. "But that's old fashioned. This sort of thing is all old fashioned, what?"

"Well, we're old-fashioned men," argued Sir John Landervorne with some heat, because he had taken much wine. "I sometimes wish to God that storytellers would get a bit more old fashioned. They'd be more entertaining."

Stoneman Wood, the American, was smiling. He contradicted all their previous ideas of Americans, dark and quiet and sardonic enough to be an American's conception of an Englishman.

"You've a fine old window here, Mr. Dunstan," observed Wood, "with some sort of curse on it, I'm told, and the ghost of a guilty monk hanging around. Possibly buried treasure. Now, all this is very old fashioned, but I'm free to confess a sneaking liking for it. Children are the only ones who are frank about it. It's all dreadfully trite and hackneyed," he added a bit nervously, for he had the usual inferiority complex of an American for an English gentleman with a manor house, "but won't you tell us a story?"

Dunstan beamed, bland and childlike.

"I will!" he said. "By Jove, I will! And you may have your voluptuous ladies, O'Riordan. I'm fond of 'em myself at—eh—past middle age. Hey, damme!" cried their host, thumping around him like a walrus. "Stobel; I say, Stobel! Get some more of that wine; don't be a damned J—[2] with it! And build up the fires; don't be so sparing with the wood!"

The manservant appeared like a family ghost. He blew the blaze with a bellows until it soared again, and all the red-coated, white-breeched gentlemen lolled about, reaching for cigarettes.

"Don't clean the dust off those bottles!" Dunstan ordered to the departing butler… Then he took a candle and went to one big window in the darkest part of the room. He had to stand on a chair to reach it. In silence wind swept along the ivy outside like a swishing stream. Dunstan stood and passed the candle along

only a rusty sword and wearing tattered clothes, travels with King Alfred to defend Britain against Guthram and the Great Heathen Army of invaders. Colan rallies Alfred's discouraged troops by slaying Guthram's "barbarian" kinsman Harold, who insults the land and its peasant defenders.

2 The original text uses the full word and is an antisemitic trope. While its use does not necessarily indicate Carr's personal views, it is an indication of how familiar antisemitism was, and how Carr did not expect its invocation to bother the reader.

the glass, so that in the candle gleam they could read the old weird lettering on it.

WHILE STANDS THE GLASS NONE SHALL BE RICH,
WHO LOOKS THROUGH IT YE SHALL NOT KNOW;
AND YET WHO STRIVES TO BREAK THE CURSE
SHALL BRING ON HIM A HEAVIER WOE.

They all spelled it out, the faint twisted script on an opaque background. Dunstan looked around with his face in the yellow light; everyone was regarding it perplexedly, lips moving, except Bencolin. The Frenchman was sitting low down in his chair, smoking a cigar. He was peering thoughtfully at a window on the other side of the room, against which ivy slithered.

"But what's it mean?" said O'Riordan.

"I wish I knew," said their host, coming down from the chair. "It's connected with the legend of the black monk, who cursed this place in the ancient terrible way. I've seen a shadow on this window myself, shaped like a monk. I'll tell you about it."

He went to the fire, where he sat down, pulled a bottle closer, and lit a churchwarden pipe. They could see him corpulently outlined in black, with the thin stem of the pipe going in rhythmical motion to and from his mouth in ghostly puffs of smoke.

"I don't profess to be a storyteller," he went on, "and this will be rather crude, but here is what is called..."

THE LEGEND OF THE BLACK MONK

It was tremendously long ago, not much after the time of Alfred. You get the idea that it was much darker around here then, and windier, and they likely had a cold time of it, with the armor rubbing their bodies. They would all grease up with oil and musk, which was the fashion of the dandy, and stick feathers in their big helmets. They were always fighting, or drunk, or home with their women in steaming hot rooms. They had minstrels who would sing at court in those green skin-tight clothes, until the hall got all full of smoke from the fires, chilly smoke that smarted your eyes. Dirty floors stamped with blood...

But there was one girl there who wasn't like that—gad, she must have been a looker! Just as remote and far-away as you please, but with a sort of hotness about her, and the deep eyes and half-opened mouth. She had yellow hair, with this thin pink-tinged skin. She was always mooning about this place, which used to be a big heavy castle; her father was the lord of the manor. When the poor devils of peasants would stumble past from the fields about dark, they'd see her maybe leaning over a battlement, in those clinging robes but with shoulders bare to her breast, hair hanging down, and up on a greenish sky where there was a star or two. The peasants would sing to her beauty like a lot of beasts growling a chant—in twilight... Hildegarde was her name.

This man Unthred, the black monk, was the power in the neighborhood. He'd grin at you, till you got the idea you were damned. He had the lord of the manor frightened out of his wits, for the lord was rather crackbrained anyhow and used to sit in a corner with a spoon for a toy. Unthred drained piles of gold out of him. More than that, he had his eye on the castle after the lord should die, for he wanted Hildegarde. He used to stand and dandle the spoon before the old lord, who looked at it like a baby at a watch, and all the while Unthred was looking out under his cowl at Hildegarde.

She had a lover. He was a powerful darkish chap who often sat on the hills and looked at the stars. Sort of childlike fierceness about him;

he tried to compose songs about Hildegarde, and his thick fingers got all fumbly at the harp. But he was an archer—by Jove! The arrow was like a bullet and a battering ram when he let it go. Whing! And the bowstring would hum like a harp after he'd bent the bow almost double, and the shaft would crack open plate armor, they say.

Often he would climb up the walls, secretly, because he was a common soldier and not for a lady like Hildegarde. There were roses then, the heavy drooping kind, that almost made Hildegarde swoon with their fragrance. So, when he came through the window of the roses, in dim oil lamps' light, she was there...pressing to him with her bared shoulders, while he kissed her mouth and her face and her closed eyes till she trembled and moved her lips on his as though she were trying to speak...Oh, Lord, it was too pretty to be coarse, even for that day.

The old lord died finally. He died in his chair, when the fires were dying out, and he kept grinning and tossing up the spoon to catch it till it fell out of his hands. He just quietly stopped breathing, rather shrunken up in the chimney corner with his foot on the huge breastplate he'd worn when he was a fighter. They found him on the floor.

Unthred got together the spearmen, locked the gates, and made himself lord. He had her now. But somehow the treasures of the house were vanishing; nobody knew where. Unthred went padding around with a silver candlestick under his arm, after which he would disappear for a time. He amused himself by making that window, chuckling at it. When the starved peasants hammered at the walls and cried for bread, Unthred leaned over from the parapet and howled with laughter and tossed some holy water down on them.

One night Hildegarde's young lover crept into the castle (some of them say he knew a secret way) with his bow slung over his shoulder. It was quite still. He got into the cold hallways and stole up to her room. When he put his head in the doorway, softly, there was a dim light burning. He gave a sort of crazy yell... Hildegarde was there, with her lovely body tinged pinker and her eyes closed, breathing... The shriveled monk was bending over her, a grotesque thing, while she suddenly trembled and curled her arm...

The young man, I think, went almost insane at the loathing bestiality of it. Ugh! Rather sick with horror...Unthred whirled around with a look of those black hidden eyes; he gave a yelp and shook himself and blundered around trying to run from him. The young man knocked over a lamp and made for him. Unthred reeled around against the walls like a bat trying to get out. He was crying out, throwing his hands at his enemy. Then he got to the door, while the girl opened her eyes stupidly.

They stumbled through the halls, Unthred's sandals going clackety-clack and his pursuer tugging at the bow to get it off his shoulder. The monk got through a door, tripping up toward the battlements. The other man saw him by the starlight, running for dear life along the wall. Then Unthred jumped up to the parapet, with a frantic idea of a jump, just when the bowman got an arrow notched on the string. Thum! Jove, you could hardly see the arrow, it smashed so fast just as Unthred sprang, and it struck him in midair. He swung around and fell in a twisted way like a big wild turkey with a shaft through it. The man on the wall did not see him, but he heard him hit the ground. Then he put the bow over his shoulder and went down the walls the way he had come.

Dunstan took a last draw at his churchwarden.

"That's all," he said.

"Eh? Demned effective, I should say," remarked Sir John, shaking himself abstractedly. He looked round at the others, who were all contemplating the fire. "What happened to the girl?"

"Why, some say he killed her too, and then went off to the woods. But I suppose there's more reason to believe they made it up and lived happily except for the times he caught her entertaining a new man..."

"But what about the ghost?" asked Stoneman Wood.

"Oh, that's the black monk. He haunts the place. It's been reported ever since that his shadow is seen on the glass of that window, a cowled head with hand holding a candlestick, and with a sort of gleaming around it like a halo. They say he is hunting for something."

"Have you ever seen the ghost?"

"Yes," said Dunstan unexpectedly.

"What the devil!—"

"Well, I saw something. I came down here once at night. There wasn't any light in the room, but the window had a sort of vague illumination around it. There's ivy all over the outside, so I knew it couldn't have been anybody looking in. I saw the cowled head all right, and it was moving. Gad, it gave me a start, just to open the door and have it appear like a man sitting in a chair."³

Dunstan was mellow with wine, so that nobody took him very seriously. They all laughed, except Bencolin.

"It's the treasure he's searching for," continued Dunstan. "These ghosts always seem to be forgetful. But there is a persistent legend about it; I heard it from the father of my man Stobel, who was here before him."

"Oh, you probably saw your own shadow," said the American.

---

3 Compare Dunstan's simile with Sir Lionel Barnstow's ("The Devil-Gun"):
"Well, I saw this thing the other night. I came in my room, and lit the lamp, and there it was just sittin' in my chair lookin' at me—"

"No, I didn't. How are you going to see a human shadow when there isn't any light to throw the shadow? It just appeared..."

O'Riordan laughed and slapped his knees.

"Let it go as a pure ghost! We may see it tonight," he urged. "But it reminds me, yes, I should say it reminds me. I've fallen in love with a lady in a story, the way I did in Constantinople the night Esmet Pasha dared me to break into a harem, and this story turned out about as disastrously as mine. If you care to hear it—"

"You're jolly well right!" Dunstan cried with enthusiasm. "I was a beau in my day," he confessed. "Especially if this is about Turkish beauties, eh? Damme, fill up those glasses again!"

"Splendid!" beamed Sir John cheerfully, but so drowsily that which proposition called forth his enthusiasm was doubtful.

O'Riordan tossed off another glass, whose warmth made him vigorous. His big body was bent forward, a hand on one knee; but there was no other hand, for his red right sleeve was empty and tucked into his pocket like an old grenadier of Napoleon's wars. He twitched the hair out of his eyes, smiling while he told them...

THE LEGEND OF THE SOFTEST LIPS

I did some secret service work for the French government in Constantinople after I got my arm shot off and they refused to send me back for active service. We knew the Huns—sorry; no offense to you, von Arnheim—we knew they were pretty nearly done, but we didn't know how close the end was. And the beautiful part was that I didn't have to go running about in disguise; I lived like a prince, until everybody in my hotel was following me like a string of gabbling ducks and pecking up the money I trailed out after me. Every one of those shiny half-n—s[4] was my servile slave. I loved it.

Constantinople was a muck of blinding heat and damp winds. The beggars wouldn't let you alone; there was always turmoil and fighting because the soldiers strutted around with their red fez-caps cocked at an angle and kicked people out of their way. I never heard such a wild babel of tongues.

Esmet Pasha started it all. I met him at the hotel. At first he sat at a table far away from mine, drinking *salep*[5] or this vile Turkish coffee that's like black molasses. I drank rum. Then he began to work around to my table like a man on a checkerboard till I found him sitting in front of me and speaking exquisite French. He was a heavyset chap with a tiny head and large ears; not dark, either, but with one of those neutral faces resembling a person from New York.

We got to be good friends. The man was French; I ascertained that he wasn't spying on me, and that he was a sort of mystery man like myself. To him, of course, I was a stranded American. One night when the smoke was thicker than usual, and Esmet Pasha sat with his

4 As in "The Devil-Gun," the editor has elided what in the original text was the full word, now considered a divisive racial slur.

5 A traditional Turkish winter beverage, made from the starchy roots of orchids.

face all curled in smoke from a long cigarette, I began to understand what he wanted of me.

"Monsieur," says he, "I have heard that Americans are a courageous lot."

"Well," says I, "I come from up in old Vermont and I guess (that's a good American expression, I *do* recall) I'm equal to 'most anything."

Nothing moved about him except the smoke around his face.

"Monsieur, in Constantinople there arrived today a great effendi.[6] He is one of the wealthiest men in Turkey, for his jewels (if I could enumerate them)—well, they would draw the eyes away from the beauty of the most beautiful woman. They would draw your eyes away from the beauty of all but one woman, monsieur. That woman is in his harem, which he takes with him like baggage animals… Monsieur is romantic. He would be pleased to know that this woman is whispered about as the lady of the softest lips. She is like a garden, a dazzling garden under the moon… *But she is a white woman, monsieur,*" cried Esmet Pasha, moving his cigarette at last. "She is imprisoned there, a German lady. Understand me, I am not romantic; I am a man of business. She could be set free by the German government if her identity could be proved—"

"Friend," says I, aping the best American manner, "I'm not a kidnapper." Nevertheless, it lit up my imagination. A lady, behind a lattice…

"It would do no good if you were. But you begin to see my meaning. No, I do not ask you to attempt to steal her away; that would be impossible, under the guards. But in the confusion attendant on the effendi's departure, she recovered the proofs of her identity which had been taken from her; a little box of papers which must reach the German ambassador… Does monsieur think that he might elude the guards himself and secure the box from her? Attend me: I am hired, I admit it. And I will hire you. In frankness, I could not do it myself. There will be much money—"

"Oh, damn the money," says I.

"And the lady of the softest lips would have a way to reward intrepid Americans… Think, I do not grow vulgar. You have never seen this woman, my friend; that is why I do not grow vulgar…"

Well, what was I to do? I was half drunk, and the crazy stars which shine nowhere else except on that Persian-carpet city were out in flying sky, and the warm winds rather blew your conscience away. I wasn't a government agent, I was wearing a sword. The world might end, or the armistice be signed, or somebody knife me in the back. For one night I was going to climb to the lights, and be hanged to common sense!

---

6 A Turkish title of nobility.

Esmet Pasha laid all my plans. I watched the great white building, wrapped with green-black trees, where sometimes lights moved like phantoms with lamps, where lay the lady of the softest lips. But there was a glow in the sky over it, a hum of Constantinople, which came back on the soft winds. Oh, I was the king of thieves that night. And I sat with one leg over the wall at the back, and the songs of the world blew around me and tossed the cobweb stars. They couldn't catch me. I was out of the Arabian Nights.

Never a false step in the garden! Hedges stood round like Ali Baba's vats, with maybe a whispering girl to tap against them, but the aisles all slept alone. I knew the very window. Only one arm, but I clung to the trees. Even before I got to the window I saw the hand lying on the sill; the slim hand with a green ring on the middle finger, melting back into an arm which was an allure...

I found her in the dark, but she had some sort of perfumed lamp, black except for tiny perforations along the top, which dappled her face vaguely. And we saw each other's faces, hung there in vagueness; but I saw the whiteness of her body too. She was fair and supple as Juno, and her eyes were fire. In a sort of plashing music like water on marble we talked in murmurings. We made a meeting place for the future. We grew to know each other in those moments as one can know a woman in danger. I took the proofs of her identity from her hands... And the little perforations in the lamp were darkened. Lady of the softest lips...

When I descended into the garden, the warmth of old spices and lands caught me again. I stole on with nary a rifle shot behind me, and I laughed as I gained the wall once more, where for sheer exultation I sat and shook the tin box at the stars. Here was the high romance.

It was not until after I had delivered the box to Esmet Pasha and heard of his disappearance from the hotel that I realized how stupid I had been. The newspapers had accounts of the jewel robbery. The lady had not been in the effendi's harem, because he had none; she had been one of his servants. The box I carried away for them must have contained, neatly swathed, the choicest gems in the effendi's collection. I never saw Esmet Pasha or his beautiful colleague again... Sometimes I wish I had.

Dunstan burst out laughing.

"Immense!" said he, when O'Riordan had denoted the conclusion by emptying his glass of wine. "Serves you right, for philandering on duty."

"What would this world be like," the Irishman muttered gloomily, "if there weren't any liquor?" He filled his glass again.

"Did you ever hear anything more about the partners?" asked Wood.

"*Von Arnheim probably knows about them,*" O'Riordan answered. "*They were the best in the business: Fritz and Elsa Rheinden—brother and sister. Bah! He looked no more like her than I do. At least, he looked like a Frenchman. That's how expert at impersonation they were.*"

It had grown drowsily hot in the room, which was faintly odorous as a wine keg and filled with slow smoke. The candles were sinking lower. Sir John Landervorne was almost asleep, smiling vaguely in the chimney corner with his booted legs sprawled at an angle. The others were all before him, so that he alone could see over their heads at the window that bore the black monk's inscription. Suddenly he sat upright.

"Look here," said Sir John, "I shall have to begin talking, or I shall begin seeing things. Look here, I actually did see something moving at that window!"

"Sir," said Dunstan loftily," you're drunk, sir."

"Sir, I am a gentleman," said Sir John. "I don't doubt that I saw something moving; stranger things than ghosts have happened to my knowledge, like the incident of the Nottinghamshire hunt!—"

Dunstan thumped the arms of his chair and cried:

"Then who will write us a hunting song,
A loving song and a fighting song?
For a drinking song is a clinking song..."

"I will," offered Sir John, "because one must keep awake, and you doubt the clearness of my head. I'll tell you about the hardest drinking, hardest riding, most glorious days we've had. The time of the Prince Regent and Beau Brummel.[7] And it's quite true; my grandfather told it to me."

There was a positive gleam in Sir John's eye. He propped himself up like an English gentleman, and enthusiasm rippled about among his audience. Dunstan was bellowing, "Hey, Stobel!" the fire was leaping up again at the mention of the flying horses of the Regency, and everybody was half rollicking except Bencolin, who still sat motionless with his eyes half closed and the cigar ash dropping on his black beard. So, in the galloping wind, Sir John began...

---

7 Beau Brummell (the story uses a variant spelling of his name) was a Regency dandy and close friend of the Prince. For years, Brummell was an arbiter of men's fashion, but he and the Prince Regent fell out. Several years later (1816), Brummell, having fallen into debt, fled to France to avoid debtor's prison. In 1835, Brummell entered debtor's prison there, where in 1840 he died impoverished and insane from syphilis.

THE LEGEND OF THE GAY DIANA

Properly, the story should begin with the sound of a hunting bugle at dawn. Mist was rising from the trees, and there were clouds of swallows twittering and beating up past the inn windows. Back in the stable yard clattered horses' hoofs, the jovial profanity of grooms in a rushing about of men with saddles, windows banging open, tall-hatted men swinging down the stairs after a merry night's drinking.

The inn was a lovely toy place, topping into peaked gables with shiny diamond-paned windows; dun-colored, but with blackening beams. The beams jutted out over doorways, mysterious doorways that had old box lamps hanging beside them. On the upper veranda the boots was whistling and polishing away at his work. Over the flagstones in the yard, redolent of heavy steps and beer cans, they all hurried: menservants with the hot water—under the archway of the low building, or merrily past the sign that swung over the front door. Oh, it was a fine sight! The nestling quaint inn, with tea steaming inside, all dun gingerbread and bright windows against the white rising mists and the dark green trees. It was going to be warm that day; there was a sweet scent of hay in the air.

Halloa! Out strode a man in a bold red coat, a glistening top hat, white breeches and black boots; all smiling and waving greetings. Out staggered another, out came two more, arm in arm and arguing; out they came all, in a jumble or singing. Fat and thin, all clad alike like soldiers. A tune was whistling gaily out of the hunting bugle. Then there was the rattle of a gate, cries and laughter, and, deeper, buffeting around the inn, the joyous, frisking bark of the dogs.

Inside, a rather striking figure was coming down the main stair. She had her hand on the black railing, and her head tossed back. Scandalously, she was in hunting costume and (which caused the hoop-skirted shy ladies to shrink with horror) she was not going to ride sidesaddle. It was the Lady Diana of Falcondene Court, always laughing—black hair wisping down under the absurd top hat, all men's costume, but woman about the eyes. She was tanned and blue-eyed, and her head flourished and her teeth showed white when she coquetted. She paused on the stairs to shake her riding crop at the man in the middle of the inn floor.

Rising sun on the floor, too; black fireplace, white walls, and the two red coats against them. Drinking cans were on the center table. The man was staring at them. He raised his head, a slender, tanned sort of young man with eyes rather wideset. The girl said:

"Good morning, George. Glorious, this is glorious! Have they got Bess saddled?—I want those girths tight, or she'll tumble me on the first wall."

"I don't know," said George.

She got suddenly suspicious, and came down toward him.

"Look here, what's the matter? Have you and that little ninny been quarreling again? Where is Tom?"

"He went back to Ravensmere; still drunk, I suppose. He was furious last night—threatened me with a pistol. It went off; there was no harm done, except that he went stamping out of here. He thinks you're in love with me."

"Well, I'm not; will that satisfy him?" She laughed, she came closer, her eyes spoke all manner of things, and none of them explicable. It baffled him and made him angry.

"Diana—"

"Now please stay back! Are you going to be foolish so early this morning..."

"But see here, I wish you wouldn't!"

"Wouldn't what?"

"Well, act this way. Go hunting, and act...not like a lady. Really, if you want to be frank, you haven't any reputation. They're saying horrible things about you; you ought to have seen them wink at me last night when I left you. Gad, you won't dare show your face—"

"Do you expect me to blush every time when they mention a man?—or thrill and be meanly lascivious with myself behind doors, and shut my eyes in wonder, and shrink and tap a parasol—"

George blushed. He fumbled with the drinking mugs.

"Diana, really—your language; please stop it! I love you, and you persist in treating me man to man. Are you human, anyhow?"

She suddenly went over to him. Her arms went around him; he felt her, quite woman, against him, mouth to mouth for an instant while her eyes closed. Then she stepped away quickly.

"That's how I feel, George..." She laughed. "Possibly ...Now never mind my reputation, because the innkeeper is watching us in a very surprised manner..."

He saw her go dazzling out of the door, and heard her laughter in the yard. He groped for his hat, feeling a bit sick, for he noticed the half-effaced bloodspot on the table. Almost immediately her voice came in.

"Lord Sturton[8], you old pot-belly, remember what I told you: keep your hands loose on those reins when you take the jumps or you'll be killed!..."

All day, from bugle to bugle, the hunt swept away. Out of the inn yard, pounding, in twos and threes, after the long leap of the dogs. Nobody missed young Tom Stevens, who had been so peering and suspicious and jealous about Diana, who was constantly bickering with George May, the fifth earl of Sandermark. Wayside taverns where the blacksmith's anvil rang on broken shoes and fidgeting huntsmen were left behind, over the fields in hot noonday, swaggering and racing after the worrying dogs! Field and ditch, where the big yellow hunter took a tumble and sent Lord Sturton grotesquely head over heels—loud on the highway and low in the marsh, on it drove into storm.

The clouds were getting black, low in the trees, where the wind hung still. The huntsmen had stopped laughing; some were woebegone, lurching in the saddle. Lady Diana's eyes were bright against the sweeping dark; her roan was still fresh, tugging the bit ever so slightly. Behind her George May clung, on a devil of a horse like a nightmare... Leap and plunge toward the wild booming of the dogs, the leader of the hunt pressing them! Only a few had stayed so far; the wind was coming out of the trees now. Up it mounted, far into the last cry. "Tally-ho!" it got into the horse's ears —"Tally-ho!" in the old way. Another horse slithered into a spill; the rider's hat bounced off absurdly...They've sighted the fox, they're driving him to his hole!...Another horse down, the rain rushing out of the black sky, but *"Tally-ho!"*

Bearing down, trampling among the dogs, they were in at the death: a gloomy bank of trees, harassed with fighting dogs and tossing hats up against a leaden sky. They were exhausted, panting, dog and man: preparing to smile and trot back over the hills for some jovial drinking and a hot bath...

The Lady Diana was off her great mare, staring at the fox's hole. Men were singing and leaning from their mounts; dogs snarled...

---

8 See the commentary following "The New Canterbury Tales," but one of the hints that Carr may be this legend's author is that there is a Viscount Sturton in *The Blind Barber*. The editor finds this insufficiently convincing; not every use of the pseudonym Eric Hirth at *The Haverfordian* was by Carr, either. It seems more likely that Carr simply borrowed the name Sturton later as his fellow students had borrowed Hirth's.

"We've made almost a circle," the Lady Diana said suddenly and harshly; "George, we're almost back at the inn…"

She was staring at the strangely large opening. Another glance followed hers. The singing choked out. The rain grew heavier on tired bodies and sodden hats…Tea and a hot bath in the English way…

What they saw in the opening was an arm projecting out, mangled by the dogs, who were tearing one bleeding hand. A body had been thrust in there.

George May did not look at it anymore. He put his face against the mud of the bank and said:

"Pull him out, for God's sake! It's Tom. I shot him last night…I thought he was hid."

While nobody moved, the virgin Diana looked at him in a strange, rather wondering way.

"What a ghastly story!" Dunstan exclaimed, after some little silence. "I thought you were going to tell us something dashing and heroic, and then you give us that…What happened to this George May?"

"Oh, some famous big-wigged counsel got hold of him and entered a plea of self-defense. They got the innkeeper to swear that Stevens had attacked him with a fire tongs, or something. He was adjudged not guilty; subsequently," said Sir John, "he married Diana. So you see the story has a happy ending after all."

Stoneman Wood, the American, made a sudden gesture. He remarked, "On the contrary, sir, I think it's the most unhappy ending I ever heard. I wish you'd left it with the murder."

"I was telling a true story, you know," returned Sir John frigidly.

"Then I'm jolly well sick of truth!" cried Dunstan. "Come, now, let's have some wild thing with a happy finish, and lovers in each other's arms. There's been nothing but gloomy occurrences so far."

There was an interruption. Stobel, the manservant who was usually so invisible as to be almost legendary, came unobtrusively toward Dunstan.

"I beg your pardon, sir," he said, "but there's a lady and gentleman outside as want to know if we can give them a pot of tea and a telephone. They've run their motor into a ditch."

"Why, of course!—Look here, don't you know any better than that?" asked Dunstan, hauling himself to his feet. "If you gentlemen will excuse me, I'll go out. I say, Stobel, they can't go out again in this; they'd never pull through the mud on the Ethandune road."

He waddled to the door with more injunctions to replenish the wine supply. In the silence after he had gone von Arnheim suddenly remarked:

"Well, then, I can tell you a story which ends with lovers in each other's arms. Rather, I'll read it to you, for the legend struck my fancy. You shall judge whether it's pleasant or not."

The old bony sardonic face blinked at them over the spectacles. Von Arnheim had capacious pockets made in his clothes, so that he could carry about all manner of odd books—mostly faded worm-eaten ones. He drew out a black-letter volume lovingly, grinned, opened it under the candlelight. "I warn you," said he, and read them the chronicle of Florimond de Rahinsauelt, named...

THE LEGEND OF THE NECKBAND OF CARNELIANS

In the pleasant little hamlet of Croissy, in the province of Touraine, whither journey all the mightiest lovers and all the mightiest drinkers in France each year in a pious pilgrimage, there is located an inn on a hill, which you may know by the name of the Green Unicorn; and the gentle hostess (a most buxom wench I do assure you, and on that point I speak with no little confidence) does say that once this Green Unicorn was the castle of a très-noble and puissant lord, Sir Joclyn of Vaurennes, on whose house had lain a curse for full three hundred years until in 1575 its territories including all the wooded lands and pastures, were taken over in the custody of the most saintly Bishop of Croissy.

In the yard of the Green Unicorn, which was in former days the court of the castle of the lords of Vaurennes, there is a circular fountain wherein six goldfish do swim about in a most pleasing fashion. Now this fountain they say must needs hold water that becomes faintly vermeil as soon as it enters the basin; and some wise-bodies say that this is no more than the red stone wherein it is held, while others aver that the sun's rays so hit the water that it forthwith grows orange in hue: but these are know-nothings and nitwits and sponge-brains and ridiculous persons I do proclaim, and those who know (which are the kitchen boys and scullery maids) have it that the water still is faintly ruddy with the blood of a certain lady of Vaurennes who was indecently treacherous and faithless. And one debonair chambermaid, Arlette by name (that you may know here, for she is a wench most adroit and generous-hearted), has sworn to me that she saw once this same Lady Joyaunce walk about this fountain of a July night, weeping so bitterly as would break your heart right in two, all the while moving her head from one side to t'other in a most pathetic fashion, and clasping her beautiful hands about her white, white throat as if 'twere paining her more than she could bear. And she (swears the package, Arlette) did go about the fountain three times and then with a grievous moan did fade into a mist that sank into the water like a bag of soggy baker's flour.

So they have this jolly legend:

One time in the city of Rouen (in fact it was none other than the year of 1275 in which there was a mighty plague of leprosy in the city of Marsayles) an eager knycht Sir Thomas of Staernten by name, a Dutchman by birth, did set it in his mind to wander joyously to the pleasant province of Touraine, whither journey all the mightiest lovers and all the mightiest drinkers of France each year on a pious pilgrimage, for no reason other than to love and to drink (and these he could do well you may rest assured, for his heart was a big and strong one and his stomach a most capable one). And they say and tell and relate how he wandered into the small hamlet of Croissy very early one July morning waking the bakers' and butchers' wives with his loud singing of how

> *The Queen of Spain she is my quean*
> *And I'm her salamander. . .*

And so well pleased was he with the pleasant faces and the wine there that straightaways he found lodging with a gentle cobbler's wife, whose husband was no longer fit for to remain with her, being eaten by the worms these seven years.

One Sunday this Sir Thomas was standing in the square in an idle fashion when there passed the most lovely lady Joyaunce, whose husband was the très noble and puissant Lord Sir Joclyn of Vaurennes, who had started for Venice on the way to the Holy Land, Jerusalem; it was a full seven months. But needs the lady must wear a veil so thick that it was like a mask and walk with two old bags-of-bones, so that the curious Thomas must wait to devise some scheme to look upon her countenance, for in sooth her figure it was most jocund and promising of even better things.

So it came that one night, having discovered the distantness of the Lord Joclyn (being a most circumspect young fellow) he climbed to the window which it had cost him a leather purse to discover (and you may yet see this same window at the Green Unicorn, for it has a jaunty conceit writ over it which you may discover for yourself, and I assure you it is worth the bother). And I need only add to this that Sir Thomas he had the most nicest way with the ladies you can possibly imagine, nor was the Lady Joyaunce an uncivil lady; and in those days when the proverb had a more direct application, Love could now and again manage to Laugh at Locksmiths most efficiently, and well it might.

So it would seem that Sir Thomas had no dislike (far from it) for the hamlet of Croissy, and the wine it was a most excellent white wine his hostess the cobbler's wife served him. But one day, a fortnight hardly after Sir Thomas first looked on his leman[9], back came from Marsayles the Lord Joclyn, none other. And the Lord Joclyn was known all over Touraine as the most sour-brained, pike-nosed, foul-cheeked, blunt-minded, disagreeablest fellow that ever wed a pretty wife. And he was sore and weary when he came to his house on the hill, and so evil-disposed that he kicked his hound so powerful in the rear that its belly was forthwith emptied of its contents. And considering that in one respect at least he had a very tangible piece of evidence that love had not only laughed at locksmiths but had in point of fact called them in to assistance, he was not entirely unjustified in certain assumptions that occasioned his rushing about in the fair Lady Joyaunce's bower roaring mighty like a bull (which we flatter ourselves is not as clumsy a similitude as it may sound).

The legend ends with the relating in an inconsequential manner how the knycht Sir Thomas did come to the castle that night, and passing the fountain in the court saw something gleaming on the edge of the basin very prettily in the white moon. This was, indeed, none other than the most cunningly fashioned neckband of carnelians gathered from the seven harems of the Emperor of Constantinople, which he had given to the Lady Joyaunce. As he raised it in his hand he saw something very like the white samite of his lady's gown, shimmering in a watery manner in the fountain. And it seems reasonable to suppose that if he'd had the time to make further investigations in the affair, he might have found a familiar body within the white samite, quite beautiful and cold. But he didn't, for a well calculated blow on the head with something or other undeniably hard made Sir Thomas unsuited for anything further involving any of the vital functions. And to make the cheese more binding, the neckband was thereupon fastened about his neck rather tighter than is customary with such articles. In short, the cobbler's wife never again saw her lodger, and in her grief swore to lead forever after a chaste and model life.

The bodies of the two sinners were allowed to rot away on unhallowed ground (which was a just punishment for so loathsome an adultery) while Lord Joclyn was esteemed by the whole community until his death, which happened not long after of a surfeit of lampreys.

"Confound it, man!" cried Sir John, when von Arnheim had closed the book, "this is getting positively insufferable. We're all either pessimists or truthful men, what with these tales about women..."

"We can only talk fairly about them," said Stoneman Wood, "when we're not with them."

---

9 Lover (mistress).

"Well, then, we shall have to begin talking unfairly," O'Riordan asserted, *"because I think I hear a woman's voice outside in the hall. Now this is the devil of a note,"* he added, fumbling at his tie and trying to smooth his hair, *"this was a nice untidy little conversation—"*

Dunstan came bustling in, escorting two people who made the other guests rise uncomfortably. One was a small thin man with elaborate whiskers and twirled hair parted in the middle, rather like a conjuror. The other was a woman, a very strikingly beautiful woman. She was almost past middle age, full-figured, with quiet gray eyes and flat dark hair. When she smiled it melted into her eyes, but her smile was a trifle long and steady. A white shawl hung over her shoulder against her yellow dress.

"Pray don't disturb yourselves," the little man begged in his nervous manner. *"Shouldn't have run in—sorry—car broke down, you see..."*

They were, it appeared, a Mr. Mortimer Grimmel and his wife; Dunstan beamed introductions on everybody. Only Bencolin stared at them a long time. Mrs. Grimmel seemed to show no surprise at being thrust into the midst of it, though her husband was agitated. She seemed to glance somewhat markedly at O'Riordan, who was the handsomest man present.

"Eh—" said Dunstan, *"if you can make yourselves comfortable while the fire is being laid in your room, I have ordered the tea sent up here. I don't really use much of the hall, you see."*

"It seems very charming," commented the woman, sitting back in the chair Dunstan had placed for her, so that the light played on her inscrutable face. *"Were you busy?"*

"Oh, no," O'Riordan hastened to say; *"we were only telling stories."*

Then something happened which was so startling that Dunstan almost dropped his wine glass. M. Henri Bencolin spoke for the first time that evening. He leaned out of his chair and said:

"Will not Madame Grimmel oblige us with a story?"

"Come, now—" protested Dunstan, *"Bencolin, you're—"*

Mrs. Grimmel inclined her head, and looked at Bencolin with pouting lips. *"Let me see,"* she smiled, *"I believe you are the great Monsieur Bencolin who had so recently one remarkable success and one remarkable failure with mysteries. There was the Fragneau case, and then that affair of M. LaGarde. Pardon me!"* She saw that O'Riordan had assumed an odd expression, and she paused. *"Why, yes, monsieur, I shall be delighted. But first let someone else tell a story. I want to see how it's done."*

Then up spoke the American, Stoneman Wood. He said:

"I can tell you an extraordinary one, if you like, and I shan't mind if you call me a liar. Your tale about the black monk put me in mind of it."

"Excellent!" Dunstan applauded, whereat the American, smiling slightly, commenced to tell...

THE LEGEND OF THE CANE IN THE DARK

The whole thing began when I read in a Pittsburgh newspaper the account of my own death. It gave me a start to see, "Mr. Stoneman Wood, for a number of years a well-known journalist and freelance writer, died at his home on North Highland Avenue yesterday. A heart-stroke..." It continued, just as matter-of-fact as you please.

I had been on a hunting trip in Canada (liquor, too) and I suppose I should have been used to shocks, after my guide almost plugged me for a moose. He was such a treacherous rat that I had to fire him, and without him it took me rather longer than I had expected to get back. It didn't matter, of course, for since I had come into my uncle's money I was taking things easy and letting my cousin handle the affairs. Lord, it was a relief, not having to hammer out a column every day for the *Gazette!*

Well, as I say, I loafed along, sending no wires, asking no questions, and assuming that Cousin Stephen was taking care of the money. I was comfortable, well fed, and knew that I could draw a check whenever I pleased. So I got back to Pittsburgh in a pleasant frame of mind —I'd surprise 'em, because I doubt anybody knew I was away.

It was on one of those smoky oil-lit milk trains that I opened my first home newspaper and saw that crazy announcement. It gave me an uncanny feeling; a mistake, but an odd and uncomfortable mistake. My eye kept going back to the headlines of the story. "Oh, what the devil!" says I, and then I would look at "STONEMAN WOOD DIES—"

I left the train at East Liberty, and started to walk out to the house on Highland Avenue. It was cool, and had been raining; there was absolutely nobody to be seen, for the streets were very wide and deserted, with nothing except a few electric signs. I could see only occasional lights on Highland Avenue, which is long and windy. Now there was none of the usual atmosphere of Pittsburgh that night: I felt as though I were walking on completely foreign ground. Sometimes it took me minutes to recognize big houses set back behind their iron fences, and I had seen those houses every day for ten years.

Then I realized that somebody must be following me. The sky looked strangely *light,* but for a while I couldn't see the person behind me, though I thought I could hear him walking. I also thought I could hear his cane going tap-tap on the pavement, slowly. Finally I turned around and saw a huge figure that looked as though it wore a high black coat. It had a cane. I began to grow afraid of that figure, though I didn't understand why. Never did it enter my head that it might be an ordinary pedestrian. I started walking faster, and it didn't walk faster—the cane tapped slowly, but every time I would look, there it was behind me.

When I reached the walk that led up to my house it was right behind me. I began to run. There was a low light behind the ground-glass door of the vestibule, the only illumination on a big rugged black house. Yet when I looked at that door (I had seen it every day for more than ten years) I thought there was lettering on it. And it was *open.* Just when I got inside, under a light in the dark hall, the door opened behind me, and in blundered that figure following me. It was even huger, and as it stared straight at me I suddenly noticed that it was *blind.*

It grinned and said, "Hello." Well, I leave it to you what I did. It would be cowardly to call out, yet I wanted to arouse the house; but my God! I thought, "What if there's nobody here, and I'm alone with this person?" I didn't even question it. I turned around and went toward the stairs; there was a revolver in my room. I stumbled up in the dark, and groped along the wall of the second floor, and found my door. From the faint light in the hall, I saw the person right behind me when I got inside the room. He was standing by the door. I rushed across the room in the dark… Then I noticed that the place had a sickening heavy sweet smell. I touched something in the dark; it was a flower, banks of flowers. And the room was shut up.

I found a lamp at last, and when I pulled the cord so that it glowed dimly in the big room, there was the blind man beside me. He took hold of my arm, stared in my face, and said in a strange voice:

"Why didn't you tell me there was a dead man in your bed?"

Well, we were right beside the bed. It had smooth sheets, smooth and white except for a motionless bulge under them. There *was* a man in the bed. His eyes were closed and his face waxy. Against the white sheets it seemed as though I were looking in a mirror, for the man was an exact counterpart of me. Maybe I was about to faint, for the room assumed a dizzy appearance; I felt sick at the stomach.

"Why don't you open your eyes?" asked the blind man, grinning.

I rushed towards the door, collided with it, and left the blind man in the middle of the room. I gave a scream.

Lights began to go up in the house, cold lights. In that dark hallway, with the faded carpet, I stood with the lights beating on me. I saw my Aunt Miranda, in a dressing gown, put her head out of one door; instead of shrieking, as she seemed about to do, she began to cry and blubber. Her head in its curl papers disappeared. Other relations looked out...

Somebody cried, "Lock the door! —Stoneman—he's walking!—"

They shrank away, they banged their doors as I tried to speak to them. Was I dead, after all?

Then I saw the open door of my cousin Stephen's room. I went in, and there was the dapper black-haired Stephen sitting on his bed. As he raised his head, he had the face of a man who feels himself falling out of a ten-story window.

"Damn you," said Stephen, yanking open the drawer of a table by his bed and pulling out a gun. After that he looked sick, and began to cry.

"What's the matter with you?" I said. "Look here, I am Stoneman—"

"No, you're not," he answered, "and you're not a ghost, either; you're an impostor. You can never prove you left this house and went to Canada. The real Stoneman Wood is lying in that other room."

I think he was gazing over my shoulder. He dropped the pistol on the bed; I think he must have seen something behind me. It scared him so that he couldn't talk straight, but out tumbled the whole story. He had planned my trip to Canada and kept it secret from everybody. He had hired the guide who was to kill me. Then he had got a body that resembled me, and, since we lived alone in the house, it was easy to pretend that I had died from a heart attack; the family doctor had not been present, but a man of Stephen's procuring. Then he had assembled the relatives, knowing, of course, that my Uncle Stoneman's fortune would go to him. The only slip-up was that the guide had not killed me... My death in Canada, if killed by a guide, might cause comment, but the death of a man from heart failure never would, especially if a tearful cousin is around...

After it was finished I sat down on the bed and watched him. I was beginning to feel better, but I was damp all over and nauseated. As I was about to ask him more questions, he shuddered, digging his face in the pillows... I heard the sound of a cane tapping on the front stairs.

"Look here," I cried, "who was the man that followed me?"

"Nobody followed you! I don't know!"

"Who was it that you saw behind me when I came in here?—over my shoulder? You did see somebody, didn't you?"

"No!"

"Answer me!"

(In silence the front door banged.)

"Did you ever see…your uncle…that died?" Stephen asked chokingly.

"No!"

"He always…carried…a cane."

When Wood had finished his audience started a little. They peered around at the window of the black monk, and Sir John exclaimed:

"Gad! What a story! It proves you can have very horrifying ghosts in America, I should think."

Wood smiled again, a bit mockingly, and relapsed into his chair. His fingers brushed some sheets of manuscripts in his pocket.

"What happened to your cousin Stephen?" questioned O'Riordan, who was regarding Wood with a rather fishy eye. "Yes, yes, the cousin!" cackled Mr. Mortimer Grimmel, like a dog barking in pursuit.

"Stephen? Oh," responded Wood vaguely, "I made him get out. Gave him a round sum, and sent him out. It made a fierce stir in the papers."

Dunstan nodded wisely, and sleepily. Abruptly Bencolin leaned out of his chair, and said:

"Now—madame's story?"

"Do you know," put in the bewhiskered little man with the conjuror's manner, "do you know, Mr.—er—Wood, I can hardly believe that story!"

He spoke rudely but triumphantly, like one making a discovery. The American shrugged.

"Well, I called it a legend," replied Wood, "remember that, Mr. Grimmel."

The fussy little man seemed to think that somebody was ridiculing him.

"Then I'll tell one, and you may take it as you please!" he announced with primness. "Are you willing? I'm considered a very good storyteller, gentlemen. My wife and I have spent some time travelling in Italy, so I assure you that each exquisite nuance of color value"—he waved his arm gracefully—"will flow from my lips."

"Go ahead, then," said the American, grinning.

Forthwith, hurrying lest somebody should stop him, he began…

THE LEGEND OF THE HAND OF IPPOLITA

The leaves of the olive tree and the many infinitesimal waves of the pool by which she sat laughed with sheer delight as she washed her alabaster arms that looked like some strange and beautiful great tropical flower; the drops of water, even, seemed most reluctant to fall from her shoulders and breast, and grew sad with the knowledge that the chances of their resting there again were practically negligible. In short, this lady Ippolita was a very splendid lady, and what was more, she was of a very chaste and modest disposition, and not one of your grandes dames who must have their crème de cacao and Three Nuns[10] or die. Which was not surprising, considering that she was of a lowly station—it was duty to her father to disembowel the venison that was to appear at the table of the great Duke of Spoleto[11] (or perhaps it was Benevento[12]).

Now it so happened that rather earlier in the morning than one would ordinarily expect so grand a duke to get up, this very Duke Ferdinand was wandering about in his garden when he happened upon the beauteous damsel in the midst of her morning ablutions. So pleased

10 A spun-rope pipe tobacco blend first introduced in Glasgow, Scotland, in the late nineteenth century. It combines tobaccos from four continents and is wrapped in Virginia leaf.

11 The Duke of Spoleto, crowned King of the region in 889 by Pope Steven V, ruled most of central Italy (the non-Papal states) going back as far as about 500, and until the fourteenth century. The earliest dukes were appointed by the King of Lombard, but functioned independently.

12 Benevento (meaning, "welcome") was the southernmost duchy of Lombard (after 774 a principality), ruled by dukes until the Normans conquered it in 1053, conveying it to the Pope, who continued appointing dukes until 1078. Benevento was returned to the Pope in 1081, after which no more dukes were appointed.

was he with the general effect that he straightaways ordered her to be garmented in the most rare of Brussels laces and Byzantine silks, and advised that her every whim should be satisfied. And it was a slightly sad irony of fate that Ippolita should have fallen sick and died shortly after, just as she was beginning to realize some of the subtler beauties of this earthly existence, and all that sort of thing. This was an occasion of great grief to the Duke Ferdinand; she had been very dear to him, more dear than anything even so great a man as he had ever known before.

In the violence of his grief and love he turned to a dark-skinned lady from Palermo, Beatrice by name, whose love was to what Ippolita's had been as a rhododendron, say, is to a crocus. But for all that she was faintly aware that her lover's thoughts still wandered all too frequently to Ippolita; and this irritated her prodigiously. Her suspicions were quite tangibly confirmed when the Duke one fine day ordered that one of the most cunning of sculptors of all Italy land should chisel out of pure white Sicilian marble a statue of the fair damsel who had died three months before; and what was more, the statue was decreed to be placed with impressive ceremonies in a sumptuous mausoleum with pictures illustrating the story of Dido and Aeneas[13] done on the outside in mosaic work, and rows of cannas and fuchsias leading up to it, sort of like the Taj Mahal, of which you must have heard.

All this, quite naturally, peeved Beatrice frightfully; and being as she had never even laid her eyes upon either the body or the statue of the object of her master's devotions, her curiosity was not a little piqued. So one night she decided to wander secretly to the tomb, having obtained the key thereto from the keeper by means of gentle insinuations, and form her own firsthand opinions as to what the woman looked like. This she did. While she was within the mausoleum, however, she was so struck and blinded by a heartbroken jealousy that she viciously broke from the statue its exquisite right hand of pure white Sicilian marble. And still more strange to relate, she treasured it in a fanatical sort of way, in a deftly carved ebony box from Grenada, lined with black velvet, even though the very sight of the hand filled her with a weird melancholy. The Duke Ferdinand, in the meanwhile having discovered his bereavement, flew into a fury, and after that developed a crabby and suspicious way about him that made the chambermaids positively fidgety.

Then a very curious thing happened. Less than eight days after

---

13 An odd tribute, given that duty-bound Aeneas abandoned Dido (the Queen of Carthage) to found Rome; after he left her, Dido committed suicide with his sword.

the stealing of the hand, Beatrice found that her right hand was growing strange and ulcerous. She feared (and with reason, for none may escape the justice of the Lord) that it was a visitation called upon her for her crime. She locked herself in her room, put on a dressing gown of black brocade chastely lined with equally black crêpe de chine[14], and sprinkled ashes on her hair; and yet, hour by hour, as she lay on her bed, she watched her hand grow leathery and dusky, until it was as dark as her gown. All her perfumes and lotions and massage creams could do nothing to alter this curious state of affairs, and she finally arrived at the conclusion that she had best swiftly gather her most necessary personal equipments, and climb into the garden below through the window, whence the keeper would make escape easy in remembrance of former favors.

As the time for her intended flight was approaching, and she was lying on her sofa, she heard angry footsteps coming down the hall. In a vague apprehension she slid her tarnished hand beneath a cushion, but not before Sir Ferdinand had opened the door. He strode over to her, and as he gazed down at her, she gave a faint cry and hysterically threw both hands over her eyes.

"O will it never be that I shall be forgiven?" she wept, and began beating the couch covers with her arms.

The Duke stood for a moment in amazement, and then said:

"I wish I had never seen you like this… And may I never so see you again."

And as he moved to the door again he glanced back at her lying there, for he felt rather sorry for the poor woman in a way.

The next evening, a little before sunset, a boat with ten oarsmen set out for a small island in the sea two miles from the Duke's palace. In it sat huddled the lady Beatrice, staring emptily at the horizon, mumbling now and again while her lips twitched nervously, like those of an old woman.

Landing finally, she stepped out without a word, walked up to a small hillock, and there sat down. The boat, with its ten oarsmen, again took the water. After it had gone a small distance, one of the men looked back. The huddled black figure was still there, soundless, motionless; but just as the last bit of sun was disappearing into the water another figure, in white, appeared next to it, and as the boat was moving farther, farther away and the island grew dimmer and dimmer, still a white figure could be seen, leaning kindly, tenderly, it seemed, over the wretched quiet black bundle there.

They say that when the body of the lady Beatrice was buried a few days later, her hands were found clasped peacefully, the one as white as

---

14 A lightweight Chinese silk.

the other. And if you wish to take the trouble, and test the verity of this tale, you may still see the mausoleum with its statue of the fair Ippolita, a bit worn and tarnished, indeed, but still exquisitely fair, with a little ebony box containing her right hand resting reverently by it, on the pedestal. All this, I say, you may still find in the garden of the present Duke of Spoleto (or perhaps it *was,* after all, Benevento).

O'Riordan coughed discreetly when the tale was ended, and exchanged glances with Wood.

"I wish you'd make up your mind," commented O'Riordan gloomily, "whether it was Spoleto or Benevento. Let's have a drink."

"You don't appreciate it," sniffed Grimmel. "Now, I suppose there are a tremendous number of stories about this very hall, ain't it?"

"Of course. The window behind you is haunted," returned his host, and Grimmel looked startled.

"My hat! Is it?—a horrifying specter?"

"Not particularly."

"But doesn't it frighten you?" asked Grimmel with earnestness. "I should simply go out of my wits, I simply should!"

"Oh, no; I don't pay much attention to it. If I did," said Dunstan, "you'd find me as cracked as old Stobel, who seems to think there's a great treasure in jewels hidden around here."

Grimmel twirled the points of his hair and fidgeted.

"The candles are going out—" muttered Sir John.

"Yes, the candles are going out," the woman cried in a sudden laughing voice, "and I am going to tell the story which my friend the detective desires."

Another candle puffed out. Now Bencolin was in complete darkness, except for the red of his cigar tip. Mrs. Grimmel turned her eyes on them, clasped her hands so that her slim exquisite arms shone, and addressed Bencolin with...

THE LEGEND OF LA BELLA DUQUESA

Her hair was still quite black, and there was a good deal of it, elaborately draped about her head; her skin was very pale and thin, her lips very red and thin, and there was a *mouche*[15] alluringly poised at the corner of her mouth. Then, too, she was dressed as a Duquesa should dress, and her feet were the tiniest ever, in their green slippers by Piccat.[16] But her specialty was perfume: today she had sprayed from a slender flask inscribed severely with the legend, "Tais-toi mon coeur!"[17]

"O you silly dear boy! What a silly *dear* boy you *are*. But ah! Some day you will learn better..." and a titter, quite silly, but alluring too. She stroked his young golden hair ever so lightly.

Finally they sat down at a table on the terrace, overlooking the gardens leading down to the lake. He was still flushed from his game of tennis, and his open blazer showed his shirt to be slightly wet.

"And now, my darling, you may fetch me a glass of Berzanto[18], and take care that it isn't Vichy water. If it is Vichy water, I assure you I shan't drink it."

As he strode along in the sunlight, finally disappearing through the glass door, she looked after him, and bit her lips, and vibrated her fingers nervously...

That evening in the boat, the sun seemed very beautiful to her, and the smell of waterlilies gave her somehow courage. The lake lay like a polished shield, and she lay back in her seat trailing her hand in the cool water. When he ceased rowing for a space, she moved up and sat

---

15 Literally meaning "fly," but an artificial beauty mark.

16 A fictional Italian fashion designer.

17 "Be still, my heart!"

18 A fictional beverage. Perhaps it is significant that unlike the cultural references in the other legends (Beau Brummell, *salep*, Three Nuns, etc.), those in the legend Mrs. Grimmel tells are fabricated.

beside him.

How young he was, and charming! Beautifully she ran her fingers along his gleaming flannels and allowed the wind tantalizingly to blow her hair in his face. Suddenly she bit him in the arm. He recoiled, partly in fear, partly in disgust; he saw a tiny drop of blood appear.

"O you horrid old lady, you horrid old woman! How disgusting you are! You think you allure us, but we really laugh at you. Why, if you only knew how funny you appear…And now you must make yourself loathsome, too. Couldn't you at least keep yourself from being utterly ridiculous?"

She laughed like a brass bell. She was quite herself again.

"You poor little boy, dear me…But you will know better someday, indeed you will…"

And he was still very angry, but the least bit dismayed too. The Duquesa Lucrezia was a clever lady; it was rarely that she missed her cues, and there was one thing she could not forget nor forgive: to be made a fool of, or even worse, to be witnessed making a little fool of herself. Her miscalculations were few, but they ate into her heart like an ulcer. She was a proud lady too, you see. She had her motto of relentlessness, *polus dum sidera pascet…*[19]

*****

It was the day after the funeral. The whole villa seemed hardly recovered from the shock—everyone went about in a sort of daze. Certainly he had seemed very healthy, and quite satisfied; the doctor said it had been something in the food, the fish, perhaps, and had shrugged his shoulders.

On the veranda, though, sat the Duquesa, with a small black-haired fellow leaning above her. She was being most charming, and the least bit provocative. She waved her beautiful fingers inconsequentially as she looked into the big beyond over the lake.

"What a dear, silly chap you are," she tinkled. "O well, some day you will know better, mark my word. How delightful you are, though!"

And her voice tripped down the terrace like a silver-footed elf.

Bencolin laughed. In the dusky red room it sounded like an answer to that laugh which the woman had described. His manner was that theatrical pose which

---

19 Virgil's *Aeneid*, I.608, a clause in Aeneas's declaration of gratitude to Dido for succoring the displaced Trojans: "While Heaven feeds the stars…" The conclusion of his sentiment (I.609), is, "Your honor, name, and praise shall live with me forever." Aeneas's profession is dramatically ironic, which Mrs. Grimmel fails to recognize.

the jovial Frenchman loved. And he rose.

"Fraulein Elsa Rheinden," he said in a loud clear voice, "you are a good loser."

Grimmel jumped up nervously and began to protest. The others forgot the warm stupor which was closing over them; the candles swished and flamed up again.

"And, Herr Fritz Rheinden, you are an excellent actor," said Bencolin.

There came a triumphant shout from O'Riordan, who slapped the table beside him and pointed to Grimmel.

"I knew I had seen you before! Why, holy saints, if I could hold my liquor like a gentleman I'd have recognized Esmet Pasha!—And I'd have recognized the Lady of the Softest Lips!"

"What on earth—" muttered Dunstan.

"Oh, come," said Bencolin, "don't blame yourself too much for not recognizing her after ten years, O'Riordan, or him either. He's as great an actor as Cyril Merton[20] ever was... But indicate me, my friend, as an utter idiot for being more than a few moments in recognizing her as this Duquesa Lucrezia about whom she has just told us. At least, I could not fail to find myself in the 'black-haired fellow' she described. Not a lover, Fraulein, but a police officer who visited you to find out the truth about that boy's death."

"It was the fish," murmured Elsa Rheinden.

Stoneman Wood was leaning back and laughing; Grimmel (or Rheinden) looked worried; Dunstan shouted, "By God, these are criminals! What are they doing in my house, then?"

"Please, not so loud," urged Bencolin. "I am sorry, but you have made a mistake, Elsa. You were misled by this crazy old man Stobel and his tales of fabulous buried jewels."

"There's no proof—" said Rheinden.

"None whatever. I will admit I am only guessing."

"Will you be so good," said Dunstan frigidly, "as to explain what you're talking about?"

"Yes," replied Bencolin. "My dear sir, you would never have recognized the truth because you are an Englishman. It is not that you lack intelligence. It is that you respect and obey all ancient curses. You preserve them as you preserve your abbeys. Tell you that a certain thing is hallowed by tradition, and you will not touch it. That is why you have not discovered the answer..." He clapped his hands like a magician. "O'Riordan, please! Light some candles! Hold one up by the black monk's window!"

Von Arnheim chuckled. O'Riordan moved over with a candle upheld, so that the old weird window stood out against darkness.

---

20 The actor who disappears from a Norman castle in the first-ever Bencolin story, "The Shadow of the Goat," which appeared in *The Haverfordian* in November-December 1926 and which Douglas Greene published in the anthology *The Door to Doom and Other Detections* (1980).

"*I am going to break the curse—*" *went on Bencolin. Abruptly he caught up a chair, and Dunstan howled in dismay as he sent it flying at the window. The old glass shattered and fell, leaving a gaping hole into which the Irishman's candle shone.*

"*—by breaking the window,*" *said Bencolin.* "*Which was exactly what the black monk meant, if you had taken his inscription literally. That was the trouble; you fastened on it some allegorical meaning. What's inside?*"

"*Why, it's an opening in the walls!*" *answered O'Riordan peering within.* "*There are two windows, apparently; the outside one is covered with ivy. Lord, it runs all along here. There's a flight of steps going down.*"

Dunstan blinked; his lips moved profanely.

"*I'm sorry not to preserve the legend,*" *Bencolin apologized,* "*but your ghost was Stobel moving inside the walls with a candle, hunting for the treasure his father had told him was here. No, no, Dunstan, don't trouble to summon Stobel yet... Madame,*" *he added,* "*it really does not matter now whether there is a treasure at the foot of the passage or not.*"

The woman stood up. She showed her age more now, but she was still beautiful, with the shaded gray eyes and the dark hair and the pouting lips. Rheinden smiled beside her.

"*I think we shall find,*" *she told Bencolin,* "*that our car is in running order. We shall not trouble our good host for a night's lodging.*"

Dunstan was bubbling with rage, but he bowed in a lopsided fashion.

"*I will see you to the door,*" *he informed them.*

The woman gave a little wave of her hand as she disappeared, and Rheinden bowed.

"*You will rise high in your profession, M. Bencolin!*" *she cried.*

When the three had gone Sir John began to swear to relieve his feelings. Von Arnheim was still chuckling, and Bencolin thoughtful.

"*I suppose you couldn't hold them,*" *said Wood,* "*but the question is—is there any treasure in that secret passage?*"

"*Not a bit!*" *responded O'Riordan, whose head appeared in the window like a genial specter. He grinned as he climbed through, shaking the dust from his clothes.* "*There's a box at the foot of the steps, cover pried off, and all there is inside are some church relics.*"

"*You search for hidden treasure, and you find—church relics a thousand years old,*" *speculated von Arnheim.* "*Shall we say a parable?*"

"*No,*" *said Sir John;* "*a jolly fine adventure. Look: two of the cleverest crooks in the business deceived by a crazy old servant who brings them to search for nonexistent jewels.*"

"*Oh, they probably picked up Stobel; not he them,*" *pointed out Wood with some incoherence.* "*They must be pretty well out of funds...Say, how did you discover the window?*"

"*It is only that people in my profession must watch for an explanation to ev-*"

erything, even ghosts," said Bencolin. "And for one thing, I heard no ivy rustling on that window, though Mr. Dunstan assured me that there was ivy outside. Moreover, is there anything that can produce a shadow on a window in a dark room except light behind the window?—Mr. Dunstan saw the ghost himself, you know."

"Well, if you ask me, it was deuced clever," asserted Sir John. "Come, let's sit down; it's early yet. And while Dunstan is out hauling Stobel over the coals, open up another bottle! Pile some more wood on the fire!"

O'Riordan came through the window. He set the candle on the table and poured out a drink.

"Right!" he agreed, toasting them. "Bencolin, you've done no work—tell us a story!"

L'ENVOI

The last story has been told. The fire is out, and even Dunstan's monumental wine supply exhausted. And, after all these impossible happenings, we end dreaming by a hearthside, with a satisfied feeling such as only the impossible can give. We have gone swashbuckling through history; we have put flesh on dead bones and conjured up ghosts, all in the gay good humor of the storytellers' group, where anything goes.

We may have butchered to make a romantic holiday. But if at any time we have toyed with an Idea, it has been in the belief that the things which lie closest to the heart are fancies, and that the old frayed banners of chivalry may rise again, be the trumpet call ever so faint. The glitter and the drumbeat will fascinate; you in your dreams will unhorse the stoutest opponent, so that you will be the man you might have been had you dared take the open road and the bright eyes of danger.

If we lived always in reality, we should all be poor things indeed. Truth? Is there anything more true than what one in his inmost self desires? Is life, then, so much fact that we should pound in only dead information—to produce a sheepskin? There is a spirit behind it that makes for a goal beyond affairs as they are. That is the spirit called gentility.

Realists are the people who look in a mirror and get disgusted. They are the ones who will explode all your fine ideas. They would pull down Kenilworth Castle[21] and substitute an efficient gas-station; they would take the Lorelei[22] off the rocks and substitute Margaret Sangers[23] and Carrie Chapman Catts[24]. Your realistic author has begun to notice a protuberant stomach and weakening eyes, so he goes right merrily to work and writes a novel exposing something as sordid. It is considered a great novel; he is awarded the Pulitzer or the

---

21 Built in the early twelfth century, Kenilworth was a storied royal castle for most of its existence. It was dismantled in 1650, but its romantic ruins have been preserved since that time.

22 Although Carr and Frederic Prokosch cowrote "The New Canterbury Tales," the reappearance of this allusion here and some others used strongly suggest Carr authored this section. See the commentary.

23 American nurse and birth-control advocate. She campaigned against the Comstock Act, which criminalized contraceptives. Carr of course would have found her to be a very unromantic figure.

24 Carrie Chapman Catt was an American women's suffrage leader who, as two-time president of the National American Woman Suffrage Association, campaigned for the Nineteenth Amendment to the U.S. Constitution, which granted women the right to vote in 1920. Even the young Carr was a strong conservative, so he hardly admired Catt.

Nobel Prize, which he refuses. Aesop once wrote a fable about this, and called it "The Dog in the Manger."[25]

But what's the difference? Open up another bottle, and pile some more wood on the fire! Let's have joyous fun-making, the Paris of Villon[26] and Jerome Coignard![27] We seek no quarrels, we try to tread on nobody's toes. If we go wrong, it will be because we have bored somebody, and that is the high sin in the calendar.[28]

There are so many magazines trying to reform something or prove something that "The New Canterbury Tales" is somewhat in the nature of an experiment. The college literary magazines, which get a smoke-drunk[29] like the Delphic Oracle and stagger away into an attempt to change their own worlds, have grown numerous of late. Somewhere along the way has been dropped the intent to amuse; when the intent to amuse is lost, they become the publications which everyone praises and no one reads.[30] Sparring with sin, Satan, and student government is an occupation best left to those most interested.

If, however, we forward romantic propaganda, that is entirely within our realm. If we assume that there is a higher thing in fiction than the realistic thump of the janitor's mop, at least we do little harm. The most dangerous trap about writing is that an author finds it so easy to be scowlingly cynical on paper that he whirls round his Byronic tie and takes a leer at romance. The college realist is grand and iconoclastic on the slightest provocation—not because he believes it, but because

---

25 The moral of Aesop's fable, in which a growling dog unnecessarily drives a hungry ox away from hay, "Do not grudge others what you cannot enjoy yourself."

26 French poet and sometime-criminal of the middle ages, and the subject of "A Lodging for the Night," a story in Stevenson's *New Arabian Nights*, one of Carr's favorite books.

27 A fictional Abbé whose biography, by a cook's son, was "edited" by Anatole France, the poet, novelist, journalist, member of the Académie Française, and winner of the Nobel Prize for Literature.

28 In his May 4,1922 screed against "realistic" writers in the *Uniontown Daily News Standard* column, "As We See It," Carr wrote that "the author's chief aim is to amuse."

29 Early twentieth-century slang for the condition in which one is simultaneously intoxicated by alcohol and nicotine. Although it requires more alcohol than otherwise to become drunk while smoking, the alcohol increases the levels of dopamine and serotonin released by nicotine.

30 Of course, Carr here is echoing Twain's definition of a classic, "a book which people praise but don't read," which Twain attributes to Pudd'nhead Wilson in the epigraph of Chapter XXV of *Following the Equator* (1897).

he wants to avoid being ridiculous at all costs. This tendency has dumped many a hearty ashcan on a marble floor. But a college author is really the most gloriously sentimental person who writes.

There they all sit around the fire, von Arnheim, Sir John, Dunstan, Wood, Bencolin, laughing as before! They have appeared before, and perhaps they will appear again. If their random talk, scattered through all the pages, has entertained one person who reads; if the dash and fire of flying hoofs has struck one responsive spark; if, when the dim window falls, it causes one person excitement or laughter, our experiment in pure romanticism will have been a success. If by such poor means we can beguile one person a moment from a world that marches with unceasing din, then surely, surely, we shall not have written in vain.

THE END

Notes for the Curious: "The New Canterbury Tales"

The eponymous inspiration for this series of "legends," Chaucer's *Canterbury Tales*, is a collection of stories told by a fictional group of pilgrims to pass the time as they wend their way toward Canterbury Cathedral. Traditionally, the faithful would undertake an annual pilgrimage to the shrine of Thomas Becket there to pray for their needs.

The Canterbury Tales provides inspirational structure and spirit for Carr and Frederic Prokosch's collaboration. Chaucer's collection of twenty-four tales is bound within an ongoing framing narrative. This includes a general prologue and an epilogue (Chaucer's tongue-in-cheek "Retraction" in which he begs the reader's forgiveness for repeating such scandalous content) combined with interstitial prologues and epilogues for the individual tales, during which the characters discuss and debate their stories (and opinions).

"The New Canterbury Tales," in addition to its mimesis of form, reproduces the sense of relationship between individual tales, too. In Chaucer's narrative, the pilgrims do not merely react as an audience to prior tales, whether with approbation or resentment; they vie as storytellers to top them. This competitive impulse emerges immediately after "The Knight's Tale," which begins the cycle with a humorless chivalric romance. (The Knight, being of the highest social order among the pilgrims, is privileged to speak first.) The Miller, who drunkenly usurps the Monk's place as the expected next speaker (based again upon social rank), declares:

> I can a noble tale for the nones,
> With which I wol now quyte the Knightes tale.

In modern English, this means, "I know a noble story appropriate to our occasion, with which I will now requite the Knight's tale." Chaucer's word "quyte," carries the modern word *requite's* connotation of refuting, overcoming, or outdoing what it answers—and indeed, as Chaucer's pilgrims offer tale after tale, some, as responses to preceding ones, are jealously intended to repay perceived slights. For instance, the Miller's "noble" tale is actually a low comedy befitting a drunk, featuring a foolishly cuckolded reeve. So naturally, immediately following the Miller's tale, the angry Reeve interjects his own narrative, which relates how a dishonest miller gets his humiliating comeuppance.

The reader can perceive similar, occasionally squabbling, transitions between the "legends" in "The New Canterbury Tales": in a given epilogue, one character, picking up on the legend he just heard, promises to juxtapose his own to it—sometimes, of course, bettering that legend's perceived deficiency. Note particularly how in the prologue, von Arnheim asks for a legend, and then, having heard what he considers only stories, tells a true legend himself; similarly, Stoneman who requested a ghost story, but has not yet been satisfied by hearing one, tells an actual ghost story.

The epilogues of "The New Canterbury Tales," though, serve a much more important function than merely bridging legends and setting them off against one another. Combined with the prologue into a framing narrative, *all these together form an independent, fair-play mystery solved by Bencolin,* who relies (as the reader can) in part on clues unknowingly divulged by the tellers of the fireside tales. As we noted in the commentary concerning "Ashes of Clues," in "The New Canterbury Tales," Carr's use of the framing narrative wholly exceeds Chaucer's example, essentially transforming it—and in doing so, Carr is giving us, by far, his cleverest presentation yet of the construction and solution of a mystery story. Carr's technique here, in both conception and execution, is far beyond the simple reveal in "The House of Terror"—even though "The New Canterbury Tales" is less than a handful of years (and only six intervening attempts) removed from it. The framing narrative in "The New Canterbury Tales" is a remarkable leap forward for Carr, especially in observance of the way his patient, intermittent revelation of clues throughout both it and the individual legends prepares him for the next writer's challenge he will face, writing longer detective fiction—beginning of course with *Grand Guignol.* In "The New Canterbury Tales," Carr drops fair-play clues in plain sight and varied contexts, practicing skills he will use (with increased sophistication) in his professional novels. With this story cycle, we can see Carr following, not violating, his own mature advice from "The Grandest Game in the World": "Your craftsman knows…that it is not necessary to mislead the reader. Merely state your evidence, and the reader will mislead himself" (p. 10).

There are other likely influences upon "The New Canterbury Tales" to consider. One is Donn Byrne's "The Story of Suleyman Bey" (from *Stories Without Women…*), which tells of an Irishman from Sligo who becomes a sheik. It has the same romantic, Arabian Nights flair that "The Legend of the Softest Lips" does, and also pivots (as does Donn Byrne's *Marco Polo*) on the ill-fated infatuation of a westerner (in this case, as in "The Legend of the Softest Lips," an expatriate Irishman) with a veiled Muslim beauty. Donn Byrne's "Suleyman Bey" could easily be one of the legends in "The New Canterbury Tales."

A more important, perhaps *the* most important influence on "The New Canterbury Tales" (even more so than Chaucer), is Washington Irving. In general, Irving had a capacity familiar to readers of

Carr to intermingle the supernatural and the humorous. Consider, for instance, this representative passage from *Tales of a Traveller*:

> In fact, he was proud of his old family chateau, for part of it was extremely old. There was a tower and cha-pel that had been built almost before the memory of man; but the rest was more modern, the castle having been nearly demolished during the wars of the league. The Marquis dwelt upon this event with great satisfac-tion, and seemed really to entertain a grateful feeling towards Henry the Fourth, for having thought his pa-ternal mansion worth battering down.[1]

This witty explanation of how an ancient family estate came to be could easily have been a passage in one of the legends in "The New Canterbury Tales"—or in one of Carr's novels. It shares a tone with the explanation of Walpole's Twickenham in *The Curse of the Bronze Lamp*, for instance. One might expect Irving's adroit wit, which mingled the supernatural and the lighthearted, to have been a conscious influence upon Carr—and perhaps it was, but only unconsciously, because in 1922, Carr criticized Irving for this style: "If you must write terror stories…disgorge your ghastly faces and bloodstains on the floor, but discard your humor."[2]

All the same, Carr borrowed from Irving just as he did from other admired authors, and in the instance of "The New Canterbury Tales," borrowed more than trivially. As much as Chaucer is, the opening sto-ry cycle of Washington Irving's *Tales of a Traveller* (1824), collectively called "Strange Stories by a Nervous Gentleman," is an influence upon this series created by Carr and Prokosch. In Irving's cycle, the opening tale, "A Hunting Dinner," is the prologue relating how, after a late din-ner, a hunting party is unable to depart their host's residence due to a heavy winter storm. They elect to sit up late in the hall, continue drink-ing, and exchange ghost tales. The host, a baronet named Sir John, hints in response to a jovial Irish captain of dragoons that there may even be a haunted room in which to lodge one of the guests.

And so begins a series of ghost stories set off against one an-other in the style of Chaucer. An old man of the hunting party starts by relating, "The Adventure of My Uncle," which occurs "some time before the French Revolution" in a haunted French chateau. In it, the titular uncle visits a friend, a gallant marquis and courtier living out of

---

1 *Tales of a Traveller*, Brentano's, 1905, p. 11. All subsequent excerpts are drawn from the same edition.
2 Cited by Greene in the biography, p. 20.

step with the Republican sentiment of his times. The marquis would later go on to make a fruitless stand at the Tuileries on the famous 10th of August in defense of Louis XVI. While staying with the marquis, the uncle is haunted overnight by the ghost of a noblewoman who met an inhospitable end, in the same bedchamber, more than a century earlier.

Another hunting party member counters the old man's tale with "The Adventure of My Aunt," in which the lady in question is apparently haunted by the ghost of her dead husband. This story, in turn, is followed by the Irish dragoon's merry retelling of his grandfather's adventure spending the night in a haunted inn. And so forth.

All these and the other ghost stories recounted by the hunting party are peppered with interjected references to one another, with the hunting party's conversation (the framing narrative) breaking in from time to time. The narrator notes: "one story of the kind produces another, and…all the company seemed fully engrossed by the topic, and disposed to bring their relatives and ancestors upon the scene" (p. 50).

The antepenultimate narrative, "The Adventure of the Mysterious Picture," is the overnight experience of the nervous gentleman himself, after the hunting party finally decides to take to bed. Sir John having reminded his guests that one of the chambers in his hall has a reputedly haunted portrait in it, the baronet assigns each of them a bedchamber without further explanation. The nervous gentleman has an uneasy night, sleeping in what he believes to be the chamber with the haunted portrait. In the morning, he confesses his experience, and suffers some good-natured chaffing by the rest of the party.

The baronet then narrates his own two-part tale explaining the haunted portrait's history. In the first, Sir John recounts how he met a tragic and mysterious young man in Venice, the artist who painted the haunted portrait. This story is told from his own perspective. The second installment recounts the tragic young man's history in the words from his own journal. This tale, then, ties together *both* preceding tales (the nervous gentleman's and Sir John's), as well as the framing narrative.

There is a brief epilogue, which concludes the entire story cycle on a note of dramatic irony: after explaining that the nervous gentleman did not in fact overnight with the haunted portrait, the baronet invites his guests to see it, one by one. Each returns to the group and explains the peculiar effect the portrait had upon him. Sir John has fooled them, though: each visitor has only projected his own imaginings upon a regular portrait. None of the hunting party ever saw the haunted one, which the baronet, in sympathy with his dead friend, did not wish to become the object of any further jests by the fox hunters.

Of course, if the reader hears echoes of Irving's elements in those of "The New Canterbury Tales"—a baronet named Sir John, a jovial Irishman in the party, a haunted uncle, etc.—it is likelier than not that at least one of them was, in fact, borrowed inspiration for Carr. In any event, we can see how Carr, after reading Irving's interpretation of Chaucer, was inspired to push his own framing story even further in "The New Canterbury Tales." Irving's denouement explains the "mystery" of the baronet's haunted portrait; the epilogue is both articulated from and inextricably tied to the themes and circumstances of the stories it closes. Carr does likewise, but puts his own stamp upon "The New Canterbury Tales" by substituting a fair-play explanation where Irving offered simpler dramatic irony.

We have discussed "The New Canterbury Tales" only with respect to Carr, but he co-authored it with Frederic Prokosch. One of the traditional preoccupations of expert readers who have examined the cycle is attempting to discern which writer was responsible for which stories. We do not have any documentation of this other than what Prokosch wrote more than six decades later in response to Greene's inquiry: "He replied that he had forgotten all about it, 'but I detect Carr's fine Italian hand (for most of it) and my own too (in parts, & to my embarrassment)'" (p. 55). Greene elaborates (on the same page):

> An examination of the stories by several experts in Carr's works has resulted in a consensus: The framing story and five of the "legends" are by Carr; two of the stories are by Prokosch; the eighth is more difficult, and it may be a collaboration.

Breaking down likely authorship story by story, the editor finds himself slightly (and respectfully!) at odds with Greene's panel. Following now are the current editor's attributions, story by story, and the rationale for each (some reasoning being in common with Greene's).

The Dedication: The poem here does not seem like typically Carrian prosody. About a dozen of Carr's poems survive; most share a distinctive prosody unlike this one. The editor believes that Prokosch was the versifier of the dedication.

The Framing Narrative: This is clearly Carr's work. There is nothing in it uncharacteristic of him, and of course, it is a fair-play mystery drawing on clues it offers, plus some hidden in the legends. Carr was a writer of mysteries; Prokosch was not. The characters were ones invented by Carr, most of whom had been used by him before, and some of whom would be again. There is no reason to suspect any contribution to the framing narrative by Prokosch.

"The Legend of the Black Monk": The plot may be spare, a tendency Carr had generally outgrown, but after all, this legend is uncommonly short. The narrative style and the voice certainly sound like Carr's, including the humor threaded throughout. What's more, this legend is the starting point for the contemporary mystery Bencolin solves. We may safely assign this story to Carr.

"The Legend of the Softest Lips": Carr rewrote this in 1939 as a new story, "Harem-Scarem." That version was published in *The Daily Mail* on March 24. (Tony Medawar is the Golden-Age literary detective who ferreted out the previously forgotten rewrite.) Not only does the plot here otherwise seem very much like Carr's work, but there is of course no chance Carr would have purloined Prokosch's work and revised it later as his own. Incidentally, the editor finds the original version markedly superior to the 1939 rewrite.

"The Legend of the Gay Diana": This is the first tale for which the present editor's attribution differs from that of Greene et al.; the current editor ascribes it to Prokosch. One reason is its lack of Carrian characteristics. This legend is short, but it is only about fifty words shorter than "The Legend of the Cane in the Dark," and, actually, more than 125 words longer than "The Legend of the Softest Lips." There are enough clearly Carrian characteristics in both those other stories to credit them confidently to Carr, but no significant ones here. One would expect Carr, for instance, to offer more and better clues foreshadowing the ending—which is not an O. Henry-worthy twist, either. The legend's ending is hinted perfunctorily and incompletely by only the single, half-effaced bloodstain on the table. Carr was, by 1927, much more adroit than this, and in fact, he ably demonstrates robust clueing in "The Legend of the Cane in the Dark." The lack of clues and of a powerful twist ending speak against this tale's being Carr's.

Similarly, the metaphorical invocation of Diana in this story as the mythical huntress is implied and undeveloped. We have seen repeatedly in Carr's preceding amateur works that if he invokes such a metaphor, Carr exploits it—whether as foreshadowing ("The Will-o'-the-Wisp") or for the sake of subtext ("The Devil-Gun"). Carr in 1927 was beyond the point of offering a gratuitous literary allusion, which he otherwise would have found "egg-headed" and uninteresting.

What is really at issue in this legend with Diana is her striving for equality with men—a subject at this point in Carr's life of, at best, antipathetic interest to him. Carr would hardly have made the story as much (more so) a showpiece of Diana's reasonable dismissals of boorish sex discrimination as of the murder.

Further, consider the style and vocabulary of this tale, using the first three paragraphs as a case study: there is a repeated construction of longer sentences, often layering parallel clauses, almost all of which clauses (parallel or not) are anchored insistently by present participles—and in the paragraphs so assembled, little or no action transpires. This isn't very Carrian; Carr, when he uses the present participle, more frequently uses it adjectivally, or in past infinitive constructions, rather than as the present-tense governing verb of a descriptive passage. While the style of "The Legend of the Gay Diana" is quite distinctive, it is very unlike Carr.

Most importantly, this legend would otherwise be unique among Carr's contributions to the cycle, were it his, in *lacking any ligatures with the rest of "The New Canterbury Tales." Not only does this story lack any Carrian atmosphere or subject matter, but there are no clues in it tying the tale back to the framing story and Bencolin's solution.*

Finally, "The Legend of the Gay Diana" lacks any subtle humor, with which Carr ripostes it in the epilogue. His doing so amounts to more than just a humorous jab at the legend's lack of dash and heroism. Rather, Carr wryly exploits the framing narrative to *change the ending and the import of the legend entirely.* "The Legend of the Gay Diana," without Carr's epilogue, is a contemporary literary tale about women's equality and a passion killing. It is an unremitted subversion of the conservative social order in which ladies act like men, independently of them, and Earls stoop so clumsily to murder that they are exposed and discredited. These would be especially strange themes for Carr in as much as he "almost never objected to a social structure" (Greene, p. 440). By virtue of the epilogue, the story is instead transformed into one of crime, arrest, trial, and acquittal—one that *upholds* the established social order. The epilogue even restores "traditional love," confirming the otherwise unforeseen marriage between the Earl and the Lady—an arrangement Diana herself discourages, protesting openly that she is not in love with her suitor.

"The Legend of the Neckband of Carnelians": Greene et al. see this as Prokosch's work, which seems correct, especially given some of the characteristics that differentiate the previous legend: this story has a relatively unoriginal and unimaginative plot; no elements tie it back to the central mystery; there is no perceptible Carrian atmosphere; there is a distinctive prose style strikingly unlike Carr's. As in "The Legend of the Gay Diana," this story's sentences tend to be long, even run on (in one or two cases, editing was required). The legend's use of polysyndeton—construction of longer syntactical structures via the repeated insertions of conjunctions—has a prolix effect similar to that of the repeated participial phrasing in "The Legend of the Gay Di-

ana." In fact, while nowhere else in his amateur writings does Carr do this, "The Legend of the Gay Diana" uses back-to-back sentences beginning with "And" five times. This includes two pairs that are part of three straight sentences beginning with "And." Yes, like many writers, Carr begins sentences with conjunctions, including in the amateur works. He almost never, however, stacks such sentences one after the other. Only once in his amateur career does Carr write consecutive sentences beginning with the same conjunction: two spoken by Girard in Part V of *Grand Guignol* beginning with "But." Having so many such sentences concentrated together in the one short tale looks to be a stylistic tell of Prokosch's.

"The Legend of the Cane in the Dark": This is as blatantly Carr's work as any of the legends. It features confidently well managed fair-play clueing. The story also demonstrates Carr's maturer grasp of how to convey horror more effectively by playing on imagination instead of a gushing surfeit of words. As well, Carr would reuse elements of "The Legend of the Cane in the Dark" in later writings.

"The Legend of the Hand of Ippolita": This tale is a sibling of "Carnelians" and "Diana." It seems clearly to be Prokosch's, in which conclusion the editor agrees (again) with his predecessor analysts. Interestingly, though, a pattern seems to have emerged for Prokosch's legends: they are more superficially medieval in their tone, settings, and subject matter. Carr's stories, even when the time period is a medieval one, as in "The Legend of the Black Monk," always involve crime. (In that legend, the important crime is not the murder committed from jealousy, it is Unthred's theft of his lord's treasure, which gives rise to the contemporary mystery Bencolin solves.) Carr's stories consistently tie back to the framing narrative, including their furnishment of clues to its solution. Prokosch's tales, on the other hand, conceal no such clues, and their simple conflicts license commonplace morals. In this sense, Prokosch's legends are literary descendants of Aesop and Chaucer, the more so than Carr's contributions are.

"The Legend of La Bella Duquesa": While the surface subject matter is more like Prokosch's, given its style and import, this story must be Carr's. One indication is that the sexual rupture in this story is of a modern temperament the reader can easily envision leading to the vengeance murder. It seems quite compatible with some of Carr's later bad romances.

This final legend also seems to be a sibling to "The Blue Garden," a 1926 Carr historical romance not reprinted in this collection. There are multiple resonances between the two stories.

"The Legend of La Bella Duquesa" demonstrates Carr's propensity for Latin quotations, too; he would go on to incorporate more than one hundred of them in his professional works.

Finally, there is the fact that this "legend" is really a thinly veiled criminal confession, not a legend like the others at all. "The Legend of La Bella Duquesa" ties straight back into the framing story, preparing the reader for Bencolin's surprise revelation and the denouement. There is no way Carr would have left the composition of this climactic tale to somebody else.

"*L'Envoi*": While Prokosch may well have helped plan this conclusion's sentiments in the same manner he and Carr probably shared responsibility for those of the opening paragraph in the Dedication, there are multiple echoes in "*L'Envoi*" to earlier and later writing by Carr. A footnote accompanying the text drew attention to the similarity between it and one of his *Uniontown Daily News Standard* columns; Carr also reincorporated several of the references here in his May, 1927 contemporary story, "The Deficiency Expert":

> "What," cried Rinkey, "would the English do to a person who pulled down Kenilworth Castle and substituted an efficient gas-station? What would the Germans do if you took the Lorelei off the rocks and substituted Margaret Sanger and Carrie Chapman Catt?"

In sum, then, while Greene and colleagues attributed just the two legends to Prokosch and five to Carr, with one undecided, the present editor awards Prokosch credit for three and for the Dedication. All the evaluators agree that the framing story is Carr's. The current editor is also convinced that, in addition to four legends and the framing narrative, "L'Envoi" is Carr's work, too. Greene and company had not explicitly addressed the epilogue, but Carr's composition of it is safely demonstrable.

"The New Canterbury Tales," for which Prokosch admitted Carr was the guiding spirit, is another demonstration of Carr's first-rate inventiveness, even when he is borrowing inspiration for premises or formats. While it, like "Ashes of Clues," was a one-time experiment for Carr, its execution is excellent. "The New Canterbury Tales" also seems to have been a creative springboard that helped Carr generate the confidence to attempt a longer narrative again. He had first tried in 1927 and then, dissatisfied, destroyed that manuscript. Carr's next attempt, *Grand Guignol*, would not only avoid incompletion or destruction, it would launch the young author into his professional career.

Grand Guignol (1929)

Mystery in Ten Parts

Performance staged under the direction of M. Henri Bencolin, prefect of police of Paris

The Cast of Characters

M. HENRI BENCOLIN.

M. ALEXANDRE LAURENT, *scholar, former husband of*

LOUISE DE SALIGNY, *the wife of*

RAOUL, *fourth Duc de Saligny, eminent sportsman.*

M. EDOUARD VAUTRELLE.

SIGNOR LUIGI FENELLI, *maestro of several enterprises.*

JACQUES GIRARD, *jockey.*

MR. SID GOLTON, *late of Lincoln, Nebraska, U.S.A.*

FRANÇOIS DILLSART, *operative of the prefecture.*

M. LE COMTE DE VILLON, *juge d'instruction,*

and others.

THE PLACE: *Paris.*

THE TIME: *1927.*

The action covers a period of twenty-four hours.

Introduction

Believing that the average reader is at least one-eighth amateur detective, the editors of THE HAVERFORDIAN *herewith present a problem for your wits as it was presented to M. Henri Bencolin, the prefect of police of Paris. Now that such things as "The Baffle Book"[1] have become the rage, and murder games are a popular indoor sport, this magazine may point out that it presented a similar game in 1926[2]—some time before "The Baffle Book" was thought of—and will not, therefore, be accused of imitating a fad.*

The first seven chapters of this problem are offered for your solution in the current number and are followed by a blank page, where it may interest you to write down the name of the person you believe to be the murderer before reading the last three chapters in the April issue to verify your guess.

As this story is considerably longer than "The Shadow of the Goat," wherein M. Bencolin first appeared, there are considerably more clues scattered about; and also, we warn the industrious sleuth, considerably more ways to go astray.

It is, in effect, a theatrical performance at the Grand Guignol of France[3], and the management expresses a wish that the members of the audience, in addition to checking off the name of the villain on the program, will remain in their seats until the final curtain.

---

1 First published in 1928, *The Baffle Book* included a collection of fifteen "10-minute mysteries" presented through crime-scene descriptions, illustrations, charts, and diagrams. At the end of each section the book challenged the reader to answer certain questions and solve the mystery. The *Second Baffle Book* appeared in 1929, and *The Third Baffle Book* in 1930.

2 Part I of Bencolin's premier, "The Shadow of the Goat," included "A Warning to the Curious": "For the impossible events in this story there is a logical and very simple solution. Should you care to attempt unraveling it in accordance with the HAVERFORDIAN's rules, published in the HAVERFORD NEWS, you will find that the key lies in plain sight. But beware of false leads! If you discover who killed Jules Fragneau you are far cleverer than most readers." Part I ended with the challenge to the reader, "(There is the problem. Can you solve it before the solution is printed next month?)"

3 A theater in the Pigalle district of Paris that specialized in naturalistic horror shows. It closed in 1962.

I

THE OVERTURE: *Danse Macabre*

"Le jeu est fait, 'seures et dames; rien ne va plus."[4]
The voices stopped. It was so quiet that from anywhere in the room you could hear the ball ticking about in the wheel. Then the shrill, bored voice chanted:
"Vingt-deux noir, 'sieurs et dames..."[5]
One man got up from the table stiffly, with an impassive face. He made a defiant gesture at lighting a cigarette, but the flame of the *briquet* wabbled in his hand; he smiled in a sickly way, and his face glistened when he looked from side to side. A woman laughed. There was the booming of an English voice, swearing triumphantly.

Paris has many such miniature casinos, which attract the most mixed throng of any places in that mixed city. This was a long red room, in a walled house of a discreet neighborhood at Passy. A harsh color scheme of red and crystal; a harsh sound of voices, and bad ventilation; a harsh jazz orchestra downstairs mangling tunes already execrable; poor cocktails supplied by the house, and a clientele at once fashionable and dowdy—above everything, a gloomy tensity of thousands being played across the table. The hard light showed worn places on faces and furniture. The women used too much perfume; men took an enormous delight in shaking out two-thousand-franc notes like tablecloths.

At a lounge near one of the windows, from which you could see the Citroën advertisement spraying colored lights up the side of the Eiffel Tower, I sat with my friend Bencolin. He idly twirled the stem of a cocktail glass; with the points of his hair whisked up, and his black

4 "The game is set, gents and ladies. No more bets."
5 "Twenty-two black, gents and ladies."

beard clipped to a sharp point, he looked even more Mephistophelian than usual. The wrinkles round his eyelids contracted in amusement, and he smiled sideways when he pointed out each newcomer
round the clicking wheel.

They were interesting. There was Madame That and the Marquise
This, octogenarian crones whose faces were masks of enamel and
rouge, dyed hair piled like a scaffolding; they smirked and ogled at
their gigolos, smooth-haired pomandered young men whose gestures
were like a woman's, but with manners and evening dress flawless. A
crone's hand would shoot out like a claw after a new pile of banknotes;
then the gigolo applauded politely, and smiled in a glittering way at
the leering woman. There was a Russian lady with a Japanese face and
a pearl collar—not beautiful, flourishing skinny arms like wings—but
several men were eager to back all her bets. There were loud Argen-
tines, the deepest plungers, and an American too drunk to follow the
play, but falling over everybody's chair and demanding to know who
wanted to start a poker game. An attendant led him suavely away to
the bar... Gestures were shriller, bolder; the hard light drew lines and
wrinkles, and showed up splotches of powder on bare backs; no fog
of smoke could eliminate the wet odor of the bar, or any amount of
music blat down that insistent song of the wheel.

"They are fools," said Bencolin idly, "to play against a double
zero." He glanced over as another burst of laughter came from the
tables. "And the foreigners will play nothing else. Baccarat, chemin-
de-fer—never. It must be quick, like a drink of whiskey, voilà!" He
snapped his fingers. "Their only system is the martingale[6], doubles or
quits, and they do not last long."

"Is the game straight?" I asked.

"Oh, yes. Cheating is quite unnecessary, and too dangerous...
Well," he added, smiling, "am I not showing you Paris, my friend
Jack?"[7]

"And much obliged. Except that I had hoped to go slumming.
This is as dull and decorous as the Latin Quarter."

"Yes, but wait," Bencolin remarked softly. "I seldom go anywhere
for pleasure. I think you will find that this is no exception."

"A case?"

He shrugged his shoulders. For a time he sat staring with blank
eyes at the crowd; then he took out a black cigar, and rolled it about

---

6 As Bencolin hints, the martingale is a gambling technique according to which
the gambler doubles down after losing bets and reduces winning bets by half.
The goal is to come from behind and break even, but for evident reasons, the
method poses a real risk of fast, large losses.

7 Carr's nickname in college was Jack.

in his fingers. Absently he continued:

"It has been in the past my good or bad fortune to be concerned only in cases of an outlandish nature; cases whose very impossible character admitted of just one solution. Cast your mind back. There was one way, and only one, in which the smuggler Mercier could have been strangled; there was one way for La Garde to have been shot, and one way for Cyril Merton[8] to have accomplished his 'disappearance.' Is a person, then, to evolve a philosophy that there is but one way for any crime to be committed? Hardly; and yet—" He scowled across the room.

"The Duc de Saligny," he went on abruptly, "is good looking, wealthy, and still young. He was married at noon today to a charming young woman. There, you will say, is a perfect cinema romance. The bride and groom are both here tonight."

"Indeed? Aren't they going on a wedding trip?"

"To the modern marriage," mused Bencolin, "there seems to be something slightly indecent about privacy. You must act in public as though you had been married twenty years, and in private as though you had not been married at all. That, however, is not my affair. There is a deeper reason for it."

"They don't love each other, then?"

"On the contrary, they seem to be violently in love... Have you ever heard of the bride?"

I shook my head.

"She was Madame Louise Laurent. Three years ago she was married to a certain man named Alexandre Laurent. Shortly afterwards, her husband was committed to an asylum for the criminally insane." He was silent a moment, thoughtfully blowing smoke at the ceiling.

"Laurent was examined at the psychopathic ward. I was present at the time, and I give you my word that Cesare Lombroso[9] would have been delighted with the case. He was a mild-appearing young man, soft-spoken and pleasant. The black spot on his brain was sadism. Usually lucid, he would have intervals in which the temptation to kill and mutilate became overpowering; and none of his crimes ever became known until after his marriage. Of course, such a neurosis could have no normal marriage, and culminated in what is known as 'lust murder.' He attacked his wife, with a razor. She contrived to lock him in his room, for she is strong, and summoned help. By that time

---

8 Another mention of Cyril Merton, from "Shadow of the Goat."

9 An Italian criminologist (1835-1909) who believed that criminality was inherited (like other genetic traits) and could be detected and diagnosed medically. He founded the Italian School of Positivistic Criminology, which rejected prior assumptions and metaphysics in favor of experience and data.

the frenzy had spent itself, but his secret was out."

Bencolin spread out his hands.

"A genius, Laurent, a scholar, a prodigy in the languages. He spent his days in the asylum very quietly, at study. The marriage, naturally, was annulled." Bencolin paused, and then said slowly, "Six months ago, he escaped from the asylum. He is at large today, and the confinement seems only to have unbalanced him more completely.

"What did he do? He set out to find a perfect disguise. In these days, my friend, they are childish who seek to disguise themselves with any stage trappings: paint, or false hair, or anything of the kind. Even an unpracticed eye, such as your own, could penetrate such subterfuges without difficulty... No, Laurent did the only perfect thing. He put himself under the care of Dr. Grafenstein, of Vienna, the greatest master of plastic surgery. He had himself remade entirely, even to his fingerprints. When this had been done, he quite coolly killed Dr. Grafenstein—the only person who had ever seen his new face. Even the nurse had never laid eyes on the patient: in the first stages, he was swathed in bandages; when he began to heal, he concealed himself in his own room. Yes, he killed Grafenstein. He is now in Paris. Two days ago, he wrote a letter to the young Duc de Saligny. It said simply, 'If you marry her, I will kill you.' And I very much fear, my friend, that he will."

I do not believe that I was ever in my life struck with so much horror as at this unemotional recital. Bencolin had never raised his voice. He smoked meditatively, watching the crowd; out of his words there grew in my mind a distorted picture of a lunatic, a Grand Guignol madman stepping through green dusk. Bencolin turned his sardonic face, shook his head, and remarked as though in response:

"No, we are not dealing with the conventional killer or the bloodcurdler, who betrays himself in public. Have I not said that Laurent is mild-mannered and pleasant?—only with that clot on his brain. And what does he look like? The good God knows. He may be that fat banker over at the roulette table; he may be the young American, or the croupier, or any of them, or he may not be (and probably is not) here at all. But I shall not forget the Duc de Saligny's face when he brought that letter to me. A tall swaggerer with bloodshot eyes and an excitable manner: he kept biting his lips, and looking round until you could see the whites of his eyes. He was frightened, but he refused to admit it. Yes, he would go through with the wedding, and so would Louise. But you will see that he longs for public places now, until my men can step out and lay their hands on Laurent."

That was the beginning of the nightmare drama. It seemed to me that the voices had grown more shrill, the gestures more elaborate;

and that some force of Bencolin's words had penetrated to everybody in the room. It was not possible for them to have heard him, and yet you would have said that everyone was conscious of it, and was looking over toward us, furtively.

"Is he always dangerous?" I asked.

"Any man who has committed one murder is always dangerous. And Laurent especially, for our pathological case has discovered how pleasant it can be."

"How does madame—*madame la duchesse* take all this?"

Bencolin was regarding a very oily and effusive J—,[10] who proclaimed his losses at the top of his voice; then the detective laid his hand on my arm.

"You will see for yourself. Here she comes now...You notice? No emotion or agitation; she looks as though she were in a drug fog."

A woman was crossing the room toward us; she moved in a rather vague way, with expressionless eyes and a slight smile. She was beautiful, but she was more than this. Even her hair had a cloudy look. The eyes were heavy-lidded and black, with not too much mascara, the lips of a sensual fullness which just escaped being coarse. In dress she was perfect, the black gown accentuating the invitation of shoulder and breast. She twisted her pearls vaguely. There was a little silver anklet under the gray stocking... She came straight up to Bencolin. When he bent over her hand she was negligent, but, closer, you could see a vein pulsing in her throat.

Bencolin introduced me, and added, "A friend of mine. You may speak freely." She looked toward me, and I had a sense of veils being drawn away. It was a look of scrutiny, not unmixed with suspicion.

"You are affiliated with the police, monsieur?" she asked me.

"Yes," said Bencolin unexpectedly.

She sat down, refused one of my cigarettes, and took her own from a little wrist bag. Leaning back, she inhaled deeply; her hand trembled, and her lips stained the tip of the cigarette as though with blood. She wore some kind of exquisite perfume; one was conscious of her nearness.

"*Monsieur le duc* is here?" asked Bencolin.

"Raoul? Yes. Raoul is getting nerves," she answered, and laughed shrilly. "I don't blame him, though. It is not a pleasant thing to think about. If you had ever seen Laurent's eyes—"

Bencolin raised his hand gently. She shivered a little, looked slowly

---

10 This is another discomfiting use of some stereotypical antisemitism. The editor has elided the ethnic term, which was originally printed in full. Note that Carr removed this passage entirely when he revised *Grand Guignol* into *It Walks By Night*.

over at me, and then said, "There goes Raoul now, into the card room."
She nodded toward a broad back disappearing through a door at the
far end of the room. I saw no more than that, for I happened to be
looking at my wristwatch. I looked at it twice, absently, before I noticed
that the hour was eleven-thirty.

"Orange blossoms!" she said, and laughed again. "Orange blossoms, lace veils. A lovely wedding, lovely bride, with even the clergyman staring at us and wondering if there were a madman in the church.
Orange blossoms, 'till death do you part'—death! Very possibly!"

This was sheer hysteria. The sights and sounds of the casino
blended in with it; the banging of the jazz band became nearly unbear-
able. That voice of the croupier rose singing over it, like the bawling
of the man who calls trains. Louise, Duchesse de Saligny, said abruptly:

"I want a cocktail. Don't mind me if I seem upset. I keep thinking
of Laurent crawling about... M. Bencolin, you're here to see that no
harm comes to Raoul, do you hear? 'Till death do you part'—" She
shivered again.

There was silence while Bencolin looked round for the boy with
the cocktail tray, a silence, and none of us intruded on each other's
thoughts. A man and woman walked past us, almost stumbling over
madame's feet; and I recall that the man was saying heatedly in English,
"Five hundred francs is entirely too damn much!—" The voices trailed
away.

Somebody had come up in front of us, and coughed discreetly. It
was a tall man; dapper, blond, with an eyeglass and an almost imper-
ceptible moustache.

"Your pardon if I'm intruding," he remarked. "Louise, I don't believe I know—" He took out his handkerchief unnecessarily, wiped his
lips, and stood fidgeting.

"Oh...yes," she murmured; "these are gentlemen from the police,
Edouard. Allow me to present M. Edouard Vautrelle."

Vautrelle bowed. "Very happy...Raoul's gone to the card room,
Louise; he's been drinking too much. Won't you play?"

"That music—" she suddenly snapped, "damn that music. I can't
stand it! I won't stand it. Tell them to stop!—"

"*Doucement, doucement!*" [11] Vautrelle urged, looking round in a nervous way. With an apologetic nod at us he took her arm and led her
toward the table; she seemed to have forgotten our existence.

Bencolin picked up the cigarette stub she had left in the ashtray.
He was juggling it in his palm, when suddenly he looked up. Madame
and Vautrelle were in the center of the room directly under one of
the large chandeliers; they stopped. We all heard the crash of breaking

---

11 "Softly, softly!" ("Lower your voice.")

glass, and saw the white-coated servant leaning against the door of the card room. He had let fall the tray of cocktails, and was staring stupidly at the wreckage.

Everyone turned to look. With the cessation of voices, the jazz band had stopped too. The manager, his fat stomach wabbling, was hurrying across the room. But most distinctly emerged the drawn, shiny face of the servant—who had seen something, and was desperately afraid.

Bencolin did not seem to hurry, but he was across the room immediately. I was directly behind him; he extended in his palm, for the manager's gaze, the little card with the circle, the eagle, and the three words, "prefecture of police." Together we went through the door of the card room.

My sensations were the same as those I had experienced once at a sideshow when I had seen some mountebank swallow a snake. The room was not well lighted; its leprous red was hung with weapons, and a redshaded lamp burned beside a divan at the far end. A man had fallen forward before the divan, as though in the act of kneeling—but the man had no head. Instead there was a bloody stump propped on the floor. The head itself stood in the center of the room, upright on its neck; it showed white eyeballs, and grinned at us in the low red light. A breeze through an open window blew at us a heavy, sweet smell.

II
RED FOOTLIGHTS

With the utmost coolness, Bencolin turned to the manager.

"Two of my men," he said, "are on guard at your door. Summon them; all the doors are to be locked, and nobody must leave. Keep them playing, if it is possible. In the meantime, come in yourself and lock this door."

The manager stammered something to an attendant, and added, "Nobody is to know about this, understand?" He was a fat man, who looked as though he were melting; a monstrous moustache curled up to his eyes, which bulged like a frog's. Tumbling against the door, he stood and pulled idiotically at his moustache. Bencolin, twisting a handkerchief over his fingers, turned the key in the lock.

There was another door in the wall to our right, at the left side of the dead man as he lay before the divan. Bencolin went over to it; it was ajar, and he peered outside.

"This is the main hall, monsieur?" he asked.

"Yes," said the manager. "It—it—"

"Here is one of my men." Bencolin beckoned from the door, and held a short consultation with the man outside. "Nobody has come out *there*," he observed, closing the door. "François was watching. Now!"

All of us were looking about the room. I tried to keep my eyes off the head, which appeared to be gazing at me sideways; the wind blew on my face, and it felt very cold. Bencolin walked over to the body, where he stood and peered down, smoothing his moustache. Beside the neck stump I could see projecting from the shadow a part of a heavy sword—it had come, apparently, from a group on the wall, and though the edge was mostly dulled with blood, a part near the handle emerged in a sharp, glittering line.

"Butcher's work," said Bencolin, twitching his shoulders. "See, it has been recently sharpened." He stepped daintily over the red soaking against the lighter red of the carpet, and went to the window at our left. "Forty feet from the street…inaccessible."

He turned, and stood against the blowing curtains. The black eyes were bright and sunken; in them you could see rage at himself, nervousness, indecision. He beat his hands softly together, made a gesture, and returned to the body, where he avoided the blood by kneeling over the divan.

"Jack," he said suddenly, looking up, "pick up the head and bring it over here."

No doubt about it, I was growing ill.

"Pick up—the *head*, did you say?"

"Certainly; bring it here. Watch out, now; don't get the blood on your trousers…"

In a daze, I approached the thing, shut my eyes, and picked it up by the hair. The hair felt cold and greasy, the head much heavier than I had thought. While I was going toward Bencolin, I recall that the jazz band started playing again downstairs, dinning over and over, "*Whe-en ca-res pur-suoo-yah, sing hal-le-loo-jah—*"[12]

"I shouldn't tamper with this," Bencolin observed, "but nobody can give me orders; and I don't think we need a coroner's report about the manner of his death." He fitted the head against the trunk and stood back, frowning. I sat down heavily on the divan.

"Come here, monsieur," said Bencolin to the proprietor. "This sword: it comes from the room here?"

The manager began talking excitedly. His syllables exploded like a string of little firecrackers popping over the room; the almost unintelligible clipped speech of the *Midi*.[13] Yes, the sword belonged here. It had hung with another, like itself, crossed over a Frankish shield on the wall near the divan. It was an imitation antique. Oh, yes, it was razor-sharp; this lent such a semblance of reality, and the patrons like reality.

"The handle," remarked the detective, "is studded with round brass nail heads; we shall get no clear fingerprints from it, I fear… Do you ever use this room, monsieur?"

"Oh, yes; frequently. But we haven't used it tonight. See, the card tables are folded against the wall. Nobody wanted to play. It was all that roulette." Volubly eager, the manager waggled his fat hands. "Do you think it can be hushed up, monsieur? My trade—"

"Do you know this dead man?"

"Yes, monsieur; it is M. le Duc de Saligny. He often comes here."

---

12 The song, "Hallelujah," is one of the songs from the musical *Hit the Deck*, which opened April 25, 1927 (based upon a 1922 novel).

13 The southern region of France, e.g., Aquitaine, Languedoc, and Provence.

"Did you see him go in here tonight?"

"No, monsieur. The last I saw him was early in the evening."

"Was he with anybody then?"

"With M. Edouard Vautrelle. The two were great friends—"

"Very good, then. You may go out now and inform *madame la duchesse;* be as quiet about it as possible—better take her out in the hall, in case she makes a scene. Tell M. Vautrelle to step in here."

He went out by the hall door, leering over his shoulder with tiny wrinkled eyes. Bencolin turned to me.

"Well, what do you make of it?"

I could not collect my thoughts, and blurted dully, "They were fortunate to keep it from the crowd out there—"

"No, no: the murder?"

"It was a terrific blow. It must have taken a madman's strength."

"I wonder!" said Bencolin, beginning to pace up and down. "Not necessarily, my friend. It was a two-handed blow, but, as our manager says, that sword is razor-sharp. I do not think that such gigantic strength was essential. You could have done it yourself...Look at the position of the body; does it convey nothing to you?"

"Only that there seems to have been no struggle."

"Obviously not. He was struck from behind. We may assume that he was sitting on the divan before he was struck; but he got to his feet. Mark that: he got to his feet also before he was killed—you note that he is some distance out from the divan..."

"Well?"

"Yes, there are a number of pillows on the divan."[14]

"Pillows?"

"Certainly. Great God! Where are your wits? Don't you understand?"

"It suggests nothing except—except an amorous implication."

"Amorous the devil!" snapped Bencolin. "There was nothing amorous about the situation here." He laughed wryly, and added, "Our madman is now in these gaming rooms. Nobody has left, unless my agents were asleep."

"By the hall door?—"

"François has been there since eleven-thirty. Do you know what time Saligny came in here?"

"I recall exactly, because when madame pointed him out I was looking at my watch. It was eleven-thirty."

Bencolin looked at his own watch. "Just twelve; it should be easy to check alibis... How do you account for the fact that the head lies at

---

14 Bencolin's (and Carr's) first enigmatic clue, which (per the introduction) Carr learned from Doyle and Chesterton.

some distance from the body, standing up?"

"It certainly couldn't have rolled to that position."

"Well, stranger things have happened, but it didn't—you can see that there is no blood trail between the head and the body. No, the murderer put it there."

"Why?"

"You forget that this is no sane mind. Can't you imagine it? The murderer triumphantly holding up the head of his victim; mocking it, addressing words to it while he walked round shaking it by the hair—"

"What a cheerful imagination _you_ have!"

"But it is necessary," he murmured, shrugging. Then he bent down gingerly and started to go through Saligny's pockets. Presently he straightened up and indicated a pile of articles on the divan. There was a queer smile on his face.

"The crowning touch...his pockets are filled with pictures of himself. Yes. See?" He ran his hands through clippings and pasteboards. "Newspaper pictures, and a few cabinet photographs. Photographs of himself, every conceivable sort; pictures where he looks handsome, pictures where he looks ghastly...here is one on horse-back; another at the golf links... Hm. Nothing else except some banknotes, a watch, and a lighter. Why these photographs at all? And especially why are they carried in evening clothes?"

"Conceited ass!"

Bencolin shook his head. He was squatting by the divan, idly turning over the clippings. "No, my friend, there may be another reason—which is the peak of all this odd business. Cabinet photographs. Diable!"[15]

We were suddenly startled by a tearing, rattling sound. The door to the hall was pushed open despite a protesting officer in plain clothes; there lurched into the room a short, pudgy, wild-eyed young man with a paper hat stuck on the back of his head. He grinned foolishly, his clothes were awry, and the noise was being made by one of those wooden twirlers they give as favors at nightclubs. He gave that sort of drunken leer very popular at weddings, shook the rattler at us, and smirked at the silly sounds it emitted.

"Party here," he said in English, "'scort couple home. Always do't 'scort to the home to, as it were. Let's have a drink. Got any liquor?" he demanded interestedly of the plain-clothes man.

"_Mais monsieur, c'est défendu d'entrer—_"[16]

"Cutta frog talk. No comprey. Got any liquor? Hey?"

---

15 "The devil!"

16 "Sir, it is forbidden to enter—"

"Monsieur, je vous ai dit!—"[17]

"N'lissen! Gotta see m' friend Raool. He's married; hellva thingta do!—"

The young man was pleading and persistent. I went over hurriedly and spoke in English:

"Better go out, old top. You'll get to see him—"

"By God, you're m' friend!" crowed the young man, opening his eyes wide and thrusting out his hand. "Got any liquor? I've been drinkin'," he confided in a low tone, "but gotta see Raool. He's married. Let's have a drink." Suddenly he sat down in a chair near the door and fell into a half stupor, still twirling the rattle.

"Monsieur!" cried the policeman.

"I'm gonna pop *you*," said the newcomer, opening his eyes again and pointing his finger at the policeman with a curiously intense look, "sure'z hell I'm gonna pop you 'fyou don't gettaway! C'mon, get back, 'm gonna pop 'im!" He relapsed again.

"Who is this?" I asked Bencolin.

"I have seen him before, with Saligny," the detective replied. "His name is Golton, or something of the sort: an American, naturally."

"We had better put him—"

Again there was an interruption. We heard a woman moaning, "I can't stand it! I can't stand it!" and other feminine tones urging her to be quiet. It was Madame Louise's voice. The door to the hall opened, and Edouard Vautrelle entered. He was very pale, but supercilious; he polished the eyeglass on his handkerchief, and looked round coldly.

"Was this necessary?" he said.

Supported by a little wizened woman attendant, Madame Louise came after him. She glanced at the thing on the floor; then she stood stoically, upright and motionless, with the rouge glaring out on her cheeks. Her eyes were dry and hot.

There was a space of silence, so that we could hear the curtains rustling at the window. Suddenly Golton, the American, looked up from a glassy contemplation of the floor, and saw her. He emitted a crow of delight. Never noticing the body, he rose unsteadily, made a flamboyant bow, and seized madame's hand.

"My heartiest congratulations," he said, "on this, the happiest day 've your whole life!—"

It was a ghastly moment. We all stood there frozen, except Golton, who was wabbling with hand extended in his bow. Golton's eyes travelled up to Vautrelle, and he added waggishly:

"Sorry you got the gate[18], Eddie; Raool's got more money'n you, anyhow…"

17 "Sir, I told you—"

18 The equivalent idiom today is to be shown the door: sent away, dismissed, or asked to leave.

III
DEATH GUIDES THE CLOCKS

Vautrelle snarled, "Get that drunken dog out of here!" and made a movement that was restrained by Bencolin.

"Take him out," the detective whispered to me, and added under his breath: "*Learn what you can.*"

Golton was more easily led away by one of his nationality; besides, at that moment he gave signs of becoming unwell. The policeman passed us out into the hall, and I supported him down its length to the men's lounging room, which was equipped with deep chairs and many ashtrays. Stoutly denying the need of assistance, he disappeared for a time and presently emerged looking pale but considerably more sober.

"Sorry to be such an inconvenience," he said, sinking into a chair. "Can't hold it. All right now." After a time of staring at the floor he said irritably: "What's alla fuss about?"

"Your friend, Raoul."

"Yeah; he's been married."

I adopted the easy camaraderie of Americans in a strange country. "Known him long?"

"Two'r three months. Met him when I was on a trip to Austria."

"He and his wife have been engaged a long time, haven't they?"

"I'll say! Must be two years. I don't know what's been delaying 'em. Ever since I've been in France, I guess... Say, lemme introduce myself. Sid Golton's the name, from Nebraska. I think I could stand a drink."

"You were an intimate of his, then?"

"Not exactly, but I knew him pretty well. Way I met him, I saw his picture in the papers—great horseman; so'm I. Walked up on the train and says, 'I'm Sid Golton. I wanta shake your hand.'"

"That was very tactful."

"Sure. Well, he spoke English all right. But I never got a chance to go riding with him. Useta drop round to his house. It was a swell wedding they had…" It suddenly penetrated Golton's mind that something was wrong. His face was assuming normal lines after a squashed-clay appearance, and resolved into pudgy, reddish features under thinning hair. He demanded: "What's all this about, anyhow?"

"Mr. Golton, I am sorry to say that the Duc de Saligny has been murdered—"

Golton's eyes turned as glassy as marbles. He was halfway out of his chair when the door to the hall opened, and Bencolin entered with Edouard Vautrelle. The ensuing few minutes showed Golton, maudlin and fearful, grotesque with his scared features under the paper cap, insisting that he "didn't know a damn thing about it, and if he wasn't let out of there right away there'd be trouble, because he was a sick man."

"You are at liberty to go, of course," Bencolin said. "But please leave your address."

Golton blundered out the door, loudly declaring that he was headed for Harry's New York Bar. His address he gave as 324 Avenue Henri Martin.

"Sit down, please, M. Vautrelle," Bencolin requested.

Vautrelle was the essence of coolness. His shirtfront did not bulge when he sat down, the wings of his white tie were exactly in line; even the colorless face had no wrinkles, but the movements of his eyes jarred it in quick darts. He crossed one leg over the other in a bored way.

"A few questions, please, monsieur. You understand that this is necessary…" (Vautrelle inclined his head)…"May I ask the last time you saw M. de Saligny alive?"

"I can't recall the exact hour. It may have been ten o'clock."

"Where was he then?"

"He had just left Louise with some of her feminine friends. He was going toward the tables. He seemed in high spirits. 'I'm going to play the red, Edouard,' he cried; 'red is my lucky color tonight…'"

I could have sworn that there was a faint smile on Vautrelle's face.

"Then," Vautrelle continued, "he turned to me as though with an afterthought. 'By the way,' he said, 'what was that cocktail you were describing to me: the one the man makes in the American Bar at the Ambassador?' I told him. 'Well, then, do me a favor, will you?' he said. 'Get hold of the bar steward here and tell him to mix me a shaker of them, will you? I'm expecting a man on something very important tonight. And, oh, yes! While you're there, you might tell him to bring it to the card room when I ring. I expect the man about eleven-thirty o'clock. Thanks.' I rejoined some friends—"

"One moment, please," interposed Bencolin. He pulled the bell cord at his elbow. Presently there entered the white-coated servant who had dropped the tray on entering the room of the murder. He was freckled and ill at ease and his huge hands tugged at the bottom of his jacket.

Bencolin, standing with one elbow on the mantelpiece, extended his hand.

"Steward, you were the person who discovered the dead man?" he asked.

"Yes, monsieur. Monsieur there," he nodded towards Vautrelle, "had told me to expect a ring around eleven-thirty from the card room and I took in the cocktails monsieur had ordered. I saw..." His eyes wrinkled up, and he protested: "I could not help breaking those glasses, monsieur! Really, I could not! If you will speak on my behalf to—"

"Never mind the glasses. You heard the bell ring, then? At what time was this?'"

"At about half past eleven; I know, because I was watching the clock for it. M. de Saligny always tips—tipped—well."

"Where were you at the time?"

"In the bar, monsieur."

"Where is the bell cord in the card room?"

"By the door into the main hallway, monsieur. You may see for yourself."

"You came immediately?"

"Not immediately. The bar steward took his time about mixing the cocktails, and insisted that I wash some sherbet glasses. It must have been ten minutes before I answered the ring."

"By which door did you enter?"

"By the door into the hallway; it is closer to the smoking room on which the bar gives. The light in the card room was bad, and when I entered (I got no reply to my knock)—" He began to speak very fast, and shift his glance from side to side. "I did not at first perceive the—that anything was wrong. I...*mère de Dieu!*[19] I walked across, and almost stumbled over the head. I cried out; I reached the door of the main salon, and I could hold my tray no longer. That is all, monsieur! I swear to you before all—"

He fidgeted, and backed towards the door. Abruptly, not at all muffled by the closed door, the orchestra downstairs commenced again on another ancient tune which had just come to Paris; a throaty voice warbled in English:

> "*Pack up all mah ca-re and woe,*
> *Here I go, singing low—*" [20]

---

19 "Mother of God!"

20 The song here is "Bye Bye Blackbird"; note the correct lyric is, "Pack up all my cares and woe..."

Bencolin turned his back and stood for a time looking out of the window. Then he motioned the steward to go. He returned to the table beside which Vautrelle sat bolt upright with an amused smile.

"Here," he said, sketching rapidly and tearing out a leaf of his notebook, "is a rough plan of the floor. I have consulted the clocks in the smoking room and on the staircase. They agree with my watch that it is now… What hour have you, M. Vautrelle?"

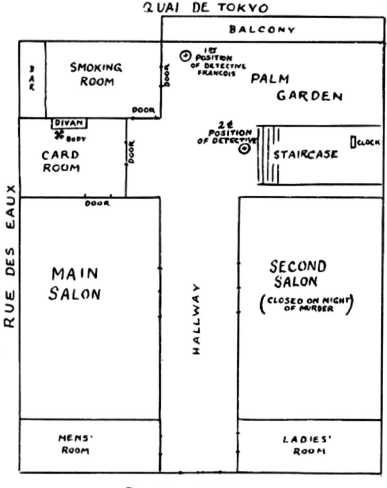

PLAN of 3rd FLOOR

Vautrelle turned over a thin silver watch in his palm. He consulted it with great deliberation, and announced: "Exactly twenty-five minutes past twelve."

"To the second," agreed Bencolin. He turned to me. "You have—?"

"Twenty-four and a half minutes, to the second."

Bencolin scowled at the plan.

"Very well. To proceed, M. Vautrelle, can you tell me your whereabouts at half past eleven, when M. de Saligny entered the card room?"

"Within a few seconds, monsieur, I can." Vautrelle hesitated; then, startlingly, he burst into a roar of laughter. "I was speaking to your detective on guard at the end of the hall, and I stayed with him for over five minutes, when I walked into the main salon under his observation and was introduced to you."

Bencolin nearly lost his temper. After an interval of silence, during which he stared at Vautrelle, he yanked the bell cord. François, the plain-clothes detective, came in with an air of importance, rubbing his large nose.

"Why, yes, monsieur, the gentleman there was with me," he replied. "I was sitting in a chair reading *La Sourire*[21], when he came up to me, and offered me a cigarette, and said, 'Can you by any chance tell me the right time? My watch seems to be slow.' 'I am positive,' said I, 'that my watch is right—eleven-thirty—However, we can consult the clock on the staircase.'"

François refreshed himself with a glance at all of us. He resumed: "We walked to the head of the stairs, and, as I knew, the clock confirmed my watch. He set his own, and we stood there talking—"

"So," interrupted Bencolin, "that you were directly before the hall door into the card room within a minute after M. de Saligny entered the room from the gaming salon?"

"Yes. We stayed there over five minutes, and then monsieur there walked down the hall and entered the main salon. I remained at the head of the stairs… Incidentally, I saw the boy go in with the tray."

"You are positive, then, that nobody left by the hall door."

"Positive, monsieur."

"That is all."

Bencolin sat at the table with his chin in his hands. After a time Vautrelle remarked: "Of course, you are at liberty to imagine that there has been tampering with clocks."

"There has been no tampering with the clocks, nor with my friend's watch, nor with mine. I have made certain of that."

"Then I suppose that I am at liberty to go? I dare say madame needs attention, and I shall be glad to take her home—"

"Where is madame now?"

"In the ladies' room, I believe, with an attendant."

---

21 *The Smile*. This was a weekly men's magazine that included satire, pinups, and some other risqué content.

"I presume," observed Bencolin, with a crooked smile, "that you will not take her to the home of M. de Saligny?"

Vautrelle appeared to take the question seriously. He put the glass in his eye and answered: "No, of course not; I shall take her to the apartments she occupied previously in the Avenue du Bois. In case you want my own address," he extracted a card case, "here is my card. I shall be pleased to present you with a duplicate at any time in the future you feel called on to be as insulting as you have tonight."

He preened himself as he rose, and his manner said, There's no reply to *that!* Standing in the doorway, he called for his wraps. Bencolin, thoughtfully turning the card over in his fingers, looked up with wrinkled forehead.

"Saligny was a great swordsman, too, I take it," he said softly. "Tell me, M. Vautrelle: did he speak English?"

"Raoul? That is the most amusing question yet. Raoul was essentially a sportsman, and nothing else. Yes, he was a swordsman, and a spectacular tennis player—he had a service that nearly stopped Lacoste—and the best of steeplechase riders. Of course," Vautrelle added smugly, "he *did* sustain a fall that nearly paralyzed his wrist and spine, and had to see a foreign specialist about it; but yes, he was a fine athlete. Books he never opened. Tiens,[22] Raoul speaking English! The only words he knew were 'five o'clock tea.'"

A servant had brought in Vautrelle's coat—long and dark, with a great sable collar, and hooked with a silver chain, it was like a piece of stage property. He pulled down on his head a soft black hat, and the monocle gleamed from its shadow. Then he produced a long ivory holder, into which he fitted a cigarette. Standing in the doorway, tall, theatrical, with the holder stuck at an angle in his mouth, he smiled.

"You will not forget my card, M. Bencolin?"

"Since you force me to it," said Bencolin, shrugging, "I must say that I would much prefer to see your identity card, monsieur."

Vautrelle took the holder out of his mouth.

"Which is your way of saying that I am not a Frenchman?"

"You are a Russian, I believe."

"That is quite correct. I came to Paris ten years ago. I have since taken out citizenship papers."

"Oh! And you were?"

"Major, Feydorf battalion, ninth Cossack cavalry in the army of his imperial majesty the Czar."

Mockingly Vautrelle clicked his heels together, bowed from the hips, and was gone.

---

22 An interjection. The literal translation makes no sense in this context, but the meaning is, "Fancy that."

HASHISH AND OPIUM

Bencolin looked across at me and raised his eyebrows.

"Alibi Baby!" I said. "I don't see how you're going to shake it, Bencolin."

"For the present, it is not necessary that I should. Question: where does this species of fire-eater get the income to go about with a millionaire like Saligny?"

"You suspect that he is our madman?"

"Frankly, I don't. But I very much suspect that he has been in the habit of supplying *madame la duchesse* with drugs."

"Drugs?"

"When she came over to us this evening," went on Bencolin, hunching up in the chair, "I remarked that she looked as though she were in a drug fog. I did not know it at the time, but that was the literal truth. Did you see me pick up the cigarette she left in the ashtray near us?" He fished it out of his vest pocket. "It is very thoroughly doctored; with what, I can't say until our chemists analyze it. It is either *marihuana,* the Indian hemp plant—the Mexicans use its dried leaves as a cigarette filler—or the Egyptian *hashish.* She is a confirmed user, or would have made her violently ill. You noticed the expression of her eyes and the wildness of her conversation: she is no novice in its use. It kills, you know, within five years. Somebody is most earnestly trying to do away with her."

He was silent, tapping the pencil against the table; and because I was busy forming a theory I made no comment. He viewed the case with sardonic eyes, sour and unsurprised.

"Well, I want to speak to one other person," he said at length. "Then we shall have to go on a little errand I have in mind. François!—Send the proprietor in."

The gentleman came in wild-eyed, his moustache drooping like a dog's ears. "Monsieur," he cried, before his stomach had preceded him through the door, "I beg of you, you must countermand that order that nobody is to leave! Several have tried to go, and your men downstairs stopped them. They demanded to know why. I said it was a suicide. There are reporters—"

"Sit down, please. You need not worry; a suicide will enhance the reputation of your establishment. Is the medical examiner here?"

"He has just arrived."

"Good. Now… Before coming here this evening, I consulted the files for some information about you—"

"It is a lie, of course."

"Of course," agreed Bencolin composedly. "Chiefly I want to know if there are any patrons here tonight who are unknown to you?"

"None. One must have a card to enter, and I investigate them all: unless, of course, it is the police. I should be grateful if my compliment to you were returned." He was drawn up in offended dignity, rather like a laundry bag attempting to resemble a gold shipment.

Bencolin's pencil clicked regularly against the table.

"Your name, I am informed, is Luigi Fenelli; not a common patronymic in France. Is it true that some years ago the good Signor Mussolini objected to your running an establishment for the purpose of escorting weary people through the Gate of the Hundred Sorrows?[23] Briefly, monsieur, were you ever arrested for selling opium?"

Fenelli lifted his arms to heaven and swore by the blood of the Madonna, the face of St. Luke, and the bleeding feet of the apostles that such a charge was infamous.

"You give good authority," said the detective thoughtfully. "Nevertheless, I am inclined to be curious. Does it require a card, for example, to be admitted to the fourth floor of this establishment? Or is the soothing poppy dispensed, like the cocktails, by the courtesy of the house?"

Fenelli's voice raised to a shout; Bencolin's hand silenced him.

"Please!" said the detective. "The information was mine before I came here. I give you twelve hours to throw into the Seine whatever shipment you have on hand. This leeway I grant you on one condition: that you answer me a question."

"Even the illustrious Garibaldi,"[24] said the other dramatically, "was sometimes forced to compromise. I deny your charge, but as a good citizen I cannot refuse to assist the police with any information at my command."

23 The title of Rudyard Kipling's 1884 short story (which features an opium den of that name), "The Gate of the Hundred Sorrows" connotes crossing into opium addiction.

24 A nineteenth-century Italian general sometimes called the George Washington of Italy. He was an important force in unifying Italy.

"How long has M. le Duc de Saligny been a user of opium? Don't deny it! He has been known to come here."

"Well, then, within the last month, monsieur. I was shocked and grieved that such a fine young man—"

"No doubt, no doubt. Did the woman who is now his wife contract any charming habits here also?"

"Each," replied the manager loftily, "was very much concerned about concealing it from the other."

"Ah, yes. Who instigated this?"

"You asked for one question, M. Bencolin, and I have answered you two. That is all I will tell you if they subject me to torture!"

"Such a contingency is hardly likely. At any rate, I advise you become busy turning your fourth floor in to a bar or a bagnio or something equally harmless... That is all, Fenelli."

When the manager had gone, I looked up from an ostentatious studying of the floor plan, and said: "May I ask how much of your information you're concealing, Bencolin? This was the first mention of that angle: Saligny as a drug taker."

"Ah, but that's another pair of sleeves completely. I was not sure it had any bearing on the case. Now I am morally certain it has."

"How did you learn about Fenelli's private parlor on the fourth floor?"

"Saligny told me about it."

"*Saligny* told you about it?—You don't mean Saligny, do you?"

"Yes." With an injured and virtuous air: "Jack, find me a person in this whole affair who is acting rationally, and I'll make you chief of detectives! Now in a moment we shall be invaded by the whole horde—I hear screamings and protestings out there—and I want you to accompany me on an expedition I have in mind. But first let us argue the case a bit. I am curious to get a layman's reaction."

He rose and began to pace about, hands clasped behind his back, head bent forward. Mephistopheles smoking a cigar, several of him reflected in the mirrors around the walls as he passed up and down; a queer and absurd little figure in motion, but Paris's avenger of broken laws.

"You want me to name the man I think is Laurent?" I inquired.

"Hm...that would be deducing from insufficient evidence, at this stage of the game. You have not seen everybody here, nor one fifth of the people who might be Laurent. I imagine that all our characters have not yet appeared... But proceed. You think you know the man who killed Saligny?"

"The chances are I'm wrong, naturally. But I'll have a guess."

"Well?"

"The American, Golton."

Bencolin stopped abruptly and removed the cigar. "Tiens, this is interesting! Why? Do you have reasons, or are you guessing detective-story fashion?"

"I give them to you for what they're worth. Reason number one: Golton's behavior. It doesn't ring true; it is overdone; it is a little *too* American. That byplay in the card room, for example. It doesn't seem possible that any man, no matter how drunk, should fail to notice such a shambles directly before him."

"An American should be the best judge of that, I confess. Still, the servant seems to have walked halfway across the room without... I wonder... No matter; go on."

"His behavior, then. He sobered up remarkably fast, too, after telling that bit about Vautrelle being cut out by Saligny in madame's affections. Reason number two: He says he met Saligny when he was returning from Austria. I may point out that it was from Vienna that Laurent escaped."

"If he is Laurent, he would be a lunatic indeed to tell you that voluntarily. Austria, moreover, has several cities besides Vienna."

"Reason number three: According to every bit of evidence we have, Saligny could not speak English. Yet according to what Golton told me, we have him speaking English quite well. More than that, we have Golton, who says *he* speaks no French, going about constantly with a man who speaks no English! How is that to be explained?"

"Touch!" said Bencolin, snapping his fingers. "You score there, certainly. Golton seems to have slipped up in that respect. However, it is hardly an indication that he is the murderer."

"You yourself have told me that Laurent is a genius as a linguist. Certainly, if Golton is Laurent, he is amazingly adept with the idiom."

"Now let us carry this on. What is Golton's procedure? How has he contrived to kill Saligny?"

"Let me ask a question. Do you subscribe to the theory that Laurent, in whatever guise, killed Saligny?"

"Most emphatically yes...Proceed."

"He might very well have been the man whom Saligny proposed to entertain."

"He might, of course. Which way did he go into the card room?"

"By either door. He might have been there early."

"Yes. Now let me ask you, " Bencolin suddenly leaned across the table and pointed his cigar—"*which way did he go out?*"

During the silence, while the detective stood motionless, I realized the significance of that remark, and I swore at myself for dropping into the trap. But there was a chasm at our feet much wider than this.

"The murderer," I said slowly, "did not go out by the hall door—"

"Because my detective was standing directly before it a few seconds after Saligny entered the room from the salon side, and he did not leave it until after the murder was committed!"

"And the murderer did not go out by the other door into the salon—"

"Because I myself was watching it from the time Saligny entered to the time we ourselves went in! In other words, we have a locked-room situation worse than any I have ever encountered, since I myself can swear nobody came out one door, and one of my most trusted men swears that nobody came out the other!"

Still he did not move, but he looked as haggard as a man crucified.

"I wondered," he said in a low voice, "how long it would take you to see that situation. It doesn't seem to have occurred to these people even now. I examined the window immediately, you remember: forty feet above the street, no other windows within yards of it, the walls smooth stone. No 'human fly' in existence could have entered or left that way...No place in the room for a cat to hide; I searched for that, too. No possibility of false walls, for you can stand in any door and see the entire partition of the next room. Tear open floor or ceiling, and you find only the floor or ceiling of another room; that way is blocked. Yet we know, in this of all cases, that the dead man did not kill himself... It is the master puzzle of them all."

He turned round, and slouched across to the window, bent shoulders silhouetted against a faint glow from the street. There was a clamor of excited voices in the hall. Hands thudded at the door.

I cried, "Bencolin!" and leaped up. "Bencolin, do you realize— the boy who brought the cocktails! The only one who could have been in the room—alone with Saligny—hired by Fenelli to kill the informer!—"

I was so excited that I did not at first understand his wry smile...

"Likewise impossible, Jack," he answered softly. "Did you not hear him, how he protested he could not help dropping the tray? How he kept his hands along the bottom of his jacket; did you not notice? The fingers of his right hand were amputated long ago."

V
THE TRUNK FROM VIENNA

It was two o'clock when Bencolin and I left the house. Sounds threw sharp, brittle echoes in the cul-de-sac of the rue des Eaux; there was a thin mist, and a wind blew from the river the raw spring moonlight. The tops of apartment houses were drawn against the sky as on glass, and a few windows were alight against their black walls. The rumble of a metro train swelled out of its tunnel and passed on the trestle over the rue Beethoven…distantly you could hear the motor of a cruising taxi.

Bencolin's car was parked not far from the Avenue de Tokyo. He had not spoken for some time, and when he climbed in at the wheel I asked:

"Incidentally, where are we going?"

"Put your hand down in the pocket of the door there," he said. "What do you find?"

"It appears to be the handle of a rather heavy pistol."

"Precisely; put it in your pocket…Do you still want to go?"

"Delighted, if I can contrive to hit anything."

"That was all I wanted to know; the thing isn't loaded. Put it back where you found it." When he had got the engine started, he tapped his breast pocket. "This one," he added absently, "*is* loaded."

We turned into the Avenue de Tokyo, a vast plain, with the parapet lamps of the river marching away in curved lines to the right. Beyond them the high fretwork of the tower was printed spider-black against the moonlit sky. The river breeze smelled of rain. Bencolin's big *Voisin* roared past the Pont d'Iena, and one had a sensation as of wings.

At length he volunteered, "We are going to the home of the Duc de Saligny."

"Oh…then why the gun parade? That isn't dangerous, is it?"

"I have reason to believe that there are things in his house which a certain somebody will be very anxious to remove—if that person doesn't get there before us. The address, by the way, is number 326 Avenue Henri Martin. Which means—" He looked sideways.

"That our friend Golton lives next door. But you have pretty well exploded my theory of the murder."

"Pardon, I didn't say you were wrong. I said we must examine the evidence from all sides."

He relapsed into silence. I sat back and closed my eyes. From Paris you can get no distant vibration, no far heavy rumble of traffic such as one hears in London. When the siren of the flying car screamed, horns picked it up and answered as from a gulf. There was the rattle of a late tram in the pale glitter of the Place de l'Alma. We swerved to the left up the hill, and presently the gray Arch dawned among hooting taxis. A few drops of rain blurred the windshield... and the head of Saligny floated against the dark...

The wan sheen of thoroughfares dwindled away; we were in a street of trees where the headlights showed flashes of budding green, but a black arch devoid of movement.

Before the gate of 326 we stopped. Twin globes of light burned yellow on either side, and shone on the dark windows of the concierge's lodge. Bencolin's fingers clicked a tattoo against the glass.

" '*Sieur et dame!*"[25] said a sleepy voice inside, "my felicitations—"

When the iron gate swung back, we were looking into the sleepy face of a woman in curl papers. The concierge was about to dart back in alarm when Bencolin intervened:

"Prefecture of police. I must ask you to admit us."

He received the key from the babbling woman, and ordered her back into the lodge. We could hear her wailing, "Murdered! Murdered! I knew it—wake up, Jules!—"

"Be silent!" Bencolin snarled over his shoulder.

Fitting the key into the lock of the house door, he whispered: "There are no servants here. If I find anybody prowling, it will be necessary to shoot."

We entered a dark hallway which smelled of flowers. I could hear Bencolin's steady breathing. He guided my arm across toward the vast curve of a stairway, down whose railing moonlight shone from a window. A rug slipped under my foot on the hardwood floor...We reached the top of the staircase; Bencolin turned, cloaked and weird against the moonlight. He nodded towards a door at the other end of the second floor. There was a thread of light under the sill.

When he put his right hand softly on the knob of that door, his

25 "Sir and Lady."

left was inside his breast pocket. He threw the door back.

A man sprang round to face us. He was standing in the middle of a room fully lighted, though the shutters were up. There was a great canopied bed nearby, and you noticed at its head a woman's blue fur-trimmed slippers... The man was small, with thick red hair, and when his mouth opened in surprise it disclosed many missing teeth. He had the cut of an overweight athlete. Bencolin closed the door.

"Hello, Girard," he said. "I had hardly expected to find *you* here. Turn out those lights, and lower your voice—"

"M. Bencolin!"

"Quite; what are you doing here?"

"I am *monseigneur's* most personal servant," said the man called Girard. He wagged his head, and grinned proudly. "I have been with him for over a month. I was preparing the bridal—" he leered and rubbed his hands.

Bencolin whistled. He gestured towards Girard. "Formerly," he explained, "the hero of Auteuil; a jockey I have put my money on in preference to the horse... *Dame de Treflu*, three to one, Girard up..."

"But overweight, monsieur. I have been out of the game for some time. See..." He lifted a tawdry affair of red roses, shaped like a horse-shoe, and inscribed in white roses with the legend, "*Bonne chance*"...

"My tribute; it brings good luck."

Bencolin stared at him speculatively.

"You're up late, Girard."

"Yes, but—monsieur, why are *you* here?"

"I want you to turn out those lights; then tell me about your new position."

The room went dark. The puzzled, suspicious Girard hung the wreath around his neck and stood gesturing in a vague glow from over the transom.

"Why—monsieur, I do not understand this. But whatever M. Bencolin says, I will do without question. I used to know M. de Saligny in the old days; once I rode his filly *Drapeau Bleu*. But then, you know how it is, I could not make the weight; rubber suits, blankets, diet, roadwork, still I could not make forty-six; you know—no, no!... I went to Marseilles. At last, in that despair, you know, I returned. I sought out M. de Saligny, but of course he did not remember me. 'A bit of work round the stables, monsieur,' I pleaded. 'Ah, Girard,' he said, 'you speak like a man of education, though not of intelligence. Can you use a typewriter? And give my stable a workout if I am not able to do so?' 'But certainly, *monseigneur*,' I say. 'I have hurt myself,' he explained, and I went into a frenzy of grief—*monseigneur*, the great horseman! 'I cannot use my hand well; therefore I shall dictate my correspondence—'

Et puis voilà![26]

He drew a long breath. "And this lady that he has married, I would die for her! She is so lovely; if anyone sought to—"

The sentimental soul paused. Bencolin inquired:

"*Monseigneur* had much correspondence?"

"Oh, yes; he is very prominent. And he receives many things—that trunk—you can see how everyone likes him—"

"What trunk?"

"Why, the trunk that arrived two days ago. It was comical, you know. He had been in Vienna, and when he sent on his trunks one was misdirected. It wandered about from one address to another, and was returned to his hotel in Vienna. It had no name on it, but they recognized it, like that!" There came a snapping of Girard's fingers. "And they sent it on to him—"

"Where is it now?"

"Why, in his study—"

Bencolin said very slowly, "Is—it—possible..." There was a silence, among the night creakings of the house. The horror of an unknown thing jumped back to a vital force when we heard the tone of his next words.

"Girard, don't ask any questions. Do exactly as I tell you. Go to your room now, and whatever happens don't stir out of it! There is, or will be, somebody in this house—"

"Who, monsieur?"

"A killer," said the detective. He opened the door softly. Against the faint moonlight I could see that he had a pistol in his hand.

---

26 "And there it is!"

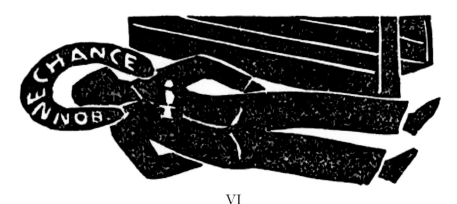

VI

WHITE ROSES FOR MURDER

I felt a sickly empty sensation around my stomach when we went up another flight of stairs toward Saligny's study, whose location Bencolin seemed to know very well.

"Stand in the door," he whispered; "I want to see that the shutters are up."... There was a space when I stood with my back to the hallway and heard Bencolin lightly trying the windows. The study smelt stuffy, and there was another queer odor... He returned presently, took off his cloak, and when he closed the door behind him he laid the cloak along the bottom of the door.

"Now turn on that lamp at your elbow. Keep your hand on the button, and if you hear any movement anywhere, shut it off."

It was a dull lamp, with a globed shade set in green glass, and its light made crooked shadows in a small room hung with pictures. Beside the door was a large trunk, on which I sat down to watch the detective.

"Hm," he muttered, talking fast and in a low voice: "Dozens of sport pictures—himself with silver cups—Ascot, Longchamps, Wimbledon amateur fencing team—fine stag's head, that—yes, and big game—gun case—Manchurian leopards—that racquet needs restringing—"

He was walking about, glancing at this and that, picking up articles and laying them down; powerful, imbued with terrific wiry energy. The table in the middle of the room claimed his attention.

"Typewriter... What's this? Books. Open here; drawers are filled with them. The works of Edgar Allan Poe. Barbey D'Aurevilly, the *Di-*

aboliques.[27] Odd fare for a sporting man... Baudelaire[28], Hoffmann[29]; *La Vie de Gilles de Rais*[30]—"

He closed one book with a snap. "That settles it."

The idea I had in mind seemed too outlandish and appalling; but I suddenly got up. We stood face to face, and by the expression of his eyes I could see we both knew...

"The man," I said slowly, "who for the past two months has been posing as the Duc de Saligny is in reality—"

"Laurent himself," supplied Bencolin. "Laurent, a master of irony! Laurent, with an eye to what he thinks is poetic justice. Over a year ago the engagement of the Duc de Saligny to Madame Louise was announced in every newspaper of Europe. There were a hundred pictures of Saligny to draw from. He had the plastic surgeon make him into such a perfect image of Saligny that Madame Louise herself does not even now know the difference. I have never encountered such an artistic cutthroat!—he planned and succeeded in marrying her a second time, and tonight, in that room downstairs, he would have avenged himself, if somebody had not discovered it—"

In one blinding glare every piece of contradiction showed up as one perfect whole. Bencolin, leaning across the desk, checked off the points on his fingers:

"First, we have Saligny taking a trip to Vienna two months or so ago. When he leaves, he is the master sportsman: rider, swordsman, hunter, tennis player, but a not over-bright individual who rarely reads a printed line and speaks no language but his own. When he returns, he has unaccountably acquired an excellent knowledge of English, such that one of his closest companions is an American who speaks no French. His whole character changes. He does not ride, play tennis, or indulge in any sports whatever—even sports where his injury would not prevent him. He refuses: because he no longer knows how—he is another man. Instead, he takes to opium smoking! He

---

27 *The She-Devils* (1875), considered D'Aurevilly's masterpiece, is a short-story collection in which each of six stories recounts a violent or vengeful crime committed by a woman.

28 Baudelaire was a French symbolist poet whose poems were of a decadent character, in the tradition of Romanticism. He admired and translated Poe. His own best-known work was *Les Fleurs du mal* (*The Flowers of Evil*), a collection of Romantic poems concerned with sex and death.

29 E.T.A. Hoffman was a German Romanticist who wrote Gothic horror novels.

30 Gilles de Rais was a fifteenth-century baron and Marshal of France who was tried for Satanism, child abduction, and murder. He was found guilty and executed in 1440.

hires a jockey—whom he does not recognize, although that jockey formerly rode his best horse—to inspect his stables for him. He hires this man to take dictation, because otherwise his handwriting would be recognized as not that of the man he is impersonating. He cultivates a new circle of friends (witness Golton), and goes in for the life of the boulevards. Yet here, as the marked books of this man who 'never reads,' we have volumes in three languages and of a sort which shows an entire change of mind."

The detective shrugged. "Yes, that is the way I read it. He intended, of course, to come to Paris and do away with Saligny here; but by a circumstance fortunate for him Saligny *did* go to Vienna, where somehow Laurent got into his hotel—and I very much suspect that the trunk on which you are sitting contains the body of the real Saligny."

I was no longer sitting on it. I had backed away, and in the weird green light the thing explained possibly that odor...

"Bencolin," I said, and with a calm not very convincing, "the trunk is unlocked."

"Chance tripped him up... Yes, you see what he did?" the detective was rambling on. "He sent the trunk to a false address; to be rid of it, he thought, and make another 'trunk murder' to baffle the police. But the trunk came back, and the manager of the hotel recognizing it, shipped it on to—"

"The trunk is unlocked," I repeated monotonously. And then I reached down and threw open the lid.

Bencolin came over swiftly. It was nearly full of sawdust, sawdust tossed about as though something very heavy had been removed from its packings. There were brown stains streaked through the mass.

"Laurent removed the body before he was married!" I said. "But... what are you doing?"

The detective's head was bent down into the trunk.

"No, Jack. This sawdust on top is damp and fresh; it came from the bottom of the trunk. The body was disturbed more recently than that. Probably—tonight."

For a moment he let the sawdust run through his fingers. "Don't you see? We are dealing with a man much more dangerous than Laurent himself, whom this man killed. We have found out about Laurent, but we are still at the beginning of the riddle. It is even less explicable now than it was before, for we have no madman on which to saddle a motiveless crime."

"Who is the man, then? You seem to—"

"*Turn off that light!*"

I reached over, fumbling, and switched it off. For a time there was absolute silence; then a faint creak as Bencolin eased open the door.

Against the lesser darkness I could see his dim shape, motionless in the aperture. From the chasm below I thought I could hear a faint rasping noise, as of a shovel scraped over stone...

Bencolin's figure moved forward, soundlessly. I edged out beside him, planting my steps to avoid creaky boards. Again he stopped; somewhere, a person was treading on stairs. There was the pale oblong of the window at the stairhead, and dull moonlight on the pattern of a carpet. So slowly we edged toward those stairs that the window grew on one's vision, like a scene through shortening opera glasses. He bent down when we reached the window, bent down and peered around the newel post, and I through the balustrades. Darkness... But the footsteps were coming up the second flight of stairs. They hesitated on the second floor, and crept round to the third. Suddenly switched into our faces was the glare of a flashlight.

"Haut les mains!"—[31]

Bencolin fired two shots, very deliberately, into the beam of light. Their flat bang was like the burst of an explosion. The light vanished, and the footsteps thudded in leaps down the other flight of stairs. I stumbled, brought my hand in numbing contact with the stair wall, and blundered down into the dark. Down to the first floor... There was a crash as a door was flung open, and other running footsteps joined the first. We heard a blubbering cry.

Somehow I found myself, trembling, unable to speak, leaning on a table in the lower hall. When the lights came on I blinked; the lights swam, and came into slow focus. Bencolin stood near the switch, the fingers of his hand crooked before his face, breathing heavily... In the center of the Aubusson[32] carpet, Girard lay on his back with a knife driven through his side. His oyster eyeballs lolled, and he gurgled through brimming lips when he tried to move his head. His arms were thrown wide, fingers picking at the carpet, and one leg was drawn up as though in an attempt to rise. Around his neck was still a crumpled horseshoe of red roses, and framed his head with the white inscription, "Good luck..."

---

31 "Put up your hands!"

32 A town in central France famous for its carpets and tapestries. The patterns for Aubusson carpets are hand carved. Then, when the woolen carpets are hand-knotted, the visual patterns actually stand off their faces.

VII
"ALL THROUGH THE NIGHT—"

At four o'clock A. M. the events of this amazing night were over, at least so far as the butcheries were concerned. But for Bencolin the work was just beginning. I never saw him so upset as at this latest development, the murder of Girard by the prowler: his hand shook when he telephoned the prefecture; he cursed himself in a low bitter monotone, like a man praying; and he cursed Girard for not following his advice. As nearly as it could be reconstructed, Girard had retired to his room on the ground floor. When he heard the shots he came from the back of the house, saw the intruder running down the stairs, and interfered at the cost of his life. Bencolin's bullets had apparently taken no effect. Both were buried in the floor, one having shattered the flashlight and the other nicking the newel post about three feet from the floor. From the remnants of the flashlight, a long Tungsten with a head much broader than the barrel, it was clear that the bullet had pierced the reflector without even grazing the hand of the man who had held it... In the cellar we found the reason for the sound we had heard. Fresh mortar between the bricks behind a pile of debris, and a trowel concealed under some straw, led to the discovery of a hollow. Inside a body was doubled up, horribly decomposed but recognizable as that of Saligny; Laurent, it seemed, was not the only person in the case who had read well in the works of Poe. The knife with which Girard had been stabbed had first been used to pry out the loose bricks; bits of dust and mortar still clung to the underside of the haft. After the murder, the assassin had gone out the cellar door by which he had entered... To this day I can see Bencolin, holding up a lantern as he looked into the ghastly hollow behind the bricks. The chill damp of the cellar, the wind banging the open door, the rat that scurried past my foot: they are details indelible.

When we left the house at four o'clock in possession of the police, Bencolin gave his last instructions: "Above all, give nothing out to the press. I do not think you will find fingerprints, for the handle of the knife is dusty and has prints of what seem to be gloves—but make the test. I will 'phone in an hour." And then he said to me:

"We will go to my rooms and get coffee. Do you mind driving? I want to study this…Avenue George V; if you're not sure of the way, get back to the Champs Elysées and then you can't miss it."

On the return drive he sat strained forward, head between his hands, staring at nothingness.

"We know hardly more than before—" I murmured. He turned savagely.

"Yes? You say that to *me?* I tell you I know the whole devilish plan. I know the height of the murderer, and that he wore evening clothes; I know when he came and why he came; I know the reason he tried to come upstairs, and what his connection was with Saligny; in short, I can draw you a picture of Girard's assassin. But—well, that is to be seen. Our organization is a devil-fish[33], which can extend a thousand arms—"

"And, according to the natural histories, it can throw out from itself a quantity of dense black liquid to obscure the view—"

"*Peste*[34], you needn't snap! And your hands are trembling on that wheel; well, it's an ordeal to turn anyone's stomach. We shall both need brandy… Turn to the right here."

Between weariness and the horror of recollection, we exchanged no more words. Bencolin's rooms were in an apartment building not far from the American church. He kept such irregular hours that he had his own key, and we did not rouse the concierge at the front door. The automatic elevator made a slow ascent to the sixth floor.

"My servant," Bencolin explained, "never knows when I shall be here; there is always coffee on the stove, and a fire in the study."

It was a formal apartment, stiff and luxurious in a stereotyped fashion, with the customary mirrors and Louis Quinze furniture—all except the study… A tiny balcony, books to the ceiling, and a fire. Certainly the most untidy room I have ever seen. There were great padded chairs with inclined backs before the fireplace. A letter had been thrown down carelessly on the hearth, beside a tabouret with brandies and cigars; and the first sentence of the letter caught my eye, "*De la part de sa majesté, le roi d'Angleterre—*"[35]

"Clean off that chair and sit down," said Bencolin. He began to

33 Bencolin here refers to an octopus, not to a devil ray.

34 Literally "plague"; an interjection connoting irritation.

35 "From His Majesty, the King of England—"

sweep a pile of debris from the neighborhood of the hearth; a flutter of red fell from it, and I said:

"My Lord, man, be careful! That's the ribbon of the Legion of Honor."

"I know it," he returned irritably. "Make yourself comfortable…"

Presently I fell into a doze, and vaguely heard him fuming at something in the kitchen. The prospect of the evening danced in my brain; became linked with a crazy jingle, "Heads and knives, swords and wives, how many are going to St. —"[36] and there swam across it the vision of Vautrelle polishing his monocle, of the flashlight in our faces… I stirred, and opened my eyes. Bencolin was sitting across the hearth in one of the great chairs, with the firelight on his sardonic face. He pointed to a cup of coffee at my elbow.

"In a moment," he said, "you are going to hear the prefecture in action. This," he tapped a telephone beside him, "is my private wire. There is another 'phone on that table at your left—push the books away—there. Listen to them, now."

Both of us picked up the 'phones. "Hello!" he said, "*bureau centrale.* Bencolin speaking."

There was a prolonged clicking. "*Bureau centrale,*" a voice answered.

"Dulure's laboratory, please… I want the reports on the Saligny case. Have they finished?"

"Two-eleven speaking," said another voice. "Report as follows: There are no clear fingerprints, due to the brass nail heads on the handle of the sword; an identification is impossible. There are several prints on the glass of the window, but they do not correspond to any in our files. The dust of the carpet and that of the cover on the divan has been swept up; the glass here sifts out nothing but cigarette ashes, mud traces, and a few grains of candy."

"Have these been analyzed?"

"Not yet. There will be a report by morning as to whether the ashes are of the same quality as those of the cigarette submitted. This cigarette contains hashish."

"Very good. Shift me to the general office; one-thirteen…One-thirteen speaking? You followed the American, Golton, from Passy?"

"Yes. He took a taxi to Harry's New York Bar, Boulevard des Italiens. He remained there half an hour; on emerging, spoke to two women but went with none; walked to the opera and there took another taxi. He returned to his home, 324 Avenue Henri Martin, arriving there at one forty-five."

---

36 Jack has remade a line from an English nursery rhyme in the form of a riddle, "As I was going to St. Ives." There were no swords or (dismembered) heads accompanying the wives in the nursery rhyme, only sacks and cats.

"You looked him up in the files?"

"Resident of Paris for two years, no occupation, reputable account at Lloyd's Bank. I have a list of his associates."

"It will keep. I will speak to one-eleven now... One-eleven?"

"Edouard Vautrelle," said still another voice, "left the house in Passy at twenty minutes to one. In his own car he escorted Madame de Saligny to her home, 144 Avenue du Bois. He left there in five minutes, returned to his car, and drove downtown to Maxim's, rue Royale. I lost him, monsieur; he apparently left through a door into a neighboring shop. I questioned the proprietor, but he will say nothing. Very sorry."

"No matter... His antecedents?"

"Came to Paris in 1917, during the Russian revolution. Enlisted for military service; army of occupation until 1922. Gives his occupation as that of playwright—"

"Questions to the theaters?"

"The managers of all theaters in Paris are being sent a blank form asking if any plays by a person of that name have been submitted."

"Good. Now forty-six, please... Luigi Fenelli? What of him?"

"To the best of my knowledge, he has not left his establishment tonight. Seventy-one is still at the corner; no 'phone message yet. Fenelli came to Paris a year ago, and sent circulars of his new house to prominent people. Twice arrested in Italy, but never imprisoned. Charges: peddling opium in Naples; aggravated assault and battery."

"That is all... Head central! 'Phone me if any report comes from the laboratory. Instruct them to examine Saligny's fingernails. I want fingerprint samples from all these people. Post a man at the concierge's box in the Fenelli house."

"Any further instructions?"

"None until tomorrow. Make me an appointment with the *juge d'instruction.*"

Slowly Bencolin replaced the 'phone.

"You see," he remarked, "the octopus reaching. It is a gigantic system. I can, at this hour, ascertain the whereabouts of any man in Paris. And you also note how it fails!" He slapped the chair arm; his eyes were bright, and he knocked over a glass with a nervous arm when he reached for a cigar. "They do not sleep, these men. I have my hands on all Paris as on a map; a finger moves across streets, up squares, and pauses at a house—a few words into this 'phone, and the police trap snaps like a deadfall. But the brain of one man opposing us renders all this organization useless. You can fight him only with the brain." He brooded, head in his hands. Then he growled:

"Drink your coffee. It's getting cold."

This was another person from Bencolin the suave and mocking, the Voltaire of detectives and the Petronius[37] of the boulevards: the man himself, in carpet slippers. I sipped the coffee, but it gave only a whirling sensation to my drowsiness. He sat there in the chair, motionless, with the smoke thickening about him and the ash sliding down his shirt front. As though slow curtains were drawn, it faded—the gaunt face with its pointed beard, staring blindly into the red firelight. Somewhere a clock chimed. The glow of the fire played on the ceiling, made deep shadows round his chair, glimmered on the nickeled telephone...

When I roused out of confused dreams, dawn was creeping up the opposite wall. The whole room had turned to gray and shadows, and it was deadly cold; colored like ashes, the whole littered, and shivered with the rattling of the window. The fire was out. Dimly I could see Bencolin's figure detach itself from the gloom of the tall chair across the hearth. He had not altered his position, though the hearth was strewn with cigar stumps and an empty bottle of brandy hung from his hand. He still sat, chin in his fist, staring into the empty fireplace.

To those who may care to inscribe on the opposite page their solution of the mystery as thus far presented, we offer for what it may be worth one further clue: When the narrator happens to meet Mr. Sid Golton in a café the afternoon immediately following the events just described, the Nebraskan winces at his handshake and complains of a sore hand.

---

37 Petronius was a courtier and author during the reign of Nero to whom *The Satyricon* is attributed, which mocked first-century Rome. Jack is attributing to Bencolin both rationality (Voltaire) and acerbic humor (Petronius).

Readers of the Chapbook will remember how the Duc de Salig-
ny was found decapitated in a carefully watched room, how M.
Henri Bencolin discovered that the murdered man was really
the much-feared Laurent, and how Bencolin was interrupted in
his investigations by a second murder. Those who accepted the
editors' challenge to solve the mystery for themselves may now
compare their results with the actual solution attained by M.
Bencolin.

VIII
(Continued)
WHEREIN THE DOUBLE DOORS ARE OPENED

Others have written of the finale to this case; my own account can
have no virtue except that of an eyewitness. There were wild accounts
in most of the papers, and what irritated us all most was *Le Figaro's*
smug assertion that "it is amazing that the only person to see the truth
was M. Bencolin, since all the details were before the eyes of the witnesses from the first." Whatever the general public may think of that,
it will probably agree with me that the reason why Bencolin staged his
denouement in the fashion he employed was rather for a psychological
vengeance on his adversary than any real desire to extract a confession.
You shall judge.

Around eight in the morning, I went to my rooms in the Square
Rapp for a bath and a change of clothes. My charitable landlady drew
her own conclusions, and solicitously inquired after the health of "my
little girl." Then she found a couple of blood spots when I sent my
dinner clothes out to be pressed, and became sympathetic to such an
extent that I hesitated to tell her they had been caused by a severed
head. Madame Hirondelle is prone to hysterics.

Unquestionably, I thought when I was drinking chocolate by my
own fire, it had been a Night. In retrospect, which is the best way to
enjoy excitement anyhow, I contemplated it with entire satisfaction. I
had had my murder. "We will forget the matter until this evening. I am
going to have you all as my guests at the central office," Bencolin had
said. "In the meantime, I suggest you call up some girl and go to an
afternoon dance as an antidote against the future."

When I did use the telephone to suggest this—it is a hall phone,
and Madame Hirondelle's door is always open—my astonished landlady inquired after this and that, and fell to dietary suggestions of more
theoretical than real usefulness.

Paris was preening its finery that day; the gigolos were all a-cackle
on the Champs Elysées, there was a warm wine-like air made luminous
around the green of the Tuileries, whose aisles were in bloom with

the early spring crop of artists painting the vista toward the Arc de Triomphe. It was all highlights and watercolor, with the gray face of the Madeleine peering down her street at the obelisk from the Nile. I very nearly forgot the black business of last night in mingling with the whirligig life in the company of my friend (she was a *demi*[38], which is the word customarily used with *tasse*), until we entered one of those dancing places where the extra charge is put on the champagne instead of the cover, and the cover is therefore permitted to be dirty. There the inspired orchestra played "Hallelujah," and followed it up with "Bye, Bye, Blackbird"...then, over in a corner, I saw Mr. Sid Golton. He had just neared that mild state of happiness wherein flipping water in a spoon seems highly humorous, and this he was doing to calculate his range when he should begin in earnest. I saw him look at me, seem puzzled, and then he waved in recognition. His shiny cheeks were freshly shaven and blooming as a baby's; his thin hair was plastered down, and the blue eyes far less bloodshot. A smile dawned. He waddled over, after an appraising glance at the lady beside me.

It was the stage for an experiment. I rose, and thrust out my hand deliberately. He responded.

Now I have normally anything but a strong grip, yet under the pressure when he shook hands Mr. Golton perceptibly winced.

"Geez, go easy!" he protested. "Got a sore hand; fell on it last night—it's no fun."

"Nor is the sensation pleasant," said I, "when a bullet hits a flashlight."

"You're drunk," observed Mr. Golton casually. "Wouldn't have thought it, but you are. Well, order 'em up. Hey, garsong, oon Marteeni, see?"

The afternoon passed somehow. I was a bit preoccupied, and Golton took care of the amusement of my companion, reciting droll stories of his adventures as ranger in Yellowstone until somebody had discovered on his property an oil gusher spouting—he illustrated the spouting of the gusher with appropriate pantomime—and delivered to him what he described as bokoo dough. Various parlor tricks served to keep the company at the nearby tables interested in his life.

We separated at six-thirty, and Marguérite, being philosophical, was content to regard one's mood and one's friends as just another of those things. Golton said that he had got a message from Bencolin to "be on hand, pronto, at nine o'clock, at the police station." Undoubtedly there hung over us the shadow of that night...

---

38 A demimondaine, or woman of questionable social standing, possibly of questionable morality.

When I returned to my rooms, I found Madame Hirondelle in possession of the afternoon paper; she had even violated an ancient French custom and bought two. All such ladies being embryo tabloid sheets, there is no reason for the tabloid in French life. She brought me in a special tray of tea and croissants in order to dilate on broken romances, which particularly reminded her of the case of her cousin by marriage, who had blue eyes and lived in Bordeaux, and was (figure to yourself, monsieur!) only the bride of a night when, etc..... I pondered the etiquette of wearing evening clothes to Bencolin's party, which seemed rather like debating the correctness of a morning coat to attend a guillotining. Then, upstairs, somebody's insufferable gramophone started to scratch through "Hallelujah"...

Everything made a person's thoughts all out of proportion. I gagged at the thought of food, but something was necessary to take one's mind off a killer. A taxi took me to the grand boulevards, already flowering with pink lights, and I dropped into a cinema. The player piano rang with a flat stereotyped sound, like a newspaper editorial, and the peanut shells... Then the picture leaped out at me, and I was struck with the extraordinary resemblance of the star to Bencolin. Except for the latter's beard, the likeness was perfect. Nor could I imagine Bencolin plunged in the amorous intrigue whose chief purpose seemed to lead the hero as many times as possible into the wrong bedroom. But there was no getting away from that likeness. The piece was called *La Blonde ou la Brune?* and featured Mr. Adolphe Menjou. Presently, in one of the feminine leads, who bore the flamboyant name of Miss Arlette Marchal, I began to see a resemblance to Madame Louise de Saligny. This is a state called nerves, and is not at all pleasant.

It was eight-thirty when I arrived at the vast Palais de Justice. You cannot imagine the size of this Palace, which resembles a pictureless Louvre; so I naturally wandered into the department whose purpose, I learned, was inquiring into the whereabouts of lost dogs. This was laudable but uninteresting. I penetrated three or four corridors before I was found at last by a clever detective and escorted through a maze of rooms to the office of Bencolin.

It was a small room paneled in dark wood and lighted by green-shaded lamps. Bencolin stood behind the desk, in no wise like the man I had seen the night before. His suavity was a mask, his voice low and clear, his beard freshly barbered. In a chair beside his desk sat a great lump of a man, like a bald Buddha, with flabby hands folded in his lap; his eyes blinked slowly, automaton fashion, and his jaw was buried in his collar.

"M. le Comte de Villon, the *juge d'instruction*," Bencolin introduced.

The judge looked me over craftily, so that I had an uncomfortable idea he would ask for my fingerprints. He grunted, and closed his eyes.

Bencolin indicated a pair of closed folding doors behind him.

"The room of my entertainment," he said.

That was all, except for a faint glittery smile. I sat down, and for many minutes there was no sound except a deep humming from somewhere in the building. A watch on the table ticked audibly.

"M. Luigi Fenelli," a voice suddenly announced. I jumped around, and saw Fenelli being escorted in. He was very haughty; he fingered his curled moustache, and his hair positively bubbled with oil, so that some of the oil seemed to be spread over his fat face. Tiny eyes darted round.

"Me, I am here," he proclaimed, and thrust his hand under the breast of his coat. Cloak and hat he offered to the escorting detective.

"Sit down, please," requested Bencolin.

Again that silence, and the ticking of the watch.

Presently Golton came in like a landslide, exuding geniality. But the atmosphere of the room awed him before long. He demanded to know "why they didn't have magazines here, like any good dentist's office," but his facetiousness trickled away; he sat down and shifted his feet nervously. François, the detective who had been on duty in the hall the night before, entered and stood in one corner.

Bencolin began to click a pencil against the table, just as he had the night before when he was questioning....

"Madame Louise de Saligny and M. Edouard Vautrelle."

The circle was complete. Madame wore a black wrap with a collar of ermine. From this collar she looked out lazily, and her face was like a lovely photograph slightly out of focus. But her black hair was bound back to a knot tonight, which seemed to make the countenance thinner, and her mouth slashed with lipstick. Only the dark speculative eyes were the same. She greeted Bencolin without the slightest semblance of interest... Vautrelle, ostentatiously cool, ran the tip of his finger along the thin line of his moustache. His colorless eyebrows were raised.

"We are all present," Bencolin said... "M. Vautrelle, will you be so good as to tell me the time?"

"Your questions seldom vary, do they, monsieur?" asked the other. "Again subject to confirmation, it is five minutes past nine."

Bencolin contemplated the watch on his desk.

"Yes. But for the purpose of this meeting," he remarked softly, "I prefer that the hour be *fifteen minutes to eleven*. François, will you be so good as to open those double doors?"

The distant humming died away. The demonstration had begun.

IX
THE LAST ACT

Bencolin asked us all to enter the room disclosed when the double doors were opened. It was very large, the walls and floor covered with white tile, so that it resembled an operating room in a hospital. Four lamps with green shades hung from the ceiling, immediately above six chairs ranged in two lines in such a way that the chairs of the second row were in the open spaces between those of the first, all of them three feet apart. The first row was about fifteen feet from the opposite end of the room. There were no windows.

"We have often been asked," Bencolin continued, "why the prefecture has no psychological laboratory such as that suggested many years ago by Professor Münsterberg[39] of Harvard. I wish to show you now that we have our own conception of a psychological laboratory. It is eminently a practical one, and, so far as I know, there is no duplicate of it in the world. I am going to ask you to assist me in a parlor game which has often caused much amusement.

"I am going to ask you all," he continued after a silence, "to be secured firmly in these chairs, and also gagged, for all the world as though you had been kidnapped by a cinema-inspired villain. I promise that the fastenings will not chafe you, and that you will suffer no annoyance from the gag. I should prefer that everyone accede in this, including you," he turned to me, "François, and Madame de Saligny—although madame will be excepted, if she prefers."

I looked round at the group. Vautrelle laughed.

"It is obvious," he remarked, "that children's games are not confined to the nursery. Well, I have no objection, if you don't mean to rob us while we are helpless. Hein, Louise? I—"

"This is an outrage!" bellowed Fenelli. His coat rose on his back like feathers. "To such proceedings—"

"You are, of course, at liberty to refuse," said Bencolin carelessly.

Fenelli worked his mouth a moment, and added, "But if the others agree—" Bowing, Bencolin turned to Golton and rapidly translated his words into English.

"Sure, it's all right with me. But no funny business, mind!" Golton amended. He stared at the detective, and whispered to me, "Wise guy, that one!"

Madame de Saligny showed no more agreement or disagreement than before. She simply shrugged. "I do not care."

Manacles, felt-lined, were on the arms and legs of the chairs. Ben-

---

39 A German-American forensic psychologist.

colin left us all to the selection of our chairs, standing before the group like a professor before his class. There was hesitation; we all glanced at each other, and it was madame who first sat down in the end chair of the first row to our left. Vautrelle took the one beside her, then Fenelli. Golton took the end chair to the right in the second row; then François, finally myself. Two attendants appeared out of a door I had not previously seen, and went about fastening the manacles on our wrists and legs with snap locks. They produced half a dozen gags, like moustache smoothers, with cotton for the covering of the mouth.

"Before these are fastened," said Bencolin, "I should like to ask one question... M. Fenelli, how should you describe the late Saligny?"

I could see Fenelli's profile partly turned in astonishment.

"Why—why, monsieur—he was tall, and good-looking, and blond; he was—" The manager hesitated, and chewed at his moustache. "I don't know that I can make it clearer—he was—"

"Can *you* make it any clearer; describe Saligny?" Golton was asked next.

"Why—sure—big fellow, always wore mighty fine clothes."

"M. Vautrelle?"

"Precisely six feet tall," responded Vautrelle amusedly, "weight, 70 kilos; eyes, brown; nose, convex; teeth, perfect; mole on right eyebrow...is this detailed enough for you?"

"You may apply the gags, messieurs."

The gags did not make one uncomfortable, but the helpless feeling these and the manacles engendered caused uneasiness. It was final; no matter what happened, you stayed; a murderer could... Suddenly the lights went out, all except a drop lamp over Bencolin's head where he stood immediately at our left, causing us all to turn our eyes. He stood weird and inscrutable in that spot of light, which showed the hollows in his face. The face became Satanic; he smiled, and for some reason I felt a shiver of nervousness. Darkness, tied and gagged in one's chair. There was not a sound in that vast building until Bencolin spoke.

"The last light, please..."

We were in total darkness now. My heart was beating heavily... Fully ten minutes passed...

"The first thing which enters one's mind," Bencolin continued in a low monotone which drifted from another corner as though he were no longer there, "is the idea of a church..."

Was somebody talking? A mass of people? I heard a deep but very faint humming of voices, broken with tinny laughter; the sounds of people shuffling. An auto horn honked; two of them. Distinctly I could smell the scent of banked flowers, hear a rustling. The blackness whirled before one's eyes, resolved into shapes and twistings; those tiny voices made a laughing, rising blur. Suddenly, there crashed through the room the sweep of an organ swelling the "Wedding March" from *Lohengrin*...

The organ died away. There was a faint, rasping sob. The darkness assumed gigantic and horrible shapes, wove and broke like foam on water. After a silence Bencolin's voice drifted dully:

"Certain people have discovered that this man who stands as bridegroom at the altar is not the true Saligny. No, the true Saligny—"

That sound, far away in the dark; the bumping of a trunk being hauled upstairs. *Thump...thump...*the wheeze of panting breath.

"It was six months ago, in another city, that something came to that trunk—"

At first it seemed an illusion, and yet the darkness changed color, shifted with a weird green light as against gauze; the sound of lapping water...violins in the waltz of *The Blue Danube*... A shadow shot across this light before our eyes, the monstrous shadow of a man upreared in profile. Something sprang at it, and there lashed down a *knife;* a thud from sudden darkness again, and a faint groan. Then I no longer heard lapping water but a slow drip, as of thick fluid. The violins pulsed, were joined by other instruments...

"The people have discovered all this before the marriage. But the marriage takes place... Night comes to Paris—"

Now that distant muted music blew faster, a hysterical note that swung to "Hallelujah." The song beat against one's ears in tinny resonance. Over it drifted a hum of conversation, the high laughter, the shrill chant of a croupier, the clicking dance of the ball in the wheel. The air was overpoweringly hot, and dense with a smell of powder; and the orchestra beat shook against it like a madman on a cage.

"It is not loud," said Bencolin's far voice, "because you are in the card room. The clock—"

Yes, the clock was striking. It tinkled with eerie chimes; then it sounded clear notes. One. Two. Three. Four. Five. Six. Seven. Eight. Nine. Ten. Eleven, with maddening deliberation.

"Already," Bencolin's voice was becoming more swift, "the assassin is preparing. The sword has been taken down from the wall, and hidden beneath a row of pillows on the divan for use later. *Look! The assassin is closing the door!*"

It had been so vivid that I had a mental picture of the card room before me. Then it was that I realized it was no mental picture at all. Staring into the dark, eyes growing used to it, I could *see* the inside of the card room. I looked at it from the side on which the window would be. There were the leprous red walls. There was the door to the salon at my right; in the wall directly ahead the door to the hall. There at the left was the divan, dull old rose with its pillows, and the redshaded lamp on the table throwing a subdued light over it. But I saw that scene as through a faint mist, hazy and unreal, a stage for ghosts, and yet with those sounds and that human laughter pulsing around… Yes, and the door into the hall was being softly closed, so softly that it hardly swayed the bell rope beside it; the knob turned, the latch clicked, and was still. Just a few minutes after eleven. The murderer had planted his sword, and left the room…

Faint music in a long interval. The knob was turning again! I could feel that the gag against my mouth was dryly rubbing my teeth; the scene whirled. *The dead man walked into the room;* Saligny—or, rather, Laurent posing as Saligny—vital, alive, carrying on his shoulders that head I had seen grinning from the floor. Behind him came the woman who was his wife, Louise, languorous, feverish-eyed. Not a word was spoken. The two moved like phantoms. They stopped in the middle of the room, and the horrible marionettes kissed.

Kissed… he seemed to be speaking inaudible words, and she was replying. She lighted a cigarette, inhaled deeply a few moments, and laughed soundlessly; you could see him smirking sideways at you now. She ground out the cigarette against an ashtray. Her eyes moved toward the place where the window should be, and I stared into them. Then she pointed to the button of her slipper, which had become unfastened; she advanced almost to the divan, and put out her left foot. While he knelt over the slipper, she threw her weight to the right, as though leaning against the divan…Catlike, she leaped aside. In her hands the great sword flashed aloft and fell.

His head seemed to leap like a grisly toy, springing out on wires… The scene went dark. Somewhere the orchestra banged into the last bar of "Hallelujah!"

"It is not yet eleven-fifteen," Bencolin's voice snapped. "See, she looks around. She shakes the head aloft in triumph, for she has smoked the hashish that drives people to murder. She picks up the head and gestures like Salomé[40]—this man, who would have killed her, *she* has killed. Then she becomes tense, ready, watchful. She has left a cigarette; that must be destroyed. She drops it into her wrist

---

40 The allusion is of course to the dancer who demanded of her stepfather the head of John the Baptist. The editor is surprised that Carr did not choose, instead, the story of Judith and Holofernes (the apocryphal Book of Judith), in which the Assyrian general designs to seduce the righteous widow, taken as a prisoner. One evening, when Holofernes is intoxicated, Judith enters his tent and decapitates him.

bag. There are some ashes on the rug; she grinds them into the nap with her heel. Then she leaves again by the hall door, having raised the window to let the smoke out.

"And why has she done this? Why has she not denounced this man, whom she knows to be an impostor, to the police? So that the world will never know he is not the real Saligny; so that she, having married him, will inherit his fortune—which she can enjoy with her confederate… Vautrelle! Now, the murder committed, Vautrelle, who planned all this, must supply her with an alibi…

"She knows that the detective Bencolin is sitting in the main salon, down at its far end. Very soon she joins him. To all outward appearances, Saligny (or Laurent) is not yet dead; she talks of him. At precisely eleven-thirty, according to a prearranged signal, a man walks through the door of the card room from the salon. His back is turned, and he is thirty feet away from the people she has joined, but he is tall and blond. She says, 'There goes Raoul now…' But that man was Vautrelle."

(As one puzzles at a cryptogram, and slowly sees the letters click into place, one by one, fewer gaps and fewer)…

"Vautrelle simply walked through the card room, pulling the bell cord deliberately as he went, walked out into the hall. *But* he turned to his left and entered the smoking room by the door in the projection of the wall (remember your plan) which conceals the card room door from the eyes of the detective seated at the end of the hall. Vautrelle walks out the door of the smoking room into the hall, and speaks to the detective. The whole process, by time tests, consumes just twelve and one-half seconds. His own alibi was now complete, as well as that of his colleague. He has summoned the boy with the cocktails, by pulling the bell, so that the body may be discovered and he can possess this alibi.

"Ladies and gentlemen," Bencolin cried out of the dark, "there will be no more pictures, no more stage effects. You see now that these two were working together to gain control of Saligny's fortune; Mr. Golton blurted out the truth about their affair. That was why it was necessary to go through with the marriage.

"But the body of the real Saligny must be disposed of. This body was then in a trunk at the home of Saligny, and Vautrelle must have known of it. He left the gambling house, took madame home, and then (knowing that he was followed) he eluded my shadower at Maxim's and drove to the back door of Saligny's house, arriving there around one-thirty. He carried the body downstairs, having wrapped it in a blanket; then he walled it up in the cellar. By that time my companion and I had arrived. He did not know of our presence, and tried to come upstairs—probably to get rid of the blood-stained sawdust or dispose of the trunk by carrying it away. The intervention of Girard led him to murder. He escaped by the cellar door, having stolen a bunch of keys on a previous visit to Saligny. Just when he learned that Saligny was the madman Laurent we shall have to ask him to tell us himself."

The single drop light appeared over Bencolin's head, but the rest of us were in shadow. I leaned back limply, and I was exhausted.

"And now," said Bencolin, "before turning on the lights over you, I may tell you the purpose of this experiment. I venture to predict that M. Vautrelle's chair is empty. If you will examine your manacles, you will see that with a little easy manipulation you could have slid them off without difficulty. None of you has tried to slip them: off, I venture to assert; this was because you were innocent. The crux of our practical psychology, and the reason why this test was tried, is that *the guilty person always does."*

The room appeared in a flood of light. There was a nervous, exhausted calm, and a strained silence. The sweated hair clung to Golton's forehead and I could hear him wheezing behind his gag. Fenelli seemed about to melt. Madame lay back in her chair, head lolling, one wrist free. Vautrelle's chair was empty.

Bencolin walked to the middle of the room, but he did not speak. The tile walls lent that room the chill semblance of a morgue. Laboriously madame worked herself free. She rose, swayed a little; tried to untie the gag, and finally ripped it off. Her ermine collar lay back from her throat, and she was panting. The face was sunken, a Madonna out of which peeped a vulture, and the dry lipstick cracked on her mouth. Her eyes, as she turned her head from side to side, were empty and frightening; a ruin.

Hard, harsh light…then the sound of steps on the tile floor. Two gendarmes appeared, escorting Vautrelle between them. He carried his coat over his arm, and he had casually lighted a cigarette.

"You weak-knees!" Louise de Saligny said, with sudden shrillness. "You left, did you?—Damn you." She leaned crookedly against the chair. The beauty and languor peeled away from her. "Well, tell them—go on—frightened at a lot of stage traps—tell them!—"

Vautrelle was breaking. He tried to keep his mouth straight, but his forehead was a glitter of sweat; he tried to be contemptuous, but the ivory cigarette holder trembled.

"You fixed up that story about ordering the cocktails," madame said, giggling. "I knew it—wouldn't go. *You* wanted me to kill him; *you* hadn't the nerve…in a public place where we could prove an alibi…if you'd listened to me," she smirked. "Yes, I'll tell them! Do you think *I* care about my precious neck?…Or do you want to kiss my neck now—as you used to. 'Ah, that divine neck'—goat of a Russian!—well, go on; it will be your last chance before the guillotine hits it." She drew her hand across her throat, and her laugh echoed against the walls.

Vautrelle's face was ghastly. The coat slid from his arm, and the cigarette spilled fire down his chin. With a terrific gritting of his nerves, he drew himself up. In a clear, defiant voice he sneered at Bencolin:

"Why, yes, I left your performance. I thought I would go up and see the Grand Guignol. If your men hadn't interfered, I should have been just in time for the second act."

He essayed a bow towards the detective; then he lurched, and slid down in a dead faint. High and shrill against the tile rang the laughter of Louise de Saligny.

X
BENCOLIN TAKES A CURTAIN CALL

"You will want some explanations, I take it," said Bencolin. "Well, there were certain features of the case which were clear from the moment I entered the room of the murder, and others which baffled me for the extraordinary time of nearly twelve hours."

Again we were sitting in his littered study, before a fire which looked a great deal more cheerful than that of the night before. He had mellowed under the influence of an appalling quantity of *Veuve Cliquot*,[41] and I was far from taciturn myself. He lighted a cigar luxuriously, and leaned back to blow thoughtful rings at the firelight.

"Let us take it from the beginning. Before Madame Louise was supposed to know about the murder, when we were all sitting there in the salon, you remember that I salvaged her cigarette, as I told you. Possibly the implication of much hashish has not occurred to you. It is the killer's drug. If you doubt it, look up the origin of the word 'assassin,' which is a direct derivation. A confirmed user is at any time liable to go amuck—we get that phrase from the drug, too—and within five years is dead. It makes them nearly as insane as our first troublemaker, Laurent.

"Then we were called into the room of the murder. You probably noted that heavy, sweet odor; if you ever dabble with this case in fiction, be sure to include it. It suggested hashish. She smoked before us, in the other room, but the overpowering collection of other smells made it confused with powder and perfume. Now that room was perfectly clear, and it appeared quite distinctly. The window was up, which might or might not have been an indication that it was raised to drive out the odor. At any rate, it created a strong suspicion that madame had been there *a short time before*. A short time, or the odor would have been entirely dissipated.

"Next we examined the position of the body. It was in a grotesque *kneeling* position; showed no sign of a struggle, and indicated that he had been hit from behind, as I pointed out. The body of a decapitated man, as we discover at the guillotine, has a habit of freezing into its position. Now imagine to yourself the only way in the world it would have been possible to *get* him into that position, so that he could be struck from behind! Why, attending to the fastening of a lady's slipper! It is not normally necessary to demand masculine attention to the stocking or the garter—well, or the roll, if you insist.

---

41 A French champagne house in Reims that produced the first vintage champagne (1810), and was the first, six years later, to introduce the process for clarifying champagne.

My comment about pillows, which seems to have puzzled you, was perfectly simple. It might surprise the victim to see a sharp sword lying in full view on the divan, and pillows in a line would very effectually conceal it.

"Thus far, it was a woman's crime; and I thought I could name the woman. Strength? Remember that *once before* Madame Louise had over-powered a madman, as I told you; and so it was no very far stretch of the imagination to conceive of her wielding that sword.

"Was it possible, I thought, that the time of the crime might have been *before* half past eleven? I would pigeonhole the idea with the question, 'Who was the man who actually entered, and why?'

"Before I came there, I already had a suspicion that the man posing as Saligny was Laurent. When we found the pictures of himself in his pockets, it suggested not so much conceit as an endless studying of his prototype; especially since some of the pictures were not at all flattering. Find me the beau who preserves pictures that make him look hideous! Then that question of a weapon in his pockets—it was curious—"[42]

"But we found no weapon in his pocket!" I protested.

"Ah, that was the curious thing. Put yourself in the place of a man who fears for his life from an unknown assailant. Would you go around entirely unarmed, particularly if you were one of the finest pistol shots in Europe? Now, I thought to myself, is it possible that Madame Louise knew this too? Might she have killed him because of it? If so, why in the devil's name does she not speak and exonerate herself? Hold that idea in mind, please. Remember that Laurent is a cunning villain, who sends notes to himself and, when he knows he is being shadowed at the opium house, voluntarily tells the police so that we shall believe he has merely been collecting evidence.

"Then came the crux: that outlandish business of the bell being rung. The question is, 'Who rang it; the false Saligny or the murderer?' If Saligny rang it, the murderer certainly was insane, for, after his victim has rung a bell which will summon a witness quite soon, he coolly kills Saligny anyhow! If the murderer rang it, the same rule applies: he blithely rang for a witness to see him commit the murder, since he could not have known that the boy would be delayed in answering the bell. The only tenable hypothesis, however, is that the man whom we saw enter the room rang the bell. If it was not Saligny, who was it; and (here is the locked room) where did that man go?

---

42 As he has several times before, by showing Bencolin pacing like Holmes, or pondering a mystery before the fireplace like Holmes, Carr here pays homage to Conan Doyle's detective with a variation of the curious incident of the dog in the night-time, complete with an enigmatic clue echoing that most famous one.

"I now switch back to the idea that when the bell was rung the victim had already been killed, and the evidence points to Louise de Saligny. Who could have been the man who entered the room? By his size and the color of his hair, only Vautrelle! Well, then, Vautrelle knew about the crime; and madame knew it was he who entered, if she had just left her husband without a head. It was pretty evidence of collusion, when coupled with Golton's drunken assertion about a possible affair there.

"Collusion *why?* The answer is obvious. They know about the false Saligny, but they must keep the world thinking it was Saligny, or there would be no fortune. But how could they have known this? The probability was that the false Saligny's refusal to indulge in sports had aroused Vautrelle's suspicions, and he investigated Saligny's house— indicated by the fact that he stole the cellar keys.

"When he learned about the trunk we shall not know until the *juge d'instruction* gets his confession, but clearly he had to hurry to Saligny's house and destroy that damning evidence that an impostor was about. The house would have been gone over by the attorneys and the appraisers of the estate, and a conspicuous trunk in the study would assuredly have been opened.

"Having already proved an alibi for madame and for himself, Vautrelle would return to Saligny's home as soon as he could. I did not, naturally, know about the trunk until we ourselves reached the premises; but it seemed probable that there was in that house some evidence of a false Saligny which Vautrelle would wish destroyed. I shall be very much surprised if the executors do not unearth a diary, some letters in Laurent's handwriting, or other suspicious material. That Vautrelle had visited Saligny's home on the day before the murder is fairly clear since he knew about and suspected the trunk. This was probably when he stole the keys of the cellar door... So after the killing of Laurent he gave my shadower the slip (recall the operative's report over the telephone), and went back to hide the body of the real Saligny. Fresh mortar does not ordinarily lie about loose in cellars, and presents another indication that not only was the prowler familiar with the house, but that he had prepared for his work that or the preceding day.

"The intruder was, then, a close friend of Saligny—"

"But why didn't Golton fit in as well? He lived next door, too."

"*Zut alors!* That Golton hypothesis of yours is an *idée fixe!*"

I narrated the experiment of the handshake in the cafe, and added, "That was why I suspected him to the very last minute—"

Bencolin chuckled. "Well, some of our evidence hinges round the flashlight; let us take that into consideration. Golton's bad hand was no evidence at all that he was guilty. Have you ever had anything knocked out of your own hand by a pistol bullet?"

I confessed to no such charming experience.

"A light object would cause no more disastrous result than a momentary jar. Something very heavy, of course, might numb one's hand; but certainly not an electric torch. Did you think for a moment that I was trying to hit the intruder with my shots?"

"Since you fired pointblank at him, it seemed highly probable."

"Why? I knew who the intruder was and I also was morally certain he carried no pistol—why should he? He expected to find the house deserted. But remember above all that we ourselves were fully as guilty of house breaking as he. I hardly wanted to complicate matters by unnecessary shooting. Had I known that Girard was in danger I would have dropped him, but I cannot lay claim to omniscience. What I was doing—sound as it may like the master detective of fiction—was estimating his height... How? Well, if you are holding an electric torch, what is the natural position of your hand? Try it. You see—waist high. Now I took good aim—I couldn't have had a better target—and put two bullets through the flashlight firing from the stairs. One of the bullets nicked the newel post at the precise height of the electric torch, and then entered the floor. Calculating from my own position on the stairs, and estimating the mark on the newel post as indicating the man's waist, it was not too difficult to estimate his height at about six feet."

"It is without doubt a unique, if somewhat too spectacular, method of taking a man's measurements. But it seems to this hard-headed person that it would have been much simpler neatly to put those bullets through both legs—"

"My dear fellow, you are saturated with traditions of American gunplay! In France the police shoot only as a last resort. Besides, a sense of drama prevented me from pouncing too soon on my victim."

"And thereby cost a man's life. But proceed."

"So the height of the murderer," went on Bencolin expansively, "excludes definitely your roly-poly candidate, M. Golton. Your last remarks indicate why I did not give you a loaded pistol. Had you been in my place, you would have felt an overwhelming urge to clutter up the premises with bullets on the slightest provocation. You would have caught the machine-gun urge of New York and Chicago—in which cities, I am told, under the beneficent American government, a man has no personal liberties except the full and free right to commit murder."

"Thereby," I said, "causing French detectives to talk like United States senators..."

"It is true!" he protested. "That is the philosophy of your great country. It is even so bad that every time I see in the newsreels a picture of your president M. Coolidge, he is either wearing a cowboy suit or indulging in rifle practice. Diable! The crime situation must be terrible."

"It is certainly a branch of crime," I said, "sponsored by the W. C. T. U.[43] and kindred producers of nausea... You were saying?"

"About the murder. When you add the evidence of the cigarette ashes in the card room containing hashish, the fingerprints on the window being those of madame, you add a couple of details which never interested me, but which would be highly valuable in a court of law. A search of Vautrelle's house tonight produced the gloves he had worn to bury Saligny and kill Girard—"

"What is the evidence in a pair of soiled gloves? I have a pair myself."

"I would warn you never to discount the efforts of our tireless laboratory. Did you know that the fibers of certain fabrics, impressed on a receptive surface, will print their individual weave exactly like fingerprints? And that no two weaves, even on a machine-made article, are precisely similar under a microscope? No, Jack, it is no longer safe even to use gloves. The fiber prints on the dust of the knife that stabbed Girard correspond with the soiled gloves Vautrelle had neglected to throw away."

"Is there any more of this scientific evidence?"

"All the evidence which will convict those two is scientific. You recall my request to examine the false Saligny's fingernails. Clinging to the inside of the nail on the first finger of his right hand was a bit of silk, about a sixteenth of an inch long, scratched from madame's stocking when he fell. Of course, I could not see it; I did not know it was there. But I trusted to the laboratory to discover anything that *might* be there. The octopus has eyes, too..."

"You neglect nothing, do you?...Then all that mummery of reproducing the crime was unnecessary!"

"Oh, well, I had to have a little personal satisfaction," he explained, somewhat apologetically. "I am inherently a mountebank. It is our national weakness as constant gunplay is yours. When I can be aided by dummy tile walls, pleasing musical effects, shadow graphs, and certain actors expertly made up (one with a wax head, which will fall at the application of a tin sword), I cannot resist the temptation to become a disciple of Hollywood. Besides, I am fond of sticking pins in my fellow mortals to see how they will react...I studied Vau-

---

43 The Women's Christian Temperance Union, which was devoted to a variety of social reforms based upon religious teachings.

trelle, and I fancied he would break before madame. It was a test…" He sat a long while silent in the firelight, so motionless that the ash did not fall from his cigar. "Examine closely, my friend," he said at last, "the extremely contained person who never cuts loose; who never indulges in a good, healthy, plebeian brawl; who affects indifference and boredom—that man is the extreme in self-consciousness. He is never sure of himself, and at the climax he will crack. Madame, on the other hand, was the opposite; you recall how she was willing to speak so freely and personally before you, a stranger. I rather imagined she would outlast him. And I was curious about both Golton and Fenelli." He chuckled. "Again I guessed correctly. The American had nothing on his mind; it scared him to a shadow, and thus he enjoyed it thoroughly. And, at least, it will furnish a better subject for conversation than Yellowstone Park. As for Fenelli, it was almost necessary to escort him home in an ambulance…

"And now," he concluded, reaching over to take the champagne bottle from its cooler, "we have finished. I give you a wish, the conclusion of all cases—"

The broad glasses clicked together in the firelight. Then, at Bencolin's elbow, the telephone rang. The pieces of his overturned glass lay shattered on the hearth, and, as he picked up the 'phone eagerly, the spilled champagne crawled and sizzled about the burning logs.

Notes for the Curious: Grand Guignol

The reader is warned: This commentary discusses vital clues in Carr's *It Walks By Night.* If you have not yet read that novel, the editor strongly encourages you to do so before reading the following remarks.

Grand Guignol is the culmination of Carr's amateur career in every sense. It is his last, longest, and best amateur composition. The novella's incorporation of, and improvement upon, so many of the techniques in the works preceding it demonstrates that Carr has successfully passed out of his juvenile state and is on the threshold of becoming a young master—after only seven years, and at the ripe young age of 22. While *Grand Guignol* is a pleasure to read for its own sake, its tipping-point correlations to works already written and to Carr's coming premier novel, based upon the novella, are worth scrutiny.

To begin, the narrator, Jack, is Carr's least disguised stand-in. At Haverford, John was known to his friends by that nickname. Young Jack Carr, when he finished writing *Grand Guignol,* was not long returned from Paris, where, recall, he avoided studying and undoubtedly drank too much, like Hugh Donovan of *The Eight of Swords*— but where also, perhaps, the "dull and decorous" Latin Quarter and his other haunts were insufficiently inspirational to Carr to finish his first attempted longer work, the intended historical romance full of "swashbuckling stuff, not altogether free of gadzookses," which Carr abandoned and then destroyed.

We may speculate, instead, that Carr realized there was a shorter step into a twentieth-century romance, one he was better prepared to imagine: a detective-fiction romance, in which Carr's creation, Henri Bencolin, would become Jack's friend, father figure, and tour guide to the dark and adventurous Paris existing in a febrile twilight adjacent to the real one. Jack himself would become a detective, or at least, the detective's apprentice. At last, Carr would not need to select a veiled surrogate to express his desire for adventure in the grand manner. As entertaining as Carter, Baire, and Cullen had been, or either of the O'Riordans, finally, Jack would have his own adventure—and so *Grand Guignol* was begun.

There is even some of Jack Carr (the author) in Bencolin. *Grand Guignol*'s Bencolin shares that stature of which Carr was self-conscious all his life, while nonetheless possessing an ineffaceable dignity: "a queer and absurd little figure…but Paris's avenger of broken laws." In later works, Bencolin will no longer resemble Carr physically, having (among other changes) by *The Lost Gallows* apparently enjoyed a late-life growth spurt: "The Frenchman opposite him was a tall and lazy Mephisto—Mephisto with a lifted eyebrow" (p. 2). The *juge d'instruction* will come more to resemble Holmes in stature, but at his inception, there is that understated likeness between author and French policeman. In another playfully superficial similarity, Bencolin (as we discover in *It Walks By Night*, p. 177) was, like both Carr and his surrogate narrator, the pupil of a great fencing master. In Bencolin's case, it is Lucien Mérignac.[1] Little depends upon these resemblances; they merely declare once more Carr's characteristic playfulness and one of his life loves, harnessed to undertake some of this adventurous fantasy through the detective himself, not only through the Watson figure.

There are deeper likenesses between author and detective, though, which have implications in Bencolin's character development. Carr, as previously noted, was by turns "punctilious and devil-may-care." So too is Bencolin—unsurprisingly, because like many characters, he is modeled in significant ways upon his author. Where else than to himself, after all, would a young author turn to breathe complexity into his main character? If, as the novelist Arnold Bennett charged in his review of *It Walks By Night*, Carr's "French characters never show a sign of French mentality,"[2] this is not simply because *Grand Guignol* and *It Walks By Night* exist in Carr's fictional Paris, but because Bencolin is a Frenchman imbued with the young American's percipiency. It was natural for Carr to transplant his own satanic cleverness and his writer's imaginative grasp of those around him into Bencolin, who solves crimes using his insights into human character, not by depending primarily upon physical evidence. Further, Bencolin's contradictory nature, as both the law's defender and a man whose conscience allows him to bypass it and deliver less conventional justice, derives, essentially, from the conflicting allegiance many young adults feel between justice as defined by the state and justice as it is passionately felt, on a case-by-case basis, in the truth of their hearts. How easy it is for Carr, a young writer cultivating the image of an up-and-coming writer living a life of Jazz-Age pleasures, to moderate and couple this behavior with his own old-fashioned sense of gallantry, his lifelong conservative impulse to defend the social order. Growing into adulthood is, after all, in good part about successfully mediating, even resolving, these sometimes-conflicting ethics. As an author, Carr wisely clung to both, and so in *It Walks By Night*, Carr humanizes Bencolin by imprinting his own engrams into the detective.

1 Mérignac was a real-life fencing legend, a gold medalist at the 1900 Olympics— held, by coincidence, in Paris.

2 *Evening Standard*, March 27, 1930.

One reason Carr can better develop Bencolin is because he has the luxury of more than 50,000 additional words as compared to the novella. We might slightly rewrite *The Haverfordian*'s introduction to *Grand Guignol* to depict its relationship to *It Walks By Night*, which is comparable to the one between "The Shadow of the Goat" and *Grand Guignol*:

> *As this story is considerably longer than* Grand Guignol, *wherein M. Bencolin lately appeared, there are considerably more clues scattered about; and also, we warn the industrious sleuth, considerably more ways to go astray.*

Carr devotes some of the expanded format, in a considered manner, to the detective's person, here from the perspective of Jeff Marle:

> Your first impression...was one of liking and respect. You felt that you could tell him anything, however foolish it sounded, and he would be neither surprised nor inclined to laugh at you. Then you studied the face, turned partly sideways—the droop of the eyelids, at once quizzical and tolerant, under hooked eyebrows, and the dark veiled light of the eyes themselves. The nose was thin and aquiline, with deep lines running down past his mouth. A faint smile was lost in a small moustache and pointed black beard—the black hair, parted in the middle and twirled up like horns, had begun to turn grey...it was a head from the Renaissance... He rarely gestured when he spoke, except to shrug his shoulders, and he never raised his voice; but whenever you were in this man's company in public, you felt uncomfortably conspicuous. (pp. 2-3)

The Bencolin of *Grand Guignol*, by comparison, is more of a Mephistophelian thinking machine, lean in both conception and description. Bencolin's image in the *Haverfordian* novella is most strongly conjured not in words, but by the frontispiece illustration accompanying the second half's publication. As to words, only a single one, "sardonic," is used (three times) in *Grand Guignol* to describe Bencolin's visage. Nonetheless, the detective is in the novella also a personal reflection of Carr.

All the young Carr's demonstrated passion in the amateur works for adventure in the grand manner comes to a climax with *Grand Guignol*. Hardly has Jack had time, for instance, to deplore the se-

date atmosphere of the gambling club to which Bencolin has escorted him before he is assisting the prefect to investigate a beheading:

> "Jack," he said suddenly, looking up, "pick up the head
> and bring it over here."
> No doubt about it, I was growing ill.
> "Pick up—the head, did you say?"
> "Certainly; bring it here. Watch out, now; don't get the
> blood on your trousers…"
> In a daze, I approached the thing, shut my eyes, and
> picked it up by the hair. The hair felt cold and greasy,
> the head much heavier than I had thought.

This is a scene calculated to make a college-age audience laugh;
the different manner in which Carr handles the same scene in *It
Walks By Night* (which we will examine) is a telling indication of the
transformation from amateur novella to professional novel.

Grand Guignol's imagery and dialogue are milestone indicators of
the young Carr's progress: the novella is the most adroitly gothic of
his amateur works, building its atmosphere of fear with economical
yet effective language. It is so far advanced from "The House of
Terror" and "The Marked Bullet," for instance, that *Grand Guignol*
almost seems written by a different author. And while "The Riddle
of the Laughing Lord" and "The Devil-Gun" are, linguistically, quite
effective, their language is showier. With *Grand Guignol*, we meet the
earliest version of the John Dickson Carr whom Dorothy Sayers
lauded in her review of *The Mystery of the Mad Hatter*:

> Mr. Carr can lead us away from the small, artificial,
> brightly-lit stage of the ordinary detective plot into the
> menace of outer darkness. He can create atmosphere
> with an adjective, and make a picture from a wet iron
> railing, a dusty table, a gas-lamp blurred by the fog. He
> can alarm with an illusion, or delight with a rollicking
> absurdity. He can invent a passage from a lost work of
> Edgar Allan Poe which sounds like the real thing. In
> short, he can write—not merely in the negative sense
> of observing the rules of syntax, but in the sense that
> every sentence gives a thrill of positive pleasure.[3]

As to dialogue, putting aside the occasional dated vernacular (e.g.,
"Alibi Baby!…I don't see how you're going to shake it, Bencolin."),
with it, Carr maintains the novella's pace marvelously, providing the

---

3 "Mystery Out of the Ordinary," *Sunday Times*, Sep 24, 1933, p. 7.

speaking cast of characters energetic exchanges and distinct, contending personalities. So much of the novella's suspense and execution is dependent upon how the characters interact with one another that *Grand Guignol* requires a near-professional level in handling them.

Grand Guignol's problem construction also reflects and improves upon previous efforts: the novella poses the same initial challenge as "Ashes of Clues" does, and in nearly the same inverted-mystery format: we learn that Laurent, the murderer, has disguised himself—through plastic surgery, as opposed to Saunders' stage make-up—and then slain Raoul, the Duc de Saligny. All this is quickly established. As in the earlier short story, the detective must discover what new identity the murderer has assumed. Differently than in "Ashes of Clues," Carr unmasks Laurent not much more than halfway through the novella, in Part VI, rather than at the climax. Afterward, the remainder of the novella leverages a more "traditional" problem: Bencolin and Jack must discover who the murderer's murderer is, and the motive. As in the mature Carr's novels, discovering *how* the impossible crime was committed reveals with it *who* committed the crime, as well as illuminating *why*. *Grand Guignol*'s deceptiveness regarding these questions is more sophisticated than that of any of its predecessors: for the first time, Carr baits his "at least one-eighth" amateur-detective readers with enough red-herring clues for them to stumble into false solutions. Both Vautrelle and Sid Golton seem, at points, to be the leading suspect. In fact, late in the novella, Jack himself offers a reasonably constructed theory as to why Golton is the murderer. In a manner approaching that of his mature style, after perpetrating these misdirections, Carr has Bencolin explain away both men's apparent guilt.

Carr does not carry over exactly the same solution mechanics into *It Walks By Night*. The key difference is that the novel delays the discovery of Laurent's identity until Chapter XVI ("How a Man Spoke from a Coffin"): Carr extends the pseudo inverted-mystery format almost to the end of the novel. While Bencolin quickly realizes that Laurent, having killed Saligny nearly a month earlier and replaced him, is the beheading victim, the other characters do not—nor, likely, do most readers. Carr leaves only a chapter for these disoriented readers to reassess everything they believed they knew before the shortly promised identification of the murderer pursued during the novel: fewer than twenty pages not merely to find a new suspect, but to begin asking themselves replacement questions—chiefly, *who murdered Laurent*, rather than *who is Laurent*—in order to unmask the correct suspect.

What do this and other differences with *Grand Guignol* tell us about the novel's divergent approach, and what does this mean for Carr's nascent professional technique? Let us begin comparing the two versions by their titles, which illuminate the inspirational conception of each. *Grand Guignol*, as noted in an earlier footnote to the text, is the name of the macabre Parisian theater that Carr attended in 1927 and/or 1928. Invoking it as a stage-performance metaphor for the novella's framework, Carr names the opening and closing pairs of chapters for elements of live theater: the overture, the footlights, the last act, and the curtain call. In this amateur version's climax, Bencolin, with his flair for theatricality, mounts a startling recreation of the crime—a cinematic one, actually, which even includes sound and (improbably) scent.

The novel's title is inspired by the mid-fifteenth-century text concerning the occult that opens it, a fictive source that Carr attributes to an imaginary French Archbishop, Batognolles of Rouen.[4] In it, the archbishop warns readers of the difference between the beguiling daytime comeliness of lycanthropes in their human forms and their moonlit misshapenness, especially the beasts' "blood-bedabbled claws" (p. 1).[5] This governing metaphor, of human duality, deceptive appearances, and the violent animal within each of us, is more integral to the subtext and tensions of Carr's tale than the artificial showiness of the novella's is to essentially the same story. *Grand Guignol*, from the start offers us entertainment—if gruesome, nonetheless, entertainment. *It Walks By Night* offers us fear. The improvement in the title's suggestive utility, which sheds all overt implications of burlesque in favor of the grotesque, is comparable to Carr's improved handling of tropes between "The House of Terror" and "The Will-o'-the-Wisp." Carr makes the new title, and many similar small elements, work harder and better to deliver the unified effect he intends.

The initial passage of the novel also sets the tone by casting its atmosphere into "the field of its own assumptions" which "holds the nerves...of the reader pliant to its mood and happenings."[6] The Archbishop's warning (from the book Laurent owned, given by Bencolin to Jeff Marle) psychologically prepares both narrator and reader to interpret subsequent events emotionally and subconsciously as a

4 The two actual mid-fifteenth-century Archbishops of Rouen were Raoul Roussel, notable for having been a participant at the trial of Joan of Arc, and Guillaume d'Estouteville, who posthumously exonerated her.

5 Those blood-bedabbled claws of the book's opening passage, cast in black shadow against an arterial red background, also inspired the striking jacket artwork of the novel's first edition.

6 "It Walks By Night," *Saturday Review of Literature*, April 5, 1930.

modern-day journey into a gothic nightmare. The past, in Laurent's inchoate form, is lurching forward to swallow the present.

Carr's conversion from novella to novel is no lazy one. Carr reuses almost none of the novella's material after Part IV. He even rewrites much of what he retains.

Note, in one representative example, how much fuller Carr's description of Fenelli's club is, and how well, functionally, this serves the novel. In *Grand Guignol*, Carr briefly sketches the gambling house as one of "many such miniature casinos" in Paris, having a décor of red and crystal, its air stagnating with stale ventilation and bad jazz. In *It Walks By Night*, Carr adds many particulars until the gambling house becomes a tangle in his knotted mystery. At Fenelli's, the victim's and suspects' vices, motivations, and conflicts intertwine; so Bencolin must untangle these underlying circumstances on his way to identifying the murderer. Carr complicates the reader's understanding of the setting and its significance by taking the bare floor plan he presented relatively quickly in *Grand Guignol* and supplementing it in *It Walks By Night* with a detailed description consuming a number of additional paragraphs over several pages. In the reader's mind, the club's details become important and carry an implicit suggestion that to figure out not just "whodunit," but "howdunit," the reader must pay careful attention to where people were and when—carefully consulting the floor plan and the timeline with which Carr complements it near the end of Chapter V. But all this extra level of detail is more distraction than substance: little, almost nothing, from either layout or timeline is necessary for a clever reader to solve the mystery. What this really is is the Carrian game of bamboozling, played in just the manner Carr describes it in "The Grandest Game in the World." In another Golden-Age puzzler, the physical layout of the murder scene and the timeline would be indispensable clues. Carr exploits this expectation, adeptly turning these genre conventions into fair-play distractions. Of course, having done so, Carr sneaks the genuinely important clues past the reader in plain sight.

On the other hand, sometimes additional detail is simply a richer set of clues. Consider the expanded testimony of Sid Golton. His (less drunken) recounting of his acquaintance with "Raoul" provides the reader clearer and better opportunity to focus on the significance of Raoul's injury and of his incongruous ability to speak English. Consider as well how the addition of *Alice in Wonderland* and the evocation of Poe both add subtext hinting at the murder's solution and the concealment of Raoul's body.

In the comparison of narrators between these two versions,

the change between Jeff Marle and Jack is much more than a name. To begin, if Jack is transparently a surrogate for the author, and secondarily one for the reader, in *It Walks By Night*, that balance is reversed. As LeRoy Panek summarizes him (commenting upon Jeff's exploits generally, not only those of the first novel):

> Carr also uses Jeff as the adventure surrogate for the readers. This is why he gets mixed up with Bencolin—to find adventure. Of course he gets it. People get killed in his presence, he chases murderers in dark attics, he breaks into an illicit sex club and is chased by French Apaches with guns and knives, and he tags along when Bencolin goes hunting. (p. 148)

In *It Walks By Night*, Carr carefully puts away the teenage frivolity he paraded in *Grand Guignol*. Revisiting that comic moment in which Jack, Carr's surrogate, picks up—upon Bencolin's instruction, no less—Laurent's severed head, we recognize that in *It Walks By Night*, this will not do. For a wider, adult audience, Bencolin must behave like the professional head of police he is, while Jeff, the reader's perspective character, cannot seem foolish. So instead, Carr has—perhaps predictably, given Carr's attitude toward Grafenstein's profession—the psychiatrist pick up the head of his own volition, making him the buffoon who obtusely tampers with evidence.

It is in fact Grafenstein in the novel, not Jeff, who makes the mistakes Jack commits in *Grand Guignol*. An important initial change between the versions, of course, is that the novel "rescues" Dr. Grafenstein from his early offstage death in *Grand Guignol*. There, he is the masterful plastic surgeon who obligingly changes Laurent's appearance and is repaid by being murdered. In *It Walks By Night*, Carr assigns this fate to a Dr. Rothswold. In an ironic foreshadowing of his own fate, Laurent deposits that good doctor's head into a specimen jar filled with alcohol on a shelf in the doctor's laboratory (p. 19). Ever the wag, Carr has Bencolin apostrophize Laurent's brutality (p. 18) with the comment, "For a man of imagination, what a Grand Guignol picture!"

Grafenstein, having been spared that early fate, becomes a psychiatrist in the novel, as well as the sullen ground against which Bencolin's bright metal glitters over his faults—of which the psychiatrist demonstrates a litany, not just the ones he inherits conveniently from Jack. Dr. Grafenstein is, for instance, despite having treated Laurent personally—and with Laurent being his favorite case, no less—unaware that Louise was his patient's wife (p. 13).

The psychiatrist is further unable to detect the difference between Louise's having experienced a hallucination due to "self-hypnosis" (p. 29) and her simply having lied. Bencolin scolds him (pp. 42-43), "Please! You are so occupied with what the murderer thought that you are completely forgetting what he did."

Grafenstein's own insufficiencies make the ones he inherits from Jack more believable. Despite his declared disinterest in criminal investigations—"I am not a detective. Crime in the course of being traced is not interesting; love of God, no!" (p. 22)—Grafenstein dutifully accompanies Bencolin and Jeff at each point of the investigation, exchanging theories with Bencolin, challenging him with questions, and being, invariably, corrected. Notably, the psychiatrist attributes the photographs of Saligny in Laurent's pockets to "conceit" (Jack's interpretation in *Grand Guignol*); fails to appreciate the significance of the pillows on the divan (the point of an enigmatic clue from Bencolin to Jack in the novella); does not apprehend that the victim's keys are missing, or the importance of this; and equally overlooks that the murderer, who could not apparently have exited the card room, is also missing. In *Grand Guignol*, Bencolin pointedly reinforces this to Jack by asking, "Now let me ask you…*which way did he go out?*" In *It Walks By Night*, he asks exactly the same question, but to Dr. Grafenstein.

If Grafenstein is not, as he admits, a detective, he is nonetheless an excellent (if unwitting) source of clues, both to detective and reader. He discloses that Madame Laurent was "possessed of unusual strength," which she used to repel the razor attack by her murderous spouse (p. 13); he confirms that Saligny was "one of the most accomplished linguists I have ever met. He spoke German perfectly, without any accent" (p. 14); he summarizes Laurent's reading habits, which provide insight into Laurent's depravity as well as foreshadowing and subtext to the reader. In all this Carr demonstrates his understanding that a longer narrative requires "a ladder of clues, a pattern of evidence, joined together with such cunning that even the experienced reader may be deceived: until, in the blast of the surprise ending, he suddenly sees the whole design" ("The Grandest Game in the World," p. 10).

Dr. Grafenstein's assuming the role of mistaken foil, in place of Jack, leaves Carr room to fashion Jeff Marle into a different and more sympathetic perspective character than Jack. There are still echoes in Jeff of Carr himself, of course—we will learn later for instance, in *Poison In Jest*, that Jeff, like his author, was raised in Pennsylvania—but Jeff is simply a better stand-in for the reader. He has, for instance, a clearer relationship with Bencolin, which transitively humanizes Bencolin for the reader. Marle explains their relationship:

> I have known him all my life, for he was my father's best friend when the two were at college in America. When I was very young he used to visit us every year, bringing me toys from the boulevards and telling me the most delightful hair-raising stories. But I never understood his knowledge or position until I came to live in his own city. (p. 3)

Jeff also offers the reader an everyday contextualization of the murders that, however spectacular they are, similarly keep the reader invested in the novel as something of a human drama, not merely the flashy stage performance of *Grand Guignol*:

> I do not know whether the reader has ever been entangled in any such gruesome mess as this, or even peeped into the events surrounding any mysterious and violent death, not seeing them through the medium of the newspapers—where the worst tragedy seems unreal, incomprehensive, and often absurd—but terribly close in the company of the people who produced them... Crime, in written outline, is as far off and unconvincing as the account of a battle in a history book, full of unreal sound and fury...so that you find difficulty in imagining that it ever happened at all. If, then, you who read this have never experienced the hopeless and caged uncertainty, the bewilderment and black suspicion of everybody, that comes with such things in your own life, I cannot make it clear... Yet here it is. It is like looking in a mirror and seeing hideous things reflected in one's own face. (pp. 252-253)

Because of passages like these, the reader has sympathy and concern for this pair of friends as they investigate the novel's grim murders, rather than reading *It Walks By Night* solely as some sort of extended *Baffle Book*.

The longer format of the novel also allows Carr to introduce more characters, more distinctly developed. In delivering them, he also delivers the reader more potential suspects and more clues. Consider Kilard, Raoul's lawyer, who unknowingly confirms that the Saligny who returned from Venice was not the same one who left Paris:

> Technically, I have been Raoul's adviser since his birth, but I seldom saw him. He was not a young man who interested himself in financial affairs. So long as he could draw a cheque he was incurious.... And I must say... that having had several talks with him as his marriage-day approached, I formed a much higher opinion of the young man than I had originally possessed. (p. 129)

Kilard also lends the narrative pathos once he finally understands that it was Laurent, not Saligny, who died in Fenelli's gambling club:

> "You know," said Kilard, raising his head and speaking in a strained voice, "something is off my mind at last. For one thing I am very glad. It is nonsensical—it is unimportant I suppose—but I did not like to see the spectacle of a Saligny in such cringing fear of death as the false Raoul was when he came to me... The Salignys were soldiers!"

The most important character added in *It Walks By Night* is Sharon Grey, who supplies not only clues, but a romantic interest for Jeff. This is a Carrian commonplace that is missing from *Grand Guignol*. *It Walks By Night* is not a novel flattering to its women, unfortunately. Perhaps improbably, considering how problematic she is, Sharon is the better and more sympathetic of the two. Sharon's first appearance, slouched semiconscious in a drug-induced stupor, is a typically Carrian, inauspicious fantasy that mixes sexuality, mystery, and danger:

> To see the face of a beautiful woman looking up into a match-flame is another part of the dream. The eyes were amber, turning to brown, and terror-stricken against a white face. The hair, waved and parted in dull gold, lay upon her shoulders. Except for a kimono over one shoulder she was unclothed, a breathless mystery of flesh and shadow against the pillows in faint light... (p. 106)

When Sharon speaks for herself, it only makes her seem worse. The clue Sharon unknowingly discloses concerning Laurent's identity comes at the expense of her own integrity:

> "Only recently he changed. Before that, he wouldn't have anything to do with me. I wanted to be loved; I had to have him. But that injury did something to him;

he was moodier, and when he came back from Austria I think he was maimed for life, and he knew it.
He'd been acting like—like one of those silly people
in books," bitterly, "and talking about honor and the
girl he was going to marry. But when he came back,
he—took me." (p. 111)

Jeff's vision of Louise, although parsed in a thoughtfulness
wholly beyond *Grand Guignol*, is no healthier in its Cabellian conception. His response to Louise's graphic confession that she meant to
split Laurent's face in half with the sword, disturbingly, is sexualized:

The ivory face and slow lips moving, the dark-clouded
hair and eyes fixed…curiously enough, she had never
seemed so alluring as in this moment of revelation;
and I thought of those women of the renaissance,
who derive a part of their very fascination from the
poisoned cruelty of their beauty, and their moist lips
whose charm blots out the dagger behind the back.
(pp. 315-316)

The denouement of the novel, during which Louise's confession
is offered, is indeed disturbing, but it is actually less disturbing than
that of *Grand Guignol*—and in either event, more believable. There,
Bencolin's recreation of the crime is so unbelievable as to be distracting: could his staff have created its cinematic presentation in a matter of hours, overnight, including that improbable incorporation of
olfactory elements and cutting-edge sound? If so, perhaps Bencolin
should have been the artistic director, and his men the stagehands,
of the Grand Guignol theater, which required much more time to
mount a production featuring even less illusory accomplishment. Of
course, Bencolin's explanation here is Carr's response to and exploitation of the then-recent introduction of "talking pictures," the first
of which, *The Jazz Singer* (1927) preceded *Grand Guignol* by barely two
years. "Talkies" quickly became a global sensation, so the incorporation of one into a work of fiction would have thrilled and interested
Carr's collegiate readers.

On the other hand, Bencolin's restraint of his viewers is unpleas-
ant to say the least, bearing an utterly coincidental resemblance to
the Ludovico treatment in *A Clockwork Orange* (preceding the latter
as *Grand Guignol* did by more than three decades). As the conclusion
to a detective story, it is a more grisly than satisfying one. That the
restraints Bencolin claps on each of the attendees are harmless and
easily slipped does not mitigate the revulsion the reader might under-

standably feel.

The Bencolin who would perpetrate such a traumatizing joke upon multiple innocent witnesses, merely to secure a confession he does not even require for conviction, is perhaps a more manageable horror than the murders he solves—but he is still a horror. Carr clearly had difficulty mitigating this, and Bencolin became something of a problematic protagonist for him. At first, Carr took half an experimental step away from Bencolin with Patrick Rossiter, the featured detective in 1932's *Poison In Jest*, also narrated by Jeff Marle. The reader may likewise construe this as half a step *toward* Dr. Fell and Henry Merrivale, neither of whom existed at that point, but both of whom would by the time Carr returned to Bencolin in 1937's *The Four False Weapons*. In 1933, Carr created another one-time experiment, John Gaunt, in *The Bowstring Murders*. By then, though, Dr. Fell, more appealing to Carr personally given the jovial detective's association with G.K. Chesterton, and being well received, became Carr's focus. He would of course be followed quickly by Sir Henry Merrivale, equally more compelling than the interim detectives. Of Gaunt, LeRoy Panek wrote that he had "too much of the Romantic side of the Great Detective and too little of the anti-detective" (p. 150). Carr would not return to the anti-detective at all: even when Bencolin takes a final bow in *The Four False Weapons*, he is a completely changed man, almost unrecognizable. Martin Edwards observes:

> Carr had, it seems, decided that the satanic protagonist of his early stories no longer suited him; his writing style had matured, and as Bencolin retired from his official position and mellowed, he became a rather less striking character.[7]

In fact, Carr's withdrawal from Bencolin was stronger than that, much stronger. In a letter written May 8, 1970 to Rick Sneary, an early Carr bibliographer, Carr wrote baldly:

> Though I can't check publication dates offhand, the bibliography seems complete and contains only a couple of minor misstatements. Bencolin of the Paris stories, which I wish I had never written, was not Inspector Bencolin; he is described as juge d'instruction, usually translated as police magistrate…

What an extraordinary statement! It is one thing to retire a character. It is another for the author to wish he had never created him in

---

7 Introduction, *The Corpse in the Waxworks*, British Library Crime Classics, 2021.

the first place. Why?

Any answer is at this point merely speculative, but as is often the case whenever Carr is concerned, it probably lies in the observations of Douglas Greene. His explanation of why Carr stopped writing Bencolin is:

> ...it is clear that Carr found some of the formulas of *It Walks By Night* constraining...the crimes [in the succeeding novels] continued to be grisly... To explain such horrors, Carr had to assume that the criminal was mad and therefore not limited to rational behavior and motives. Since Bencolin was supposedly with the Paris police, it became more difficult to ignore police procedure... Carr, moreover, came to believe that he had made Bencolin too cruel in the novels. In 1937, some years after he had invented other detectives, he revived Bencolin in *The Four False Weapons* to show that the original Bencolin of the short stories was the genuine version of the detective. In *The Four False Weapons* Bencolin is again kind-hearted, and we learn that his sadism and theatricalism were merely "careful stage-trappings, which he found useful in his business".... When Carr reacted against the flamboyant Bencolin...he invented detectives in the opposite extreme... Detectives must be memorable, and Rossiter and Gaunt were too easily forgotten; but no one could forget Carr's great detectives invented in 1933 and 1934, Dr. Gideon Fell and Sir Henry Merrivale.[8]

In any event, Bencolin was the pinnacle of Carr's amateur career and the first glory of his long, professional one—which would be filled with many, to the gratification of readers for at least the next hundred years.

---

8 Introduction, *The Door to Doom and Other Detections*, Harper and Row, 1980, pp. 17-18.

The Kindling Spark

The Kindling Spark: Early Tales of Mystery, Horror, and Adventure by John Dickson Carr is printed on 60-pound paper, and is designed by Jeffrey Marks using InDesign. The type is Garamond, a group of fonts named for French engraver Claude Garamon. The cover is by Ezra Cumbo. The first edition was published in a perfect-bound softcover edition and a clothbound edition accompanied by a separate pamphlet of John Dickson Carr's "The Cloak of D'Artagnan." *The Kindling Spark: Early Tales of Mystery, Horror, and Adventure* was printed by Southern Ohio Printers and bound by Cincinnati Bindery. The book was published in September 2022 by Crippen & Landru Publishers.

Crippen & Landru, Publishers
P. O. Box 532057
Cincinnati, OH 45253

Web: www.Crippenlandru.com
E-mail: orders@crippenlandru.com

Since 1994, Crippen & Landru has published more than 100 first editions of short-story collections by important detective and mystery writers.

This is the best edited, most attractively packaged line of mystery books introduced in this decade. The books are equally valuable to collectors and readers. [Mystery Scene Magazine]

The specialty publisher with the most star-studded list is Crippen & Landru, which has produced short story collections by some of the biggest names in contemporary crime fiction. [Ellery Queen's Mystery Magazine]

God bless Crippen & Landru. [The Strand Magazine]

A monument in the making is appearing year by year from Crippen & Landru, a small press devoted exclusively to publishing the criminous short story. [Alfred Hitchcock's Mystery Magazine]

Previous Crippen & Landru Publications

Challenge the Impossible: The Impossible Files of Dr. Sam Hawthorne by Edward D. Hoch. Full cloth in dust jacket, signed and numbered by Josh Pachter, $45.00. Trade softcover, $19.00.

Nothing Is Impossible: Further Problems of Dr. Sam Hawthorne by Edward D. Hoch. Full cloth in dust jacket, signed and numbered by the publisher, $45.00. Trade softcover, $19.00.

Swords, Sandals And Sirens by Marilyn Todd. Murder, conmen, elephants. Who knew ancient times could be such fun? Many of the stories feature Claudia Seferius, the super-bitch heroine of Marilyn Todd's critically acclaimed mystery series set in ancient Rome. Others feature Cleopatra, the Olympian gods, and high priestess Ilion blackmailed to work with Sparta's feared secret police. Full cloth in dust jacket, signed and numbered by the author, $45.00. Trade softcover, $19.00.

All But Impossible: The Impossible Files of Dr. Sam Hawthorne by Edward D. Hoch. Full cloth in dust jacket, signed and numbered by the publisher, $45.00. Trade softcover, $19.00.

Sequel to Murder by Anthony Gilbert, edited by John Cooper. Full cloth in dust jacket, $29.00. Trade softcover, $19.00.

Hildegarde Withers: Final Riddles? by Stuart Palmer with an introduction by Steven Saylor. Full cloth in dust jacket, $29.00. Trade softcover, $19.00

Shooting Script by William Link and Richard Levinson, edited by Joseph Goodrich. Full cloth in dust jacket, signed and numbered by the families, $47.00. Trade softcover, $22.00.

The Man Who Solved Mysteries by William Brittain with an introduction by Josh Pachter. Full cloth in dust jacket, $29.00. Trade softcover, $19.00

Constant Hearses and Other Revolutionary Mysteries by Edward D. Hoch. Full cloth in dust jacket, signed and numbered by Brian Skupin, $45.00. Trade softcover, $19.00.

Subscriptions

Subscribers agree to purchase each forthcoming publication, either the Regular Series or the Lost Classics or (preferably) both. Collectors can thereby guarantee receiving limited editions, and readers won't miss any favorite stories.

Subscribers receive a discount of 20% off the list price (and the same discount on our backlist) and a specially commissioned short story by a major writer in a deluxe edition as a gift at the end of the year.

The point for us is that, since customers don't pick and choose which books they want, we have a guaranteed sale even before the book is published, and that allows us to be more imaginative in choosing short story collections to issue.

That's worth the 20% discount for us. Sign up now and start saving. Email us at orders@crippenlandru.com or visit our website at www.crippenlandru.com on our subscription page.